'Is                 he
real                l of
pa               of

'Ric           tyn's
*M*           ion,
         o

l         h a
        ance
        ng
n        he life
       and

       *y*;

      n

with a surprisingly mode

own terms.'

—An           ional bestselling
         thor

Published in Great Britain 2013
by Mills & Boon, an imprint of Harlequin (UK) Limited, Eton House, 18-24 Paradise Road, Richmond, Surrey TW9 1SR

© Isolde Martyn 2013

ISBN: 978 0 263 91012 4

024-0613

Harlequin (UK) policy is to use papers that are natural, renewable and recyclable products and made from wood grown in sustainable forests. The logging and manufacturing processes conform to the legal environmental regulations of the country of origin.

Printed and bound by
CPI Group (UK) Ltd, Croydon, CR0 4YY

# ISOLDE MARTYN

*Mistress to the Crown*

**Isolde Martyn** is originally from England and has an Honours degree in History, with a specialisation in the Wars of the Roses. She ended up in Australia after meeting a rather nice geologist at a bus stop. Since then she has worked as a university tutor, an archivist and for six years as a researcher in historical geography at Macquarie University. She spent a year researching sedition in early colonial Australia and then became heavily involved in the Bicentenary History project and researched all the towns in Australia for the Bicentenary volume *Events and Places*.

Her more recent career was as a senior book editor with a major international publisher before taking up writing full time.

Isolde enjoys using turbulent historical events as the backdrop of her books. Her debut novel was the first book by an Australian writer to win the prestigious RITA® award in the USA and her first two novels have won the 'Romantic Book of the Year Award' in Australia.

She is a former chair of the Richard III Society and Vice-Chair of the Plantagenet Society of Australia, which she co-founded with five other enthusiasts twelve years ago. *Mistress to the Crown* is her fifth novel.

For my cousins, Rita and Yvonne, and for Simone,
who was once my youngest reader and who
overcame illness with such courage

# The Plantagenets and Related Families in the Late Fifteenth Century

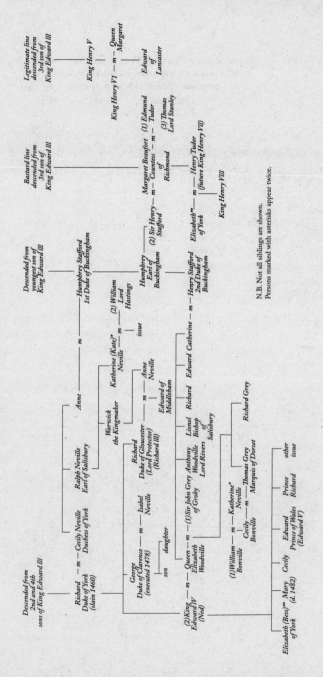

N.B. Not all siblings are shown.
Persons marked with asterisks appear twice.

# Characters appearing in this novel

Nearly all these persons are historical. Where the given name of a person is unknown and it has been necessary to create one, these are marked with one asterisk. Fictional characters are marked with two asterisks.

## THE CITIZENS

| | |
|---|---|
| ELIZABETH LAMBARD | known to history as 'Jane' Shore; married to William Shore |
| WILLIAM SHORE | Elizabeth's husband, a mercer, originally from Derby |
| JOHN LAMBARD | Elizabeth's father, a London mercer and alderman for Farringdon; Sheriff of London in 1460–61 |
| ANNE | Elizabeth's mother, daughter of merchant grocer, Robert Marshall |
| ROBERT<br>JACK<br>WILL | Elizabeth's brothers |
| JOHN AGARD | Shore's brother-in-law from Foston, Derbyshire |
| MARGERY* SHAA<br>ALYS* RAWSON | Elizabeth's friends, daughters of London merchants |
| HUGH PADDESLEY<br>SHELLEY<br>COLET<br>RALPH JOSSELYN THE YOUNGER | guildsmen and friends of William Shore |
| EDMUND SHAA | Margery's father, a merchant goldsmith; later knighted; Lord Mayor of London in 1483 |

| | |
|---|---|
| JULIANA SHAA | Edmund's wife and Margery's mother |
| WILLIAM CATESBY | lawyer and councillor to various noblemen |
| ISABEL<br>LUBBE**<br>HIKKE**<br>ROGER* YOUNG | servants to Elizabeth |

## THE COURT

| | |
|---|---|
| WILLIAM, LORD HASTINGS | Lord Chamberlain, Lord Lieutenant of Calais and Master of the Royal Mint; King Edward IV's close friend |
| KING EDWARD IV ('NED') | Yorkist King of England |
| QUEEN ELIZABETH WOODVILLE | Edward's queen, daughter of the Duchess of Bedford and formerly wed to Sir John Grey |
| THOMAS GREY ('TOM') MARQUIS OF DORSET | the Queen's eldest son by her first marriage, betrothed to Lord Hastings' stepdaughter, Cecily |
| SIR RICHARD GREY | the Queen's son by her first marriage |
| PRINCESS ELIZABETH ('BESS') PRINCESS MARY | King Edward's elder daughters |
| EDWARD, PRINCE OF WALES | King Edward's eldest son and heir (the future King Edward V), domiciled in Ludlow |
| PRINCE RICHARD ('DICKON') | youngest son of King Edward |
| GEORGE, DUKE OF CLARENCE RICHARD, DUKE OF GLOUCESTER | King Edward's younger brothers, both married to daughters of Warwick the Kingmaker |
| HARRY, DUKE OF BUCKINGHAM | last lawful heir of the House of Lancaster and cousin to King Edward and his brothers |

| | |
|---|---|
| THOMAS LYNOM | Crown Solicitor to King Richard III |
| ANTHONY WOODVILLE, LORD RIVERS | the Queen's eldest brother, tutor to the Prince of Wales at Ludlow |
| SIR EDWARD BRAMPTON | Portuguese friend of King Edward |
| SIR EDWARD WOODVILLE<br>SIR RICHARD WOODVILLE<br>LIONEL WOODVILLE, BISHOP<br>OF SALISBURY | the Queen's younger brothers |
| BRYAN MYDDELTON | Yeoman usher of the King's Chamber |
| CECILY NEVILLE, DUCHESS OF YORK | King Edward's mother |
| JOHN MORTON, BISHOP OF ELY<br>JAMES GOLDWELL, BISHOP<br>OF NORWICH | royal councillors |

## OTHERS MENTIONED

| | |
|---|---|
| RICHARD, DUKE OF YORK | King Edward's father, slain at Wakefield 1460 |
| KING HENRY VI | former King of England, died in the Tower of London in 1471 |
| QUEEN MARGARET | imprisoned Lancastrian Queen of England, wife to Henry VI; daughter of René of Anjou |
| WARWICK THE KINGMAKER | King Edward's cousin, died at Battle of Barnet 1471 |
| KATHERINE ('KATE') NEVILLE | wife to Lord Hastings and sister to Warwick |
| LADY CECILY BONVILLE | stepdaughter to Lord Hastings; betrothed to Thomas Grey, Marquis of Dorset |
| KING LOUIS XI | King of France |

| | |
|---|---|
| DR WESTBURY | Provost of the College of Our Lady at Eton |
| ROBERT STILLINGTON, BISHOP OF BATH AND WELLS THOMAS BURDETT DR STACEY BLAKE | supporters of George, Duke of Clarence |
| MARGARET BURDETT MARION STACEY | wives of accused men |
| MARGARET ('Meg') DOWAGER DUCHESS OF BURGUNDY | King Edward's youngest sister |
| GERARD CANIZIANI | Medici banker resident in London |
| PETER BEAUPIE | Clerk of the Green Cloth |
| THOMAS KEMPE, BISHOP OF LONDON | |
| JOHN MATHEW | mercer; Sheriff of London 1483 |
| THOMAS MYLLINGTON, BISHOP OF HEREFORD JOHN WOODMAN, BISHOP OF ROSS WILLIAM WESTECARRE, BISHOP OF SIDON | Judges at the Court of Arches |
| THOMAS, LORD STANLEY | Steward of the King's Household; married to Margaret Beaufort; stepfather to Henry Tudor |
| LADY MARGARET | wife to Lord Stanley and mother of Henry Tudor |
| HENRY TUDOR | exile in Brittany; claimant to English crown |

# Maiden

# Soper's Lane, the City of London, 1463

At fourteen, we make mistakes. I had been a fool to come to this old man's chamber on my own, but I was desperate for legal advice on how to annul my marriage. He had told me he was a former proctor, a church lawyer – exactly what I needed – and he had seemed as friendly as a kindly grandfather when I spoke to him after Mass on Sunday. But now he was tonguing his cheek as he eyed my body, and dancing his fingers slowly on the table between us. Behind him, in the corner, I could see his half-made bed.

I would not scream, I decided, slowly rising to my feet. Shrieking for help would mean my name would be all over the city by suppertime. No, I had to deal with this on my own.

'Thank you, sir, I shall pass your counsel on to my friend, but now I have to go.' My voice emerged creakily. I had meant to sound brisk.

He smiled, nastily now, no longer bothering to mask his purpose. Both of us had been lying. In truth, I was 'the friend' who desired advice, and his legal counsel was not 'free'; it came with a fee that was still to be exacted.

'If you are desperate, Mistress Shore,' he declared, rising heavily to his feet, 'you'll be willing to please me.'

Yes, I was desperate for an annulment, but I had rather be hanged than 'please' this revolting old goat. My maidenhead was intact and I intended to keep it that way.

'I made no such bargain,' I said, fisting my hands within the folds of my skirts, cursing I had not brought a bodkin to defend myself.

'We won't go all the way because that would spoil the evidence,' he wheezed, fumbling at the ties beneath his tunic. 'Some fondling will do. *For now.*'

'Oh, just fondling,' I said with a pretend smile of relief. 'I thought you meant—'

I rushed to the door but the latch tongue stuck. He grabbed my left forearm, dragging me back.

This was the moment, or never. I swung my right fist with all the fury I possessed into his face. I heard something crunch. He went staggering back and crashed against the table, the bright blood spurting from his nostrils. That and the toppling inkpots would spoil his clothes, or so I hoped as I ran down the stairs.

It was realising the enormity of my folly that rearranged the contents of my stomach once I reached the street. I did manage to hide my face as I retched, and the moment I could stand upright, I ran past the tenements up to Cheapside, and with a gasp of relief, plunged into the chaos of carts, pigs and people. My mind was still in panic. What if the old man threatened to blab to my husband or to my wealthy father?

My slow progress through the crowd calmed my shakiness. I felt concealed. Outsiders might be afraid of London cutpurses, but this wonderful, raucous hub of noise was my neighbourhood, safer to me than any quieter lane. I pushed further along to where a tight press of people was clogging the thoroughfare and wriggled in amongst them. In their midst, a hosier's apprentice was standing on a barrow. I had heard his silver-tongued babble before. He was good.

'The best price in Cheapside,' the lad was yelling, waving a pair of frothy scarlet garters. 'Just imagine your wife's legs in these, sir.' Laughter rumbled around me. His gaze scanned our faces. 'And what about the jays and robin redbreasts among you sparrows?' he challenged, flourishing a pair of men's hose – one leg pea green, the other violet, and then his cheeky stare sauntered back to my face and slid lower.

Lordy! Squinting downwards at the gap in my cloak, I realised what the proctor had glimpsed as well – a woman's breasts straining against an outgrown gown. And it was not just on the outside that my body was changing. I knew that. Dear God, that was why I needed the urgent annulment. I was an apple almost ripe for plucking, and my husband, Shore, was watching – waiting – like a hungry orchard thief.

I gave the apprentice a hands-off glare, tugged my cloak tightly across my front and, aware that the proctor's neighbours might still raise the alarm, I determined to stay where I was with every sense alert.

No hue-and-cry was coming from the direction of Soper's Lane and I said a silent prayer of thanks for that. Maybe the foul old fellow was as fearful for his reputation as I was for mine. That welcome thought made my shoulders relax. And, apart from learning that men of all ages were not to be trusted, I had at least gleaned one piece of useful advice. The proctor had told me that 'my friend' needed to have her case heard by the Court of Arches, the Archbishop of Canterbury's especial court for hearing divorce petitions. St Mary-le-Bow, the church, which housed the court on weekdays, was just a few moments' walk back along Cheapside.

Perhaps the Almighty was watching over me, after all. If I went to St Mary's straight away...

'Pretty mistress? Hey? Anybody home?' Lapis-blue garters pranced before my eyes. The glib-tongued apprentice had singled me out again. 'Pet, you're not listening,' he declared with feigned dismay, reaching out to tweak my nose. 'Come, give your husband a surp—'

'Exactly my thoughts!' I exclaimed fervently and elbowed my way out.

One of St Anthony's wretched sows blundered along in front of me, as though she had some similar mission. At least she cleared my path.

St Mary-le-Bow lay almost a stone's throw from the alley off Bow Lane where I now lived. Richard Lambard, my grandfather, was buried beneath the church's nave so that was why my family sometimes worshipped there to pray for his soul. My brothers used to tease me that the steeple was haunted, and if you stood in the churchyard for long enough, you were sure to see a chunk of masonry fall from the roof, and that was Grandfather's ghost making mischief.

To my relief, the doors of St Mary's stood open. I crossed myself and prayed to Our Lady the Virgin to give me strength. After all, Our Lady's marriage had been arranged, too, and I doubt she had cared for St Joseph at first, especially when he was so angry about the Angel Gabriel.

I could, would, do this now – go in, swear on the Gospels that I had been wed against my will and that the marriage had not been consummated. They might insist upon a midwife to examine me, but my body's evidence would prove I was no liar. Of course, I'd need to move back to my parents' house and I could not be sure Father would take me in; but first things first. With a deep breath I grabbed up my skirts. Freedom was just steps away.

But I was wrong. A pikestaff dropped obliquely across my path. I had not noticed the sergeant on duty.

'I have business inside, sir,' I announced, imitating my mother's tone when she addressed the household. 'It's a matter of urgency.'

The soldier jerked a thumb at a parchment nailed on the door. 'Plaintiff or defendant, mistress? What time is your hearing?'

'I…ah…er…'

He propped the pikestaff against the wall and shook his head at me. 'The rule is you cannot go in unless you are on today's list.'

'But I need a marriage annulment, sir. By the end of this week. Today, if possible.'

'Bless me, young woman,' he clucked. 'Have you been sleeping in some toadstool ring? Don't you know it takes months, sometimes years, to get a hearing?'

Months? Years? My first monthly flow might be only days away.

'They'll understand the matter is urgent,' I assured him, wondering if I could duck beneath his arm, but he was no fool.

'Listen, first you find a proctor to write your petition, then it has to go all the way to Rome, and the Pope himself must be told of it. His Holiness may say you have a case to be heard or he may not.'

'But I do. Oh, please, let me through.'

'How old are you?'

'Almost fifteen, sir.'

'Fourteen then. Well, pardon me for asking, but does this husband of yours cuff you around when he's had a bellyful of ale?' He peered down, inspecting my face for bruises. 'Is he unkind to you?'

'No, sir.' This was becoming embarrassing. Next he would ask whether Shore had lain with me. Instead he said, 'Does your father know you've come here?' And that angered me.

'No, sir, this is my business. I am quite capable of handling it.'

'I can see that.' I could tell he was trying not to laugh. 'So, who is to pay the legal fees?' He cocked his head towards the door. 'None of the carrion crows in there will take your part unless you pay 'em. They can't live on air, you know. It's business, see.'

How naïve of me. I thought it a matter of justice.

Dismayed, I stared down into the churchyard, biting back my tears, looking so forlorn, I daresay, that the soldier creaked down upon his haunches and took my gloved hands. 'Give your marriage time,' he advised, with a kindly tug on the end of my blonde plait that must have been showing beneath my coif. 'Lovely girl like you can twirl your husband round your little finger if you play it right. Now you go home and make him his supper, eh?'

Someone cleared his throat impatiently behind me. Three churchmen were waiting to pass. My self-appointed counsel snapped up to standing, his chin turning a dull red beneath his stubble. 'Go home an' forget all about this, eh?' he muttered after he had waved them through.

Forget? The rest of my life is staked out unless I cut the ropes.

How easily Life can flick us. Like an idle boy's fingernail against a tiny fly. We are so fragile, our destinies changed so easily by a quarrel, a smile, a death – or marriage.

I was twelve years old – that's two years ago – when I was wed to William Shore. He was twenty-six and already a freeman of the Mercers' Guild when he became my suitor. My father considered him an honest man with good prospects.

Once I reached thirteen, I was sent to live with him. I found him kindly, but whenever he stepped inside the door at the end of the day he seemed to bring a weariness that settled like a dust upon my chatter. He still does. I have no idea how to engage him save to inquire dutifully about his business, and most times he will not speak of it. Nor does he wish me to play music or read to him, save from the scriptures.

He is dull, dull, dull. I don't mean like a numbskull, but dull like an old coin dug up by the city wall. Maybe some other bride might have brushed the earth away and shined him up, but I do not have that urge, and the thought of him taking my maidenhead makes me shudder. Shore likes the way he is; it is me he desires to mint to his liking, but I'm not a yes-sir-please-you-sir girl.

He chose me for my looks and because I was a Lambard, and he did everything wrong. He and his brother-in-law from Derbyshire, John Agard, *inspected* me before I even met them. I don't mean they stared at me across the pews or during a sermon in St Paul's Yard. No, really *inspected*. I awoke one January morning to find my night robe up around my thighs and the sheet drawn back. It is quite commonplace for parents to permit prospective husbands to view a daughter naked, but how demeaning.

The bargaining was done swiftly after that. Both Shore and my father were in haste to shake hands on the contract. Shore saw himself acquiring a useful patron, because, besides being a wealthy merchant and influential in the Mercers' Guild, my father, John Lambard, is Alderman for Farringdon, which contains St Paul's Cathedral and the rich abbeys of the Franciscan and Dominican Friars. What's more, Father was also Sheriff of London that year, second only to the Lord Mayor. Anne, my mother, is the daughter of Robert Marshall, a reputable merchant of the Grocers' Guild.

What Shore did not know when he offered for me was that Father had loaned a huge sum to the Duke of York for the war against Queen Margaret, and when the news reached us that her grace had just nailed the duke's head up on a gatehouse at York, and her army was marching south to enter London, my father was in terror of his life. If the Queen found out which aldermen had lent money to the duke's cause, it was good odds she would execute them for high treason – hanging, drawing and quartering – or, at the least, exact huge fines.

Father was in haste to provide for us children before all his possessions were seized. He arranged apprenticeships for my two older brothers, Robert and Jack. My younger brother, Will, was promised to the church. I was the only daughter and Father feared if he did not find me a husband straight away, he never would.

Do not think I did not protest. I wanted to be apprenticed like my brothers. I wanted to be the first woman to sit on the Council of Aldermen, to have my name in the Great Chronicle of London, maybe become the first woman Lord Mayor, but no one would listen and the rod across my shoulders was a painful argument.

Well, my father has not had his innards ripped out on Tower Hill. The Duke of York's son, handsome Edward, has seized the throne, driven Queen Margaret into exile and locked up old, mad King Henry in the Tower of London. (He has even outraged everyone by marrying a steward's daughter.) Father's business is prospering, although he is disappointed not to have received a knighthood, but he carries on his life as a highly renowned alderman, while I am stuck in this loveless marriage.

I believe there is a way to unlock the chains of wedlock, even for a woman. I won't give up. I won't. I won't.

# LOVER

# I
# Bow Lane, London, 1475

How easily Life can flick us. Like an idle boy's fingernail against a tiny fly. We are so fragile, our destinies changed so easily by a marriage, a death, a quarrel or a smile. I have been waiting a long time for Life to edge his finger close again.

You see, I am twenty-five now and still tied to William Shore despite all my efforts to break free. At times I have considered murder and adultery, but I have resisted both, despite immense temptation to do the former and insufficient enticement to enjoy the latter.

My mind aches for challenge. When my father was sheriff of London, our family house was ever full of esteemed and knowledgeable men, and their talk at table was of kings and dukes, of battles and parliaments, of laws and verdicts, trade and strategy. I learned what went on at the Council of Aldermen, the quarrels between the guilds, the jostling for advancement, the give and take between the city fathers and the King. I miss that rich discourse. When Shore bids fellow liverymen to dine with us, such matters are only for the men; we wives are banished to the parlour. I mean no disrespect, but much of the women's talk is about their children. And I am childless. Oh, you might look at me and notice no discontent. I am like some tree with ring upon ring of thick armour around my heart, waiting for the woodcutter.

But there is a rainbow promise in the sky. Shore has become impotent, and at last he has agreed that we should no longer share a bed. I also have a little money of my own coming in because he has grudgingly allowed me to set up a workshop of silkwomen, and I am going to save up until I can find an honest lawyer to present my case to his Holiness in Rome. Yes, there is hope.

That was my thinking as I climbed onto a set of steps behind the counter in Shore's shop. So thankful to be alone, I was looking forward to making a display of the jewelled girdles that my silkwomen had finished the day before. Outside, a fierce April shower was cleansing the street so there would be no customers until the sun showed her countenance again, and I could take my time.

Behind the counter, I draped four falls of fabric from the uppermost shelf. The ruby velvet and the blue-black brocade, wefted with silver thread, were borrowed from my family's shop in Silver Street. The other two were brunette and russet, the humdrum fabrics that my husband sold.

I had already arranged the most expensive girdle around the brocade in semblance of a noblewoman's waist. It was so beautiful — a sliver of silver samite stitched with tiny seed pearls and completed with a trio of teardrop pearls set at either end. By contrast, the belt that I took up next was a plain, silk cord, but its shining blue would enhance the brown cloth behind it like the flash of azure on a mallard's wings.

I was concentrating so diligently with the pinning that the sudden sound of someone's cough nearly toppled me. On the other side of the counter stood a man in expensive apparel and he looked to be enjoying a view of my ankles. Can ankles blush?

'I beg your pardon, sir,' I exclaimed with a gasp of surprise. 'I did not hear the bell.'

'I did not ring it.' His voice was utterly beautiful. What's more, he had a smile to make my toes curl. Not lascivious, but as though we shared a jest and the rest of the world could go and be hanged.

I descended as gracefully as I could and smoothed my tawny skirts, trying to glance up at him with modesty when I so longed to stare. I knew Shore supplied several noblemen with livery cloth for their households, but such men never came to the shop.

A brooch of pearls and peridot lit the black velvet of this stranger's cap and he wore a fine murrey riding cloak loosely cordled at his throat. Raindrops showered to the floor as he shrugged the cloak off and laid it across the end of the counter against the wall. I was intrigued to notice that the velvet of his slate-blue cote was flattened across each shoulder. This was a man who usually wore a heavy collar of great office.

I curtsied low. 'How may I help you, my lord?'

He did not correct my address of him. That smile again. 'Sir Edward Brampton has recommended your silken belts,' he murmured, looking up at the samite and pearls. 'I desire to buy one for my stepdaughter. She is almost sixteen and soon to be married.'

Well, I wished her happiness in her marriage, but more than that, I wished myself in her shoes, able to feast in this man's company.

'May I show you some that may be more appealing to her youth, my lord?' I fetched out half a dozen belts and laid them in a row for his consideration.

He did not inquire the prices like most would. Instead, he seemed genuinely interested in the craft and beauty. Drawing off his gloves, he set them at the end of the counter beside his cloak. I was curious to observe his hands.

*Look behind the outward show*, my father always advises every new apprentice. *Observe a man's fingernails when he takes off his gloves to feel the quality of the cloth you are selling. See if his nails be clean beneath and filed smooth. A rogue may dress like a lord but his hands will show the truth.*

This man's nails were clean, buffed crescents, and his hands would have thrilled a sculptor for they were robust yet slender, unblemished by the sun. A flat diamond adorned his third finger. It was one of the largest gemstones I had ever glimpsed.

Together we peered over the merchandise, our foreheads almost touching. I could smell the imber-gres and chypre essence this man was wearing and, oh, it stirred my senses, and I prayed that no other customers would venture in.

'You do not sell expensive cloth, mistress,' he observed, glancing round at the bales leaning against the walls. 'Who supplies the jewels, then, for these belts?'

'The goldsmith, Alderman Edmund Shaa. He has also given my silkwomen a workroom so they may be together.' Then lest my business relationship be misconstrued, I added swiftly, 'He is the father of a good friend of mine, my lord, and this is a new venture on my part. I am praying it will succeed.'

'I am sure it will,' he replied courteously. 'I am well acquainted with Master Shaa. He must think very highly of you.'

I blushed, honestly delighted by his remark. I so longed to ask him who he was but courtesy bridled my tongue.

By now we had reduced his choice to three. He was taking his time in reaching a decision.

'Forgive my impertinence, mistress,' he said, observing the tiny wisps of blonde hair that had escaped from my cap. 'Your hair and colouring are similar to my stepdaughter's and she often wears that same blue there.' He half-crossed himself, his third finger drawing a line from his heart. I glanced down at the bright blue modesty inset within my collar, and grew hot within my gown. He took up one of the belts and held it out to me. 'If you please, it would help me if you could hold each of these in turn.'

So I obeyed, lifting each pretty girdle to gleam against the square of bluebell velvet that crossed my cleavage.

Thinking much about this encounter later, I realised it gave him plentiful opportunity to stare at my bosom, and yet at the time it did not strike me as sinful. If he was interested in more than the ornate belts, he was subtle.

'That one!' he declared finally. It was expensive – honey silk shot with gold, lined with taffeta and embroidered with tiny scallop shells, each with a pearl nestling in its heart. A row of little tinkling shells weighted the ends, promising that it would hang gracefully. A lively girl would find it delightfully frivolous.

'A good choice. I think your stepdaughter will be very pleased,' I answered honestly as I fetched out a shiny drawstring bag to match his purchase. He watched me wind the belt into a coil and nestle it safe in a little nest of rabbit fur before I slid it inside. 'Actually, my lord, Lambard's shop in Silver Street has some Toulouse silk shipped in only this week that may please your stepdaughter if her marriage chest is not yet full. A bright blue embroidered with white *milles fleurs*. Toulouse dyes are fast and the quality is excellent.'

'Lambard's, you say?' There was flicker of amusement.

'Yes, my lord.' I did not tell him John Lambard was my father. 'And if you do visit, pray say you came from here.'

'Thank you.' He looked genuinely grateful, but then he teased me. 'Now before you recommend some other delightful ways of emptying my purse, we must negotiate for this.'

Curse it, I'd forgotten to bargain. 'Oh,' I exclaimed, touching my left-hand fingertips to my lips in innocent confusion. The girdle had only been finished last night and I had not put a price on it. Yes, that sounds as though I was poor at selling, but in truth this man had me dazed, so delicious was his company. As if he sensed my dilemma, my handsome customer came to my rescue.

'I see you stock murrey broadcloth here. My steward can visit tomorrow to bargain with your master.' His words caught me on the raw.

'There is no master.' I flared swiftly with a lift of chin and then thought myself an utter fool for behaving so. 'Your pardon, my lord, my husband owns this shop but the girdles are my enterprise. You may have the belt for six shillings.'

He took the coins from his leather pouch. 'And you are Mistress...?'

'Shore, my lord.'

'Then I give you good morrow, Mistress Shore.'

I knew my duty and hastened to open the door for him. Outside, huddled beneath the lintel, were two men in livery. They arranged their lord's cloak about him and stepped back. His groom straight away led up a fine chestnut stallion, but my noble customer was in no hurry. He stared out into the rain pensively and then turned his head to me.

'I think perhaps I should discuss the livery cloth myself, Mistress Shore. What time may I come to speak with your husband?'

'My lord,' I gasped. 'I pray you tell me which hour is convenient to you and he will oblige.'

'Shall we say one o'clock tomorrow, then?'

'So please you.' I curtsied, my hand in deference across my heart. 'And pray you, my lord, may I tell my husband your name?'

'Hastings.'

My jaw slackened. The King's Chamberlain, Lord Lieutenant of Calais and Master of the Royal Mint! I could not answer for shock, but I managed to make a deeper obeisance. After he had stepped forth, I closed the door, gave a squeal of delight, grabbed up my skirts and, humming, spun around our showing room as though I had found the crock of gold at the foot of the rainbow.

*Tomorrow shall be my dancing day;*
*I would my true love did so chance*
*To see the legend of my play,*
*To call my true love to my dance.*

'Ahem.'

Jesu save me! He stood within the shop again. What was worse, he had glimpsed me prancing like a merry five-year-old. My face must have looked mighty sheepish because he burst out laughing.

'I-I like d-dancing,' I explained, smoothing my skirts.

'And does Master Shore *dance* with you?'

I shook my head.

He looked downwards, smoothing the fingers of his right hand glove to make a better fit; even that was done with a languid grace. 'Pardon my curiosity, but is it that Master Shore will not or cannot *dance*?' He raised his gaze slowly. There was nothing improper in his expression and yet...

'My husband cannot, my lord.'

'That's a pity. But I forget my purpose. I have other business to transact after noon tomorrow so tell your husband I shall come at ten o' the clock. It was pleasant talking to you, Mistress Shore.'

O Heaven! I should not sleep that night. Lord Hastings' presence lingered with me like a fragrance upon my wrist. Every phrase he had spoken I lifted gently from my memory and examined over and over again with a collector's care.

I was humming to myself when Shore returned to the shop an hour later. Even he could sense that something had changed. I must have looked more alive.

'I have good news for you,' I said triumphantly. 'You missed an important customer, no less than the King's Chamberlain.'

'Lord *Hastings*?' Shore nearly had an apoplexy on the spot. Disappointment to have missed the noble lord shone from every pore.

'Ah trust Howe treated him well?' His Derbyshire dialect was always stronger when he was upset.

'No, I served him,' I replied proudly. 'He purchased a lady's belt and he is returning to see you at ten tomorrow to bargain over the broadcl—'

'*You*?' He cut in with such disgust that I recoiled. 'By the Saints! You fool of a woman, why did you not summon Howe?'

Howe was our oldest apprentice but I was just as capable.

'Because he was gone to Blackfriars to negotiate the dagswain order, remember? What was I supposed to do, sirrah? Close the door in Lord Hastings's face?'

'No need for that kind of tongue,' Shore admonished. 'It's just that ah've a large order from Lord Rivers' steward an' if word gets around that ah'm dealing with Lord Hastings as well, they may cancel it. Happened to one of the Drapers' Guild.'

'I wish you had told me,' I said wearily. Not that it would have made any difference.

'Lord Rivers, the Queen's brother, and Lord Hastings have fallen out over who should be governing Calais, see, and if you look to be dealing wi' one of them, the other will ha' none of you.'

'That's ludicrous,' I declared. 'King Edward must find it hard to deal with their quarrels.'

'Very likely. That's probably one of the reasons the King sent Lord Rivers to ha' charge of the Prince of Wales at Ludlow. Anyroad, like ah said, you should have sent for me straightway.'

'But you won't turn down Lord Hastings' business, surely?'

'Tha's summat for tomorrow.' Shore was looking at me strangely. 'Why didn't you send to find me, Elizabeth?'

'I did not know rightly where you were, sir,' I answered, although I was certain he had been trying to raise himself with a gap-toothed seamstress, who lived two streets away. 'But I'll obey in future. Next time her grace the Queen knocks and you are out, I'll hide beneath the counter and pretend we are closed.'

'Aye,' he grunted. 'Do that.'

During supper that evening, he said not a word until we had finished eating. 'Lord Hastings is a great lord, wife. You should ha' said ah would attend him at t'Palace.'

'But he offered to come back tomorrow. Anyway, being such a "great lord", I daresay he may take his leisure where it pleases him, and it pleases him to return tomorrow morning. Are you decided? Shall you accept his business?'

He set his alejack down and made a face. 'Depends whether he makes an offer. Ah hope you asked a good price for the girdle?'

'I think so. It was for his stepdaughter.'

'Aye, that would be the Bonville girl. Worth a fortune, she is.'

'Well, he took much trouble in choosing it for her and he was pleasant and not high-saddled at all. You should have seen the clothes he was wearing.' I shook my head, still marvelling. 'I advised him go to Father's and see the new delivery.'

His face creased in disapproval. 'Jesu! You presumed to direct a great lord like him?'

'But he didn't mind at all.'

Shore's eyes narrowed. 'Mayhap it was not just the girdles that interested him.'

This conversation was travelling onto hazardous ground. Shore had not agreed easily to me employing some silkwomen and making a little money of my own.

My hands fisted in my lap. 'What are you saying?'

He snorted and clambered from the trestle. 'Have you not noticed that when you are in t'shop, we have more men come to buy?'

Foolish logic! How could I notice the difference when I was not there?

'I do not like your implication, sir,' I said, swivelling round to face him. 'Nor do you make any sense. Just tell me how would men know whether I am in the shop or not before they come in?'

He was looking down at me as if my dress was immodest. 'Because ah've seen them staring though the doorway as they pass, or else they traipse in, feign interest in summat and then leave if you are not around. God's truth, when you are there, they dawdle like sniffin' dogs. Ah've observed it's only the men, not the women.'

'And ah observe that you have a great imagination,' I muttered, gathering up the platters for our maidservant to remove.

He grabbed my shoulder and growled, 'Are you calling me a liar, wife? Why do you think ah've always been reluctant all these years to have you in the showing room?'

I shook his hand away as I stood up. I knew very well but I said, 'Well, I always thought it was in case people believed you too poor to employ sufficient apprentices. If I am good for business because my manners please people, sir, then you should be content. I am not like my friend, Alys Rawson, using my looks to turn men into fawning lapdogs.'

He looked so peevish that I could not resist tormenting him further.

'Oh Heavens, Shore, you surely do not fear I shall cuckold you? What would Lord Hastings want with a lowly creature like me?' There is such a thing as a husbandly grunt and Shore's was perfected. 'Anyway,' I added, pouring some more ale into his cup, 'let us not quarrel but celebrate our good fortune. If you can be cunning and sell to both lords, you shall have much profit.'

But Shore's jealousy was pricked. Next morning, the sly knave sent out an invitation to his friends' wives to come at a quarter to ten and take refreshment so that when Lord Hastings arrived, I should be making petty talk upstairs and unable to come down. Oh, how his distrust made me seethe.

No bargain was made with Lord Hastings that morning, but I noticed later that he had left his gloves behind, not on the open counter by the measuring rule, but tucked at the end between a shallow basket of remnants and the wall.

What should I do? Send an apprentice to Westminster or my lord's house? Tell Shore? Take the gloves myself? Was this forgetfulness deliberate? Ha, vain fantasy on my part to suppose such a thing. This great lord would no doubt send some menial to retrieve the gloves, yet I stood there holding them and dared to dream.

# II

I met Lord Hastings again within a few days. He summoned my father to bring samples of silks and gauzes to Beaumont's Inn, his London house. The request read: *Since the fabrics are to be purchased for my lord's stepdaughter and Mistress Shore resembles her, would Master Lambard please ask his daughter to accompany him!* So Lord Hastings had discovered the family connection. I felt very flattered. Of course, Shore would have made trouble had he known, but he had gone to Suffolk to collect cargo that had arrived from a manufactory he part-owned across the water in Bergen-ap-Zoom.

I had visited the houses of wealthy merchants, but I had never stepped inside a noble lord's dwelling, and Beaumont's Inn, with its two gables and three storeys, looked to be extremely modest. It lay at the south-east end of Thames Street, close to Paul's wharf and neighbour to Baynard's Castle, where King Edward's mother, the Duchess of York, lived. Only a strip of garden and a laneway separated the two properties.

Father and I were shown up into a hall with long windows that looked westwards towards the River Fleet. Two immense tapestries adorned the facing wall. I do not know a great deal about the stitching but the dyes I do know. Indigo, woad and madder

24

predominated and I would have wagered these hangings had been made in Anjou and come to England as part of Queen Margaret's dowry when she married King Henry. In fact, the golden salt upon the high table might have been hers as well for it was shaped as a swan, one of her badges.

The man who had been privileged to receive this spoil was in conversation with two men from the Tailors' Guild and all three were leaning over drawings set out on the high table. When the steward announced us, Lord Hastings dismissed them and stepped down to greet us.

Ah, I am a mercer's daughter to my fingertips! There is such beauty in a well-dressed man. Lord Hastings had excellent taste. He clearly understood colour, and his long robe of Saxon blue velvet was tailored skilfully across his shoulders. Falls of gilt brocade hung from his padded sleeves just above the elbows and his indoor shoes were finely tapered and made of dark blue leather embroidered with his maunche in white and violet thread.

'Ah, I see you have brought my gloves, Mistress Shore.' My senses picked up a descant to that plainsong remark. 'Bring the samples to the windows, Master Lambard, if you please.'

As he stood with his steward flicking through our squares of cloth, the sunlight showed me a lord who was far older than I had first thought. His forehead was lapped by fine, plentiful hair of a lustrous fairness, a pale scar angled up from his left eyebrow and a frown mark slashed his brow above his nose. Otherwise, the lines in his face hinted at a kind and generous disposition.

'Your daughter is of my stepdaughter's complexion,' he said, looking round at Father. 'It would please me if she could remove her headdress.'

'Of course, my lord,' agreed Father, his mind utterly on selling.

What choice had I? I took off the velvet and buckram cone that sat upon my coiled plaits and let the steward take it into his care.

'Since she is not yet wed, my stepdaughter, Lady Cecily, wears her hair loose. If you would oblige me, Mistress Shore?'

I did not take my gaze from Lord Hastings' face as I reached up and removed the pins, one by one, and let my blonde plait fall. There was something deliciously sinful in him asking this of me. A married woman's hair is for her husband or her lover.

'Unbraided!' commanded Lord Hastings, his gaze touching my hair and coming to linger on my lips. In obedience, I brought my plait forward over my right shoulder and slowly loosened the braid and with a toss of my head sent the strands swirling across my shoulders like an unfurled cloak.

'You have beautiful hair, Mistress Shore.' So had he. I could have clawed through his and drawn his face to mine. I had never experienced the power of kisses, but this lord would know the craft of lips, the delicate thrusting, the *petite mesure parfaite*.

My father, fussing which brocade to proffer first, had missed the dance of stares, but he knew what to advise. The choosing was swift and decisive, and leaving my father to bargain with Hyrst, his steward, Lord Hastings led me up to the dais.

'Tell me what you think of these.'

'Are they for a tapestry, my lord?' I asked, picking up the nearest paper – a charcoal sketch of a helmed man wearing a mask, breast-plate, leather skirt, greaves and sandals.

'No, it's an entertainment for the court. *The Siege of Troy*. Lord Rivers' notion. Unfortunately I doubt I'll have time to put it on this year. Here's the Lady Helen.'

The drawing showed a creature in a long, yellow wig and volu-minous white gown. Metal cones armoured her massive breasts and steel tassets protected her broad thighs. She looked like a fishwife playing Joan of Arc.

'Why are you smiling, Mistress Shore?'

'Your pardon, my lord, but unless your desire to is to make

people laugh, I cannot imagine anyone stealing this lady from her husband. Why, Prince Paris would need a derrick to get her on board his ship. Oh, but I suppose she is to be played by a man.'

He took the cartoon from me. 'Do you believe any of this tale is true?'

'That a princess could leave her husband for a handsome Trojan? I am sure that has been happening since time began. However, I do not suppose the war lasted ten years. That is probably the storyteller's exaggeration. Or if it did, I expect the Greeks went home at Christmas and Easter.'

'They were heathens, Mistress Shore.'

I shrugged. 'Ah, well, perhaps they had orgies to attend.'

I was flattered by his company. There must be weighty matters on this great man's mind and yet he was making every effort to be pleasant.

'My lord, is it true we shall be soon be at war with the French?'

'Yes, Mistress Shore.'

'That is not good news for the city. Is it to punish the King of France?'

King Louis had funded a mighty rebellion a few years earlier. He had brokered an alliance between King Edward's cousin, Warwick, the King's younger brother, George, and the exiled former queen, Margaret of Anjou. The result was an invasion that drove King Edward and Lord Hastings out of England for the winter, but they returned in the spring and after two bloody battles at Barnet and Tewkesbury, King Edward slid back onto the cushions on his throne at Westminster and clapped on his crown again.

'To punish the King of France?' replied Lord Hastings, humouring me. 'Yes, Mistress Shore, it could be seen that way but there are better reasons. You do not approve of the King's enterprise?'

'I know that King Louis has invaded Brittany and would like
to conquer Burgundy, my lord. I understand also that England
has treaty obligations with Burgundy, but I wish the realm might
have continual peace so our trade may prosper. War means higher
taxes and good men risking their lives. Hasn't there been enough
killing in the quarrel between the Houses of York and Lancaster?
No, I do not uphold a war with France.'

He seemed amused by my outspokenness. 'I shall inform his
grace the King of your opinion, little mistress.'

'I pray you do not, my lord,' I said genially, for I knew he was
teasing me, but inside I was bristling for I dislike being belittled.
'As for taxes, a man may milk a cow, for sure, but there comes a
time if there is insufficient grass when—'

His gasp of laughter interrupted me. 'Mistress Shore! And there
was I believing you only get milk if you pump a cow's tail, but
now you tell me it's a matter of grass.'

For an instant I thought to clamp my lips closed and wallow in
mortification but instead the she-devil in me brazenly retorted,
'My lord, you may believe what you will. Perhaps in Leicester-
shire there are a lot of cows with aching tails!'

Hastings drew a breath at my audacity, for he was from those
parts, then laughed heartily, slamming his hand upon the table. It
was fortunate that his steward's polite cough ended the conversation for although you can push the boat out far when you are
younger and female, it is best not to get into unfamiliar waters.

Lord Hastings' hand between my shoulder blades was extremely
agreeable as he escorted me back to Father. 'Your daughter has a
sharp wit, Master Lambard.'

'Oh, please do not tell him that, my lord, or he will start
noticing.'

Father pushed an armful of samples at me with a glare to hold
my tongue.

As we walked back to Silver Street, he said, 'That man will seek to have you, Elizabeth.'

When I made no answer, he added, 'You'll not encourage him. I'll not have any daughter of mine causing a scandal. The Guild won't like it.'

'I do not think you have any right to preach to me, sir.' I watched his handsome profile redden.

'Damn it, I suppose you'll never forget I made a fool of myself.'

We walked on in silence, both of us remembering how he had stupidly leased a house in Wood Street for his mistress and then when he had finished with her, she had moved out taking everything that could be lifted, unscrewed or levered off. Because the dwelling was rented from the Goldsmiths' Guild and Father did not have the coin in hand to pay for the woman's thievery, his reputation would have been ruined. Fortunately Alderman Shaa forewarned me and provided a list of all that was owed. It took all my savings to pay my father's debts.

'I helped you then with what little money I had, Father,' I exclaimed, hastening to keep up with his angry stride. 'But now all your cargoes have been safely delivered, you might consider helping me.'

He halted. 'To grease some slimy lawyer's palm, Elizabeth, so he'll write to His Holiness in Rome on your behalf? Jesu! If divorce was easy, princes would change their wives like they change their cotes. Besides, you and Shore have managed all these years.'

'Managed!' I echoed indignantly, tempted to toss Father's precious samples in the nearest sewer. 'Shore's been impotent since he had that quarrel with the cooper's cart, and before that was not much better.'

I knew what I was missing. I had discovered how to pleasure myself.

'I concede that Shore is not of the right temperament for you, Elizabeth,' Father was saying, 'but as I've told you many times before, he's no sluggard and the Mercer's Guild thinks highly of him. Why, I'll wager he could become an alderman like me in a few years' time. Just be patient.'

'Patient for what? I did not want this marriage when I was twelve and now I am twenty-five and childless, I am even more resolved to end it.'

Several passers-by were eyeing us now and Father rapidly dredged up his pat-on-the-head-and-she-will-calm expression that he used with Mama when she was angry.

'Sweetheart,' he cajoled, putting his free arm about my shoulder to urge me forward, 'taking a husband to law is not how a decent woman behaves. Marriage is for life. It is God's will.'

'God, sir, was never *married*.' I shoved his merchandise back into his arms and fisting my skirts marched on alone.

'You try my patience, Elizabeth,' he grumbled, hastening after me. 'Even if you had the money for a petition to Rome, his Holiness in Rome would never listen to a woman.'

'I'll make somebody listen,' I vowed.

And maybe it would be Lord Hastings.

# III

'What's going on, Margery?' I whispered to Alderman Shaa's daughter on Sunday, a week later after we had heard the sermon at St Paul's Cross. I could see that her parents and mine were heading off together to their favourite tavern for ale and pies, but Margery was blocking my way, insisting that Shore and I remain with her in the stands at St Paul's Yard beside the cathedral. She had more flesh to keep her warm; I was feeling chilled and ravenous.

I had always trusted Margery. We had become friends at the Cripplegate School for merchants' daughters and neither of us had found marriage easy. But there was something else that bound me to her family. Not just their help in strangling the scandal that would have dishonoured my father, but Master Shaa's kindness in persuading Shore to let me have my little enterprise with the silkwomen.

'Wait-and-see!' My friend tapped the side of her nose. 'A surprise.'

'Oh lord, we haven't got to watch another pair of priests being flailed around the yard, have we?' I sat down again with great reluctance. The hour's sermon on Divine Love, delivered by a

Franciscan with a blocked nose, had been tedious. 'Won't your children be missing you?' I muttered.

'Lizbeth! Be patient!'

The last thing I wanted was to watch some poor wretch doing penance for their sins. God's mercy! I was the last person to desire to cast the first stone. Part of me was bursting to tell Margery about my encounters with Lord Hastings, but her tolerance of others' foibles had narrowed since her marriage to the goldsmith Hugh Paddesley, a man I did not care for. Sometimes she sounded more like Paddesley than he did.

'Ah, here we go,' she exclaimed, nudging me with her elbow.

A ragtag mob of people, who had not heard the sermon, was thickening the crowd. Alarm bells sounded in my head. Adultery! It had to be adultery! I cast a sharp look at my friend. Had she suspected I was dreaming of taking a lover? No, that was lighting a bonfire with green wood for I read no rebuke in her eyes, and Shore and Paddesley were discussing cockfighting with their friend Shelley. Nothing was untoward.

'I promise you, Lizbeth!' she exclaimed. 'You'll be glad you stayed.'

There was only one penitent in the open cart, a woman in a white shift with her long dark hair unbound about her shoulders. Not a common strumpet by the way she held herself. Well nourished, too, neither scrawny nor obese. The crowd whooped as the sheriff's soldiers pulled her roughly down onto the cobbles and untied her wrists. A priest handed her a lit taper, and then with two soldiers ahead of her and two behind her with their halberd blades prodding her forwards, she began her journey of contrition around St Paul's Yard.

I had seen these walks of penitence before, but today the crowd's jeers made me shudder as though someone had walked across my grave. The human cockroaches from the back lanes had brought buckets slopping with excrement. Soon the woman's shift would resemble a filthy rag.

At first she tried to keep her dignity, but as the pelting grew, she started to flinch, her body jerking this way and that like a thief on a hangman's rope. As she approached our stand, I could see she was about ten years older than I. Her forehead and left cheek were bleeding, and spittle and dung spattered her hair and skin. The thin, putrid shift showed her nipples and she was shivering as though she had the marsh disease.

Shore and Margery's husband leaned over to spit at her.

'Come on! *Hiss!*' Margery sprang to her feet and, like the other merchant's wives, shook her fist and jeered. I stood up with the rest but I could not abuse the poor creature. This was no prostitute snared to give the crowd its monthly dose of titillation. She could have been an erring wife or a courtesan; just a woman who had fallen into temptation.

'Vile,' I muttered, wincing as I watched the woman whimper and fling up her hands as the stoning began again.

Flushed and pleased, Margery subsided on the bench and put her mouth to my ear. 'That was your father's greedy whore. She was caught last week fleecing a merchant from the Grocers' Guild. Didn't you hear all the hubbub? The guild has expelled him.'

'Sweet Christ!' Now I understood why her parents had hurried mine away. Or had my father done the hurrying?

I searched the faces around me. Did our husbands know?

'Too tame,' Paddesley was complaining, with a sneer of nostril. 'They could have whipped the whore around the yard.'

'Aye, better sport,' agreed Shore, which made me want to stick a dagger in him.

'For my part, I cannot see what charm she held for the poor dotard,' Master Shelley was saying. 'Breasts like a beggar's purse. Whereas that cherrylips a month ago.' He whistled. His eyes skewed covertly in my direction. 'Legs to her armpits, but this hag...'

'Ah, but...' Paddesley whispered something behind his hand. The other two laughed.

Margery, excluded, reddened. 'You might give me thanks,' she muttered, taking out her annoyance on me. 'I thought you'd be pleased.'

'Pleased! I found it offensive.'

'Twaddle, Lizbeth! Women like her make it harder for the rest of us.'

'Make what harder, Mistress Paddesley,' quipped Shelley, elbowing her husband.

'Yes, what are you trying to say, pet?' Paddesley asked, trying to exchange a grin with me.

Margery was already in a nose-up huff. 'No matter. Can we go now?'

'Yes, Margery, what did you mean?' I whispered as we descended the stairs ahead of the others.

She had to be coaxed. 'Just that respectable wives like us are not supposed to play the games in bed that she does. If we do, we're accused of being wanton.'

'So it's a sin to enjoy a husband's lovemaking? How very absurd, but then I wouldn't know, would I?' How bitter I must have sounded.

'Well, I think the whore deserved her punishment, Lizbeth. She's the worse sort, tempting husbands to be unfaithful.'

'What, you think she's worse than a common strumpet?'

'Winchester geese do it to stay alive. And it's a business transaction for men who have too much—' She gestured. 'You know.'

'Ah, "the fiery men who become ill if they do not have regular intercourse with a woman",' I said, quoting a treatise on the issue.

'Exactly,' agreed Margery. 'Whereas that bitch's sort does it because they enjoy it.'

'So it's her pleasure you take issue with?'

'Well, yes.'

It was a point of view I had once shared. The sisterhood of respectability. Guild wives were supposed to uphold God's commandments to the letter. But poor Margery was feeding the incubus of Envy. If she could not enjoy the sport of the bedchamber, she did not want anyone else to either.

I, too, had never enjoyed a man's lovemaking. Suffered, yes. Shore had first used me when I was fourteen years old. His recent impotence was a blessing. Alas, now I was five and twenty! More than half my life gone already. But none of the London guildsmen had measured to my taste. No man except... And into my mind at that moment crept a scheme so outrageously sinful that I halted on the cobbles with a gasp.

'Lizbeth, what's wrong? Are you ill?'

'Possibly.' I laughed. Crazed might be the word.

Yes, wild, fevered, CRAZED! Deliciously mad with a spire-high, illuminated 'C'.

# IV

I took matters – and courage – into my own hands and trounced off to Beaumont's Inn.

'You'll 'ave to wait in line,' the porter growled at me.

*Wait?* There I was, anxious to give, my heart beating frantically, and ahead of me were forty people, and more arriving.

'Be patient, dearie,' said the woman behind me as she heard me sigh. 'It's always like this on petition days.'

But then I saw his lordship's steward come out and linger as though counting us. I left the line and hastened towards him but he vanished inside and the two guards protecting the entrance to the hall slammed their halberds across my path.

'Take your turn, mistress,' chortled one of them, 'unless you'd like to take your turn wi' me.'

I bit my lip. 'Very tempting, sirrah, but it's not that business I had in mind. I'm a mercer come to see Master Hyrst about an order.'

'Why was yous standing wi' the petitioners, then?' demanded the other guard.

'I thought...well, no matter. A silver penny for whichever of you can take me to Master Hyrst.'

Coin and a woman's smile are better than battering rams to open doors. Eventually a servant beckoned me through. Master Hyrst stood waiting in the passageway.

'Good day to you, sir,' I said with a curtsy. 'I should like to see my lord.'

'Oh, would you! Well, you can whistle for that, mistress.' But then as fortune would have it, Lord Hastings himself came by. The yearning creature inside my body gave a wriggle of delight at seeing him.

'Mistress Shore, whatever are you doing here?' He took my hand as I made obeisance and drew me to my feet.

'I...' How could I state my real purpose with his steward standing there like a busybody? I had to think swiftly. 'My gracious lord, I came to ask if you could recommend an honest lawyer. It is a very personal matter.'

Hyrst gave a whoosh of impatience.

'Fetch the next one in!' ordered his master and turned his attention back to me.

'Your pardon,' I said, looking up at Lord Hastings in utter humility. 'I truly had no understanding how many people were...' I half-turned to the door with a lift of hands. 'Forgive me, I'll leave at once.' But his curiosity was whetted.

'Wait,' he called out with concern.

Perhaps this was not meant to be, I thought, judging myself such a fool to even believe that he...

'Why should you need a lawyer, Mistress Shore?' he asked, pursuing me.

I halted. Could hesitation be honest yet contrived?

'It's a very private matter. I...I've tried several proctors too and not one was worthy.'

He glanced towards the next petitioner being escorted in and drew a deep breath. 'Is there an action in process against you?'

'No, my lord, I wish to bring one against my husband.'

This was a man who could defend himself in battle. He recovered instantly. 'Hyrst, ask Peter to write a letter of recommendation to William Catesby. If you wait here, Mistress Shore, it will be brought to you.'

'My lord, I cannot thank you enough.'

'What else are friends for? Good morrow to you, then.'

Friends? The doors of my life were at last letting in the frightening, sweet breath of the wild woods. The King's Chamberlain had called me friend.

Master Catesby was my age, the son of a knight and the nephew of Sir John Catesby, who was Justice of the Court of Common Pleas. Sleek auburn hair, the hue of weasel fur, pranced about his shoulders. He was one of those men who lean back nonchalantly when they talk to you.

I had no intention of sleeping with him. Nor he with me, and how assiduous he was in explaining that his clients were dukes rather than housewives and that he dealt in demesnes and not divorce. However, he did not show me to the door before the hour bell had finished striking.

Since Lord Hastings already had an 'interest' (Catesby underscored that word rather prematurely), yes, he would recommend a proctor to help me, but there was no precedent for bringing a charge of impotence against a husband. It was clear he thought I had a walnut for a brain.

'To be frank, Mistress Shore, as far as obtaining a divorce after ten years of marriage you have not got a leg to stand on, but money can open any door, even His Holiness's in Rome. Money and powerful friends. You have beauteous legs, I'm sure. Do not stand on them, spread them!'

To be truthful, he couched that advice with more circumambulation, but that was the sum of the matter. And the initial cost?

I offered him what I could afford, but to my relief he pushed the purse back at me.

'I do this as a favour to Lord Hastings. Which reminds me, Mistress Shore.' He waved my lord's letter. 'He's asked me to give you a message. He desires you to wait upon him tomorrow at a quarter to ten. And, be warned, there is always a price to pay.' I presumed he meant Lord Hastings expected reimbursement of a horizontal nature, but I was wrong.

'Divorce is an ugly process, Mistress Shore. Once you are recognised as an oath-breaker and outside the protection of your husband, your credit and reputation will be at stake.'

I rose to my feet. 'You clearly still think me rash and head-strong, Master Catesby, but women should be free to make their own decisions. If I had a mark for every girl compelled into wedlock, I should be passing rich.'

The lawyer's smile was as smooth as polished alabaster as he came to see me out. 'I'll not argue that one. But on the practical side, what else can girls of respectable family do save marry?'

'Take up the law, perhaps, Master Catesby?'

'Heaven forbid, Mistress Shore,' he laughed, and unlatched the door. 'Farewell and good fortune! I'd sin my way to matrimonial freedom if I were you.'

Can any prince or ploughman put an estimate on freedom? Freedom to walk alone or with friends? Freedom to choose with whom you share a bed? Freedom to laugh?

Freedom at last to love?


Mornings were not difficult for me to extricate myself from our house; I regularly visited my silkwomen, shopped in Cheapside or, much to Shore's annoyance, took provisions to feed the street children in our neighbourhood

That hour, as I set foot in Beaumont's Inn, my courage was wound tighter than a tailor's yarn. Except... Except if Lord Hastings granted me an audience in his private chamber, could I *thank* him enough?

Hyrst showed me into the hall and loftily bade me wait there. I did not sit down for I wanted to keep my rose gown free of creases. I'd barbered the nap to make it look new.

Two men servants came past bearing fresh bed linen. They eyed me speculatively as they made their way to the door behind the high table. I did not like their interest. It made me feel cheap.

Hyrst returned less haughty. 'Mistress Shore, my lord requests that you join him in the garden. This way, if you please.'

My sight of Lord Hastings could have adorned the margin of *The Garden of Earthly Delights*: a noble lord reading beneath a lathed arbor of vines and *rosa alba*, with a mazer and a flagon at his knee and a page in attendance.

'Mistress Shore.' He set aside his book and stood to take my hand, then bestowed me upon the nearby cushioned bench and sat down again upon his cross-legged chair, beckoning his page to pour me a beaker of perry. The welcome in his face showed I was anticipated and not a pother.

He was clothed simply. A loose-sleeved slate blue mantle, edged with coney, reached to his knees. His shirt was belted and its tails just covered his codpiece. Above the neck of his honey-hued stomacher, the cordals of his shirt were undone and I could see the tendrils of blond hair that must span his chest. To hell with his age! The lusty creature inside me was wide awake. I no longer needed to ratchet up my determination, but I was as nervous as a fieldmouse in short grass.

'Was Master Catesby able to help you?'

'Thank you, my lord, he has given me the name of a worthy cleric at the Court of Arches. I am very grateful.' I was prepared to show him how much.

'Hell, be done with thanks. Can't blame you for being wary of lawyers. Escrew you soon as look at you.' He removed the mazer lid and took a mouthful, grinning at me across the rim. 'Pretty headdress.'

I smiled, sipped and looked around. Wild strawberries and periwinkles lapped the flagstones where we sat and a chequer-board of well-scythed turves and beds of seedlings was spread before us. 'This...this is a very fine garden, my lord.'

'Not of my making, sorry to say. All rented.'

'Have you lived here for very long?' Oh, this was not easy.

'Only since I returned with the King from Burgundy. Before the rebellion, I had rooms at the palace. Still have. This is an extravagance, really. I spend more time at Westminster or Eltham than I do here.' He leaned forward, his elbows on his knees. 'What was yesterday really about, Elizabeth?'

Elizabeth – my given name – the way he said it was a caress.

'Are you sure you want to know, my lord?'

He leaned back languidly. His eyes, narrowed against the sunlight, searched my face. 'Maybe I can assist you.'

I looked down at my lap. 'I believe you can, my lord, but not in any way you can imagine.'

'Oh, I can imagine.' The garland of words was strung out evenly. I glanced up, took breath, trying to ascertain his meaning. Ambiguity might be a delight for diplomats and barons, but for the likes of me? Was this just courtly teasing? If I swept away all artifice and asked him outright, what then?

His blue gaze gleamed as though he guessed my dilemma and swept on past me. A she-blackbird, a creature of carnality so the bestiaries say, was waiting hopefully for a crumb. Like me.

*Do it*! cried the other creature inside of me, her fists hammering against my ribs.

The hour bells made his mouth tighten. I was but a swift meeting in today's agendum.

*Do it*!

'If it would please you, my lord, I should be willing to lie with you.' I drew a ragged breath and plunged in even further. 'Indeed, I should count it as an honour.'

His eyebrows arched like chevrons. 'My dear, I've been solicited by the rich and the ragged but...' I was studied anew as though he had picked up a magnifying glass to inspect every lesion in my soul. 'Devil take it,' he muttered, frowning, 'you are in earnest.'

I cursed at having cheapened myself in his estimation. This precious friendship would be over now. Desire, spoken, could not be scraped away like errata on vellum.

'Does Shore's cockerel not crow enough for you, Elizabeth?' I must have shaken as though the very air was bruising, because the cynical lines in his expression softened. 'Hell! Forgive me, that was stable talk.'

Well, I deserved stable talk if I was begging to be treated like a milkmaid, and I could speak it, too.

'Shore's cockerel sits on the perch all day and all night, my lord, and so it has been for most of the marriage. We are ill-matched.' I shook my head in sadness, and then clasped my hands to my lips in contrition. 'I ask your pardon, my lord. It was presumptuous, pathetic of me to have asked you.'

A gentle finger lifted my chin. Compassionate eyes searched my face. 'You, the most beautiful woman in London? Oh, Elizabeth.'

His voice held the kindness of a friend once again, but my self-worth was as fragile as a jenny wren's egg. I did not believe his flattery, of course, but if only he knew the depth, the desperation, of my longing to be held in his arms, valued not judged, and loved,

loved for the fledgling lonely girl within me and not my shell. The hope in my eyes must have appalled him. It was probably my imagination but there was certainly a quickening of interest in his.

'But you could take a lover so easily,' he said, sitting back and shaking his head in wry amazement as he looked at me. 'Damn it, any merchant in England worth his salt would fall before you on his knees and beg.'

'I don't know about that, my lord. They certainly hang around my doorway like flies in search of fresh meat. See, I, too, disdain ragged manners and gutter purposes.'

It was too painful to tell him that, after one of my husband's married friends had tried to assault me, Shore had blamed me and then monstrously suggested I lie with the man. 'What in fucking hell does it matter if he tups you?' Shore had said. 'He's a worthy fellow. At least that way you might provide me with an heir. You like playing with his children well enough.'

I looked across at Lord Hastings with a wry smile, trying to reclothe my vulnerability.

'Then I must count myself most favoured,' he was saying, 'however...' He stood up and paced to the edge of the arbor. I watched in dismay as he thrust his hands on his waist and cast his gaze upwards, letting out his breath with a sigh of amused wonder before he swung round to face me. 'And you consider me as manna from Heaven?'

I bowed my head in respect. 'I know you would be kind with my ignorance and gentle in teaching me.'

'Teaching!' He dragged his fingers across his jaw. 'Oh, sweetheart, was ever man so tempted?'

'Then you agree?' Excitement eddied through me. Would this divine man initiate me into Paradise? Oh, when, when? This moment even? Except his fingers were plucking at his golden troth ring. O Jesu, no!

'Do not take this wrongly.' A refusal? Please God, make him say yes. 'This is not a simple matter, Mistress Elizabeth.' He leaned a raised elbow against the weathered lathes. 'I was just thinking – remembering a Christian woman I once knew who fell in love with a Jew, loved him so much that she converted to his religion and became more devout than he.

'Now, from what you have told me and from what I have observed, it seems you have behaved with propriety all these years and suddenly you want to change your coat. Dangerous waters, Elizabeth. If you throw your values overboard, what chart shall you steer by?' His expression was telling me of an even deeper concern.

'I thank you for the warning, my lord,' I murmured with my head bowed like a daughter and then I looked up with a wicked grin. 'So your concern is I shall become an apostle of the creed of lust, and end up raddled with the crabs?' And before he could answer, I added soberly, 'Or are you afeared I shall fall in love with you?'

Relief swept into his face. 'By the Saints, you never hide your meaning, do you?'

I smiled, my heart aching. 'You have been a light in the darkness of my world, my lord. Surely friends can be honest with each other?'

He nodded, not guessing me a liar. 'Then, to be honest and speak plainly, I have a wife and family I love dearly. Kate and I do not spend much time together. I have my court duties. She has the children. Since her brother Warwick's death, she rarely steps foot in Westminster for reasons I am sure you can understand. Yes, I admit I am not faithful to her in body.' He grimaced in self-judgment. 'But where my heart is not engaged, making love does not seem like such a betrayal.'

'Then make love to me.' I tried not to sound like a desperate beggar.

'I'm grown fond of you, Elizabeth. You've been a temptation since I first saw you. Ah, a plague on it!'

I watched him drive his bejewelled fingers through his fine, fair hair. *Must I go down on my knees?*

'I am not assured this is the path for you.'

'Path, my lord?' I retorted, looking at him through my lashes. 'Blind alley, rather! I'm stitched in a cered cloth shroud on my way to the grave if I don't struggle out while I have the life force still in me.'

'The path to Hell, sweetheart,' he repeated firmly.

I rose and held my hands out to him. 'Then lead me down it.'

We stared at each other not like friends or lovers but like two knights agreed to a tournament. I was waiting for an invisible marshal to give us leave to gallop at each other, but Hastings stepped back, laughing, hands raised

'Christ save me! Not now, you hungry puss, we've insufficient time.'

'Ohhh,' I protested. 'How long do you need? Shore only took a heave and a groan when he managed it at all. Do you want me to undress, is that the reason?'

He smiled, reached out to draw my face towards him, and kissed my brow. 'My poor innocent Elizabeth. Tomorrow, then. Tomorrow at two.' A finger under my chin to make me listen. 'Put on a veil so no one will recognise you and come to Gerrard's Hall in Basing Lane. Ask for the chamber for Master Ashby.' I must have looked shocked for he added, 'See, I sound heartless and you are offended.' He turned away, dragging his fingers down his face as if he was disgusted with himself.

'No,' I lied, picking up his book. 'But should I not come here? I could creep through the postern like a thief before curfew.'

'No, Gerrard's will preserve your reputation and my privacy. And now, I'm afraid, I must ask you to leave.' Oh, he was all instructions and purpose now, other business tugging at his thoughts, but how could I resent that?

My fingers stroked the leather cover.

'My lord?'

'Yes?'

'The others? Are they always married women?'

He nodded, glad, I daresay, not to look into my face as he took the book from me and pressed the clasp closed. 'Elizabeth, if you change your mind – and you well might – send word here. Tell your servant to say, "Master Shore seeks an audience".'

'And if you change yours, my lord?'

He drew a deep breath. Clearly, the prospect of lying with me still bothered him, but as he kissed my hand, he smiled down at me.

'I promise you I won't.'

# V

Basing Lane was off Bread Street, near St Mildred's, two streets south of West Cheap. I decided to go there now on my way home, inspect the battlefield, so to speak.

The respectability of the gates at Gerrard's Hall was daunting. The house was not one of those timber and daub hostelries like those along Knightrider Street, but a turreted building discreetly tucked away behind a high wall and a beautifully carved archway of Caen stone. I had always assumed it was a nobleman's dwelling.

The porter's room was inside the gate. What if he did not let me in straight away? What if an acquaintance recognised me as I stood a-knocking? I should just have to keep my veil from blowing about and try not to look furtive.

And how long would be required? Shore always expected me to have a supper ready for him at four o'clock. If lying had to be done, it must be done well – in both senses. I laughed aloud. Lord Hastings was right. I still had too much respectability strapped to my spine. Well, a murrain on that! Tomorrow could not come soon enough.

★

I do not know how I managed to stay calm through the repast with Shore next day. He brought one of his friends up to dine with us. Ralph Josselyn the younger, who decided to show me his latest samples for striped bed hangings. I was not pleased; Ralph's eagerness for showing me things in the past had not been confined to drapery and I was in no mood for the 'I'll give you a good price' and nudge of foot beneath the table. His presence prolonged the meal and then Shore wanted to discuss cobblers. How can you sanely suggest who can repair your husband's shoes when your soul is ripe for the Devil's taking?

As soon as they had gone back down to the shop, I hastened upstairs and abandoned my house gown. Because it was one of those rare early summer's days when you can wrap the warm air in your arms, I took off my chemise and drew on a petticote of soft fine cotton. I was going to wear my best damask because it was a butterfly blue that made me feel at my best. It had tight fitting sleeves with embroidered cuffs. For modesty, I'd loosely stitched a triangle of silvery silk into the 'v' of the collar to cover the lower part of my cleavage. I pulled on my best headdress and hoped the wires would not bend under the extra dark lawn, veil I needed to hide my face. It seemed to hold up. Finally I tried on my light, tawny cloak, which tied snugly at the throat. There! I held up my small hand mirror and a mysterious veiled creature stared back at me. Most excellent!

If I was Salome, the lascivious dancer of King Herod's Court, how would I lift my veil and remove my cloak? I practised taking my outer garments off. Then I looked into the mirror again and bit my lips to make them red. Should I have plucked my eyebrows and drawn high arches like noble women did? No, that was not for me. Friends would remark upon it. So would Shore.

Betrayal versus fulfilment. Treason versus seduction. My hands were a-tremble with wicked excitement as I trickled perfume between my breasts. Two hours! Must I wait two hours? Two hours to change my mind. And would I?

Suffice to say that when I stepped into Basing Lane for my sinful meeting, my misgivings were clamouring like a flock of starlings and the what-ifs were back in abundance. But mercifully the saint of the timid and adulterous took a hand. Not only were the gates of the inn already open but a large party of horsemen was leaving.

I slipped through without being noticed and sped across the cobbles to the front steps only to be loudly 'ahemmed' by a massive serving man.

The flying phallus badge in his green hat unnerved me. Was this some kind of expensive stewhouse? His tabard bore the curious picture of a giant holding a pine tree and his hose was pied – Lincoln green and tansy, the colours of a mocking demon. I controlled the urge to cross myself.

'State your business, madame!'

'Yes, yes, of course,' I exclaimed, trying to be matter of fact, but it was hard with this fellow eyeing me with a mixture of officious sentinel and speculating pander. 'Please give me direction to Master Ashby's room.'

'Ah.' His massive shoulders seemed to heave a sigh of relief. 'That's all right then. Come this way, my lady. Can't be too careful, see. Our customers value their privacy when they stay with us. We like them to know that they won't have their belongings pilfered or pick up bedbugs or something more 'orrible. Know what I mean? No rubbing shoulders with the vulgar, eh?' Another checking stare. 'Not been here before then, madame?'

'No.'

'Ah, this place is full of surprises.'

He led me along a flagstone passageway and we emerged in the centre of a round great hall. Centuries earlier it would have been spacious and seated many, but a more recent owner had built an upstairs gallery with chambers leading off. Surrounding us were several rooms divided by oaken panelling. However, it was the trunk of a massive fir tree that the fellow wanted me to admire.

It was indeed amazing. Cathedral dimensions! Two priests holding hands could have hugged its girth. Generations of visitors had gouged their initials, and gazing up through my veil, I made out plenty of scurrilous Latin doggerels about women that made me blush. The sauciness increased with altitude, and perhaps the ladder bolted onto the tree was entirely for that purpose. Good luck to the scribblers! It would have taken a whole firkin of wine to get me on the first rung let alone the fortieth.

'Different, eh, madame?'

'I suppose the tree holds up the roof?'

'Aye, it does. Let me tell you, this hall belonged to one of the tallest creatures that ever walked God's earth, Gerrard the Giant, and that there tree was the staff he used in battle. A wonder, eh?'

'Gerrard the Giant?' It would have been rude to show disbelief. I would have put my money on a monastery refectory.

One of the doors behind me opened and yet another serving man of huge stature emerged with a cloth in hand. My escort chuckled at my astonishment.

'Aye, no one small is ever employed here. Take a look through!'

I was expecting something sordid like a daybed flung about with cushions and furs, not the silver goblets set out on the glossy buffed table. A carved chair fine enough for any nobleman stood at the end of the board between two great candleholders, and the cushioned benches would have seated a half dozen. White and red dragon heads with fiery tongues and lashing tails were painted on the walls.

'These lower rooms are for guests who wish to dine privily with friends, et cetera. A lot of deals are done here, I can tell you.

The Welsh like this room, because of the dragons, but we also have the unicorn, dolphin, peacock and lion chambers. The Scots always favour the unicorns. Now this way, if you please.'

And what did mercers choose? Did my father ever come here? Lord, I hoped not. I could have sworn it was he who first told me this was an earl's dwelling.

'Do I need to go back into Basing Lane when I leave, sirrah?' I asked as I followed the huge fellow up the spiral stairwell adjoining the hall.

He grinned. 'Like that, is it? There's a postern into an alley that will take you out to Bread Street or there's a stone staircase in the far wall that will deliver you further down Basing Lane. Yonder's the chamber for Master Ashby. Third door along.'

I paid him a groat and ignored the lascivious gleam in his eyes as he bowed and wished me a pleasurable stay.


Left alone by the rail, I stood beguiled by the peace that surrounded me. Come the evening, the servants would light the four candelabra that hung around the tree and I imagined this gallery would look beautiful and mysterious with the flicker of candles dancing across the cavernous ceiling. But not for me. Not yet. And I was glad. There was something calming and reassuring about the light tumbling lazily through the grisailled glass of the high upper windows, a sleepy serenity about this place that was as false as its purpose. The murmur of men's conversation reached me from one of the dining chambers below my feet, and through the open door of another came the sound of platters being cleared as quietly as possible.

Beyond the thick stone walls I heard the deep bell of St Paul's and the tinnier chime of St Mildred's striking the hour. This very moment I had the chance to flee, but my yearning other self held

me fast like a determined sister. I walked along the gallery to the
door of the bedchamber. No lover answered my knock. Biting my
lip, I tried the latch and let myself into my future.

The chamber designated for 'Master Ashby' was the most
spacious bedroom I had ever seen. Meadowsweet rushes were
freshly strewn across the floor. Upon one wall hung a stained cloth
of a huntsman and his hound, the wooden ceiling was spangled
with a delicate profusion of white butterflies and crimson flowers,
and scented candles flickered in the two tall wooden candelabra
on either side of the bed.

Ah, the bed! The bed was vast, large enough to accommodate at least five. With a jolt, I recognised the striped satin bed
hangings of lilady and primrose, and then I laughed. Oh, by the
Saints, I was about to sacrifice the virtue of my entire life within
inches of Ralph the Younger's curtaining!

'What is the jest?'

I squealed in shock as Lord Hastings stepped laughing from a
recess that had escaped my notice. The warmth of his smile made
me feel beautiful and welcome.

'It is these,' I laughed, giving the tethered drapery a playful tug
before I curtsied.

'Devil take it,' he groaned, 'you are not going to tell me their
price?'

'No, but I'll have you know the man who imports this made
me a very generous offer today,' I boasted wickedly, setting back
my veil. 'A tester and coverlet of best brocade – providing I lay
with him beneath it.'

'This to him.' He raised an insulting finger. His mouth was a
narrow slit of determination as he studied me, and his blue gaze
was deep enough to drown in. There was restraint in the way he
stood, as though he fought against invisible chains to reach out
and embrace me. 'Still certain, Elizabeth?'

I swallowed, realising that he had already discarded his day clothes. A blue robe, loosely tied about the waist, was all that screened his naked body.

'Satisfactory?' he teased, mistaking my stare. 'Bought from your father and stitched by the house of Claver.'

My silkwomen's rivals! Never mind. I let my gaze climb from his bare calves up to the gold haze of hair across his chest. 'I was thinking of what lay beneath, my lord.'

'Well, so am I.' He was eyeing my neckline, the only patch of skin showing beneath the cords of my cloak. 'Am I to climb the ramparts or…?' He gestured to the curtained recess. 'There's a wrap behind there.'

I imagined other women using it. 'Ramparts, please.' I half-turned to the window, like a good housewife. 'Shall I snuff the candles?'

'No.' Male and a dash indignant. Surprise must have flashed across my face before realisation enlightened him. 'Lord love us, Elizabeth, have you only done the deed in darkness?'

'Yes,' I hung my head and swallowed. Would this be a disaster? I was so miserably tutored, and a man like this, so experienced, so worldly.

'I can blindfold you. It might be the right thing.' And amusing too, his tone hinted.

'As it pleases you.' Uncertainty was beginning to undermine me and with it a tiresome trembling as though my body was as nervous as my mind.

'Well, first let's unpeel you. No, let me!' He stepped behind me and his body touched mine as he unfastened the cords of my cloak from around my neck. It was sensuous having him so close, so intimate. With husbandly dexterity, he eased off the cap, wire and veiling that covered my hair and gave a whistle of admiration.

'By the Lord, you certainly have an angel's beauty.' His breath was sweet upon my cheek and neck. He kissed me behind the ear.

'Hmmm.' I purred, letting my head fall back slightly. 'I rather like that. Can you do it some more, please?'

'My poor starved kitten.' He kissed me on the other side and then in the little hollow between my neck and shoulders. Already his fingers were round my waist, unfastening the knot of my silken belt. My gown was eased up and tossed across the end of the bed. His adroit fingers tested the ties of my underskirt and then rose instead to sprawl across my breasts. His thumbs caressed my nipples, sending waves of delicious feeling to between my thighs. I sighed with delight as his right hand slid down over my belly into the shield of tiny curls.

'Have you never done this by yourself, sweetheart?'

'I have, my lord,' I admitted.

Hastings laughed and turned me to face him. He was utterly naked, but before I could see him properly, he kissed me. I had never been kissed in such a way in my entire life. The fire and wildness in it melted me to my very soul. I wound my arms about his neck. He slid his hands down my back and held me hard against him. I could feel his prick hard against my lower belly, and when we paused to draw breath, I put my hand down to feel him. Compared to Shore, he was huge.

'I thought you said you were a new apprentice, sweetheart.'

'Book learning,' I lied.

'Which library?' he teased. Our foreheads were touching. He was loosening my hair and combing his fingers through it so it shawled my back. Oh, if only marriage had been like this.

Then with a laugh he bent swiftly, and suddenly I was lifted in his arms like a rescued maiden and laid upon the coverlet of the bed. With a knee upon the bed, he sprang up beside me, turned me over and loosened the back laces of my chemise. Then with my breasts free, he began to tease the tips of my nipples with his tongue. I was able at last to bury my fingers in his hair, free to delight and gasp with pleasure, free to arch my body at the beautiful sensations thrilling through my entire being.

Then he swept his hand down to the badge of hair and eased his fingers into me, touching me where my body burned for his coming. He gave a satisfied growl.

'I am on fire,' I gasped. Was the Devil inside me, driving me so?

He laughed softly and, to my dismay, slid from the bed.

'No, no,' I protested. 'You are not leaving me?'

He touched a finger to my lips and walked across to take something from the small table. Was he doing this to torment me? My body was crying out for him to enter.

'We need to be careful, sweetheart. I'm going to push this inside you.'

Whatever it was – a tiny sponge I discovered later – it smelled of vinegar. I was not pleased – this was a strumpet's device.

'No, you need not concern yourself,' I protested, writhing away from him. If I had not wanted him so much, I might have fled. 'I cannot conceive, my lord!'

'Maybe you can. Behave, and let me put this in.' He kissed me on the mouth to silence my argument and his fingers parted my cleft and forced the sponge well into me. His greater strength, the sternness of his voice in demanding my obedience, enhanced my appetite for him even further, and within seconds of him entering me, my body convulsed about him and I shuddered with an ecstasy that was not holy and yet divine.

So divine that we did it again.

And again.

★

No wonder Holy Church called this a sin. With Lord Hastings the act was not faith, it was a visitation. The songs of the troubadours were true. Lust by consent with skill. Perhaps my lover was right, I might become addicted to this pleasure.

'By the Saints!' he exclaimed, collapsing beside me after our third coupling with a satisfied groan. 'Not bad for an old lad. That was...' But I never heard. I drifted into sleep in his arms, blissful and at peace, and I think he slept too.

A rude knocking roused us. Neither of us had thought to bar the door. I struggled to pull the coverlet across me, afraid it was Shore, but the stranger who barged in was too tall for my husband, thank God. For an instant I thought he was one of the serving men, but this man's broad hat and riding cloak proclaimed 'outsider'.

'Ha! Master Ashby!' He disappeared into the alcove as though he knew it well and the next instant, Lord Hastings' clothes fell across us. Surely even a trusted servant would not behave so. This had to be some friend from the court.

'The pretty fellows from Brittany,' the stranger said cryptically. It was the closest he came to an apology.

'Excellent!' Hastings exclaimed gleefully, and grabbed for his shirt.

'Caught me unawares too!' the interloper replied. I could not see much of the man's face beneath the deep brimmed hat but he was staring at me. I was like a helpless moth caught in a candle flame.

'I must go, sweetheart,' Hastings laughed, turning to kiss me. He seemed quite unaware of my predicament. I dared not move since my scant covering was precarious already. 'Fare you well.' He stroked a playful finger along my lips. 'The tariff is paid, by the way, so take your time in leaving.'

'Well, don't take yours,' admonished the stranger with extraordinary rudeness, pelting Lord Hastings' hose at him. 'Where's your other boot.' He disappeared again behind the curtain. 'Not in here,' he called out.

I instantly scrambled to hide myself within the sheets.

'Hey, sweetheart, help me with my points!' Hastings made it a plea not a command. I cursed inwardly but how could I refuse after his generosity to me? Then I espied his discarded robe upon the rushes and swiftly scurried from the bed and drew it on. The silken belt was missing but at least its folds bestowed some modesty and my loosened hair would hide my face as I stooped to tie my lover's hose points to his gypon.

'Who is this?' the stranger asked, prowling as I performed a servant's duty.

Hastings ignored him. 'Find my other boot, sweetheart.'

It lay within the shadow of the bedsteps and he took it from me with thanks. 'You can leave my robe here when you are finished.' A command that mightily displeased me, but I smiled up at him in gratitude, my only act of defiance to his friend's impatience. The strategy worked. Lord Hastings touched his lips to mine and then, as if to stoke the other man's annoyance, he gave me a deep farewell kiss that told me we should couple again before long.

'God keep you, my lord,' I whispered huskily as he lifted his face back from mine, and still I kept my arms defiantly wrapped about his neck.

The stranger's spurs jingled as he strode to the door and held it open. 'Are you done, Will?' he demanded impatiently. Then they were gone and I was left alone with Hastings' kiss drying on my lips.

Fragrance in a vial of Venetian glass was discreetly delivered by a servant next day with a spoken message of thanks but no explanation of why my lover had left in such a hurry. My imagination had a fearful riot all by itself. Did the Lord Chamberlain and his swaggering friend have an appetite for 'pretty fellows' or had they been promised to some drinking orgy? Then a few days later I heard Shore talking about how the King had signed a military treaty with Duke Francis of Brittany. Oh dear, perhaps my lascivious sodomites had been the silver-haired Breton ambassadors desperate for a pledge of military aid against the King of France?

Had I shown too much ardour or not enough? Alas, I heard nothing more from Lord Hastings and I wanted nothing but more. Had Heloise burned so for Abelard? Ah, I burned night after night and waited day after day, my blood seething with anticipation, my tide of hope rising with the dawn and ebbing at nightfall.

Like some fantastical sea creature, my tendrils snared each morsel of gossip that eddied out from the court. Was my lord gone with the court to Eltham? Did he attend King Edward's meeting with the Merchants of the Staple? Oh, I was tempted to loiter outside Beaumont's Inn or take a wherry to Westminster and lurk like a stalking hunter. But what man wants a stinging gadfly pursuing his hide? Ah, I am amused now, remembering my impatience, but at the time, it was like having your tongue cut out when you have tasted the elixir of the angels.

I was returning from Mass at St Mary's Aldermary when, at last, a retainer with Hastings' badge stitched upon his cap waylaid me.

'My lord begs that you will meet him at five o'clock on Monday evening for supper. The same chamber as before.' The servant's eyes slid over my person with approval. I made pretence of gravely considering the matter, before I nodded graciously.

# VI

I took the same trouble as before in choosing my apparel. My rose madder gown had a splash upon the skirt, but ashes-in-lye took care of that.

Attempting to be inconspicuous on the street and alluring in the bedchamber was not easy. The day was windy and it was going to be a battle to keep my veil from fluttering up, but at least most passers-by would have their eyes down to avoid the dust. I resolved to wear my voluminous dark blue cloak, and instead of the silly affected headdress, all wires and stiffened gauze, which my lover no doubt had found a nuisance, I plaited my hair loosely and pinned on a simple cap that had a hood at the back to hide my hair.

What concerned me most was finding an excuse to leave our house after four o'clock supper. Earlier in the day it was easier because Shore would be down in the workshop or busy with customers, but at four he would leave Howe in charge and come up to supper and unless he was meeting with friends, he would linger at the board. In case he decided not to go out, I told our cook to make a batch of oatcakes that I might take to a poor family down off Cornhill. And so it was that I had to sneak out with my basket by the back postern, for Shore was still at home.

It was not just the fear of his questions later that had me anxious; I was very unhappy at being on the street at this hour for there were plenty of braggarts strolling between taverns and the watch did not start their rounds until nine o'clock. Safeguarding my good name from tittle-tattle bothered me as well. I was certain Hastings would arrange an escort to see me safely back to Cheapside before curfew but the less his people knew of me, the happier I should be. I resolved to bid his servants leave me at the nearest corner to my house and then scurry on alone.

Gerrard's Hall was still serving supper as I arrived and this time I made my way alone past the tree. I could hear laughter and talk from all the lower chambers and to my dismay I espied several well-clothed men leaning upon the gallery rail as they conversed. A trio of hawks. I understood now why rabbits and voles dart so fast. Resolving that I would never agree to come at this time again, I affected the dignity of a noble married traveller and made my way upstairs.

Not only did the men at the rail watch me pass but I found two retainers sitting cross-legged outside 'Ashby's' door playing at dice. Both scrambled to their feet at my arrival. One touched his cap to me with a wink.

'Mas'er Ashby be 'ere shortly, Mistress.'

'Then go and buy yourselves some ale,' I said sweetly finding them each a coin. I did not want any eavesdroppers. They seemed surprised at my largesse – or perhaps the paucity of it – but they politely accepted.

The small oil lamp hanging above the bed was lit and a potkin of sweet violets neighboured a bowl of blushing apples on the small table beside the bed.

I hung up my cloak and veil behind the door, set my basket

down upon the bed and then I leaned against the bedpost to let my heartbeat settle.

A rustle disturbed me. Turning, I saw the hem of the recess curtain billow subtly. I smiled. Ah, so his servants had dissembled; my lover was already here.

Mischievously I tiptoed across to make a gleeful pounce, but it was the breeze from the window light that teased the curtain. The alcove was pristine. Fresh napkins were folded on the wooden rail above the washstand. I lifted the jug beside the ewer and took a deep breath. Today the water was perfumed with sandalwood; last time it had been rosemary. But I could still smell rosemary; yes, a ribboned spray of silvery spikes and tiny mauve flowers lay upon the cloth that disguised the stool of ease.

Lord Hastings' blue robe was hanging on a wall hook with a bronze hued wrap beneath it. I dreamily lifted a silken fold of the blue to my cheek, trying not to think about how many other women had worn the bronze. No worse than a communion cup at Easter, I consoled my conscience, but I would not put it on.

He was late. The bell struck the quarter before swift, heavy footsteps stopped outside. The latch rose. But it was not Hastings. It was the stranger who had disturbed us last time. He was wearing the same black hat tugged forward over his face and I remembered the broadness of him.

I glared at him with dislike, sure now that he was not a courtier. The corner of his earth brown cloak was thrust up over the opposite shoulder like a night thief's, but the huge gloves and creaking leather doublet trumpeted soldier – soldier with a message from Hastings that would render this evening's subterfuge a waste of time.

No, I was wrong. He was removing his gloves with the air of a man who was staying. If only I had not sent Hastings' servants away!

'Mistress Shore, I believe.' He touched his hat brim with a slight bow.

I did not curtsy. I was so angry, so hurt. This was betrayal.

'Ah you must not blame Will,' he said cheerfully, unwinding his cloak. 'We hauled him down into the Tower dungeons, thrust him upon the Duke of Exeter's daughter and turned the screws.'

I had not one iota what he was talking about. 'Pray do not make yourself at home,' I said, with contempt underscoring every syllable.

'It could be a threesome if you insist.'

I must have looked shocked, for he quickly added, 'Except Will doesn't know I am here. Listen, I do apologise for tricking you but he's up at Ashby-de-la-Zouch and I thought you might lack for decent company.'

'Please leave, sirrah.'

'Oh,' he lamented, cocking his head like a crestfallen rooster. 'I beg you give me a fighting chance.'

I remembered my father's lectures. 'Three things,' I growled, restraining the urge to stick my fists on my hips. 'Firstly, I am not a harlot; secondly, if I have any arrangement with Lord Hastings, it is none of your business; and thirdly, I am leaving. Now remove yourself from between me and the door or I shall kick you so hard in the ballocks you will have difficulty walking, let alone procreating with your wife or anyone else.'

'*What!*' He was laughing but in ridicule. 'Firstly,' he spluttered, 'whether you are no harlot does not matter; secondly, I do not think you are giving us a fair chance to be acquainted; and thirdly, although you may be tall for a woman, I am six foot-three inches tall and long in the arm, so I think your chance of getting anywhere near my ballocks – with your clothes on, that is – will be highly unlikely.'

A scratch at the door. He opened it and the two retainers carried in trays, set them upon the bed, bowed and departed. I cursed inwardly. Why had I not noticed earlier that neither of the fellows had worn Hastings' livery?

'Hungry?' My unwelcome host uncovered the platter, crossed himself with his right hand and a mutter of grace, then spiked a twirl of beef and held it out to me.

'I hope you choke,' I said coldly.

'No!' He ate the meat himself, followed it with a sliver of fruit, and then drew a fastidious finger across his lips. 'No, you can't wish that. It's against the law.'

'Not in my book, it's not.' This was ridiculous. I grabbed my basket and swept to the door. 'Good day to you, sir.' I inclined my head with a dignity he did not deserve.

'In my book, it's treason, Mistress Shore.' His voice had changed.

The threat in it brought me up short. My hand froze upon my cloak. I had no idea who this man was. If he was the same rank as Hastings, then he had the power to destroy my reputation. Malice is a cruel enemy. I had no intention of staying, but if he was going to set a torch to my honour, maybe I still had a chance to staunch the flame.

I turned. 'I beg your pardon then, sir, but the jest is on Lord Hastings not me.'

'Please do not go, Mistress Shore.' His voice had grown kind again. 'I realise we have not been introduced and you are at a disadvantage.' He swept off his hat. The lion mane of bushy, brown hair tiptoeing on those broad, high shoulders seemed coarse and exuberant compared to Hastings' sleek fairness. His face surprised me: not the fist-in-your-teeth features that usually went with a large body and stubborn nature but fine hazel eyes, a noble nose and delicate mouth. Now I could see him better, he reminded me of someone. He bowed, not deeply, more a teasing concession, a curl of shoulder, his head remaining superior. 'My name is Edward, I am the King of England.'

'Oh yes, and I am the Holy Roman Em—' The words jammed in my throat. Without his hat... O Blessed Christ defend me!

I had only ever seen King Edward from a distance in recent years — a playing card, cloth-of-gold figure watching the tournaments at Smithfield or else just a gloved hand, resting on velvet, half-hidden by purple curtains aboard the royal barge. But I knew the triumphant bow of this man's lips, the victor of Mortimer's Cross and bloody Towton, the nemesis of Warwick, Queen Margaret and King Henry; the upthrust fist that betokened the victorious conqueror.

Trembling, I sank in the lowest curtsy I had ever made, wishing the rushes and floor might swallow me out of sight. As if in punishment, I was left to wobble there in misery. Then he relented. A strong hand grasped my arm and helped me to my feet.

'Now we have that out the way...' He kept hold of me like a diligent groom until I was steady, before he stepped back.

I could not answer the look of inquiry. It would need a hue and cry to find my voice.

'It will come back,' he assured me affably. 'Always does.' Then, as if giving me time to regain my wits, he prowled across to inspect my basket and, like a curious child, flicked up its cover. 'Mm-mmm, oatcakes! May I?'

I nodded, still in shock.

'Ah, I've not had one of these for years,' he exclaimed joyously, healthy white teeth taking a bite. 'Hmm-mm, just the right hint of cinnamon. Good, very good.' And then he astonished me even more. 'Lambard's girl, aren't you?' he said, savouring another mouthful and observing me with the curiosity of a lion that could crush a mouse with a swipe of his paw. 'Stout heart and generous, your sire. Loaned my father money when he was at low ebb. Helped me out as well back in '61, convinced the city to let me in so I could be proclaimed king. Not forgotten, I assure you.' Then his friendly tone weathervaned to a cool north again. 'Now are you recovered enough to have some supper? Some poor beast has died to give us food and we should be grateful.'

Refusal was impossible. 'So please you, gracious lord.'

He gestured me to sit on the bedsteps, filled a platter for me and passed it down. 'Usually takes half an hour for it to pass,' he told me as he selected some viands for himself.

'To p-pass, your highness?'

'The awe,' he said dryly, licking the sauce from his fingers and then wiping them on a napkin. 'Eat!'

I was not sure I could, but I watched in fascination as he moved the tray bearing the jug and goblets to the floor and heaved out the nearest bolster from beneath the pillows. Doubled against the wall, it made a reasonable seat and he lowered himself down. With a wifely instinct that might have passed for repentance, I poured out the wine and that pleased him. He took up his mazer and held it out. I lifted mine, and the surface of the wine quivered as my hand shook. Metal kissed metal.

I found my regular voice again, albeit humble and wary. 'Good health, my lord.'

He took a gulp and winced. 'Too sweet, more my brother George's taste. What do you think, Mistress Shore?'

Me? My first thought was that he was gulling me; the second that he meant it.

'I prefer a red, fuller-flavoured wine with beef, my lord.'

The answer satisfied him. He settled back watching me still and at last I retrieved my appetite. It was part expedience. I could hardly sit opposite him idle. Later, I would laugh to myself that King Edward had sat on the floor to dine with me like some itinerant tinker. In fact, I suppose it was in deference to my sensibility that we were not seated in comfort upon the bed and I was grateful.

On the same level, without his great height towering over me, I found him less daunting. His complexion was pale with a sprinkling of freckles and he had a Cupid's bow mouth, narrow but full-lipped. I reckon his worst feature was his chin – too dimpled – and his neck might thicken with age – but he had intelligent eyes, hazel with flecks of green gold, which reminded me of sunlight shining through a meadow pool. Hastings' eyes were more handsome, possessing translucence like clean-sheared crystal, yet there was a playfulness in the King's that was very charming.

'Is he in good health, old John, your father?'

'Yes, I thank your highness. A touch of stiffness in the knees but otherwise quite hale.'

'And your mother, Anne…no, Amy, yes?'

'Anne. Very well, I thank you. Father has bought some land in Hertfordshire and is gradually letting my brothers take over the business. Robert is in Calais and Jack runs the shop.'

'Jack? Ah, John Lambard the younger. Doing well?'

I nodded. 'Yes, your highness.'

'I'm not surprised. Robert Cousin, my Master of the Wardrobe, bought some Florentine sarsynett from your brother this week for seven shillings a yard.'

'That's ridiculously high,' I exclaimed and then clapped my hand to my lips mortified.

The King's face hardened. 'Are you saying my officer was fleeced?' A glimmer of humour that did not quite flatten the corners of his mouth replenished my courage.

'Shorn might be a better word,' I replied demurely, shaking some crumbs from my skirts.

My audacity amused him. 'So what should he have paid?'

'No more than five shillings and sixpence.'

'Hmm.' He swished his mouth sideways. 'I'd better have a word with Rob.'

'There are some really beautiful summer brocades due in any day now. I saw the samples a few months ago. The Queen has—'

He grinned. 'Ah, gotten an order in already, has she?' He took a gulp of wine and waved a hand while he swallowed. 'Separate household, see. 'Course being in business, you'd know how it all works. Can I have another of your cakes, if you please?' I reached up for the basket and passed two across.

He demolished one and took a bite of the other. 'So how long have you been married?'

'Since I was twelve.'

'Any whelps?'

'Whelps?'

'Children. I have five princesses, two princes and at least two bastards.' He thought about it. 'No, more, I daresay.'

'I haven't any, your grace.'

'What, none?' He thumbed the crumbs from his lips. 'No… no…' A languid flourish of fingers sufficed as though the word for stillbirth was only for a woman's use.

'No, your highness, I believe I was wed too soon.'

He frowned, his eyes sympathetic. 'Happened to Lady Margaret Beaufort, the Countess of Richmond. Not even fourteen when she birthed her son, Henry Tudor. Tudor, heard of him, yes? Lives on crumbs from the Count of Brittany's trenchers. She never had any more progeny, thank the Lord.' He had a most heart-rending smile, I discovered, and he was using it on me now. 'Does it sadden you, Mistress Shore?'

It? Being barren?

'Not any more, your highness. I am happy to go down on all fours and play bears with my friends' children, but at the end of the day I am content to hand them back.'

'All fours?' he echoed wickedly, laughter breeding with speculation in his expression and I could see he was imagining – O Jesu!

'I growl very fiercely,' I said quickly, hoping that he could not see my blushes. He really was sinfully attractive.

'Oh, do you?'

The neighbourhood bells tolled six and I was still in the lion's den. Children would have been a useful excuse to leave.

The King of England read my mind. 'Curfew is three hours hence.' *Wriggle out of that*, his expression told me.

'Yes, your highness, but it is later than when I met Lord Hastings before and my husband—'

'Is of no consequence, Will tells me.'

'I am sorry,' I murmured, rising to my feet, and again shaking the crumbs from my skirts. 'I have the cakes to deliver…to the poor, otherwise…'

His highness stood up as if out of courtesy but his lower lip betrayed displeasure. Then he twisted, retrieved the bolster and, holding it against his body with one arm, sensuously slid his other hand down it. 'I thought we might…' A jerk of his head towards the bed finished the question. At least it *was* a question.

I shook my head treasonously and Lord knows what else of me shook. Oh yes, my senses were stirred. Not just his handsome looks but the aura of power had me wondrously thrilled.

The bolster was flung aside with a deliberate menace. I briskly picked up my basket and hugged it to my waist. There was no way I could withstand him if he chose to stop me leaving so I stood there, my chin raised defiantly. It was his decision.

Tight, calculating tucks appeared in his cheeks. King Edward was watching me as though I was his assailant in the combat yard; all I had was basketwork. I clasped it tighter to my waist and stared up at him defiantly, my heartbeat frantic.

A woman shrieked playfully outside. The floorboards creaked lightly as she ran across them. Heavier footsteps chased her. A guffaw of laughter. A door opening. No one would care if I screamed, and what difference would it make? The hawks outside were probably royal servants on subtle sentry duty.

At a loss in this impasse, I primly pulled the napkin back over the remaining cakes like a diligent housewife, without taking my eyes from my antagonist, and suddenly, mercifully, the swords between us were lowered. The King's cheeks grew full again, a smile grew and grew and then he laughed.

I took one step towards the door but his voice snapped out like a whip. 'The King has not given you leave, Mistress Shore.'

I looked around. 'Does he need to?' I chided gently.

'By the Devil,' he murmured, but it was amusement not arrogance that graced his face. 'Yes he does. Before you utterly devastate me by leaving, let us just get matters straight.'

I swallowed, glanced at the door, and then back at him, put down my basket and gave a shallow curtsy.

'Thank you,' he said sarcastically. The large gems on his pale hands flashed in the candlelight as he made a steeple of his fingers. 'Now let me understand this aright. You will lie with Will but not with me?' *Even though I am your king, younger and better looking,* the lift of eyebrows seemed to be saying.

I nodded, more apprehensive than ever. Apparently the bell had sounded for the second bout.

He swayed forward slightly but I did not dare recoil. I was not going to let him close me in with the bed at my back.

'You do confound me, Mistress Shore,' he murmured. 'I understood that your liaison with my chamberlain is for the purpose of…education?'

These two men had discussed me? Curse it! As what? A silly hen ripe for plucking?

'Th—that is t-true, your highness. I wanted to find out...' I bit my lip, horrified at what he must believe about me. 'It is most... most generous of you to offer to...to further the tuition but thank you, no.'

I curtsied, trying to hide my hurt. It was as if God had tipped burning oil upon my soul. Hastings had betrayed me. I was nothing but a jest.

'Kings rarely make *offers* except to other royalty,' he replied with hauteur. He strode from me and turned, his voice growing dryer with each syllable: 'Kings tend to make commands.'

How should I escape him? Sweet Mother of God! I could hardly argue that I was virtuous.

'It shames me that Lord Hastings told you of my circumstances, your highness.'

'But you have signed an indenture with him and must keep loyal. Poor Mistress Shore, alas, how terrifying the consequences if you disobey. No doubt Hastings will slap my face with his glove on his return and slit my throat in fury. You'll probably be hanged in one of your pretty garters.'

It was belittling.

'I thank your grace most honestly for supper.' I curtsied deeply.

He inclined his head haughtily. 'Go, then.'

'Please,' I said to the King of England, and proffered my basket. 'Would you like to take these back to the palace for your children?'

'Where have you been?' growled Shore, as I came in through the yard door.

'Taking cakes to the poor.' To a man poor in humility! God have mercy! What a fool I'd proved. I must be the laughing stock of Westminster.

'Without a basket?'

'Oh bother, I left the cursed thing behind.' Was my face scarlet?

'Tell me where you left it and ah'll send one of the boys.' By his tone, he was determined to make a liar of me.

'Lordy, I cannot remember.' I turned away, tucking my waist-cloth into my belt.

'Like that, is it?'

I closed my eyes, knowing the lid was off the seething pot. Was truth the best way, slid in cleanly like a dagger rather than administered in a slow poison? But it was he who astonished me. I knew all week that he had something on his mind and here at last came confession.

'There's summat ah have to tell you, wife. There was this cher-rylips came into the shop last week when ah was serving on my own. Tricked out in finery she was like a real lady. She swished abaht in her furs and trinkets, and when she'd made her choice, she offered to pay for t'cloth by spreadin' her legs. Ah said, yes, but she'd better be quick. Anyroad, ah locked the door and led her to t'stairs so as no one could see us from the street. She bared her breasts and eased her skirts slowly above her thigh. Had me in a raight sweat...'

Please Heaven, it never rose, I prayed, imagining my argument for a divorce evaporating with Shore's resurrection. 'Did you...'

'No, No, damn it, ah could not manage it, even with her! Christ!' He smote so hard upon the board that the inkpot jumped and then he grabbed the alejack and hurled it furiously at the wall. I stared open mouthed at the liquid, pale as urine, trickling down the whitewash.

He was breathing hard, staring at me like a cornered beast. I feared he might strike me. His mouth arced into an ugly loop of pain and tight slits of skin swallowed his eyes. 'O Jesu, Jesu, Jesu!' He sank to his knees, cradling his ribs and began an anguished keening.

I flung myself on my knees and drew him to me. 'There, there!' I soothed, stifling his howls against my bosom. I rocked him until the shudders ceased.

'Ah'm so sorry, Elizabeth,' he sobbed. 'All these years. Ah'm so sorry.' He tried to pull away but I held him fast.

'There is more to a man than his prick, William Shore. The whole world knows that. You should not judge yourself so cruelly.'

'But ah'm no true man. I am cursed by God.'

'Then we both are, William.'

Still reeling from Hastings' betrayal, I needed a few moments to grasp the implications of Shore's confession. He was no longer blaming me for not giving him a child. I was unsaddled at last. No more guilt to carry like a weary packhorse.

'There is something I should tell *you,*' I said, holding by his sleeves so he could not pull away. 'I went with another man.' His reaction was a fierce start to free himself but I held on. 'So, you see, you must forgive me also. Two weeks ago for the first time. Just once. I wanted to know what it was like.'

'An' what was it like?'

'It was satisfactory. There was no commitment.'

'Yer tuphead,' he snarled. 'Dinna you make sure he was... clean?'

My heart lurched. Whore's pox as well as a broken heart? By Heaven, I hoped not.

'Can you forgive me, William?'

His face was as chill as a Derby winter. 'Does it matter if ah can't?'

# VII

'You ignored my messengers.' Hastings came striding up into my solar. It was the first time he had visited upstairs. He sounded peevish, great lord peevish. Not a surprise; I had ignored three notes and two nosegays. Shore followed him in, mumbling about broadcloth.

'Broadcloth, be damned!' The Lord Chamberlain neatly slammed the door in my husband's face. Then he opened it again. 'Oh, Hell take it! Forgive the discourtesy, Shore. I thank you for your offer of assistance but pray don't let me detain you. My steward will deal with the order.' He waited until my stunned husband was downstairs before he dropped the latch. '*Well*?'

'My lord.' I rose from my curtsy, smoothed my skirts and looked up at him with my best businesslike face. 'There was intervention.'

The frost melted slightly. He folded his arms and his elegant black sleeves flashed their amber taffeta linings.

'Him?' A condescending jerk of head towards the door

'No, my lord, your friend, the one who charged in on us.'

'That friend! I see. My abrupt departure annoyed you!' He tossed his hat onto the small table and surprisingly donned the manner of sackcloth and ashes. 'Well, I cannot blame you and I do apologise, but the Breton diplomats were anxious to sign the treaty and get back to Duke Francis.'

'Your pardon, I did not understand that at the time.' I poured him out some wine in a forgiving fashion.

He grinned sheepishly at me across the rim of our best goblet. 'Just as well "my friend" interrupted, my luscious Elizabeth. I do not think I could have managed a fourth coupling.' At least he had remembered the other three. 'Anyway, I ask you to excuse my friend's churlish manners. Sometimes he needs a boot on his arse.'

'Do you bow, my lord, before you kick him?'

My question caused a little silence. He chewed his cheeks before he answered.

'Ah. Clever of you to realise.'

'I didn't, my lord. Until I had a command from you to meet me at Gerrard's Hall. Except you did not arrive, he did.'

Although Hastings seemed to be considering the revelation, I wondered if he had already known. 'I see,' he murmured with the cool worldliness that was still so alien to me, 'and I daresay my "friend" usurped my favour with you.'

Such a conclusion mightily annoyed me. The bed-swapping habits of the palace might be commonplace to him but they were unacceptable to me.

'He did not usurp anything, my lord, save two little oatcakes. I declined his request.'

Hastings' beautiful eyes widened and emotion returned to his face, even if it was merely surprise. 'Is my hearing amiss, Elizabeth? *You* said "no" to the King?'

'Of course,' I exclaimed passionately. 'I do have some honour.' Did he think of me only as fresh city meat? 'I assure you I am no whore to be prancing in and out of gentlemen's beds.'

'Just so.' His mouth was a grave slash now. Oh, such a diplomat, shifting position to accommodate my vehemence. A token flurry of jealousy would have been more acceptable. 'Was that your only reason, Elizabeth?'

'I felt some loyalty to you, my lord.' *Some* – my fledgling attempt at Westminster nonchalance. 'Please do not mistake me,' I added swiftly to reassure him that I was not infatuated. 'I certainly do not seek to put any obligation on you. We had an agreement – just you and I.'

'Elizabeth, I hope you are not thinking that I put his grace up to this?'

'No, of course not,' I lied, resolving to sieve my feelings later. 'He—' I cleared my throat. 'His highness explained you were at Ashleigh.'

'Ashby,' he corrected. 'My castle at Ashby-de-la-Zouch.' His hand rose in a flourish as to how I should find it. 'West of Leicester.'

'Oh, west,' I echoed dryly.

'We were celebrating my stepdaughter's name day. I bought the jewelled girdle for her, remember?'

'Yes.' I was not a jealous person but I felt it now. Unreasonable of me. I desired his affection. But I had no right. I did not own him. What else had I expected?

'Cecily was introduced to her future husband.' With a scowl, he took a sweet wafer from the platter and carried his goblet to the window, where he stood, his back turned. With King Edward active on the board, perhaps, like me, he was uncertain of the next move in this game of seduction. *If there was a next move?* At the moment, trust lay between us like a bleeding corpse.

His fidelity was a matter of geography. I must accept that. And did Lady Katherine up at Ashby accept that? By Heaven, if his marriage vows could be bent, what rules *did* he play by? His loyalty to his king? Was that the only standard in his world? If King Edward said, 'Give me that bread you are eating, that ring

from your finger, that woman you are escrewing!' Did he ever
refuse? If his royal master wanted to sample Lady Cecily, his stepdaughter, what then?

'Was she pleased, my lord?'

He turned. 'Your pardon, she?'

'Your stepdaughter. Was she pleased by her future husband?'

A sneer spoilt his face. 'Yes, for now. That's one hedge that
won't need jumping. His horns and the forked tail will only come
out after they're married.' He took an angry swig of wine.

'Who is *he*?' I probed gently, seating myself on the footstool.

'Queen's eldest boy by her first marriage. Tom Grey, Marquis
of Dorset. Cecily is a great heiress – vast estates in Devonshire. Fly
in the web, poor child. If lightning strikes Tom Grey dead, there's
still his brother to snaffle her up.'

'Can you not withhold your consent?'

Hastings shook his head. 'I might as well piss in the wind.' He
downed the wine and slammed the goblet on the small table. 'And
what is so ironic, sweetheart, is that before Ned married Elizabeth
Grey – Baroness Ferrers of Groby, as she called herself – she and
I had a neighbours' agreement that if Kate and I had a daughter,
Tom would marry her.'

God's mercy, before the poor mite was even born!

I refilled his wine cup, flattered he felt free to speak his mind
or was this a means to lull me back to trusting him?

'So Grey was not considered for Lady Cecily back then?'
I asked.

'Hell, no. A landless nobody, son of an attainted traitor? No,
Cecily was far too wealthy for the likes of him. It was sheer charity
on my part to have any dealings with "the Widow Grey".' He
took a gulp of wine. 'Of course, once Elizabeth became queen,
she set her sights on Cecily's inheritance.'

'But you could delay the marriage, my lord. If Cecily is only fifteen, I beg of you, don't let her go to him yet.' I should not have spoken so but Hastings did not take offence.

With a fond look, he reached out a hand and caressed my cheek. 'You speak from the heart, do you not, sweetheart?'

I nodded and felt the tears pricking behind my lashes at the kindness of the gesture. I kissed his palm. 'My lord...' I began but his mind had moved on.

'So have you've begun rattling the bars of Holy Church yet for your divorce?'

'Rattling, yes. I've made a start.'

'I'm glad to hear it. These matters take a millennium. If you don't start proceedings straight away, you'll still be waiting at the Second Coming.' Then he realised his improper choice of words.

I pleated my lips trying not to giggle and then we both laughed. He rose to his feet and slid his arms about my thighs and drew me to him. 'Let's go and sup at Gerrard's Hall. Time for another lesson, my beauteous scholar.'

Such cunning I learned from the tryst that evening: the act of love does not have to be with the woman underneath; a woman may straddle a man and, what's more, a man and woman may lie busy tip to tail.

'It is about power as well as passion, Elizabeth, conquest and surrender. A game of subtlety and strategy until you bring the protagonist to their knees, so to speak.' That disarming smile. He encouraged me to use my imagination and to play out one of my fantasies. I had thought that the reality would spoil it, but with Hastings, I was wrong.

'Soon there will be nothing left to teach you, mercer's daughter.' He whacked my behind playfully as I lay on my front after we had sported, and kissed the hollow of my back. 'And now I desire to ask a favour. Remember I told you one of my duties was to organise revels for the court.'

'Yes, my lord. You were considering *The Siege of Troy*.'

'Well, the damned siege ladders are going up the walls tomorrow after supper if I haven't fallen on my sword by then.'

Ah, if only he would give me a pass to witness such a spectacle. 'I'm sure it will be a marvel, my lord.'

He gave a humpf. 'Not with the citadel unfinished and Helen of Troy breaking her ankle in the palace yard last night.' His gaze swerved to meet mine. 'I don't suppose you'd like to take the part?'

'Me? You'd be better with a duck from the Thames. The last time I was in a pageant I had lost my two front teeth and was warned not to smile or the Devil would carry me off. No, I lie. I did dance once before Queen Margaret. Goodness, you are serious.'

'You can be a damnably acute mimic when it pleases you.'

'Yes, but that's just between us. Shore's hair would stand on end if I said yes.'

'I'm glad we would get a rise out of him somehow.'

I clapped my hand to my lips. 'That was unkind, my lord.' I spluttered, battling my guilt anew and ignoring his beseeching expression. 'Absolutely no. It would be like taking hemlock. Why, Shore and I could be struck off the guest list for next year's mayor-making.' I tried to keep a straight face but dissolved into laughter.

'Worse than death, eh? But seriously, Elizabeth Lambard, you'll enjoy yourself, I promise. It's very simple. Prince Paris watches you dance, scoops you off to Troy and the rest of the time you are on the Troy battlements watching the duels until Menelaus, your husband, carries you back to Greece. Not much to it.'

'If she's "carried off" most of the time, I shouldn't think the broken ankle matters.' I turned away from him. 'And it doesn't have a happy ending if she has to go back to her husband.' I cradled my body, wondering how long these snatched moments with Hastings could last. 'I'm a real Helen and tonight I have to go back and there's no happy ending.'

'There will be if Catesby keeps your proctor's nose to the grindstone.' He kissed my shoulder. 'Humour me, play Helen. You said you would like to see the court.'

'*See* them, not hop around in front of them like a demented rabbit.'

'You can dance, my dear. I saw you in the shop and it was most charming.'

'I'm a mercer's wife, my lord, not a handmaiden from the court of Solomon.'

'Hmmm,' he put a hand on my backside again and shook me playfully. 'We could disguise you and it's a very pretty costume. I took your advice and got rid of the breast cones. Except...'

'No!'

How many times can a woman say no? Clearly, denial was not a word in Hastings' vocabulum. Next day at three o'clock, the shop had two visitors. The first was a servant of Sir Edward Brampton's requesting Shore to bring sample cloths to his house without delay. The second was one dainty Master Matthew Talwood, who carried an urgent letter from the Lord Chamberlain asking me how he could put on *The Siege of Troy* without the Lady Helen? What's more, Hastings pledged he would buy me a wagon of lawyers and a score of girdles if I saved his reputation as Master of the King's Revels.

Ha, I did not believe a word but Talwood was insistent: my lord's barge was awaiting me at Puddle Wharf beside Beaumont's Inn. *His barge*! He'd sent an entire barge?

'A word for the wise, Mistress Shore,' said my visitor, flicking back his long grey locks. 'Save for his grace the King and his royal brothers, Lord Hastings is the most powerful nobleman in England. That letter is not a request, it's a command. There are plenty like you, Mistress Shore, but only one of him.'

# VIII

The rebellious wench inside me was prancing with gleeful excitement as we boarded the barge, but behind my veil my lips were tense, and my knuckles gleamed white in my lap as I seated myself beneath the awning. Talwood started to tell me about the play and what was expected – just one dance, he said. Did he realise it could destroy my reputation forever if word reached the city? Just one dance! *Be brave*, I chided myself, *if you stumble and they laugh at you, it doesn't matter. At least you may glimpse King Edward in all his magnificence.* Yes, I admit I had been thinking much about King Edward.

Talwood had passes that saw us through a succession of courtyards and sentries until we reached the postern of a half-timbered building adjoining the Great Hall. The players' chamber proved a chaotic hell of spangles and peevish hubbub. At one end, men in wigs and leather kilts were in mock combat; at the other a large man with faux breasts and a wig that Medusa would have envied, was having red powder rubbed below his cheekbones. My destination was a side chamber where a baker's dozen of minstrels were practising.

Talwood introduced me to Walter Haliday, the hoary-headed Marshall of the King's Minstrels, and delivered a warning to the rest: 'Be diligent with our dancer, my masters. This is her only chance to practise and then she needs to get into costume with great haste. The disports begin in an hour.'

An hour! I could have encircled Hastings' neck with a cord and tugged it tight.

I was supposed to rattle a timbrel as I danced but I asked Haliday if the tabor player could provide the rhythm instead.

'Pretend you have a mirror, dear. Gives you something to do with your hands,' suggested Talwood, and he kept directing me until he was satisfied.

The sound of clapping coming from the doorway made me turn. Hastings was standing behind me in his full court dress.

'As always, you underestimated your ability, mistress.'

I stared speechless at his splendour – the high-crowned, black hat with a jewelled band; the silver collar of Yorkist sunnes-and-roses straddling his shoulders; and the Order of the Garter encircling his thigh. Such tailoring, too; the way his slashed, damson sleeves were stitched in – pouched to give breadth at the shoulders.

He thanked the musicians and ushered me from the room. As no one was in sight in the passageway, he kissed me on the mouth. I imagine he tasted my nervousness.

'You are doing well, sweetheart.'

'My lord, in all honesty I am fearful.'

'Elizabeth, you will outshine the rest, believe me.'

I tried to smile. 'It's just that in your magnificence, you are like a stranger. Is every noble lord like to be dressed so? It dazzles me. I feel like a country mouse.'

'But I know you are a proud little city mouse.' He pinched my cheek. 'You will surpass us all, believe me. And Talwood will look after you throughout. Do exactly as he says and all will go smoothly. Now, we must make haste. There's a tailor standing by to make adjustments to your costume.'

I followed him back to the confusion of the greater chamber. The instant he entered, the room hushed. I swiftly curtsied to him with the rest.

'Friends,' Hastings began, addressing the players, 'Remember the purpose of the disguising is to provide joy and laughter. If aught goes wrong, do not put on a grim visage but bluff it out. Are the battlements and wooden horse at the ready, Master Curthoyse?'

An officer straightened and stepped forward. 'They are, my lord.'

'Excellent. As you were, good friends. I leave you in the Master of the Wardrobe's capable hands.'

No one moved.

'Your pardon, my good lord,' called out one of the actors, 'but we 'ave no Helen.'

Hastings gave a nod to Talwood to deal with the matter and left the chamber.

Talwood gestured me to my feet. 'This is Helen.'

'But she's a woman.'

O Blessed Christ, I thought, I'm the only woman here. This is wrong, very wrong.

Beside me, Talwood bristled, 'And your point, sirrah?'

'Our point,' yelled someone else, 'is that only men can be players.'

Talwood was primed. 'This woman is a dancer. She has no lines. *Pirouette, darling, pirouette*!' he hissed. Scarlet-faced, I turned, swirling my skirt as gracefully as I might.

*A dancer*! I blew the actors a kiss and sank in a deep curtsy. Christ's mercy, what if this reached the Guild? Shore would turn me out of doors. I could find myself begging on the streets tomorrow. I must be lunatic.

Appeased, the players returned to their preparations.

'Thank Heaven for that,' Talwood said, fanning himself. 'Oh, they are so precious. Now, let's get you dressed.'

There was no privacy and I had to swallow my sense of niceties. I had imagined a gorgeous robe with purfiled hem; the tailor presented me with two lengths of thin blue silk. Secured at the shoulders and cinched with a narrow cloth-of-gold belt, this was Helen's costume. That unravelled my excitement. The fabric scarcely covered my knees; the side slits – 'devils' windows'– would expose me to the thigh; and the flesh-coloured hose and garters had gone missing. I refused to dance without a petticote.

'You're a beautiful ancient Greek, remember, dearie,' clucked the tailor from his knees as I insisted he close up the side seams. 'Them maidens went bare-legged because of the heat, and bare-arsed too in case they met any of those lovely pagan gods. There, I'm not sewing the windows any lower.'

I refused the uncomfortable saffron wig. At least the pretty half-mask of white satin, edged with silver braid, was perfect, but as I began to tie it on, Master Talwood twittered in protest. Frantic gestures on his part summoned a man with several tubby facebrushes poking out of his waistcloth. Along with him came a boy with a peddler's tray – a minute woodland of charcoal sticks, kohl and pastes of all colours.

They smudged blushes across my cheekbones, puffed a fulsome shimmer of gold dust wherever my skin was uncovered and added red to my lips. Fine dark lines were gently drawn around my eyes and my hair was unbraided, draped over my right shoulder and tethered with a golden clasp.

Finally, Talwood took out a wrapper from his doublet and drew back its folds to reveal a necklace of gilded leaves. 'It's only lent to you by my lord, you understand,' he warned.

The boy offered me a silver mirror. Mistress Shore had vanished behind the pagan artifice. Caparisoned in mask and silks, I felt as skittish as an inexperienced tournament horse, and these last moments of waiting while the trestles of the great hall were stacked away could have been torture save some of the players joked with me in friendly fashion and smoothed away my fears.

Hastings came back to make a final inspection of us. 'Is Lord Paris not here yet?' he exclaimed wearily. 'Curthoyse, fetch him hither NOW!' He moved along the line and halted before me. 'Where in Hell is Helen's coronet?'

'Lordy!' The tailor scuttled out and returned with a circlet of tinsel threaded with artifice cornflowers, poppies and laurel.

'Princess.' Hastings clicked his fingers for the diadem. With the smile of a sinful archbishop, he crowned me.

Westminster Palace Hall was in shadow save for the bright ring of candles in the centre where we were to strut. We were herded behind a screen and there we huddled awaiting the return of the royal retinue. I was not the only player who gasped at the massive dimensions of the hall. Huge oaken beams, carved with angels' heads, thrust out from the walls above our heads and higher still was a great row of embrasured windows, set in jowls of stone, and in each stood a stern, crowned statue.

I knew from Father that a huge stone table ran along the dais. Peering between my companions' shoulders, I made out the glimmering stretch of white cloth. No one was seated there; the two thrones and benches were empty.

Below the dais at the sides of the hall stood massive cupboards with shelves of glinting platters and flagons. Every other inch of wall was lined with trestle tables propped lengthways. In front of these were the benches and here sat the rest of the court using the trestle supports as backrests.

A trumpet sounded. I heard the assembly rise in a rustle of apparel to make obeisance. Crammed as I was amongst the sweaty bodies jostling for a view, my mouth went dry and my heart panicked, but then the small pipes began and the Greek kings stepped forward leaving me space to breathe. I forced my lungs to calm and crossed myself against evil. Vigilant Talwood patted my arm; I had no choice but to screw up my courage.

Our disport began with poetry but no one in the court was listening. Only when several gentlemen began to call out ribald comments to the players, did the fine lords hush to listen to the jests.

As each Greek king was introduced, I had the chance to distinguish the chief players. The man portraying my husband, King Menelaus of Sparta, was a scrag end of a creature. His brother and blustering overlord, King Agamemnon, looked fit to run a tavern. Achilles had such a magnificent body, all bronzed with metallic paint, that he had me wondering if the King, England's own 'Achilles', had stooped to play a part. No, as the warrior drew back, I heard a shrewish whine: ''Ere, why 'as 'ector been given betta armour than me?'

Prince Paris, thank Heaven, was sufficiently manly to be Helen's lover. He drew great applause as he swaggered forth. Except for a glittering baldric, his chest was bare. I was shocked by his immodest kilt. The leather straps scarcely covered his breech clout.

'Be ready!' Talwood whispered as the Greek kings returned behind the screen.

The flute's voice sounded sensuously.

*And now Prince Paris, blessed by moonless sky,*
*Like a night thief hides among the shadows*
*To see this beauteous lady—*

'Now!' Talwood shoved me forth and there were whoops and cheers as I curtsied.

Hill, the tabor player, began a sensual beat and the beguiling notes of the small pipes softly slid into the rhythm.

Snared in the circle of light, I lifted my invisible hand mirror at arm's length and danced with my reflection. Hidden behind my mask, Elizabeth Lambard was unshackled, free to become Helen of Troy, a princess who knew she could make men kill to possess her. As I stilled, sensing Paris' presence, like a doe hearing her hunter, it was no longer Hastings' face in my make-believe mirror but a lover I'd always dreamed of.

When the music ended and the applause took over, my practical self dashed out from her temporary prison beneath my heart, trying to seize back control and dampen down her twin's sinful exuberance. I held her back a few moments longer, acknowledging the huzzahs like I imagined a real princess might with a gracious lowering of the head. Oh, this was heady, wonderful. I should not sleep tonight.

Paris grew impatient. He strode over and embraced me from behind, his prick hard beneath his kilt. Bastard! While the narrator tediously droned out the story for anyone thick as a London piecrust, this cursed Trojan was rubbing his groin against me. Sloppy kisses gushed up my arm from wrist to neck. Worse, he turned me in his embrace and went for my mouth. I resisted; his breath stank of wine but the fellow kept firm hold of my thighs.

'Don't overdo the virtue,' he muttered against my lips. 'Be craaaazed with love.' He held me tight against his belly. When he adventured his hand down my throat to my breast, I was doing the stiffening.

'Lovely,' he murmured, leering down the gap. 'Fancy a bit of ravishing afterwards?'

'Squeeze either an' you'll be a coun'er tenor by tonight,' I hissed back sweetly.

The verses ended. Paris neatly scooped me up with an arm beneath my knees. I pretended to look up at him lovingly. It was a shame he could not have kept my draperies secure. I think the whistles were for a side view of my thigh.

There was no time to chide. While the Greek princes were whining that Helen had been snatched by a Trojan and resolving to go to war to fetch her home, Talwood hauled me through the side door and we raced through passageways until we reached the mock barbican of Troy, where it stood outside the far end of the great hall. An icing of players already clung to its battlements.

Talwood pointed to the ladder. 'Up! Be quick!'

Before I could get both feet on the plank that served as rampart, the ardent assistants whipped the ladder away. Queen Hecuba's brawny arm saved me.

'A squeeze, ain't it?' He evidently liked garlic in his stew.

'God's Blood,' I muttered in an alley voice. 'I feel like one of them jars too broad for a pantry shelf.'

'An' I'm a barrel. Move, you lardcakes! 'Elen should be in the middle.'

The 'lardcakes' obeyed. Cassandra, a youth in a long black wig, deftly swung around Hecuba, and we performed an intricate, perilous reversal so that I ended up midway next to Prince Hector's wife and son.

'Have to get it right, dearie,' Hecuba whispered. 'You bein' the last to leave.' He straightened his false bosom and then nudged me: 'Did Paris feel you up?'

'Aye, 'e did.'

The others laughed. 'Oooh, lucky you.'

'Tell me,' I whispered. ''Ow's the player who was to be 'elen? Is 'is ankle mending?'

'He ain't done nothing to his ankle, luv. His lordship didn't want 'im to do it no more.'

Aha, I was beginning to suspect as much.

'So wot's your name, precious?' asked Hector's wife, but before I could answer, the edifice shook as the attendants grabbed hold.

''Ere we go, ladies,' chortled Hecuba, as the doors opened. 'Wave graciously. We're royalty, remember.'

The damnable barbican wobbled perilously as it was pushed forwards. Would the timber brackets break, spew us out across the flagstone plain of Troy in a tangle of gauze and wigs? The courtiers were laughing.

'Oh, I adore playing a queen to a queen,' Hecuba gushed, waving airily towards the heart of the dais. 'Ready to blub, Mistress Hector? Got your onion, darlin'?'

With nothing to do save pose like a princess at a tournament, I began to enjoy myself. Although Hector and Achilles' wooden swords could not strike sparks, there was sufficient force in their combat to have the courtiers cheering. When Hector received the death blow, he pierced the bag hidden beneath his waist, and enacted copious spluttering and staggering as the blood oozed between his fingers.

The onion smell was strong but I wasn't prepared for the horrific scream right next to me. A shrieking Mistress Hector and son scrambled down to do a 'woe is me' over the corpse.

'Employed for 'is screeches,' Hecuba informed me.

Then came the death of Achilles. He grabbed an arrow to his heel and died with a great deal of twitching. Finally, the Wooden Horse rumbled in. I was disappointed. It was just scaffolding with a painted great horse head sticking out on a pole. Its body was made up of warriors, each holding a curved, dun-coloured shield to resemble a horse's flanks.

'Doom, doom!' Cassandra, who had already climbed down, rushed at the horse waving his arms like a housewife chasing the pigeons from a pea crop. He was carried off in the mêlée as the

Greek soldiers sprang down and some thirty men waged battle.

When the swords and verse came to a standstill, Hecuba descended to wring his huge hands over dead Paris. I tried to look bereft as 'she' was led away sobbing. Once all the corpses were dragged into the shadows, the fields of Troy lay deserted and I realised with a jolt that I was the only player left on the battlements

Oh, for more onions. Broken hearted, I held my wrist to my eyes so I could glance back at Talwood. He was firmly signalling me to stay in place.

What in Heaven…? Ah, phew, the narrator stepped back into the candlelight and King Menelaus strode up to the wall of Troy. The cascade of poetry stopped abruptly. Menelaus held out his hand, waiting for me to return with him to Sparta.

Devilment crept into me. Poor Helen. Had Menelaus been a William Shore? I gravely shook my head at his highness of Sparta and flapped my fingers like ass's ears. The court began to chuckle and then shriek with laughter as the player became really angry.

His overlord, King Agamemnon, joined him. He also held out his hand to me. Still I refused and then suddenly there was a scraping of chair, a movement across the high table, followed by applause. A third king! Tall and magnificent, King Edward halted before the gates of Troy, looked up at me and held out his hand.

By the Saints, I'd never intended this. How I managed that narrow ladder behind the edifice with my heart trying to escape my body, I'll never know.

England's king was a huge haze of gold and sable. I inclined my head to him like Princess Helen should, and he graciously led me forward to make a player's curtsey to the court, then keeping firm hold of my hand, he grinned down at me like a lion viewing dinner.

'I knew you'd come to me eventually,' he said.

# Mistress

# I

Paris saved me from answering. Not to be excluded from the tumult of clapping and stamping, he materialised on my left, grabbed my hand with surprising assurance for an artisan, snatched off his wig and bowed. Tethered ash blond hair and smiling teeth gleamed in the candlelight. A young man with dangerous ebullience. He had to be one of the court, I realised, but I was so euphoric it did not matter. I tugged my hand free from his and beckoned the rest of the players out of the darkness. Just because they were not nobles, it did not diminish their right to tributes.

We all made obeisance again and then – thank God – proud hands clasped my shoulders. I knew Hastings was standing behind me.

'Excellent, Will!' exclaimed King Edward, but his eyes were on me. 'Heard you helped out at the final moment, Mistress Shore. Our thanks to you and our compliments on your dancing.'

I could scarce whisper a thank you as I was high on the huzzahs. Sweet Heaven, name a woman who wouldn't be!

'I'm Dorset, by the way,' said Paris in my ear, as if the revelation would ensure I melted. He kissed my hand.

'Ignore him,' said King Edward. 'Paris has been defeated. Let us leave it that way.'

Hastings' fingers tightened. '"Helen" needs to change.'

'Only her mind,' murmured the King, 'or is that now done?'

Too dazed to follow the footwork of this conversation, I did not dare stare above the diamond clasps of his highness' doublet. 'Later, then,' he was saying to somebody.

'Can we all come?' quipped Dorset, his lascivious gaze upon my breasts.

And then the atmosphere chilled.

'Elizabeth,' purred King Edward.

I thought for a foolish instant that he spoke to me and then *she* appeared from the shadows, a woman in her late thirties, her belly high with child. His queen, Elizabeth Woodville, with emeralds glittering around her throat and golden threads criss-crossing her headdress. Behind the transparent demi-veil, a frown marred her perfect forehead and her full lower lip betrayed her to be somewhat out of temper. I was overwhelmed, not by her ill-humour, but because she was wearing one of Tabby's girdles over her magnificent brocade gown. I gasped in delight and sank in a deep curtsy, far too euphoric to shiver at the malevolence flowing off her.

'Ah, the Trojan horse,' she remarked cryptically, setting her hand upon the King's proffered wrist. 'They say, "Beware the Greeks when they bring gifts".' Her moon-cool radiance beamed straight across my head at her husband's friend.

'Indeed, madame,' agreed Hastings dryly. 'Indeed.'

I expected no less than the promise of an escort home as soon as I had cleansed the colours from my face and wriggled back into my own apparel, but when Lord Hastings sent a page requesting me to join him in his chambers, I agreed with delight. Even though the bells of St Martin-le-Grand would soon be sounding curfew in the city, I cheerfully followed Talwood through the coney warren of servants' passageways.

Hastings was sprawled with his feet upon a footstool and a fine glass goblet in his hand. His doublet and stomacher were gone, the collar of office dangled from the back of his chair, and only a gemmed cross glittered among the loosened laces of his shirt. He bestirred himself in welcome and kissed my cheek.

'Here is the necklace back, my lord,' I said, laying the golden leaves upon a little painted table.

'No, keep it as your player's fee, my dear Elizabeth. You exceeded all my expectations. Here, let me!' He fastened it back about my throat, before he poured me wine. Feeling the necklace against my skin and the costly goblet between my fingers, my senses thrilled. Elizabeth Lambard was in Westminster Palace drinking with the King's close friend. Except he looked haggard in the candlelight – utterly forgivable – *The Siege of Troy* would have leeched anyone's vitality.

We touched rims. 'You did well,' he said, raising his glass to me.

I shook my head with genuine modesty. 'By the skin of my teeth. The other players were very kind and Master Talwood made a wondrous guardian angel. No, it is certainly you who deserve all the praise, my lord.' I drank to him.

There was no return sparkle in his eyes. No hint that he desired to make love tonight. Sometimes I forgot he was so much older. Around us, the silence seemed suddenly precipitous and my delight began to ebb. I took another sip of wine.

'I noticed her highness was wearing one of my women's girdles. Was that your doing, my lord?'

His forehead puckered as if the remark was not worthy of his attention. 'No, I believe Lady Brampton presented it to her grace. Pray sit down, Elizabeth. I need to talk to you.'

Apprehensive, I made myself comfortable on a cross-legged chair and, with mounting dismay, watched him prowl across to the hearth and turn.

'Elizabeth, you and I have come to a crossroads.'

I had anticipated this. But not so soon. Nothing lasts. I know that. The petals of the violet shrivel; its perfume lingers only in the memory.

'You want no more to do with me?' Had I behaved inappropriately tonight? Did I still lack the bedroom skills to please him? Or was I some matter to be tidied up before he left for France?

'Stop it!' he scolded. 'I see all manner of thoughts flitting through your mind. Of course your company is a delight, my dear, but I can no longer be your lover. You need a younger man.'

'But you are—'

'Older than you by almost twenty years.' I had thought him scarce forty. Astonishment must have blazed across my face for he added: 'How kind of you to look surprised.'

'I am, I truly am. But, please, do not think that—'

He held a finger to his lips. '*Doucement*, little one. Our arrangement was temporary as we both agreed.' He drew a deep breath and I should have expected what came next. 'Out of loyalty to me or because of your sense of virtue, you have already said no to the King of England. Tonight you have a chance to reconsider.'

'*Tonight?*' Deep inside me, excitement began to stir but it was shackled by a suspicious anger. 'Was this your agendum all along, my lord? I know the man supposed to play Helen did not break his ankle.'

'Yes, you are right, he didn't. The opportunity was provided at royal request and now it is up to you, Elizabeth.' He took a taste of wine, watching me over the glass. 'I have brought the horse to water. You do not have to drink.'

So, broken in for the next rider, I was to be sold on.

'I trusted you, my lord.' Hurt underscored each word. My hand shook as I set down the glass. I intended to leave but he stepped into my path. '*Please-let-me-pass!*'

'No!' he said, holding up his palms. 'You must hear me out and…and stop looking like an outraged virgin in a soldiers' bath-house!'

I sat down but I kept my back poker-stiff.

He dropped on his haunches beside me and his voice was gentler. 'Elizabeth, you offered yourself to me for no other reason than you wanted to learn and, by Heaven, I was happy to teach. All you asked of me was the name of a worthy lawyer, and in this world of venality I found that unselfishness remarkable, a breath of purest air. Now I am asking a favour. You have a choice tonight. The favour I ask is that you do not make your decision rashly.'

'A choice? Do I?' Disbelief spiked my voice; tears mustered behind my eyelids.

'Of course, you do, my dear.' He set a reassuring hand across mine. 'You can go back to your husband before curfew and nothing more will be asked of you ever again.' Back to my little kerchief of bleak space beyond the partition? A future of respectable celibacy – the worsted world of William Shore and lecherous Ralph the Younger?

The haughtiness left my spine and I stared unhappily down at my lap like a chastened child. His thumb scuffed my wrist. 'Can you not see that Life is challenging you, Elizabeth? Are you going to ride into the joust or watch from the crowd with everyone else?'

'Christ's mercy!' I rose to my feet in anguish. 'I *am* everyone else. His grace said the awe would wear off but it hasn't. I am *nobody*, my lord.'

Hastings stayed where he was. 'Elizabeth, my dear, King Edward can have any woman in this entire kingdom – and he desires *you*.'

'Ha! Only because he saw me naked at Gerrard's Hall!'
I exclaimed in disgust, rising and pacing to the window. 'I am
a toy on a stall. He just wants what you have, like a child that
cannot bear to be left out.'

I heard the rustle of taffeta sleeves. He had climbed to his feet.

'You're wrong. He wants your company because he enjoyed
the supper with you at Gerrard's and you gave him cakes for his
children. Gave, not took. You were yourself, open and honest.'

I knuckled away the moisture at the edges of my eyes and
stared up at the darkening sky. The King's face came into my
mind. Teasing, challenging but with a kindness, too – he had not
ravished me at Gerrard's Hall.

Wasn't this the miracle I had longed for all my life? The chance
to be someone, to make a difference? But how many years in
Purgatory would this cost? A housewife like me being offered
temporal power? Wasn't this an offence against God's order?

Hastings came to stand beside me. 'Can you feel *no* alchemy
with Ned?' Alchemy? An attraction that had my pulse racing and
my heart beating like a tabor? '*Elizabeth*?'

'I daresay he might be goodly company.'

Hastings started laughing and I turned upon him. 'I am in
earnest about this. I am not some strumpet you've plucked out of
the gutter.'

'I know you are not, but, Christ, my dear, calm down!' With
an arm about me, he turned me towards the open window. 'Try
and look beyond the horizon.'

I stared up at the huge feast of stars and planets stretching into
infinity and remembered as a little girl looking up at that self-
same canopy of sky and daring to dream. What had happened to
that hopeful child? Was she still crushed inside me?

'You will be good for Ned because you will be doing this for
the right reasons.'

'Are there "right reasons", my lord?' I chided, stepping away from him. 'Aren't royal concubines supposed to be greedy, selfish bitches? They already say that about the Queen, his lawful wife. What will they say about *me*?'

'That's up to you.' He lidded the air with his palms. 'Stay calm.'

'Lord's sake,' I exclaimed, looking around in panic. 'Is his grace behind the arras, listening to all this?'

'Indeed not! He is above such things and so am I. However, you would do well to keep your voice soft.'

Lest servants heard and carried the tittle-tattle to those who would pay for it? I wanted none of this. 'Supposing his grace finds one night enough, my lord?' I asked wearily. 'Even one night will ruin me if word of this reaches Mercers' Hall.'

'Elizabeth, it may be one night, it may be one year. But think of the challenge and what it could bring you.'

'What will it bring *you*, my lord?'

Hastings' eyes glittered. Had I provoked anger or courtly amusement?

'I am requesting you to do this for the good of the realm.' Reading disbelief in my face, he added, 'No, I swear to God that's the truth. I…I try to do my best.' With a sigh, he drew his fingers wearily across his brow, searching for the words to persuade me. 'Listen, Elizabeth, when I was not much older than you are now, his grace's father, the Duke of York, asked me to become his son's shadow. He wanted me to make sure the lad didn't fall into bad company. I have been trying to do that ever since and at times I have failed badly. I am asking you to become Ned's friend because I think you would be wholesome and good for him, and for all of us.'

I was to be some kind of patriotic oatcake?

Someone's polite knock stopped me saying that aloud. Hastings dealt with the interruption, a brief, muttered exchange.

'The King's servant?' I asked.

He nodded reluctantly and stayed in my path to the door. 'Please, Elizabeth,' he said eventually, breaking the silence of hurt that lay between us. 'You can do much good, for yourself and for the kingdom. I had far rather you were Ned's mistress than the greedy whores Dorset tries to foist upon him.'

'I don't know,' I whispered, shaking my head as if I could toss this dilemma from my temples. It was hypocrisy for me to plead a sense of honour; I was already an adulterous wife.

'Sweetheart!'

I turned anguished eyes upon him and watched him clasp and raise the cross he wore around his neck. 'Within this is a fragment of the True Cross. I swear to you that unless you turn the King against me, which God forbid, I shall stand your friend until my dying day.' He stared at me in hope, his quiver of arguments empty at last.

The King of England's mistress! A clever woman might wield more power than London's Lord Mayor. But did I have that artfulness? Did I want that authority or wish to live in fear of the Queen's malice? No! But what I did want was *my freedom*.

At last I recognised the truth. Tonight could be the price of severance from Shore!

I stared wide-eyed at the open window light and then at Hastings. The Lord Lieutenant of Calais was watching me like a dog hoping his mistress would reach for her boots. A walk? A walk? And if I did not walk towards King Edward's bedchamber, would Hastings' friendship swiftly unravel?

'Do you wish some time alone to make up your mind?'

'But the King is waiting, isn't he?' I answered caustically, as I picked up my cloak.

Taken off guard by my change of humour, the King's great friend stared at me shrewdly, trying to estimate my capacity for rebellion.

'Are you sure?' Then he realised the ambiguity. 'Or Shore, but not for much longer.'

My face told him it was a poor jest in the circumstances and he had the grace to look contrite. I lifted my fingertips to his cheek; the lines of care were those of loyalty.

'I can see why he loves you so,' I stated. 'You would give your life for him.' And he was giving him me as well. But I understood now what the Queen had meant.

I was the Trojan Horse.

# II

Like a great beast, the palace was easing down onto its haunches for the night as Hastings led me, an icily silent sacrifice, through the torchlit passageways. The guards at the arched portal to the King's Chamber did not bar my way. They stared ahead as though I was invisible. And would I become invisible to my family and friends by giving my body to the King?

'My blessing on you.' A fatherly squeeze of my steeled shoulders, then Hastings stepped between the soldiers and thrust open the door. Oh, how I hated him at that moment.

Before me, the chill, ceremonial chamber was in shadow, save at one end where two great floor candles flickered either side a door. The soft cadences of a single lute came from there. So I was to be lured in with sweet music like a besotted insect. To my right, I espied a huge bed with turgid murals flanking its dark canopy, and a painting of an ancient coronation louring from above. Glinting stretches of battles decorated the wall that faced me.

A manservant slid from the shadows behind me and strode to the slit of light streaking out from beneath the inner door. I started to follow and gasped as a rat ran across my foot. Mercy

God! My resolution faltered. For an instant of weakness, I looked back. Hastings' face was in shadow as he seized both ring handles and drew the doors closed behind me.

'Mistress?' The servant had knocked upon that inner door. Now it was open, blazing with candlelight and silhouetted within it, dark and faceless, like the Devil waiting for my soul, stood the King himself. His long shadow fell across my path and I had no choice but to walk towards him.

And to give myself strength, I conjured guardian angels on my either hand – the young, ambitious girl who had daydreamed of greatness before she married Shore, and the wanton, reckless Eve whom Hastings had bestirred.

The King's hand fastened round my fingers.

A silken robe, the hue of the wild woods, the green of the hunt, was knotted loosely about his body. I breathed in musky perfume as his lips brushed my wrist and he drew me into that bright, warm chamber. How long would it take him to unpeel my clothing and use me? Would it be done on the daybed, against the door or on that monstrous bed? And afterwards, a mutter of thanks as he fastened back his points? Probably. With some trinket or a purse. Maybe he would order me back for tomorrow evening.

'Helen of Troy, how generous of you to come,' he murmured, offering me a broad grin and the gift of a perfect white rose. 'Not wearing the "devils' windows" then?'

'No, your highness.' I blinked, startled by the reality of the flesh and blood Achilles who stood beside me. In a few minutes he would be thrusting inside me.

The music ceased abruptly with a twang and a muttered apology as the lutanist swiftly tried to replace the string.

'Hope Will didn't have to twist your arm?' my new lover asked.

What a false question! As if the King of England, six foot three and wearing his shirt loosely laced, needed reassurance.

'Not exactly, your highness,' I replied gravely, wriggling my left shoulder as though it had been wrenched. 'I had to wait an hour for the awe to rub off again.'

It took him a moment to remember. 'And has it all gone?'

'Not quite.' Raising the rose to appreciate its perfume, I looked over its petals at him. 'During the escape from Sparta, I threatened to make a counter-tenor of Paris. Since he is your stepson I daresay it is a hanging matter.'

'Afraid so,' he replied, shaking his head at my folly. 'And you have already threatened the King of England in similar fashion. However, the King decrees he will grant you clemency if you agree to take supper with him now.'

Oh dear, all this banality. I wished he'd just throw my skirts up and have done. If the coupling proved too drawn out, how was I going to fake the passion he'd require to flatter his skill?

I bit my lip in a seductive way. 'It might be a "Last Supper" for me, your grace.'

'I am certainly hoping it won't be, Mistress Shore.' His warm hand slid behind my shoulder blades. 'Now be at ease. I can't have you looking like Jehane of Arc about to be put on trial. Come and sup.' With a possessive arm about my shoulders, he led me to a table set before a recessed windowseat. Platters of viands, fruit and sweet pastries awaited us.

'Please.' He indicated that I should sit down and he slid in beside me. I was enclosed among the opulent, satin cushions, a luxurious cage. Even the toothpicks set beside the plate we were to share were made of gold and pommelled with gems.

The royal servants were immediately in attendance, lifting the table closer to us for comfort and removing the pinnacled, jewelled lids from the exquisite goblets.

The chamber was softened by tapestries. Above the musician's head, a voluptuous Helen and sinewy Paris were escaping from

Sparta, and facing the supper table was an arras of St George, his sword bloody and his steel foot set upon the writhing dragon.

All about the room, Love and War glittered in glorious contradiction. A naked battle sword lay starkly across two wall braces but dangling from its blade was a child's drawing of a heart. Upon the little table by the hearth, a statuette of a curvaceous St Mary Magdalen presided over the stony-faced chessboard military; and a Venetian bowl of blood red glass, entwining lovers enamelled upon its curves, was at odds with the single arrow that rested across its rim. And the two books with ornate claps beside King Edward's chair of estate? A tale of Sir Lancelot du Lac weighed down beneath a tome on martial strategy?

I glanced sideways beneath my lashes at the man beside me – the muscular soldier's body, the dimpled, pleasing smile. The same contradiction – a ruler who denied his enemies the right of sanctuary yet tumbled to his knees, bewitched by a beautiful widow. But there was no sense of the Queen in this room, no reliquary of her about his neck. Was this man shallow, whimsical, a mirror to his flatterers? But then I saw beside the books a splintery old footstool, tapestried with a ragged, faded falcon-in-fetterlock. Something kept and loved.

'My lady?' A little page with a Rheims napkin across his shoulder held out a silver ewer. I dabbled my fingers in the perfumed water.

*My lady?* Were my manners good enough? Would the sovereign lord of England find me dull? Oh, I must smile and please from now on, especially since his hand was resting on my thigh and his gaze was stroking me with a lover's caress. Hypocrite! If his love for Elizabeth Woodville was past, how long could Elizabeth Lambard last – a comet that might flash a few nights in the sky and then no more?

But the King was trying to be pleasant, and the truth was that Elizabeth Lambard, the envious girl who had watched a shining,

victorious youth ride into London, was sitting alone beside him
now he was a man – and he desired her.

I must not succumb to his charm, I told myself. Stay in control,
Elizabeth. Like the other men, he sees you as a body for his use,
his pleasure. But the Eve in me was whispering that pleasure could
be shared. Hadn't I enjoyed my lessons with Hastings?

His hazel eyes were examining me with a mixture of kindness
and puzzlement.

'Be at ease, Mistress Shore,' he said, and he withdrew his arm
and stretched out both hands to select one of the strange fruit that
lay before us upon a silver platter. Six gaudy, yellow fingers joined
at the knuckles. He snapped one free.

'It's called a long apple or apple of Paradise. Peel it thus and if
you break it so, there's the Holy Cross or Trinity, see.' He held out
a span of pale creamy flesh for me to bite. 'Like it?'

It was luscious. The long flesh so soft. I did not dare consider
how much one lick of a tongue was worth. 'Perhaps.' I suggested
softly, 'this was the true apple that the serpent offered Lady Eve in
the Garden of Paradise.'

King Edward finished the other half and ran his thumb along
his lips. 'Well, I reckon she'd have certainly turned down an
apple-john or leather-coat.'

'Our homely windfalls, ravished by golden wasps?' My laughter was genuine as I shook my head. 'But these fruits are a true
wonder. Where do they come from?'

'The Fortunate Isles off Mauritania.' He broke off another of
the strange fruit. 'Here, enjoy, it's all for you.' And he watched my
fingers as I explored the skin. 'Could be the apple mentioned in
*The Travels of Sir John de Mandeville.*'

'The one that rots within a week?' Yes, like my reputation
once the gossip reached the city.

'Except these don't perish during the voyage, learned mistress,
they are packed grass green.'

I peeled down the three pieces of the fruit's strange skin and took a bite of the creamy flesh while King Edward watched my face indulgently.

'Are they a gift from Sir Edward Brampton?' I asked.

'From dear Duarte?' The King gave a flourish, mimicking his Portuguese friend, making me smile. 'Yes, you are right. Not a horse short of a shoe, are you, my pretty citizen! Ah, but, of course, you know Duarte's wife. Suppose you noted my queen was wearing one of your girdles?' His attention slid down to the samite stitched with pearls that snaked my waist, then appraisingly up over my breasts to the collar of leaves about my throat, and settled at my lips.

Warmth was stealing through my body, turning my skin to rose and my apprehension was sliding away, too, as I gazed back. Here was a man who genuinely liked women. There seemed no contempt in his demeanour; no cruel agendum hiding behind his kindness.

'You danced like a nymph tonight, Mistress Shore,' he said appreciatively. 'Did you expect me to order a repeat performance?'

'Something like that.'

'Thought so, the way you marched in.'

'I did not!'

'You dance better than you march.' His strong fingers were wielding a knife. He pierced the flesh of a fig and set its two halves before me. 'And I'll wager you skate with the same grace, too.' But his eyes were asking a different question.

I coaxed some slivers of soft cheese onto the platter between us and then tasted a piece of fig.

'I've never skated, your highness.'

'Then, come winter, you shall.' He took a swig of wine and gave me a teasing, gorgeous grin. 'You will look as sweet as a rabbit kitten with fur gauntlets and a matching cap. Once you've got the way of it, I'll teach you how to skate backwards. Would you like that?' Now his gaze was running hot fingers down my cheeks, across my lips and I was beginning to burn.

'Yes, I would, your highness,' I answered huskily. What sorcery was happening to me? How could I be yearning to feel his tongue upon my breasts, his touch between my thighs?

'No "highness" or "grace" in here. Ned will suffice.'

There were no servants now. One by one and subtly, the candle flames had been smothered so that only about the table was there sufficient light to show the sheen of skin. The musician had quietly left.

King Edward watched me take a gulp of wine, shook his head teasingly and removed the goblet from my clasp. He let his gaze fall to my cleavage and then rise once more to my eyes.

'Well, my proud Londoner, shall you let me unclothe you, adore and worship you? If not, flee now, for I've an appetite on me that needs must feed.'

'And my appetite?' I asked.

'Fire for fire, sweetheart.'

His lips touched mine teasingly and before I could respond, he drew back.

'Sweetheart, I have learned that Life is a trickster and Fortune his strumpet. You live for the moment because you don't know what he has in store for you. That sinful fellow has taught me some cruel lessons, seesawed me up, seesawed me down, set me against those I believed my friends.' He carried my hand to his lips. 'So, my beautiful mistress, let us live this night as though it is our last upon this earth. What say you?'

I nodded, watched him push the table back, stand, and turn to face me.

'Take my hand and dance, Mistress Shore, dance before the music is over.'

He held his left hand out to me, palm uppermost. Gold banded his fingers, graceful fingers for so large a man.

Our faces drew close. He looked down into my eyes and tenderly brushed his lips along mine. Had the real Helen felt like this with Paris? Then he made another pass, grazing playfully this time. And deep inside me, the she-serpent reached up her arms through mine and sensually eased her fingers through his long hair and drew his face down.

We kissed hungrily. The King's breath mingled with mine, our lips devoured, our hands were everywhere. He did not lead me out to that great state bed but gathered me up into his arms and carried me to the innermost of his private rooms, his true lair, where the bed coverlet lay glittering with silver fleur-de-lis and golden lions. He tossed it back, exposing its soft belly of fur.

'Better than that damned Bed of Ware out there?' he asked, lowering me before him.

'Infinitely better, my gracious lord.'

'Ahhh.' With a sigh of male approval, he moved behind me, slowly slid my gown down my shoulders and ran his hands over my breasts. The rub of his palms, his subtle fingers on my roused nipples had me wet and hot for him. I was liquid, ravenous. He loosed my silken belt and pushed my gown down below my hips.

'Elizabeth, my beautiful girl.' His breath caressed my throat between kisses. 'I'm glad you made me wait, for our pleasure will be infinitely greater.'

All reasoning fled. Tugged back against him, I felt his hardness pressing into me before he turned me to face him. 'See the power you have over me. Feel how much I want you, need you, want to taste you.' He slid my body across the bed and then swiftly he took off his clothes and stood looking down at me like a naked god before he took me in his arms. His mouth fed on mine as the soft ermine lapped against my skin and his hands slid up, up stockings and garters to between my legs.

'So you do want me,' he murmured with a male purr of satisfaction. 'Ripe and wet.'

'Yes, I want you,' I gasped. Although I was burning for him to slide inside me, I wanted him to be hungrier still. I pushed him back and slid a leg astride him.

He laughed, drew me down and possessed my mouth, curling his tongue about mine with open-lipped thirst while his hands played upon me like a sculptor's, creating an art of love, outside me, within me and my fingers too were skilled now, teasing, enticing.

I kissed his broad shoulders, ribs and belly, lapped him with my tongue down to the thicket of tiny curling hairs and his prick. He arched and cursed and groaned like a great golden dragon, writhing beneath me until he could bear no more. With swift strength, he had me on my back. His mouth was a slash of tension as he readied me. His skin was slicked with sweat as he thrust into me at last.

And there are no words left, try as men may, to describe that little death, that incandescent instant when, transacted with mutual love, there is no difference between sweet submission and exquisite conquest.

I reached out and fingered one of the golden tassels that adorned the pure white bedcurtains. The early sun was stealing through the glass, edging towards my lover's face. He stirred, yawned, stretched. There was no morning arousal. He was sated. We both were.

'That was a goodly night,' he murmured, drawing me closer to his side. It was the first time I had ever slept through until morning with a man I liked, and I snuggled close revelling in this glorious miracle – Elizabeth Lambard lying within the arms of King Edward of England.

'Happy?' he asked.

'This much.' I rolled back and stretched wide my arms. 'Deliriously. Exquisitely.'

He smiled and looked at me with such great tenderness. 'Excellent, I have made at least one of my subjects joyous this morning.' Then he leaned up on his elbow and jabbed me on the nose. 'Listen, wench, are you always called Elizabeth?'

'My brothers call me Lizbeth.'

He shook his head. 'Won't do. The Queen prefers Elizabeth and my daughter is Bess. What about Jehane for you?'

'No!' I had seen a Lollard's gruesome death and the memory still terrified me. 'No! They burned Jehane as a witch.'

'Pah, I don't believe that,' Ned scoffed, lying back and clasping his hands beneath his head. 'I'll wager she was no ignorant shepherdess either.'

I stared at him in astonishment. I had never questioned the tale.

'Well, some poor creature burned,' I said sadly, 'but it would be sweet to believe that Jehane escaped.' A slender maiden in armour astride a white destrier, the lion and lilies pennon fluttering above her inspired face. 'So brave for a woman, even if she was our enemy.'

'The name fits you.' He leaned over to his bedsteps and lifted up a goblet, dipped his finger in it. 'We could make it more English. What about Joan?' I must have winced. 'Or Jane? Not too many of them. Yes, I like it. What do you say, *Jane*?'

Before I could argue, he drew a cross upon my brow.

'You didn't let me *say*.'

He laughed and kissed my brow. 'Oh, feel free to disagree. I do listen sometimes.'

I clouted him.

'Stop doing that, you witch. That's treason.' He playfully nuzzled my hair. 'When I get back from the campaign in France, I want you to come and live here at Westminster.'

'Whoa, my liege, I think you put the cart before the horse.' I pleated my lips, close to crazed laughter; last evening had been so full of horses. 'Truly, you hardly know me.'

Surprised at my reluctance, he said haughtily, "If you think I am going to send a servant all the way to Farringdon past your father every time I want your company, stow that!'

'I do not live in Farringdon.'

'Ah, no, I forgot we have the feelings of poor, broken-masted Master Shore to consider. Send him along to see me.'

'My lord...Ned...'

'Going too fast for you, am I, Jane?'

I nodded, laughing. 'Just a little. I have been rebaptised, my movables shifted to Westminster, my husband about to be—'

'Placated?' Ned's eyes devoured me. 'No, how could he be unless he's blind and senseless?' For an instant it was as if the wraith of Shore hovered between us. 'Is your husband ambitious, greedy, venal? Helps to know.'

'No, my gracious lord, he is hardworking and diligent.'

My lover pulled a face. *'Respectable?'*

'With an illuminated "R".' I said with a little growl.

'Oh, one of those. Poor Jane. Well, we'll sort him out. I'll see him after Mass this morning.'

I held up my palms. 'Your gr—'

*'Ned*! Come on, I did not think you so slow-witted.'

'Ned, I feel I am on the back of a runaway horse. No, don't laugh at me!' I ran a finger down his stubbled cheek and spurred the conversation down a different path. 'Tell me, can the King of England stay in bed as long as he likes?'

'Does the earth go round the sun? No, they'll all be gathering out there like mother hens in half an hour.'

'Do they have to wash you as well as robe you?'

'Sponge me down? For pity's sake, not *en masse*. I have one servant standing by with a towel and clean underlinen and a barber who comes on Saturdays. You were lucky to get me cleanshaven last night. Mind, for you…' He blew me a kiss, slid out of bed and retrieved his robe from the floor. There were several scars on his back and buttocks. Not the badges of war from Towton, Barnet and Tewkesbury – he would have been clad from head to toe in armour – more like the vicious thwacks from a quintain.

He looked up to see me admiring him and grinned.

'There's a meeting at the Guildhall this morning. I need to squeeze more donations from your worthy Londoners for the war with France.' The golden smile flashed. 'Sometimes it only takes a kiss.'

'I'm sure the aldermen will enj—'

'I'm talking about the old wives.' He demonstrated his beseech-ing face. Cheeky wretch!

I curled round to sit upon my heels and shook my head reck-lessly. 'Wouldn't the money be better spent on new caravels or finding a swifter route to the Indies?'

He took it in good humour. 'Don't you disparage my war, mercer's daughter. I've been planning it for years.' Then he came round to my side of the bed, sat down and wrapped a friendly hand over my ankle beneath the sheet. 'And what investment may I make in this pretty vessel? Gowns to adorn your sails? A cargo of gems?'

'No,' I said softly. 'Friendship is worth far more than any worldly treasure.'

He looked surprised. 'Well, this divorce, then, where are you at with it?'

'Well,' I said, delighted that he had aired it. 'Not very far. But thanks to Lord Hastings and his lawyer, I have finally found a proctor willing to take the case but he says I have not much hope of winning. I shall plead that Shore is impotent and that I desire to become a mother and bear children – a wife's right. It's thin, I know. After so many years, I can hardly plead non-consummation.'

Ned grinned like a rascal and pinched my nose. 'Not after last night at any rate.'

I sighed. 'Well, I probably have as much chance of winning as walking on water but at least I shall have tried.'

He nodded. 'Audacious, I grant you that, but not impossible. For a start, you will have the lusty widow's testimony from the other week.'

I frowned. 'I do not understand, your gr...Ned?'

'The cherrylips who visited your husband's shop. Your poor Shore couldn't manage anything although he huffed and puffed. Didn't you know?'

'Actually, Shore told me, but how do *you* know? Hmm, I thought omniscience was confined to God.'

'I claim no divine powers, sweetheart. We sent her, that's why.'

I recoiled. '*We?*'

'Don't look daggers at me, puss. When you propositioned Lord Hastings, we deemed it wise to see if your story was true.'

There is a limit to how furious you may get with a king, especially if you are wearing nothing but a cross and a gilded collar. I was not pleased. Would he and his chamberlain discuss last night's coupling on the way to meet Mayor Basset?

'I suppose you know how many garters I have as well,' I said grumpily.

'Lordy, no, waste of money finding that out although I could have sent one of my agents to chatter with your maidservant. You've nice teeth, Jane.'

I realised I was staring at him open mouthed. 'What else do you know?' I muttered, clenching my jaw.

'Oh, that you stand by your family in trouble and that Alderman Shaa, for one, thinks the world of you. Patient Griselda where your husband is concerned, eh?'

'I hope not. Griselda was a craven milksop. But let me understand this, your...Ned. Did Lord Hastings tell you that I asked him to lie with me?'

'Well, yes, now don't go sour about it with him. I was impressed when I heard. Tremendous courage.'

'Is that why you barged in at Gerrard's Hall?'

'Ouch!' He shook his wrist as though I'd smacked him. 'Phew, I feel like I'm up before my own bench. Yes, madame magistrate, it annoyed old Will mightily and I'm sorry if it offended you. I wanted to see you for myself.' His hazel eyes beamed. 'And I did! But now everything's right as it should be. I'll make sure you get your divorce, *Mistress* Shore.'

That was a boot in the ribs of my anger. *The price of freedom. Powerful friends.*

'But how, my lord? Forgive me, but even you, though king, are not above the law of Holy Church. My proctor has warned me there is no precedent and it will cause too much uproar.'

He shook my ankle. 'So, it's a challenge. All we really need is for old Sixtus to toss the matter back to our holy fellows here and then we shall be home and hosed. A trio of well-chosen bishops and *voilà*.'

'*Voilà?*'

'Definitely *voilà*. Don't worry. Art of compromise. Might have to agree with the old fellow's nominee for the next vacant bishopric, but what's a concession now and again. A letter shall go off this afternoon. About time my agents in Rome got off their arses. Some ring-licking around the cardinals and judicious greasing of palms, but, heigh, that's the way of things.'

I held up my hands. 'Please, Ned, may I say something?'

'Madame, feel free.' He tugged at the sheet, which I had gathered round me. 'You really have the most beautiful breasts, you know.'

'I desperately would like severance from Shore but for honest reasons, not because I have the good will of the king and—'

'And you are a delight to f—'

I had leaned forward and pressed my fingers to his sinful mouth. '*But* because there is a case to answer,' I persisted firmly. 'Holy Church and...'

He slid his head free. 'And husbands everywhere will be terrified if you succeed.' He stroked a finger along my lower lips. 'You are a dangerous woman, Mistress Shore. And you definitely need subduing.'

'Do I?'

'Hmmm, definitely and thoroughly.'

But a polite knock upon the door halted him before he could kiss me. Instead, I was swung from the bed and my gown thrust into my hands. 'Best be out of here soon, my darling dear, unless you want all my gentlemen of the chamber stiff within their breech clouts.'

'Well,' I began skittishly. He silenced me with a kiss and my rebellious soul purred with delight. I might not have become the Lord Mayor of London but I had become the King of England's mistress.

# III

Being sent home in the royal barge was too extravagant for my taste; a wherry back to Puddle Wharf sufficed and I stepped ashore with my feet on the cobbles but my spirits as high as St Paul's. I wanted to shout my happiness to the entire world but instead the passers-by saw Shore's wife coifed and cloaked like any other housewife.

It was past breakfast as I slunk through the back gate like a mouser who had been out caterwauling all night. In the kitchen, our cook was beheading carrots, and my maid Isabel was singing as she measured out honey. The house smelled of ripe fruit. We were supposed to be making plum preserve this morning and an opportunistic wasp was already crawling upon the heaped basket that awaited my attention. The incongruity of my kitchen compared to the King's bedchamber made me laugh aloud.

'Oh, mistress, I am glad you are merry for he's in a right lather.' Isabel darted a meaningful glance at the rafters.

'Is that you back at last, wife?' came a furious voice from above.

Shore and I met on the stairs. He grabbed my wrist and hauled me up into the solar. 'Ah thought you were murdered, you wretched cow. Where the Devil have you been? It's him, isn't it? The poxy Lord Chamberlain.'

I bit back 'two hims' as I drew off my gloves. Instead I said, 'Your pardon if I worried you, Shore. No, it wasn't Lord Hastings. I played Helen of Troy in an entertainment at Westminster Palace and then I had a late supper with the King's grace.'

'Enow of your bamming!' He jabbed a ribbed fingernail at me. 'Ha, ah have it! Ralph Josselyn the younger!'

'Drooling Ralph?' I scoffed, untying my cloak. 'No, it's King Edward.'

Looking up, I saw Shore was wearing one of his know-better expressions that imposed a selective deafness. 'It's-the-King, husband. I lay last night with-the-King.'

He opted for a more palatable explanation. 'God save us!' he exclaimed. 'Your wits have gone asunder. I'll send the girl for a surgeon, see if old Jack Dagville can bring some leeches.'

'You might need the leeches when the truth sinks in.' I rattled the necklace. 'I am not lying. His grace the King commands you to attend him this morning at eleven after he returns from the Guildhall – by the way, aren't you supposed to be there? Never mind. Anyway, give your name at the Palace Watergate and you'll be taken straight in. I'd put on your violet livery if I were you.'

He crossed his fingers against me. 'The Devil's possessed you.'

'I warn you, Shore, he'll send an officer for you.'

'Then let him! Go and lie down, Elizabeth.'

'No, I've promised to help Isabel with the plums before they turn to pulp. Please get out of my way, sir. I need to change my gown.'

At eleven o'clock he still did not believe me. At noon two soldiers in lion and lilies surcotes clanged into the shop; they were not in the buying mood. I ran upstairs and watched from our jutting window as Shore left with them. His lirapipe scarfed his face but people were staring. The fool! I had not wanted it this way.

He arrived back past two, armoured with my father and mother's company as though my mind might be changed by a good dose of paternal chastisement. They were back from the country. Oh Heaven, I had forgotten Jack's months of negotiations for a mercer's heiress had reached fruition and his betrothal feast was just days away.

Shore folded his arms wearing an expression that would have withered an entire harvest. 'Tell them, Elizabeth.'

Mama flung her arms about me with motherly warmth. 'Oh, my love, at last! I've prayed so hard. When is it to be?'

'After the campaign in France,' I said, stiff within her embrace.

'Ah resent your attitude, Mother Lambard!' spluttered Shore. 'How can you—'

'Of course, I am cock-a-hoop after all these years. And I'm much obliged to you for letting Elizabeth tell us the news firsthand.'

Shore and I looked at one another.

'I am not with child, Mama,' I announced.

Her grey eyes lost their sparkle. 'But you said she had an important announcement, Son Shore.'

'Tell them you've become a whore, Elizabeth. Let's make a meal of it, eh! Her lover is sending me to Antwerp out of the way so ah'm not an embarrassment.'

'Antwerp!' I exclaimed. 'When?'

'When he gets back from France. Ah hope the plaguey French stick a bombard up his bloody arse.'

'Antwerp?' Father decided to join the ring at last. 'Furs? Baltic trade? You going as well, Elizabeth?'

Shore looked like he was about to burst. 'Lambard,' he began with admirable control, 'she's abaht to become the *King's Whore*!'

'Well, not about to,' I corrected.

'*The King!*' The air whooshed out of Mama and she subsided onto the nearest stool, palm clapped to her mouth.

Shore – who could blame him – was still finding the cuckold's horns an unpleasant fit. 'Your daughter has the morals of fornicatin' she-ape, John Lambard!'

My mother rallied at the insult. 'How dare you!' she exclaimed, her pointed cap all a-quiver. 'Say something, John!'

'I don't think he wants to,' I muttered. Beneath my I-dare-you stare, my handsome sire looked shiftier than a cutpurse caught with a knife. Before he could resume his 'respectable alderman' posturing, I said swiftly: 'I should mention in my defence, Father, that I did say "no" to the King the first time he asked me. In fact, I've been extremely discreet, and if Shore had bothered to believe me instead of being stubborn and superior, he wouldn't have had the street gaping when the royal guards came for him.'

Shore flung his hands in the air. 'What in God's name will our guild say?'

'Hell and damnation!' The implications of his adulterous daughter's decision were gathering in Father's mind like hungry kites. A swoop on my carcass was imminent. 'Son Shore has the right of it. The Company abhors scandal. O Jesu!'

'A husband's rights are protected,' fumed Shore. 'A king cannot be above the law. Why, ah'll...ah'll complain to Bishop Kemp and see what Holy Church has to say about this. If ah want to take my wife to Antwerp—'

'Timbuktu might be safer,' pointed out my mother witheringly; Shore's insult had drawn blood.

'Oh, you *are* going to Antwerp then?' I asked Shore.

'Ah cannot stay here in ignominy, ha' everyone laughing up their sleeves at me.' He stared at his hand. 'Look at me, ah'm all of a shek. You've shamed me, Elizabeth. If ah'd known when ah took you to wife— God help me! Ah did not deserve this, you strumpet!' Then he swung round on my parents. 'She can move out this very hour. Ah wash my hands of her.'

Matters were boiling up too fast for my liking. I had not wanted our parting to be so clumsy.

'Let's keep a lid on this,' I exclaimed, fixing my parents with a warning stare. 'Scandal likes to play the cat with its victims, but only if we let it.'

'Hmm, but if you and Shore are to live separately, it will be remarked upon.'

'Yes, it will, Mama, but the Church does not object to separation – and nor should the Mercers' Guild – if the marriage is to be annulled.'

'Annulled!' cried Shore. 'Christ Almighty! Why do you not lead me through the streets on a donkey with the placard "CUCKOLD" about my neck!'

'But surely an annulment would be for the best?' I offered. He could find some neat Dutch woman. 'You'd be free to marry again. I'd like to see you content.'

Shore sat down at last, back hunched, his head in his hands. I wanted to fill his alecup but I thought he might throw it at me.

'Easy, Son Shore.' Father set a hand on his shoulder with a grunt of male sympathy and then shifted in beside him. He grabbed the flagon of stingo and filled the alecups. 'What inducement is King Edward offering, eh?'

'Enow, daresay, though ah intend to raise the price.' Shore glared up at me. 'But money does not compensate for a man's honour. Ah thought to stand for alderman at the next wardmote but now ah'll count myself blessed if they let me stay as a liveryman.'

'You could have bargained for a knighthood,' I declared, and noted my sire's head jerk up like a dog hearing the sounds of supper.

'You still could, son,' Father pointed out. 'In fact—'

Shore knew the old hunger in my parent. 'By Heaven, Father Lambard, you may get a knighthood out of your daughter spreading her legs for the King but plague take me if ah'll ha' men saying ah made such a bargain.' He took a swig. 'Truth is ah were too cursed dumbstruck to ask *him* for anything, and ah dinna see him anyroad, it were her high-handed friend the Lord Chamberlain who spoke wi' me. Tell 'em you've lain wi' 'im as well!'

'Lord Hastings is a friend of yours, Elizabeth?' Mama's lips shaped an oval of surprise.

'Yes, that is how I met the King's grace.'

'That's the way of it,' sneered Shore, lurching up as though he was going to slap me. 'Hastings rides 'em first. Procurer of the King's Strumpets! Is that how it were, wife?'

I flinched. Treacherous blood was heating my face. God forgive me, I wanted to strike him for making me feel a filthy whore.

'An' you'll get the pox.' Smugly, he waggled a finger at me. 'There cannot be a strumpet in London that he and his royal master haven't fucked. Well, thank Heaven, ah've not slept with you o'late, you slut. At least, ah shan't die stinking.'

'That's enough!' My mother stepped between us. 'We need to discuss this when we are all calmer. It might be better if you moved back to Silver Street, Elizabeth.'

'Aye, Mother Lambard,' agreed Shore. 'Get your lewd daughter out of here, or ah'll hurl her possessions out t'window in t'gutter and St Anthony's pigs can urinate all over 'em with my blessin'!'

'I'll pack,' I conceded, anxious to leave the room before the tears rushed down my cheeks. But he was not done with me. 'Ah'll sell you to the court for the best price ah can get, Elizabeth Lambard. An' what's more, you can whistle for the return of your dowry, nor am ah payin' this month's rent or wages for your silkwomen.' Another consequence I had not thought upon. How simple of me to expect a sensible, gradual parting.

'Of course, sir!' I left the chamber with my feelings like a ransacked house.

'Mistress?' Isabel rose from the lower stair.

'You heard?' With my wrist to my upper lip, I hurtled up to my bedchamber.

'I think it right marvellous, mistress,' she exclaimed, following me in. 'An' if you please, may I come with you?'

I halted at the chest and turned. She was a looking glass of my own ambition. 'Oh, so you don't think I'll get the pox and end up in Bedlam, then?'

She beamed at me. 'Course not, mistress. He be talking out his arse, if you'll pardon me for a-sayin' so. A woman's gotta look out for herself and you're too young to end up with a blunt quill like the master.' She held out her arms and her honesty was so welcome, that we sat on the chest together like a pair of new orphans and I sobbed my heart out until I could cry no more.

But what promises could I make the girl with my own future so precarious? Better she stay with Shore until he left for Antwerp and then join me.

Satisfied with that suggestion, she went downstairs to fetch me a warm drink while I threw open my clothing chest.

'Howe and Knotte are doing an uncommon amount of business for us, mistress,' she declared on her return. 'An' every customer wants to stay and chew the cud.'

I swore beneath my breath. 'See how the infamy begins, Isabel. God's mercy on us! And how shall it end?"

'Pah, I'd rather be choosin' King Edward than the master,' she giggled. 'There, now, you're smiling again. An' Knotte says to warn you there's been a stranger watching the shop since Master Shore arrived home. The fellow looks too full-bellied to be a thief but what he be doin' hanging around like a bad smell, who can say?'

'Show me!' Alas, opening the window was a huge mistake. Coarse huzzahs and whistles greeted me.

'By Jesu,' I squealed, drawing my head in straight away.

'That's him,' Isabel whispered. Lounging against the house wall opposite was one of the men who had been dicing outside the chamber at Gerrard's Hall.

'Go ask him up to the solar, and if the master gainsays you, tell him it's his highness' man come to see me.'

I washed my face and hastened downstairs.

My visitor was not flaunting any royal livery, but a king's trust gleamed in this man's quiet confidence.

'Bryan Myddelton, yeoman usher to my lord the King. You'll pardon my presence, Mistress Shore, but in the circumstances his grace was concerned for your safety. I did not like to intervene earlier, but is there any way I may assist you now?'

My joy at Ned's consideration made me doubly sure this was the right decision.

'Have you the authority to obtain a cart to shift my belongings, good sir? I am returning to my father's house.'

'Certainly, Mistress Shore.'

It was that easy. Suddenly, I was a person of consequence. I left the solar with my head higher than before, but I wondered how great the later cost would be.

My husband slapped me hard in the face as I left.


Moving back to Silver Street was like re-entering childhood. My mirror might tell me I was a woman, but my father still regarded me as a rebellious girl. By the end of the week I was walking on nails. Jack was no longer speaking to me because the scandal of my new position had knocked the wheels off his betrothal and our quarrel was swift and snarling.

A thwarted bridegroom, buttered with disappointment and larded with resentment, he saw me as Salome and Delilah baked in the same pot. For certain, he would have thrown me out if Father hadn't waved the financial stick.

'If I say your sister may have shelter here, she shall!'

Jack glared suspiciously from Father to me. 'She's got you over some kind of barrel, hasn't she? Or are you still drooling for the sword tap on the shoulder?'

'I'm still the head of this family, lad!'

'*Lad*! I'm twenty-nine, and who runs this poxy business for you? Call Robert home from Calais if you like, but I'm your cursed workhorse and you know it. As for you, you harlot, keep out of my sight. You've ruined all my plans. I *loved* her.'

'Jack, I never meant—'

'This is as much your fault,' he snarled at Mama. 'Encouraging her to run her own business.'

I stepped between them. 'That's so unfair, Jack, you wouldn't even have a business if…if…' My father's appalled face had me faltering. I could not tell my brother how I had rescued Father's reputation with my savings when his whore had almost ruined him. Such a revelation would devastate Mama.

'If what?' prodded my brother.

Fortunately Mama was game for fisticuffs. 'And what's wrong with your sister running a business, Jack? She's got as good a mind as yours.'

'She's a woman, Mother.'

'You think I can't stand on my own two feet?' I exclaimed hotly.

'That's *exactly* what I think.' That crude swipe had me scarlet, but before I could think of a cutting answer, he stormed out.

The bruises of life often come from those within arm's length, from those we love.

His bitterness was forgivable. I wiped my tears away and made a silent pledge. I would help him to a more worthy wife if I could

– when the verbal blows had ceased to sting, when there was kindness and understanding once more between us.

'I'm sorry,' I muttered.

Father grunted. 'And this is just the beginning.'

I sat down miserably in my old bedchamber and buried my face in my hands. I still had to confront Master Shaa and my silkwomen. The business was so new and making no profit as yet, but the moneys for rent and wages were due and I must pay them. But how? Jack would not offer, my father had recently spent most of his savings purchasing some land in Hertfordshire for a country house for Mama, and the proctor's fees were rapidly depleting what money I had saved. And then, as I drew my fingers down my cheeks, the answer was given to me. My gold wedding ring! I would send that to Master Shaa to keep my women employed. What's more, I would no longer stay a-hiding in my father's house like a penitent.

I determined to brazen things out and attend the Sunday sermon at St Paul's Yard, but that proved an ordeal. Gossip had already spread like a miasma. Even though Mama went with me, none of the Mercers' Company came near us, nor my friends, Margery or Alys. There was a distinct, telltale space on the bench between my leprous skirts and the pure ones of the haberdasher's wife who neighboured me. It was ostracism, and the expectation that we should drink hemlock or stab ourselves with our bodkins was very clear in the sniffy glances sent in our direction.

'I am sorry, Mama,' I whispered, grateful that she had the courage to be seen with me. Father had stayed home, pleading a head cold.

'Do not get in the dumps, my love. We must give people time. Hmmm, I observe Juliana Shaa isn't here. I wonder where her loyalty lies.'

'Well, her daughter has a wooden neck, that's for sure.'

★

My childhood playmate, Alys Rawson, whose parents lived next door to mine, braved the persistent rain next morning, holding a cered cloth across her starched headdress as she hastened through our back gate. The back gate, mark you! Margery was with her, dragging behind like a reluctant packhorse on a leading rein. Clearly, the sudden infamy of an old friend was too juicy for Alys to ignore. No doubt she wanted to press me until she heard the pips squeak, but I put her in the stocks first.

'Thank you for not speaking to me at Paul's Yard, the pair of you.' I did not sit down with them but stood, arms folded.

'Well, you are no longer respectable, Lizbeth dear,' crooned Alys, twitching her skirts, 'and you might have warned us. We are your oldest friends.'

'Cupboard friends, it seems.'

Alys' lashes fluttered. 'Oh, do not be shrewish. Paddesley's made life very uncomfortable for poor Margery here.'

Margery was the most subdued I'd ever seen her. 'He's forbidden me to visit you, Lizbeth,' she muttered.

'But you are here, anyway, Meg. Well, a pity he is so disposed. Given time, perhaps I could have recommended his business to my lord Chamberlain.'

She hung her head. 'He says I cannot be acquainted with a fallen woman.'

I stared down at her with hurt and sadness. Where was the vibrant girl who had enlivened my childhood? 'And what does Margery say?'

That pricked her. Face thrust up, she thrust her opinion at me like poison.

'How dare you bring such scandal on us, Elizabeth! Poor Shore! He says you are determined to drag him through the mire and seek a divorce as well. A divorce! I should not wonder if the Mercers' Guild asks him to withdraw his membership and then he will have nothing, nothing! You shall have utterly ruined him.'

'He will have King Edward's protection if he bothers to come to his senses,' I replied sternly, but I was glad that Shore had unstoppered his feelings to someone. 'However, perhaps you'd care to recall my unhappiness over the last ten years, Margery.'

'Oh, you mean being childless?'

I did not argue. There was much I had not told her, like my attempts to free myself lawfully from my marriage or of the time when I had almost taken my own life.

'So what would you do in my shoes, Meg?' I challenged. 'Refuse the King of England to please the Mercers' Guild?'

'Pah, throw that at me, Elizabeth Lambard!' Her plump hands writhed on her broad lap. 'As if that could happen to me. I haven't the face and figure to be frivolous like you, and I have my children to consider.'

Frivolous? Did I not run the business of four silkwomen? Did I not help Shore with his shop? And Meg had a nursemaid and a wetnurse to help her.

'If I had children, Meg, we would not be having this quarrel.'

Alys broke into the uncomfortable silence with a different approach. Widening her lovely blue eyes, she exclaimed, 'Oh, Lizbeth darling, you are such a sly puss, and there we all thought it was Ralph the Younger who was tempting you. How did all this come about? Is King Edward as good a lover as they say? Do tell. Is he…' She measured the air, palms facing each other. 'Or…?' Her hands moved wider apart.

'Alys!' Margery turned an unpleasant scarlet.

'Since what you are referring to was covered in a golden sheath embroidered with leopards, Alys, I really cannot— Oh look at your face. As if that was true. And as if I should tell you.'

'I have to go.' Margery stood up. 'I cannot wish you well,

Elizabeth. I know some may think it a great honour for you to be admired by the King but you are another man's wife and it is still adultery when all is said and done. You will both go to Hell for it. And now I take my leave. I doubt our paths will cross again.'

'What if they do, Meg?' I answered, steely and hiding my hurt.

'Then I shall look through you, Elizabeth. I shall not see you.'

This could not be happening. My beloved friend kicking me aside.

'Please, Margery,' I exclaimed, following her to the door. 'You can't mean this. After all these years…'

She did not even turn her head as she left.

There are other Deadly Sins beside Lust, I thought in retaliation: Envy, Anger, Sloth.

'Well, I had better go, too,' announced Alys, delivering a reproachful look at me for being so secretive. 'Of course, Mother says you will always be welcome to come next door when I'm visiting, Elizabeth, but she'd prefer you to come by the back postern.' She seemed unaware she had just insulted me. But I wasn't sure. At the threshold, she turned with unfulfilled hunger.

'Elizabeth, is he—'

'He is magnanimous and magnificent, Alys.'

'Oh.'

What else could she say?

As if losing friends was insufficient punishment, my next visitors were my family's rector from St Olave's and the priest of St Mary Aldermary – Shore's parish church – both anxious to persuade this stray lamb to consort no longer with the wicked wolves of Westminster. To my unspoken horror, they threatened excommunication.

'Does that apply to the King's grace as well?' I asked sweetly, as I rose to broom them out.

Their visit deeply affected Mama, who, despite her questioning intelligence, possessed a strong faith. Could things get worse?
Would Mama summon Will from Oxford to purify me? Would
Jack ever speak to me again? He and Father were avoiding the
guild meetings and, worst of all, because I had received no fresh
message from Ned. Father had begun to believe my future as a
royal favourite was a fantasy.

Guilt, my humourless inner magistrate, took its place on the
bench. By day it admonished me on how my fall from grace had
harmed those I loved. At night it proved a snoring bedfellow;
keeping me awake, and when I supposed I had shaken it to silence,
it would produce another loud snort of judgment.

Just when I began to doubt my sanity, fearful my family might
throw me out, Master Myddelton reappeared with an invitation.
Wondrous news – except I was bidden to wear my oldest clothes.

Mama was relieved but not impressed. 'I hate to say it, my love,
but I haven't been standing by you in the teeth of a tempest so you
can swish out the palace privies. He's not got odd fancies, has he?
Some men like shoes, you know and…'

I could not enlighten her but I took Ned at his word.

Unhappy in my shabby musterdevillers – imagine a drab grey
November sky – I followed Master Myddelton past Ned's guards
into his private bedchamber. My lover was securing his hair into
a tail while his attendants unrobed him.

'Heigh, here's trust and obedience.' England's sovereign lord
beamed at my apparel and called out to someone behind him.
'First wager won, Tom.'

'Am I to be reduced to scrubbing doorsteps?' I asked, spreading
my skirts as I curtsied in the doorway.

'All fours?' His grin was villainous. 'That's for later.' He strode
across to a lidded pannier that stood upon the small table, and
the four noblemen, who were struggling to divest him of his

*mille-fleurs* doublet and tapered, embroidered shoes, moved with him. A fifth man, whom I recognised with dismay – Paris, the Marquis of Dorset – turned from arranging the heavy collar of sunnes and roses on the back of a cross-legged chair. He regarded me with a supercilious smile before he raised a mocking eyebrow at his stepfather and carried across the gooseturd leather jerkin that had been lying on the bed coverlet.

'See, Jane,' exclaimed my lover, sliding his arms into the laced-on sleeves. 'I've had a bellyful of being agreeable to people indoors all day, raising money for the campaign, *et cetera*, so we are going fishing.'

'*F-Fishing*?' Fishing? Skating? Helen of Troy! Next thing he would want me to be a steeplejack.

'Aha!' He was trying to decipher my expression. 'Putting a good face on it, are you, Jane?'

Lord! I was trying to remember fishing ventures with my brothers.

'Then you'll be after perch?' I hazarded. 'And there'll be plenty of worms after last night's rain.' I inspected the cluster of rods leaning against the carved settle. 'I have not fished since I was this high.'

'And you've hardly grown since,' Ned jested. 'Which rod do you want?'

'She'll choose yours, of course.'

I ignored Dorset's coarseness. There were five rods to choose from. I selected the smallest, best for my height, and flicked it. Then I tested the next tallest. It was far more supple. 'This is better,' I declared. The lower section felt like willow and there was probably the usual hazel insert, but the upper section had a wonderful springiness. 'Is this blackthorn?'

'It is!' Ned grabbed me up and whirled me. 'Excellent. I win the second wager as well, Tom.'

'You supposed I could not fish, my lord Marquis?' I asked Dorset as I landed back on my feet deliriously happy. After ten years of William Shore, Ned's exuberance was sheer delight.

Behind Ned's back, Dorset strived for indifference.

'Could not, would not. Most courtesans care too much about their fine clothes. Clearly you don't mind getting *dirty.* Your leave to go, Ned?'

A waggle of fingers from the King, and the Queen's son left us with a mocking bow. To report to his mother? I hoped not; I had sufficient enemies, and that was just among my friends.

# IV

In my innocence I imagined a modest long boat followed by a second vessel of bodyguards, thorny with weapons. I was wrong: roped along the quay lay the royal barge, glowing with torches and bristling with oarsmen. Fishing in *that*?

Ned ushered me up the plank and turned impatiently. 'Where's Myddelton? Be a good fellow and tell her if she's not here within sixty heartbeats, we are going without her.'

Jesu! A fishing triangle? But it was not the Queen he meant, thank God. A leggy young girl in an aproned gown came bounding down the steps. She sprang aboard and joined us in the barge's pavilion.

'This is Bess, my eldest, my child of Aquarius,' declared her proud father, tugging her ribboned plait. 'Poppet, this lady's name is Elizabeth, too, but we shall call her Jane.'

The ten-year-old princess proved to be a happy soul, neither precocious nor prying, so I was spared the jabs and digs that could have come my way. Watching her freckled face concentrating hard as she strung her rod made me sad that I had no child of my own. Was it possible I could conceive a child to Ned?

'Gathering cobwebs?' He clicked his fingers in front of my eyes.

'Something like that,' I smiled.

Fishing for perch was a serious business for Ned. We did not talk much once the barge halted beyond Lambeth Palace. Together with Bess and two of his henchmen, we climbed into the small boat that had been tethered at the stern. The King himself grasped the oars and sent us upriver. Bess trailed her fingers in the water and laughed in delight to see a heron take flight from the reeds.

I daresay most people count themselves fortunate if they experience euphoria once in their lives, let alone count those times on their fingers. I could have died that night off Chelsea Reach for I was so utterly at peace. The wash of water lapping at our little kingdom, the tiny beacons of light on the shore as the cottagers lit their candles, the warm laughter of the oarsmen floating across to us from the barge, the glorious sky a map of golden coasted islands at first and then a heavenly river of hazy stars – simple joys. But none so great as the joyfulness that came from the quiet king in our midst as he helped his daughter thread her hook or glimpsed the bob-bob of the float as the perch prepared to bite.

I shall keep that evening like a dried flower in the pages of my memory to treasure always. For a few hours I had a family of my own, even if Ned and Bess were borrowed.

God pardon this if arrogance it be, but I felt His absolution, the faith to believe that this was right.

Ignoring the evil midges, we sat out on the water for two hours with only a couple of goodly fish to make it worthwhile, but afterwards there was wine and sweetmeats by torchlight as the barge carried us back to Westminster.

After delivering Bess to her nurse, waiting at the gate, Ned took me by my hand and we went back to his apartments. Then he led me through a door behind the arras in his private bedchamber into a hell of steam and heat that made me squeal in shock – a bathhouse with a furnace. Hot water was gushing into the cloth-padded, stone bath and two sweating menservants came at once to loosen the laces of Ned's gypon.

'Leave us,' I exclaimed. 'I shall wait upon his highness.'

Ned dismissed them to please me.

'"I shall wait upon his highness",' he mimicked. 'Tell me honestly, you conniving wench, is it because you do not want to unrobe in front of my servants?'

'Partly. However...' I adventured my hand across his prick before I loosened the laces that held his hose. Ned had a delightful rich growl. He let me peel down his hose and pull his shirt over his head and then he shoved me backwards.

Water flooded up my nose and open mouth and I flailed in panic until a strong hand hauled me up by the neck of my gown and I surfaced spluttering in his arms.

He laughed at me, sank under and then surfaced with his hair sticking to his forehead like a painted statue's.

'An ancient thing, this, but I love it. Three hundred years old and patched like a miser's elbows. Old Henry III may have been a numbskull at keeping his barons in line, but he enjoyed his luxuries.'

The perfumed water lapped above the swell of my breasts. I turned about, marvelling at my billowing skirt and how my hair floated like ribbon grass.

'Heigh, sweetheart, have you never been to a bathhouse?'

'When I was little. Mama used to take me and my friends to the one in Farringdon, but it closed during the pestilence in '64.' My head must have listed like a spent poppy head for Ned put a finger beneath my chin.

'And suddenly you are sad. What's the matter, my Jane?'

'The same friends shun me now. Because I'm here with you.'

Shore would have chided me for a galloping imagination, but Ned's face held pity.

'Be patient,' he advised me, with a shrug of his magnificent shoulders. 'Had my share of betrayals, too. I tried making peace with the Beauforts and they kicked me in the teeth for it. As for my cousin, Warwick…' He grimaced. 'And there's always my Judas brother, George, who delights in spreading rumours that I'm the son of a Flemish archer! Yes, such talk can scar, like a torch thrust in your face, Jane, but, heigh, here we are, you and I. Let them suffer in their envy.

'Believe me, sweetheart, you will make many new friends from now on. Will Hastings, for instance, salt of the earth!' He kissed my furrowed forehead, and swung round to the stopcocks behind him. 'Some more hot water, eh? And I'll have that gown off you, you witch, see whether you float or sink.'

He made short work of unrobing me and long work of making love in that glorious warm water.

When we finally climbed forth onto the tiles, I had never felt so clean in my life even though I am fastidious about such matters. My king helped me wring my long hair and wound a soft towel about my head in pagan fashion, then we fell asleep together on his featherbed.

I awoke next morning alone and my sleepy calm turned into instant pother. Searching the bathchamber, I discovered my clothes had vanished, whisked away with the spent towels. Here was a fix. I opened the servants' door and peered out onto an unlit passageway that led to a stairwell. Were there guards below? I called out but no one came.

No gown, no comb. I could hardly hobble for help in a sheet nor dared I venture through to the Painted Chamber. That would be shameful. I resigned myself to wait until Ned's ushers came to make up the bed, but then I heard Ned arguing with someone in the middle chamber. It was not a voice I recognised.

'For Christ's sake, Ned!' the other man was saying. 'Either Richard or I should be regent while you are in France and I am the oldest. Besides, Richard won't stay home. He's been itching for years to grab the French by the ballocks.'

'No!' There was a silence as though Ned was trying to buckle his temper. 'Need I say it again, George! I want an appearance of unity when we confront Louis. He needs to know you stand firm with me – *for once.*'

I drew a sharp breath. God protect me! I should not be hearing any of this. *George*? Could this visitor be the treacherous Duke of Clarence, who had allied with Warwick and driven Ned out of England?

'But you need to leave a regent in England, damn it! What if you get slain or held for ransom? Remember King Hal, for Christ's sake!'

'Death from chronic flux, brother? Oh, you'd like that.'

'No, let's leave feelings out of this and think like princes, shall we? Louis would love to see you skewered, and who would stand protector for your son in that event? Dear Elizabeth? Over my dead body!'

'Christ, George! We shall only be across the Channel not down in Jerusalem. Anyway, I have no intention of getting hit by an arrow, dysentery or—'

'The French disease?' The sarcasm was poisonous. Silence and then this duke spurred in for another swipe. 'Supposing the Scots decide to break the truce? If every English lord is over in France with you, who the hell is going to withstand them? If I was King James, I'd be champing at the bit.'

Ned did not answer.

The verbal circling might go on forever. I rattled the ring handle as a warning before I opened the door a span width. Ned, in just his dressing robe, was standing at the window, his hands

were on his thighbones and his head was thrown back as if his
brother's presence starved the chamber of air.

His antagonist, a fit, fine-featured man in his twenties with
light brown hair neat beneath a cream velvet cap, was sprawled
in the carved chair, very much at home, an ankle resting on the
opposite knee. Cheveril-gloved fingers toyed with the pendant
bull upon his great gilded collar and a smirk serifed his mouth;
clearly he was enjoying the sport of brother baiting. He looked
round angrily at the disturbance.

'Who's this? The latest bed-warmer?'

'No, my lord,' I replied, much put out. If Ned did not like
this man, why should I? My glance fell on the shabby footstool.
'I'm his grace's new counsellor on furnishings, and footstools in
particular. CLOTHES?' I mouthed at my sovereign liege. Ned
sucked in his cheeks and was trying not to splutter.

George, Duke of Clarence glanced from Ned to me. His irritation subsided.

'Footstools?' he mocked. 'Old Nursie's footstool?'

'Yes, my lord,' I replied sternly. 'One has to take into account
the amount of sunlight and whether his highness may come in
wet shod. The dyes must be of the best.'

'Jane,' murmured Ned, striding across to me and setting his
hands about my sheeted waist, 'if you do not hold your tongue,
I shall die from laughter and my brother here will be so glad.'

O Jesu! So his visitor was the weathervane of the family.

'I' faith,' murmured the duke, rising to his feet to inspect me,
'maybe I could use some advice on footstools, brother. Does she
suck toes as well as lick your soles? Pray, come further in, woman,
and discuss your terms. I'll pay you more. *No*? Alas, Ned, your
adviser seems somewhat coy now.'

I glanced sideways at my lover's grinning face and tried for
dignity. 'My sovereign lord, I pray you, some dry clothes and a
comb, *please*.'

'Oh, allow me.' The duke picked up a freshly laundered shirt from the pile of laid out clothes and brought it across to me. He probably did it to shame Ned, but I took it graciously and withdrew.

I hoped to hear the ring of a hand bell to summon a servant to find me some apparel but, of course, Ned, had more important matters on his mind. Their quarrel resumed.

'I've already drawn up papers appointing the Prince of Wales nominal Keeper of the Realm in my absence. Canterbury will head the royal council, and you, George, are coming with me to France and there's an end to it.'

'And Louis will conclude you do not trust me out of your sight, won't he, Ned?'

'Ah, I forget how *well acquainted* you two are.' Gall soured every word.

I could understand Ned's bitterness. Everyone knew King Louis had brokered the duke's brief, treacherous alliance with the House of Lancaster. Then I heard Ned add, 'But no matter. You and I and Richard shall just have to put on an unparalleled display of fraternal amity, won't we, brother?'

'Brother' made no reply. Instead, the inner door was flung open, startling me.

'Mistress,' his brother purred, 'we need a judge and jury. Do you consider it sensible for England to have a five-year-old regent while my brother struts it in France?' Common sense bade me hold my tongue. The duke mockingly applauded me. 'So silent now and so garrulous before. Fur between the ears like the rest.'

'Oh, I can answer you, your grace,' I retorted. 'Firstly, I do not think we should be going to war with France at the present time and, secondly, if I may speak frankly, your highness?' Ned gestured his permission. 'Your lady mother could best stand as regent since she managed to beget so clever a family. Now would you mind giving me some privacy, my lord of Clarence?'

That raised two pairs of eyebrows. As the duke closed the door, I heard him say, 'Tsh, tsk, you've been a naughty boy. Darling Elizabeth won't like this one.'

I huddled in the bedclothes, disgusted with my impetuous tongue. To have criticised the King's enterprise in front of his sneering brother. Was there ever such a want-wit?

I hid my despair as I returned to Silver Street in borrowed clothes.

Mama waylaid me on the stairs, all purpose and decision-making. There had been a time when I had shunned her, blamed her for not talking my father out of betrothing me to William Shore, but that was long past. We were friends once more and she had been my greatest advocate in persuading Shore to let me employ the silkwomen.

'Elizabeth, my love.' She drew me swiftly into the solar. 'Your father wishes to leave for Hertfordshire, but I've told him I'll not go until you are settled at Westminster.'

'*Mama*, that won't be until the King returns from France.' If ever.

'As long as it needs, my darling,' she said pointedly.

'I am very grateful.'

'Now, harken, I've had a talk with the servants this morning. From today, they are not to allow any strangers into the kitchen.'

'Your pardon?'

'The Queen.' Her voice dropped to a fierce whisper. 'I wouldn't trust the Woodvilles an inch. Do you not remember how they ruined poor Tom Cooke, one of our best merchants? If her highness takes a hatred of you, as well she might, you could find poison in your pottage.'

'Mama, I think you should know th—'

'And another thing, Elizabeth,' she exclaimed, still prowling before the hearth, 'you will have to think up…amusements.'

'Mama!'

She blushed. 'But I also mean it in a wider sense. Make him laugh.' Then she added with a sigh, 'Look, Lizbeth, I cannot say I am happy with this…well…people treating us like lepers. But since the die are already cast, I want to see you succeed.' She sat down upon the window seat. 'There, I've had my say.'

I did not have the heart to tell her that I had already failed. I knelt, lifted her hands from her lap and kissed her knuckles. 'I know it's hard for you, Mama, but…have faith. I intend to do much good, I promise.'

I had my agenda if the King proved true to his word. My father and Shore had often been asked to oversee welfare to guild families where the father had died, but there were plenty of starving wives and widows outside the guilds. God willing, maybe I could arrange apprenticeships for some of their children by providing the means myself or persuading others to do so. Yes, it might take time. And if the London citizens continued to shun me, I should do my charity through an agent.

'My greatest dream,' I told Mama, 'is to fund a lawyer to give free advice to wronged people, especially poor women, about how to obtain justice, which bench to approach, whom to seek out, whom to avoid, that kind of thing.'

'Yes,' she murmured, 'I remember you wanted to be the first woman mayor of London and change the world, but, honestly, darling, don't run before you can walk.'

'I'll manage it…if he'll let me,' Then, sighing, I sat down beside her and leaned my elbows upon my knees. 'But it's so easy to say the wrong thing. I'm like a child stumbling through a perilous wood in darkness. This affair may be all over in an instant.' *And it probably is already, Mama*, I added silently.

She took a deep breath. 'Then you were a fool to tell Shore so soon.'

'Perhaps.' I rubbed my fingers across my eyes in weariness. 'But God willing, at least I'll be free before long.' *Except how, without the King or Hastings?*

'Free, Lizbeth? Oh, you mean this severance from Shore. Do you really want that? You'll have no crutch to lean on if… well, you know what I mean, darling. If aught should happen to your father, you'll not be able to rely on Jack to help you, not anymore. Make provision for mischance, my love. Think of Pharaoh's dream and stack the granaries while the harvest is good.' Her hand came down on mine. 'Forgive me, here I am mouthing like a cursed Cassandra when it is all so wonderful for you.'

'But you are right, Mama.'

'I just don't want you to have stars in your eyes about this.'

'No, it's the sunne-in-splendour dazzles me.'

She put an arm about me. 'Don't let him. He can never put you first, Elizabeth. His queen, his children, his noble friends, his hounds, the war against France, all have precedence over you. You will sip the dregs from his cup, the crumbs from his table and one day he will not even notice you are still there.'

'I know.' I rose to my feet. 'But it was my choice this time.'

Mama shook her head. 'No, Elizabeth, you're wrong. It was his.'

At noon I threw a gambler's dice. I sent Ned an invite to supper, bidding him meet me at Queenhithe Wharf in his humblest clothes. Risky? Presumptuous? How else could a newcomer like me seize back the reins and harness both his lust and intellect?

Mind you, my heart was in my mouth as I set out for the wharf. But, yes, there was Ned leaning against the wall alongside the wherry landing in the merchant garb he had worn to Gerrard's

Hall. He had brought his two eldest daughters as I'd requested. The princesses, shadowed by Bryan Myddelton and two hefty esquires, were happily counting the oyster and mussel boats.

Royal folded arms and the surly concave of my lover's cheeks boded ill, but I had surprise on my side as I whoaed in my father's wagon.

'Jesu!' he exclaimed as he strode across with the girls racing after him in glee.

'We are going for cherry pies at the *King David*,' I said defiantly.

He muttered something that sounded like 'Kiss my arse!' but Princess Bess was bouncing about us so he stowed his bad temper and hoisted her into the back. His other girl had inherited her mother's disdain. She already had her nose at an angle.

'I cannot ride in that,' she proclaimed. 'I've read *The Knight of the Cart*. It's is dishonourable for knights to ride in carts.'

'For knights, Mary, but not for kings,' her papa growled, shoved her aboard, and clambered up beside me. 'I will drive,' he insisted, holding his hand out for the reins.

'Are you sure you know how, Ned?'

'What about us?' wailed Master Myddelton.

Our sovereign lord shrugged and flicked the horse's back. I bit my lips not to laugh as his servants had to run and scramble aboard.

Being a man, the King of England was anxious to show off his skill and speed the cart, but Solomon the carthorse shook his mane and plodded up the hill at a pace that gave the princesses time to stare – when they weren't poking or tickling each other.

The cookshop in Thames Street was crammed as tight as a night thief's kerchief, but we squeezed onto a bench. Ned and I sat opposite one another. The girls scrambled in beside me like a pair of stepdaughters. My heart sang at this simple happiness, despite the surly looks from our escorts as they settled in at the neighbouring board.

The aroma of hot pies battled with the familiar smells of spilt ale, miry soles, sweat-slicked armpits and scents bought for a groat in Cheapside.

'How very domestic,' muttered my liege lord, mopping his brow already, unconvinced the adventure was to his taste. I knew he had imagined testing bed ropes. But he also loved good food.

'*King David's*,' I promised, 'makes pies to die for.'

'Papa,' giggled Bess, putting on a street dialect, 'can we 'ave cream an' all?'

He ignored her, fixing his stare my way. 'I thought…' Beneath the board, he nudged the beak of his shoe up my skirt.

'Later,' I mouthed.

Princess Mary gave a shriek of delight as the platters arrived. Bess pinched her to be quiet and they began to squabble, kicking each other.

A man seated two down from Ned leaned back and reached along to tap his shoulder. 'Your pardon, good sir, but could you tell your family to be quieter, please you? We are trying to converse.'

Ned drew an indignant breath but I sent him a warning glance.

'Behave!' he hissed to his girls. 'Would you have us thrown out of here like beggars?'

'Can they do that?' Princess Bess asked me.

'Yes, they can,' I answered. 'If we are unruly, it is their right to make us leave, and if we resist, they can send for the city sergeants and we shall be arrested.'

'That could be amusing,' Mary imitated her mother's voice.

'No, demoiselle, it will shame me,' growled Ned, 'and I'll tan your little hide so hard, you won't sit down for a week.'

It was then my misfortune to be recognised.

'Ah thought it wuz ya!' A fierce hand grabbed my shoulder and I froze. Shore's Derbyshire brother-in-law, John Agard. Damnation!

'Oh,' I said coolly, and turned to look up at him. 'Are you down from Foston, then?'

'Well, ah'm not there, am ah!' Seething hatred glared in his eyes.

My breath froze. How in God's name could I silence him, spare the King and his children the appalling scandal that could come of this?

'God save me, if we weren't 'ere in t'common place, ah'd give ye the back of mi 'and for the 'arm ye 'ave done m' Brother Shore. In fact, I will. Haaarken, everyone! This woman is a stroompet and she should not be allowed in respectable establishment like this wi' decent folk. Ah demand that ye ask her to leave these premises this instant!'

'Ain't she the brazen shrew what wants to divorce 'er 'usband?' said someone.

'Get you out of here, you shameless slut!' hissed a wide-girthed slopseller I recognised from Cheapside.

The royal servants tensed to defend us but I did not want a brawl. Determined to preserve Ned's anonymity, I stood and turned to face my nemesis.

'John, I—'

'Would you like to strike me as well, sirrah?' Ned cut in, rising to his magnificent altitude on the other side of the board.

Agard's Adam's apple bobbed but he held his ground like a stubborn mastiff. 'Ah can only assume ye are ignorant of her true nature, sir.' A clever parry. Then he added in a lower voice, 'Ah pray ye be advised and keep out of this 'ere quarrel.'

'What is a *stroompet*?' Princess Mary boomed out in the awkward hush.

Ned put a finger to his lips to hush her, and then he strode round the table. Benches scraped back with urgency.

'No fisticuffs in here!' yelled the mistress of the shop, waddling up. 'Settle your quarrel in the yard!'

'No fisticuffs,' promised Ned, kissing his hand to her. 'A word with you, sir, on the quiet.'

'Say it to me 'ere! Ah've nothing to hide from these good people.'

'I think you will regret this, John,' I warned, but he slapped my hand from his arm.

'Then, know, whoever you are, sir,' declared my lover, shaking his head like a disappointed parent, 'that you are breaking the King's peace.'

It was Princess Mary who forestalled Agard's rebuttal. 'Yes, you are,' she said proudly, resisting my attempt to hush her, 'because my papa is—' The slap on the back from Bess nearly knocked the child's nose into her pastry.

'Outside,' murmured Ned. '*Now!*' He forced Agard to back towards the door. Half the inn scrambled off their backsides to follow.

A moment later, he was back, flexing the fingers of his right hand. His audience returned and, last of all, his gentlemen. I had seen expressions like Ned's on the leaders of dog packs.

'As you were.' He flourished his palms at the enthralled company. 'Hostess, could we order four more helpings, please?'

'Of course, sir.' She bobbed an awkward obeisance, rubbed her sweating palms upon her skirts and disappeared in haste.

'Hmmm,' Ned murmured wickedly, squeezing in next to me. At the end of our bench, someone almost fell off but there were no complaints. 'A pity we couldn't have a decent brawl but the fellow was too puny. Myddleton dealt with him. He'll have a sore head but no broken ribs.'

'Did anyone gues—'

'No, thank the Lord. *Mary!*' He put his finger to his lips.

'Heigh, good health to you, master!' yelled a bold wight further down the board with a broad wink. 'We don't want no ill-tempered turnip from up north spoilin' things, do we?' and then the entire table were raising their jacks.

Ned bestowed a public smile on them. Miraculously no one recognised the flash of white teeth.

I was ashamed that his daughters had witnessed this unpleasantness. Dear God, my nerves were still a jangle. Could he forgive me?

'You are not angry?'

'Not unless this rabble expect me to buy a round,' he muttered stingily.

'You *are* going to invade France on their money,' I pointed out, my confidence returning.

'And *they've* just invaded my privacy. By the way,' he muttered, with a little boy look. 'I never carry a purse. Are you paying?'

'I certainly am,' I promised, hoping desperately I had sufficient. 'Knight errants like you are worth a score of pies.'

His hand slid stealthily between my legs. 'I'll expect interest as well, mercer's daughter.'

Before the city gates closed for the night, I took the reins for the ride back to Westminster. A contented, pie-filled lover hummed at my side.

Yes, I thought, it need not all be between the sheets. But while Ned was kissing his daughters goodnight and bidding them keep our adventure a secret, a furious Master Myddelton hauled me over the coals.

'You put their graces' lives in danger, Mistress Shore!' A just chastisement. Yet a risk that had paid well. That night I took another – I bound Ned's wrists to the bedposts and let my tongue and fingers rouse him until he was cursing me to hell. Only then did I slide down upon his prick and ride him until he roared with release.

# V

If I licked my finger at the end of that week, I could have drawn five strokes on Ned's bedchamber window. From famine to feast. Five nights of lovemaking. My mind was hazy from lack of sleep and my body felt tender. To be with the King was exhilarating, like dancing high on wine at a wondrous merrymaking, yet outside the sunlight of his presence, the world was shadows and I was stumbling to find where I belonged. I was not his wife but I was as dependent on him as I had been with Shore, and infinitely vulnerable.

*Make him laugh.* Mama's counsel held truth. I needed to become Ned's trusted friend as well as his concubine. Once I had my own dwelling, my strategy would be to send my menservants to harvest jests from the alehouses. To cheer, amuse and surprise Ned would become my creed.

At first I felt sorry for the Queen, the Yorkist milk-cow, forever calving. No wonder the King strayed into other pastures. Did she care? I think she did and her solution for dispensing with me was an oblique form of warfare through her son, Dorset. Several times the marquis ambushed me, trying to have me in his embrace where Ned might discover us. After his third attempt, I complained to the King.

'Does my lord of Dorset have to goose me as though I am some tapster's Jill? No wonder Lord Hastings is loath to have him as a son-in—' I froze; Ned's indulgent expression had turned frosty.

'Is that what Lord Hastings is saying, Jane?'

'No, no, that's only my opinion,' I said quickly. 'I should not want a hellhound like Dorset for my daughter.'

'He's the Queen's son.' My lover's voice was chill.

'Well, I wish "the Queen's son" would stop try to put his hand up my skirts. Why is he doing it? To provoke you or to make me seem faithless?'

He ignored my point. 'I will have this marriage between Dorset and Cecily Bonville whether Will Hastings likes it or not, and you would be wise not to express any opinion. I need to have a powerful landholder whom I can rely on in every shire. That girl owns half the West Country so I'll be damned if I'm letting her go to one of the other Devon families just because they're offering Will a better bargain.'

Time for sackcloth and a snatch of ashes?

'Forgive me, my gracious lord. What I am struggling to say is that it will be for Cecily Bonville's good as well as my peace of mind if you would kindly ask Lord Dorset to keep his hands to himself.'

Appeased, Ned sucked in his cheeks. 'So you don't prefer a younger dog?' He slid a possessive hand round my neck.

'Do you wish me to prove it?' I purred, kissing him.

His lips caressed mine, but he was not quite done with the scolding. 'Look, my darling, I know all too well that my barons see the Queen's family as upstarts but, God be thanked, her kin are loyal to me, and it's through their marriages I have established a greater hold on the kingdom. I haven't given them a choice either in who they marry. Young Tom can be a pest but he'll grow out of it.'

So the Greys and the Woodvilles, like the mosquitoes and midges of the world, were there to be endured.

'Well then, amen, Ned. I shall just have to keep slapping the marquis away.'

Unfortunately, Dorset believed in perseverance. He once more intercepted me on my way to Ned's apartments. I tried to pass him, but he halted with a jingle of spurs and adventured his hands about my waist. The passageway, usually so bustling, was cursedly deserted.

I pushed against his chest. 'His grace the King is waiting, my lord.'

'So am I.' He stroked his third finger over the satin that covered my left nipple. 'So firm. How you rouse my blood, sweet Mistress Shore.'

'As long as I don't rouse anything else,' I snapped.

He pouted, his face so close to mine I could smell wine upon his breath. 'Ah, can you not find it in your heart to yield a teensy-weensy, seeing there's no one around to notice?'

'Have you no loyalty to the King, my lord?' I chided, holding my ground.

'Oh, but we play these games, he and I. He stole a wench from me only last week.' He read the astonishment in my face. 'Did you think *him* faithful?' The tip of the riding crop teased down my bosom and belly to poke the cleft between my thighs. 'What green, green wood you are, Mistress Shore.'

I pushed him away. 'Oh, go back in the Ark!' I snapped.

Somehow that bolt penetrated his armour of conceit. 'That is not very kind of you,' he growled. 'I think you need to remember your lowly place, peddler's girl.'

Before I might defend myself, he had me pinioned against the wall with the whip-stock across my throat. His grey-blue eyes were as cold as an adder's. Malevolently, he held my gaze while his other hand groped too freely upon my bodice. 'Now you stay still and hushed like an obedient mare. What's here, such pretty silk! Bought at a bargain from your father? Let me feel.' As he tried to unhook the fent triangle, I struggled anew and the whoreson jammed the cruel crop so hard he was almost choking me. 'Maybe I can talk Ned into being more generous,' he murmured, peeling back the fent. 'I'd love a threesome.'

I'd have spat in Dorset's accursed face and damn the consequences, but we were no longer alone and there came a curt voice from behind his shoulder.

'Do you have to fornicate in the passageway, Grey?'

The pressure on my throat instantly eased. Dorset swung round with a swagger to confront the speaker, leaving me exposed to disdainful scrutiny. Two young men were standing there. The shorter one, who was closest, glared at me with so pure a contempt I had to defend myself.

'I have no plans to fornicate with Lord Dorset anywhere!' I ground out, furiously mending my appearance.

I had never seen this stranger before yet somehow his face was familiar. Spurred riding boots and the expensive, studded leather brigandine proclaimed he must be one of Ned's bannerets, newly arrived from some distant shire. His younger companion, a tall stripling with a freckled complexion and long hair the colour of gingerbread, was clad in a short doublet of quality brocade that had seen much wear.

'Oh, good day to you too, your grace,' purred Dorset, with a mocking half bow. He grabbed my arm and jerked me forwards, 'You have not met your brother's latest concubine. May I present Mistress Shore.'

'No, you may not!' There was a dab of Yorkshire in the stranger's voice.

*Your brother?* Oh no! This must be Richard, Duke of Gloucester, who ruled the north for Ned. I hastily made a deep curtsy. He ignored me.

'Some things never change,' he observed in a voice that could saw through marble.

Before I could defend myself further, a young girl's shriek of 'Uncle Richard!' burst from the end of the corridor and a bright bundle of blue that was Princess Bess hurtled towards us.

In an instant, Gloucester's harsh expression melted to delight.

'Hey, Mischief!' he yelled and we were forgotten as he gathered Bess into his arms and carried her away down the corridor, both of them laughing.

Dorset jabbed up a two-finger insult at Gloucester, raised his eyebrows in disdain at the duke's companion, and, damn him, sauntered off in the opposite direction, leaving me with my skirts precariously spread.

There was no emotion in the slate blue eyes that stared down at me; nevertheless Gloucester's companion held out a hand to help me to my feet.

'Thank you, sir,' I replied gratefully, shaking out my skirts and casting a furious glare in Dorset's direction.

His voice was just as contemptuous but not towards me. 'You should take care, Mistress Shore. The palace is full of foxes and rabbit-suckers – creatures who do not know their place.' One side of the patrician mouth curved into a sneer as he watched Dorset's retreating back.

'Then I may trust you are neither, sir,' I murmured, securing the gauze that edged my collar.

'Trust?' The cool stare came back to me. 'Trust is a very old fangled word, Mistress Shore. I haven't come across it of late.' He held out his wrist. 'May I escort you to the King's grace?'


The Painted Chamber was deserted – just like a confessor's prie-dieu on May Day morning. Ned must be still at the royal council.

My escort bowed and left me and I hastened across to Master Myddleton, who was on duty.

'Pray, can you tell me who that gentleman was?'

'What, the lord who was with you, mistress? Harry Stafford, Duke of Buckingham.'

'You jest!' I gasped.

'Do not trouble yourself about him,' Myddelton murmured and added behind his hand, 'He may be a Plantagenet but the King's grace doesn't care for him overmuch. His family always fought for Lancaster.'

Jesu mercy! Walking through this palace was like blundering into tacky threads, everywhere these covert factions. Did that mean Buckingham was to be avoided?

I tucked myself in a corner, fretting whether Gloucester might convince Ned to get rid of me. My fears increased when he and the King came in together. I tried to stay unobtrusive and slip through the peacock tail of councillors who had trailed after them, but Ned had seen me. He dismissed the entourage and, slinging an arm around Gloucester's uneven shoulders, nodded to me to follow them into his inner sanctum. When I shook my head, I was mortified to see him let go of the duke and come back to speak with me.

'What's the matter with you today, my darling dear?'

'Pray give me leave, sire,' I replied, curtsying. 'I am sure his grace your brother would enjoy spending some time with you on your own.'

He frowned. 'So he shall. Now come and serve us.'

'I do not think—'

'Oh, come on, he won't bite you.'

Tugged through the doorway, I was certainly glad of my hand secure in Ned's as Gloucester looked round at us. He did not hide his scowl.

'Richard, do you remember hearing of John Lambard, the mercer who lent money to our father? Expelled from the Council of Aldermen, too, for speaking up for us when Warwick and George marched into London? Well, here's his daughter, Elizabeth, but I call her Jane to avoid confusion. I hope you will like each other. She has bewitched me utterly.'

'We've already met.' Gloucester's tone was ironic, dismissive.

But I was resolved to show I had a backbone. 'His grace interrupted another of Lord Dorset's assaults upon me, Ned.'

'Oh ho, playing Galahad, little brother?' Ned let go my hand. As he strode across to the wine flagon, he playfully shoved Gloucester's cap over his eyes.

'Must you still do that?' Irritation flickered fiercely in the duke's voice and I could not blame him. There might be ten years between them, but Gloucester was already in his twenties.

Ned shrugged and stood by the flagon for me to serve them. I performed the task reluctantly. Had Gloucester been friendlier, I might have told him of how my older brothers had tormented me, but instead I held my tongue.

'To victory in France, Richard!'

'Amen.' Gloucester's brown hair was already trimmed for war.

Watching them clink goblets, I found it hard to believe them brothers. The duke scarcely topped Ned's shoulder. On further observation, it could be seen that the scaffolding of face, shape of head, even the cleft in chin betrayed a kindred blood. Gloucester's mouth was wider and thinner, his jaw more resolute. That surprised me.

'To the future King of France, *Edouard le Premier.*' Then he turned and looked my way. 'Mistress Lambard, you may have cast your spell over my brother, but I am sure even you would yawn at battle stratagems so I suggest you take your leave.'

Before Ned could argue, I replied swiftly: 'Phew, your grace,

I am most relieved,' and I offered a thankful smile. Almost against his will, a wholesome humour flared in his eyes, but he quickly gave his attention back to Ned.

I backed out of their presence only to have a little page plucking at my sleeve tippet, bidding me to attend Lord Hastings. It made me uncomfortable. We had avoided each other these past weeks. Was he angry that I had mentioned Dorset's wedding to Ned? Oh dear God, maybe I should have stayed a housewife.

The Lord Chamberlain's rookery at the palace proved similar to my father's accounting room save it was spacious with a high vaulted ceiling. Rookery? Its threshold resembled the drawbridge to a beehive, utterly buzzing with messengers and marshals. The alarm went up. A woman! *In here*? Every jack goggled at me as though I had three tails and a pair of flippers before their stares skewed to my cleavage. I kept my gaze downward like a modest maid as my little escort bowed me into an inner chamber.

Lord Hastings was seated at a table going through a list with two of his fellow army captains: Lord Howard, who turned and winked at me, and Sir Ralph Hastings, my lord's brother, who gave me a cursory nod.

'Pay attention, Jock. We shall not be long, Mistress Shore.'

He was so detached, as if we had never been lovers. That hurt. Relegation: Elizabeth Lambard was jarred and lidded on a high shelf. Today's repast was the war.

Ledgers and orderly stacks of opened letters were pancaked on the shelf behind him, vellum scrolls with rolling pin handles lurked in open coffers at knee level within a hand's reach and a pile of dispatches with their seals still virginal waited for attention.

Two secretaries, round-shouldered like herons, were perched on stools at either end the table with wooden writing boards slung round their necks. Each had their own tray of inkpots, penknives, quills, pine dust, pumice, candles, sand and sealing wax. One was making notes as the discussion moved from how many soldiers could be squeezed aboard a carrack to the price of arrow-shaft feathers and on to whether they could afford to pay the mounted men-at-arms 18d a day. This could go on for hours, and as I'd noticed a huge book chained onto a lectern, I wandered over to investigate.

The title page depicted a king dining in state. I turned the pages of the long preamble to the main text – written in Latin and English – and discovered it contained the duties and allowances of every officer of the king's household. Amazing how many there were.

'It interests you?' Lord Hastings joined me after the others had left. If this were Gerrard's Hall, he would have put his arm about me; now he took care that nothing touched. Common sense, no complications and yet... To be knifed out of his life like an unwanted grub was painful.

I turned the pages until I found the entry for the Lord Chamberlain.

'Oh, how unfair, you only get two esquires and two yeomen. Is there an entry for "the King's Mistress"?' I improvised:

*A mistress serving in the king's chamber shall have due care his highness shall not exhaust himself. She shall be available at all times and ensure she introduce neither goujere, pox, pestilence, lice or fleas into the royal bed. She is allowed silken chemises, down pillows, sundry perfumes and the order of the Gart—'*

'Oh, for God's Sake!'

I subsided, delighted I could still make his conscientious look evaporate, but it returned within the instant, and he was avoiding looking me in the face.

'What if I am unavailable for his highness, my lord?'

'I haven't all day. Elizabeth. The King wishes you to reside at Westminster forthwith, and since I have to inform the Exchequer and need some distraction from this cursed campaign, I'll walk across with you. Leave ahead of me. I'll meet you in Palace Yard.'

He was still in terse mood when he joined me outside.

'You should not have spent entire nights in the royal bedchamber,' he growled, 'and as for taking the King of England – and the princesses – to a common pie shop! They could have caught the pestilence.'

'It's not high summer yet but, yes, I'm sorry,' I murmured, gathering up my skirts to match his stride.

'Hell, Elizabeth, I thought you'd have more sense. Thank the Blessed Christ nothing went wrong.' He crossed himself. 'Can you imagine the danger to the realm, the anarchy that might ensue if... Well, it doesn't bear thinking about. I feel myself to blame, I should have made clear to you there are rules for his grace's mistresses that must be followed.'

My good humour ceased. 'How many of us are there, my lord? Am I only for use on Tuesdays and Saturdays?'

'You won't be for any, if you don't show sense. I heard all about you being stranded without any decent clothing. You belong only to his *private* life. The common people expect him to be contented with a beauteous queen and a brood of perfect children.'

'As if the common people are blind, deaf and stupid, my lord! Our guildwives' embroidery mornings would have been silent as a coroner's morgue if we hadn't had the tittle-tattle.'

'Elizabeth!'

'Oh, I must be as unobtrusive as a spider, lurk among the royal cobwebs until whisked down with a bunch of feathers.'

'I'm glad you understand.'

'Oh yes, my lord,' I conceded wearily. 'I shall exist in an adulterous Purgatory.'

Hastings sent a beseeching look at the featherbed of clouds overhead and continued with the pulpit admonition.

'No more rebellion, Elizabeth, your time is now the King's.' Then he added stiffly, 'I'm pleased that you have cheered Ned as I hoped you would. Now let us proceed.'

'Wholesome, merry, and capable of whamming into the bull's eye like a champion's arrow?' I muttered. 'Is that how you see me?'

'I have had my say!' His profile was stony as granite. He began striding towards a row of gabled buildings overlooking the river.

'I still have questions.' I hastened after him, bridling my hurt.

'Well?'

'If...if the court travels to another palace such as Windsor or Eltham, do I trudge along at the back with the horseboys like a camp follower or am I expected to languish with tears and swoons until his grace's return?'

He held open the door for me. 'If the King desires your presence, you will be escorted separately, usually ahead of what we call "the riding household".'

'Ah, the thrill of being trundled off before dawn on a winter's morning. Are hot bricks part of the arrangement, my lord?'

He did not answer. We had reached the Exchequer.

It was a two-storeyed building manned by an army of clerks. We did not go into the lower rooms where the king's moneys were received but upstairs where the board bearing the famous chequered cloth (albeit shined and grimy from much use) was set up. Beside it, a dispute was in full sail. I recognised the merchant grocer who was brandishing his end of a tally stick at one of the officers. He halted in mid-argument on beholding us. The frenzied hubbub hushed and every clerk put down his quill, rose and bowed to Hastings.

'As you were, gentlemen.'

Business resumed. I kept my gaze lowered, but my woman's antennae could sense the suppressed leers and speculation – did Mistress Shore lie with my Lord Chamberlain as well as the King's grace? A frolic *à trois*?

Hastings beckoned over a gorbellied man in a leather doublet. Around us, the scratching of quills began anew even if every ear was straining to hear our business.

'This is Master Peter Beaupie, Clerk of the Green Cloth, Mistress Shore. He will assist you if any problems arise. It is agreed by the Treasurer that you will be given a regular allowance of ale, wine and so forth like the rest of the household. You will be entered in the accounts as a gentleman usher of the King's chamber. There are four, Masters Young, Hervey, Talbot and Ratcliffe. You are the fifth.'

*Gentleman Usher No 5*! At least it had a ring of permanence. If I was careful, I should be able to afford to buy some apprentice-ships for some of the street boys and children of poor families. But how long would my good fortune last?

'So, my lord, is there a Gentleman Usher No 6 who wears pretty garters?' I asked coldly as we left the Exchequer.

He halted. At last his blue eyes met mine with an apology that he could not speak. But perhaps that was my imagination, for after a moment's hesitation, he asked, 'Tell me, have you heard Ned speak with Dorset about the marriage to Cecily?'

'I cannot tell you, my lord. That is the King's business.'

He drew breath to press the matter, and then nodded wearily. 'Well done, Elizabeth Lambard. You pass the test.'

I guessed he had hoped otherwise. But maybe I was wrong.

'And…it was the right decision?' he asked.

I could have pretended not to understand, to brandish my hurt, but in truth I owed him everything.

'Yes. And since the King believes it was…' Here I reached up a gloved hand to straighten the lappet of his robe. 'What other decision is there?'

# VI

I admit I was afraid of the Queen while Ned and his noblemen made war in France. Not that she was known for poisoning anyone, but rather because Pestilence stalked the London streets in high summer and a fat bribe to the coroner might ensure a convenient epitaph for a king's mistress and no questions asked in high places.

Mama was relieved when I agreed to go with her and Father to the house he had purchased at Hinxworth, a blink-as-you-gallop-through hamlet in Hertfordshire.

It was restorative to be in a shire where no one knew me save my uncle and aunt, who wanted no truck with a jezebel like me. My parents were still in the womb, so to speak, in replacing the old dwelling they had purchased, but I paid little heed to their plans for I was utterly lovesick for Ned's arms about me, so terrified he might end up with a French arrow through his visor. Every day I lit a candle and said prayers for him. With good reason, too, the tidings from across the Channel had England tense.

Leaf fall came. The Michaelmas daisies in my mother's garden let down their mauve skirts, garnet berries adorned the hawthorns in the hedgerows and bryony necklaced the thickets with berries like bright drops of blood. And Ned was still in France.

In the end, the closest he went to any 'Agincourt' was the village not the victory. In return for a massive pension for himself and his captains, a marriage for Princess Bess and a favourable trading treaty, he promised to withdraw his mighty army and bother France no more.

Like the rest of England, my father heard the news with disgust. 'What! After all those years of high taxes and forcing donations out of us?' he fumed. 'All those ships and men, and the King doesn't draw a poxy sword?' His tankard hit at the fireplace. 'Well, he should be right glad England is not a republic otherwise the daggers will be out when he gets back. And don't you try to shush me either, Elizabeth. A man has a right to his opinion in his own hall. Think I'm a fool to bellow treason in the market place? By St George, the shame of it! That oily Louis is boasting he's defeated the English army with naught but French wine and venison pies.'

Ned remained in Calais throughout September until all his soldiers had been shipped home. I thought that unwise for there was talk of rebellion in England. Although the guilds sent their liverymen to welcome him back to London, the citizens did not huzzah or fling their caps up as he rode past. He noticed. By the time he was free to visit me in my new lodgings in King Street (close to St Margaret's and just across from Westminster Great Hall), there was a tail-between-the-legs vulnerability about him.

'If our soldiers had set fire to half of France and toasted all the babies, there would be no derision,' he complained, as he lay back in my arms on the daybed in my parlour after we had made love. 'But no, I'm labelled a coward because I negotiated a peace, a very good peace.'

'You could never be a coward, Ned.'

His face was bitter. 'The common people think I am.'

I snuggled within his arm, happy to have him real to my touch. 'Give them time, my gracious lord.'

'Ha! The royal council insists I go round the southern shires and restore order. I'm leaving tomorrow.'

'But you've only just come home,' I protested. 'I've missed you so much.'

He kissed my hair. 'Darling Jane, all I really want to do is make love to you for a week and forget the world.' But I knew ignominy scorched his mind. What he needed was absolution.

I leaned up on my elbow and stroked my finger down his brow and nose. 'Is King Louis as greasy haired and spidery as people say?'

'Yes.'

'Did he understand your French?'

'Of course,' he replied immodestly. 'Didn't you know I was born in Rouen?'

'Born speaking fluently?' I teased. 'What a clever family you are.'

'Yes, born in Rouen and I'd damn well hoped to be crowned there.' He took a swig of ale. 'You know, Jane, I could have, should have, gone through with it. Ever since I became king I dreamed about invading France. I was going to seize back all the lands that old Henry lost, yes, with a glorious victory that would leave Crecy and Agincourt looking like a walk in the garden, and what happens? I let myself be talked around by that damnable French prick. Richard told me I was a blockhead.'

'Hmm, for what my humble opinion's worth, I think you behaved correctly.'

'Distaff approval. That makes me feel so much better.'

I fisted the cushion by his head. 'No, don't you dare be patronising!'

'You forget I'm the King of England, woman,' he scolded affectionately, burying his fingers in my long tresses. 'I can be what I poxy well please.'

I ran a finger across his lips. 'Listen to me, my dearest lord, if I were a French peasant woman, I'd be thanking God my family are still alive, I haven't been raped or skewered, and my haystacks haven't been torched.'

He muttered something about French peasants not having brains to know there was even a war afoot. How could I cheer this unhappy, splendid man?

I sat back on my heels. 'Oh, Ned, God was with you. He guided you although you may not realise it. Just consider how many thousands are still alive because you chose to talk matters out. And the benefits to trade!'

He snorted. 'I wish you'd go out and tell my subjects that. Whoresons! *They* didn't have to deal with damned Burgundy. If dithering Charles hadn't played shall-I-shan't-I like a green virgin, I might be King of France by now.' He clambered to his feet. 'Christ! I wish I did not have to go on this plaguey circuit to poxy Hampshire.'

I knelt up upon the daybed. 'But you'll be merciful.'

'Will I?' The ruthlessness that had seen the fugitives in Tewkesbury Abbey dragged forth and executed was naked in his eyes.

'Yes,' I said firmly, although his expression dismayed me. 'Of course, you will.'

Yuletide that year was joyous. Carol dances and disguisings. Such merriment! The palace walls and lintels were festooned with branches of holly and ivy, and everywhere you could hear minstrels. Apart from worshipping at the special Masses, we feasted and we sinned. But I also became acquainted with the stars and planets that whirled about Ned's sunne-in-splendour universe; the accomplished men with intelligent discourse, not Shore-and-Paddesley-stuff about wrestling at Smithfield, but men who had been to Russia and Arabia; travellers who had seen magical lights in the waves of the night sea and a green brilliance dancing in the northern skies.

Playing at cards, I lost a month's income to the Medici banker, Gerard de Caniziani, then I won it back at backgammon from Hastings' friend, goldsmith Hugh Bryce. Ned's Genoese acquaintances taught me the *saltarello* and the Burgundian ambassador tutored me in some wicked Flemish oaths.

Yes, I was like a child in a flower garden, tasting, touching, thrilling, but beneath my splendid robe of cheerfulness, I wore a hairshirt of anxiety because I was still bound to Shore and the Queen wanted me gone.

'So, is there a traitor among my servants?' I murmured, brushing the February snow from my hands as I joined Hastings in a sheltered triangle of sunlight. He was watching Ned and the royal children finishing a snowman in the palace yard. 'How did the investigation go?'

It was a week since I had set my suspicions before him. I was certain that someone in my household had tried to pick the lock to my private papers.

'You were right to come to me, Elizabeth,' he replied and I could tell he wasn't gulling, even though I knew it was his policy to keep me wary of the Woodvilles and reliant on his friendship.

'Oh damnation!' I growled. 'Please, don't say it is Lubbe.' Lubbe, my gap-toothed, jester of a servant.

'No, not the carousing Lubbe.'

I frowned, bracing myself further for the ugliness of Hastings' disclosure. Although the princesses' shrieks were shaking the air, I glanced about to make sure none of the King's gentlemen were close enough to hear. 'Who, then? Which viper in the bosom are we talking about?'

'Alas, Elizabeth, vipers come in all shapes and sizes especially in the vicinity of bosoms like yours.' His sideways glance was appreciative rather than predatory since a thick, fur-lined cloak muffled me to the chin. Then he glanced up at the feeble sun to mark its angle. 'I'll have to whistle the King in soon.'

'For pity's sake.' I shifted from one foot to the other. It would have been impolitic to set hands on so great a man as Hastings, but he could see I was tempted to shake him.

'It's your maidservant. She's the one in the Woodvilles' embrace.'

I gazed at him, utterly winded. My body-servant? Oh, surely not Cristina. I had come as close to trusting Cristina as I had my former maid, Isabel. This was like losing a good friend. Why, yesterday when she was braiding my hair, I had almost remarked that the Queen... Oh, Christ!

'Stings, doesn't it?'

'Yes.' How much of my private life had been betrayed? 'I feel... violated. You *are* sure, my lord? She's...she's been with me since I moved here. She seemed so trustworthy. Oh, a murrain on it!' I kicked at my petticotes. 'I wish it weren't true. And the inconvenience, too. Finding good servants is like hunting for unicorns.'

He buried his gloved hands beneath his armpits, watching Ned blasphemously shape the snowman's headwear into a mitre. 'My dear, we all do it. I've a "friend" among her grace's ladies. And one of Dorset's favourite drinking cronies is in my pocket – I purchased the fellow's debts.' His smile turned weary. 'Do you want to hear more?'

'You find the chink in the armour and hold the dagger against it?' My voice was bitter. I wondered what hold he had over the Queen's lady-in-waiting. 'Does Lubbe report to you as well?'

'Lubbe?'

'Well, it was your steward Hyrst who found him for me.'

His laughter made a plume of vapour. 'Got you scratching, have I? Next instant, you'll be accusing me of bedbugs.' He held up a hand in oath and said softly, 'No, Elizabeth, I wouldn't dare.' And then as if he suspected I had discerned some pain or self-derision within his teasing, he swiftly bent, scooped up a handful of snow and firmed it between his palms. 'Do I have your promise that you'll dismiss the girl?'

I sighed. 'Yes, of course, but in all fairness to her, I'd like to know your evidence. No, don't protest. I have to give her some reason when I dismiss her.'

'No, you don't.' He aimed it at the King. 'She's a two-faced vixen.' Ned ignored the snowy hint. The children were pelting the snow archbishop. 'You're glaring at me like an offended Mother Superior, Elizabeth. Cristina wasn't your novice.'

Chastened, I rearranged my expression. 'Better?'

He sniffed. 'Not much.' Beneath his fur hat, his eyes were narrowed on his royal bird like a cunning falconer.

The hour bell sounded and he nodded across to the cluster of idling nursemaids to advance upon the children. A lot of scream-ing and chasing ensued. Satisfied, Hastings turned to answer my question at last.

'Your girl meets with one of her grace's laundry women at the water conduit each morning. They linger as if in gossip, she makes her report and then the other woman carries the snippets to a higher servant in the Queen's household.'

'Ha, where next?' I asked, hiding my hurt. 'One of her grace's embroidery women? It must be a very garbled account by the time it reaches the royal ear.'

'Ah, interesting that you should mention that.'

'You jest,' I giggled in admiration. 'You pay an embroiderer?'

He waggled his hand. 'I pay for "embroidery". Except my "embroiderer" has been unpicked, so to speak.' He signalled for the King's esquires to present the royal hat and cloak. Ned obliged with a sideways scowl at us.

My mind was still fathoming the sense of Hastings' words. 'So, are you saying nothing that reached the Queen about me was of any use, my lord?' He nodded wickedly and I laughed, bursting to hug him in relief.

'Now promise me you'll get rid of the girl straight away. I'll get Hyrst to find you another.'

'That would be excellent. Oh, if only my former maid might come to me, but Shore hasn't left for Ant— *Ned*!' The snowball intended for Hastings thwacked into my cheek.

'Your pardon, Jane,' yelled Ned and hurled another.

'Time!' Ignoring the icy cannonballs, Hastings jabbed a finger towards the bell tower as he strode towards his master. 'You promised my Lord of Canterbury eleven o' the clock.'

'A pox on him!' Ned grinned at me, pulled a pretend visor down and in place of a cheerful father instantly stood the frowning sovereign lord of England. 'You, Will, are worse than some pesty wet nurse. I'll expect you later, Jane.' I blew him a kiss and he stomped off across the yard with his attendants falling in behind him.

Hastings slapped his hands together. 'Get you gone, Elizabeth. Warm yourself up with a cup of mulled wine before you administer the *coup de grâce* to the two-faced Cristina.'

I curtsied. 'As always, I'm very grateful to you for your care of me.'

Although he should have left, he took me by the elbows and raised me to my feet.

'Even if you feel like shooting the messenger? I know when you are hurting – you use humour as a buckler.'

'That's because I'm not very good with a bow, my lord.'

'But you are always honest with me.' His smile seemed to pain him. 'A golden honesty! Oh my dear, it sits in your aumery along with your silver platters.'

'And you are Ned's truest friend,' I said fondly, wondering what splinter was needling him.

'How kind of you to think so,' he replied, squinting at two red kites circling above the palace roof. 'Survival means we use whatever weapons we can.' And with that cryptic farewell, he marched towards the snowman and punched its head clean off.

Next day, Ned received a letter containing his Holiness the Pope's official response to my petition. My heart was brimful with foreboding when I was summoned to the royal inner sanctum.

'Here.' My lover handed me the parchment with a foxy sort of smile. I took it to the windowseat and sat down to peruse it.

'I can only understand the gist,' I muttered, frustrated that I had never mastered Latin. 'And all the names at the end here, why, I've never heard of them.'

'Not your concern, love,' Ned said, playfully tugging my veil as he stood behind me. 'That's just an addendum for me. This is the important bit.' He leaned over my shoulder and ran his finger along a sentence in the heart of the missive. 'Basically, old Sixtus has given the thumbs up for a tribunal of English bishops to hear your case and the good news is he'll abide by their decision. The names below are the men he wants elevated in return. Progress, eh?' He plucked the document from my fingers and passed it to his secretary. 'Copy the list for my lord of Canterbury, and let's hope he doesn't quibble. Now, my Jane, we need three wise monkeys.'

Doubt kicked like a babe within me. 'Three! Alas, I cannot think of one who would give the likes of me my freedom.'

Ned squeezed my shoulder. 'Cheer up. It is not that hard. For a start, Tom Myllington, Bishop of Hereford, is one of the regular tribunal. Have you met him? Abbot of Westminster when I was stuck in Burgundy. Looked after Elizabeth and the children like a father.'

I twisted round to face Ned. 'But if he is fond of the Queen, won't he—'

My lover's quicksilver mind had already moved on. 'It's the other two we have to be sure of.' He turned to his other secretary. 'Fetch me the list of bishops we were looking at this morning.'

I was not optimistic. For a start, bishops were male, celibate (well, some of them) and they all supported the sanctity of marriage. I was female, an adulteress and I was trying to do the impossible.

I waited with a sinking heart as Ned took the paper and sprawled down in his great chair. He punctuated his reading with mutters: 'Not him', 'Lunatic', 'Hmm', 'Crooked as his plaguey crozier', 'Maybe', 'Ahh, here we go.' He flicked the paper. 'The Bishop of Ross, John Woodman. Just the fellow, he's in London at the moment and he's sat on the bench many a time. And for *numero tertius*, William Westecarre, the Bishop of Sidon!' He expected applause and a fanfare.

'Isn't that in the Holy Land?' I queried unhappily. 'Tyre and Sidon?'

'Hell, no, my darling, Sidon *in Ireland*! All sheep and tussocks. Vacant for years because the godless whoresons thereabouts were too pissed to pray, and King Henry hardly got off his backside about it. Westcarre's long in the tooth and can't run up the stairs any more but he'll do. If Canterbury and Sixtus want to bellyache, they can do it later. There you are, my love, good as done.'

Three obedient bishops. Whenever this king needed a miracle, he ensured one happened, but I had a cumbersome conscience.

'I am not happy about this.'

He put his arms about my waist and tugged me against him. 'My lovely, honest darling, what alternative is there? It's not as if you can plead that you were related to Shore and didn't know it, or that your marriage was never consummated.'

I splayed my hands against his chest. 'Yes, that's so, but as I said before, I had rather my plea was judged on its truth.'

He put a finger beneath my chin and kissed me on the lips. 'Jane, love, it will be. What I am trying to avoid here is some pernickety triumvirate who will waste months tying their hose in knots over whether they are creating a mischievous precedent. Believe me, this is the only way for you to have justice.'

I was fast learning that Ned was a master of rationalisation. I appreciated his logic but it still sounded underhanded.

He shook me gently. 'Is your cause just?'

'Yes,' I asserted, 'but—'

'No more buts. Trust me.'

I talked it over later with Hastings and he said the same.

'Besides, Elizabeth,' he added, 'the world will believe only what it wants to be believe. Even if the judgment were to be given in your favour by Our Lord God himself, the gossips will still maintain the King has made sure of the outcome.'

And so the judges were appointed and the hearing began at the Court of Arches within the Church of St Mary-le-Bow, and London buzzed like an upturned hive with the scandal. A woman divorcing her husband! Everyone had an opinion. For my part, I was glad that all the proper procedures were observed. Neither Shore nor I were actually questioned before the court, but we did have to provide depositions under oath to our proctors, and these were written down and submitted to the bishops.

However, I was horrified when the bench required me to be examined by two midwives to ascertain that I was capable of penetration – I could hardly call the King and Lord Chamberlain to testify. The women were respectful, but it was an ignominious process.

Shore faced a similar Calvary. Although the cherrylips sent to our shop had made her deposition, the judges wished to be certain that that Shore had not regained his ability. It was arranged for three comely bawds to spend an hour fondling him, baring themselves and observing whether there was any stiffening of his member. Apparently there was not, and I heaved a very loud sigh of relief to hear those tidings.

I was as nervous as a maiden on her wedding night when I was finally summoned in on the day of reckoning – St George's Eve. A foul day it was, too, April behaving like a cow refusing to leave the byre for a spring meadow, and the wind buffeting me as I tried to keep my veil down.

Nor was it pleasant to stand with Shore before the court. He had brought his guild friends with him, men who had tried to seduce me into betraying him, and they sat at the back of the church, indignant and loud in their prejudice.

My servants were waiting outside the church, but I had no one with me inside the court save Master Catesby and my proctor. Mama had changed her mind at the last instant and Father insisted Jack needed him at a meeting at Mercers' Hall.

Process, pleading and proof. All in Latin. Our proctors spoke in turn, their scarlet robes the only warmth in the church. The depositions were tabled and familiar to the judges so there was no need for them to be read out. Each of the women who had borne witness against Shore (and very pretty they all were, too) made their oaths, whispering the Latin, phrase by phrase. *Jurabitis, et quilibit vestrum jurabit, quod tempore*…and kissing the holy book. Then it was the turn of the warden of the Mercers' Guild and our parish priest who had testified that Shore was a god-fearing and honest merchant.

The judges conferred and we were called to stand before them. The Bishop of Ross spoke first. I understood the gist of it. This was not the first divorce case in the kingdom on the plea of a husband's impotence, he said, and he described a similar case in York (when he was Abbot of Jedburgh), where the husband, a man in his forties, had failed to prove his fornicatory powers.

The precedent was reassuring – my proctor's eyes were twinkling with confidence – yet as I stood beside Shore before the bench, hanging upon the bishop's every syllable, I was so afraid that the law of men would prevail and I should not be set free.

My husband fidgeted, emanating loathing with his sweat as the Bishop of Sidon made his speech. I could make no sense of that judge's comments. Did he mean yea or nay?

The last was the Bishop of Hereford, the Queen's ally in adversity. He preambled his decision with such judicial terms and lengthy arguments that any man listening would not have dared wager on the outcome, but outcome there was at last – a long rumble of Latin that had me cross-eyed until seeing my blank look, he had mercy, cleared his throat and repeated it in English:

'It is the decision of the bench that the marriage between William Shore and Elizabeth Lambard be annulled for reasons of the frigidity and impotence of the defendant, William Shore.'

Catesby's 'Yea!' buffeted any further doubt from my head.

In my favour! I could have jumped with utter delight, but seeing Shore's shamed expression sobered me instantly.

'Forgive me,' I said with all sincerity, holding out my hand. 'I wish you well with all my heart.'

But his eyes held the dull look of a horse that has been whipped too often. He walked out the church with not a word to anyone.

'The first time a London court has ever upheld such a plea, Mistress Shore,' declared my proctor, turning to me from jubilantly pumping Catesby's hand. 'You are to be congratulated.'

I murmured my thanks but I felt as scared as an escaped cage-bird testing its first branch.

'And I hope you will mention my part in this to the King's grace,' murmured Catesby. But I was staring past him at the cluster of vengeful men who clogged the nave, blocking my path. Would my lawyers play my escort? Did they want their clothes spat upon? But it was the Bishop of Hereford who perceived my dilemma; he instructed his secretary and a sergeant-at-law to conduct me out through the sacristy into Bow Lane. Unfortunately, Shore's friends realised. Like a pack of dogs they raced out the main door into Cheapside and, elbowing my servants aside, came growling through the churchyard.

'You behave yourselves, gentlemen!' snarled the sergeant, brandishing his pikestaff. 'This woman is under the protection of Holy Church.'

Shelley jabbed up a lewd finger. 'Tried your weapon as well, has she?'

'Wetting your quill too, eh, inkhorn?' Paddesley jostled the skinny secretary, while Ralph Josselyn the Younger scorched me with obscenities.

'You poxy hypocrite!' I flared back.

They spat upon me and Paddesley, evading the pikestaff, kicked my ankle hard.

I stumbled, but the sergeant caught me and, hobbling in pain, I reached the gate and clung there in dismay. It was evident my enemies' shouts had drawn a crowd. Were Shore's friends going to stir up the mob? Risk a fine from the guild for breaking the peace? Where were my servants who were supposed to escort me home?

God's mercy! Lubbe, struggling through the mob, grabbed a jeering citizen by the collar and then all hell broke loose.

I screamed as someone scooped me off my feet, but it was Father's large apprentice, Barnaby.

'Give way!' he bawled. Somehow he got me beyond the fisti-cuffs and unloaded me onto a cart board into my mother's arms. Then he sprang up beside us and shook the reins. The crowd scrambled back, yelling abuse, as we galloped through. Stones and mud hit the back of the cart.

'O Jesu, Barnaby,' I exclaimed. 'What about Lubbe and Hikkes?'

'They'll be all right,' he muttered, flicking the horse's back. 'Can't risk stopping.'

I broke into tears as we turned up Foster Lane and left the jeers behind. 'You came for me, Mama.' I couldn't stop sobbing.

'There, there.' She cradled me against her as she had when I was a little girl. 'I thought this might happen, darling. I'm sorry you lost.'

I pulled away. 'But I didn't, Mama. I'm no longer married. *I'm no longer married!* I'm free at last!'

But Mama was looking at the men's spittle streaking my veil and she made no answer.


Barnaby took us to my lodging in Westminster, but Mama would not stay to celebrate. 'I've promised your father to go straight home.'

As the cart rattled away, I stood in the cold shadows with my key in my hand. Beneath the frigid afternoon sky that betokened snow, only the wind bustled, shrilling through the archways and kicking the detritus of a vanished world. The courtyards were deserted, every window shuttered. In the back streets, curls of smoke rose through the stacks and louvres that belonged to strang-ers. I looked across at the silent Great Hall. The court had gone to Windsor for Dorset's wedding.

Ostracism, the loneliness that rips our veil of self-esteem and plucks away all hope, stood before my door mocking my frail victory. No husband, no children, no loyal maid, my reputation black with adultery, my brother cursing me for shaming him, and my lover was feasting with his wife and friends. Was this liberty a mistake? What if Ned wearied of me? What would happen when my fairness faded to lead and my breasts stretched to meet my toes, where would I be then? Had I defied the will of God in setting myself against the laws of men? This should be one of the most blessed days in my life and yet my joy tasted like ashes.

A tiny ahem broke through to my panicking soul.

'Mistress Shore.'

I turned to find two of Ned's little choristers. In hose and jackets instead of their surplices, they looked more like imps than cherubs. The cruel wind had buffed their cheeks to polished crimson, their breath was vapour, but their eyes were as bright as a robin's.

'Why aren't you two at Windsor?'

'St George's have their own choir, mistress.' Elbow nudged elbow. Did they need courage to speak with an outcast like me? 'We…we were wondering if…' More elbowing. 'If you have any honeycakes that you don't need. We saw you giving some to the bridge beggars at Long Ditch yesterday.'

I made a drawstring of my lips. You must never be a bootscraper to the male sex even if they are only seven years old and missing their mothers. 'I daresay I could make some,' I said, checking my own chimney to make sure my servants had kept the fire alight.

'Oh, please, would you, mistress.' As if I had set a flint to two candlewicks, the little faces glowed.

So, I finally celebrated my freedom – not with my royal lover and wearing fine apparel, but in an apron before the kitchen fire, with dough beneath my fingernails.

Lubbe and Hikke arrived, somewhat disarrayed, to join us.

And afterwards, my two little guests, full of griddlecakes, sang us their latest anthem.

We bid the children farewell with jests that made clouds and whorls amidst the frosty air, but once the front door was bolted, I felt the cold still clinging to my soul.

# VII

During that first year Ned was so often away. It was as if I had a travelling chapman or an overzealous pilgrim for my lover. Mind, there was always a good royal reason. In the midsummer of '76, he rode north to fetch his father's body from Pontefract Priory and, together with his mother, brothers and sisters, made a solemn progress to Fotheringay where the old duke was buried with much pomp. Following that came a royal progress meandering from Nottingham to Oxford.

That long, long summer, loneliness stalked me like an unwelcome suitor. The sand fell through the daylight hourglass so slowly and at night the candlewicks took too long to burn. Taking a boat to the city once a week and spending several hours with my silk-women was like a snowflake on the face of my unhappiness, a joy quickly melted, but it helped.

The first visit to them — after my adultery had become a public scandal — had been painful. My dear women had been so tongue-tied, exchanging furtive sidelong glances that shared their embarrassment. Had they not needed the work, they might have barred the door against my knock, but I persevered, thrusting my presence on them each week to deliver their wages in person.

It was on Mama's advice that I continued the business, and in time my silkwomen were welcoming my visits once more, hungry to share morsels of gossip or the sweetmeats I always brought.

The little enterprise faced adversity. Not just the Clavers, our main rivals, but Shore and his friends telling others to refuse to do business with a whore like me. However, to my great relief, Master Shaa continued to supply the gems my silkwomen needed and let them continue in the workroom on his premises. As to finding guildsmen who would stock the pretty girdles? Ah, that proved a dilemma at first. A leper trying to sell underlinen might have fared better. However, in September, my father's apprentice, Barnaby, who had received the freedom of the Mercers' Guild, opened his own shop and he was right willing to make a display of the belts. With the return of the wealthy to the city after the plague season and the notoriety attached to the merchandise, the jewelled belts became much sought after and other shops began to stock them. I appointed a chapman to carry our ware to York, Bristol and Southampton and other cities I had never seen, but most of our profit looked to come from London. The Girdlers Guild were none too pleased that merchants in other guilds were beginning to take our belts, nor was the House of Claver, but the restrictions on who could sell what had been gradually slackening during Ned's reign, and sometimes it was a matter of swiftly removing our girdles from the counter when their guild inspector came to call.

My parents tarried in returning to the city, but in September Mama wrote from Hinxworth that Jack was newly betrothed. His marriage to a merchant draper's daughter was to be in October so that our youngest brother Will, who was promised to be priest of St Leonard's in Foster Lane, could marry them. Jack invited Shore to the wedding, but not me, so on the day of his wedding I defiantly – and sadly – waited on the opposite corner of Cheapside to glimpse his bride. A hope soon kicked away.

'We don't want your sort here,' wheezed a man's voice behind me and I swung around to discover two old people arm in arm. The man wore a draper's livery.

'Be off with you to Southwark, you harlot!' he barked, waving his walking staff at me.

'I beg your pardon, sirrah,' I said through my teeth. 'You are mistaken. I'm here to see my brother married.'

'Oh, we know who *you* are. You're the sister, the royal strumpet. Well, I'm Eleanor's grandfer and I'll not have you besmirch her wedding day. There's a law against whores like you fouling our streets. Be off or I'll send for Sheriff Stoker.'

'My father's friend!' I laughed defiantly. 'That should be amus—'

'Go!' said the old woman and spat in my face.

Shock disarmed me for a moment, and then I thought there are two paths from here; to cringe for my sins or to stand up for myself.

'Yes, I am King Edward's mistress,' I said, straightening my shoulders and ignoring the detritus drying on my cheeks. 'I am also a freewoman of this city and I have as much right to stand in this place as you have. So send for Sheriff Stoker or Sheriff Colet. If they are without sin, they can cast the first stone.'

I held my breath, dreading this might become uglier. St Leonard's bells were pealing, the neighbourhood was gathering and I could hear the shawms of the bridal procession.

'People like you should be locked away,' snarled the old man. This time *he* spat, and led his wife across to the church door.

Shaken, I turned and leaned a hand against the wall like some poor addle-witted crone.

'Is that you, Lizbeth?' The new voice was male and uncertain, making it safe to look behind me; safe to stare at the fair-haired, tonsured young man, who stood inspecting me with my father's eyes, taking in the lavender damask, the cream satin, a gold-ornamented sister.

'Will? *Will?*' I had not seen him for several years.

He held out his arms like the Good Shepherd, but his embrace was the stiff, inexperienced gesture of a celibate. Holy vows be damned, I wanted to claw down the invisible rood screen that hedged his reserve.

'Oh,' I exclaimed, holding on to his forearms and examining his face for the little boy I had loved. 'I think you've grown some more. Oh, Will.'

'Jack's seen you're here,' he said. 'He wants you to leave. It might be for the best.'

'Then I must,' I said bitterly, letting go. 'Tell Jack I wish him well. I've always wished him well.' I thrust a small casket at him. 'This is a gift for his bride. I pray you give it to her.'

'I warn you it may be returned.'

'Understood. You'd better go.'

He nodded. 'I'll see you again, Lizbeth.'

'Only if you accept who I am, Will.'

His face was official. 'It's not who you are, sister, it's what you are.'

# VIII

'"I am who I am" saith the Lord Our God,' thundered out the preacher at St Paul's Cross next morn, and that suddenly had me alert. The clanger of self-right hit my bell of guilt. No more Janus disposition, I vowed. No more picking at the scabs.

*I am who I am.* I no longer hid away at Westminster but walked through Cheapside with my shoulders at ease. There were people I wanted to help – children who needed to learn a trade but had nobody to sponsor their apprenticeships. There were only a few I could afford to help at first, but I did my best, speaking with friends of my father. Their wives might shun me, but the men listened. A small beginning and not an achievement to be written in a chronicle, but people noticed. Gradually both rich and poor began to see me as a pipe to the royal rain butt and I soon found myself as busy as a magistrate after the Feast of Misrule. I did not need to appoint a lawyer to advise people where they might find help, I seemed to be doing that myself.

Doubtful investments were suggested across the tablecloth, fat bribes nudged my way and petitions waggled in my face. Posies blossomed overnight on the doorknocker, ambitious young

182

liverymen cluttered the threshold, and poor widows wrung their hands in my parlour.

Everyone wanted me to slide in a word on their behest in the hazy, lazy aftermath of royal lovemaking. I was pleased to be useful. Sloth and loneliness no longer tarried at my heels like a pair of growly greyhounds. This was the power I had dreamed of, spoken of to Mama when Ned first took me to his bed, the chance to make a difference.

I did not take bribes, unless you count a single rose, and I only intervened when there was clear injustice. The cynical might say I was trying to scratch some years off Purgatory or show off my influence over Ned but, honestly, no. If God had given me the chance to help the poor and meek, then so I would.

'Taking business from me,' Hastings jibed, flourishing a hand at the crowd outside my door. 'Clogging up the thoroughfare. Worse than a hanging. Did you know Ned's planning to establish a Court of Mistress's Bench to handle this rabble?'

'A court for women's pleas might be very welcome,' I suggested sternly, but the Lord Chamberlain was pleased to ignore that.

'Your servants are not managing, are they? I'll get Hyrst to find you a burly porter.'


Not all my petitioners were threadbare, smelly or gutless. When Ned was in the north at Pontefract, there had come a churchman of high degree.

To be honest, I was wary of priests for I had a great fear of being excommunicated and, on the rare occasions I encountered Will, my brother, he tried to herd me back into the sheepfold of virtue. So, when my new porter, Young, brought the visitor in, I had my mental buckler raised, expecting a silver-tongued friar wanting alms.

'Provost Westbury, Mistress.'

My caller wore a simple woollen robe and hefted a shabby leather satchel. Sandals dark with age were bound around his dusty feet and the edge of his cuffs had the shiny rub that hinted at making do. His lean, pointed chin and scholarly stoop reminded me of old King Henry. Old, yes. Thick grey hair fringed his tonsure and the blue of his right eye was clouded.

'Mistress Shore, my name is Westbury. I am the Provost of the College of Our Lady at Eton. Perhaps you have heard of us? Many of our scholars go on to study at King's College, Cambridge.'

*Cambridge?* This might not involve me at all. 'Are you seeking the whereabouts of my brother, William Lambard, Father?'

'No, Mistress Shore, I'm seeking your help.' Help? The lightening of my purse, perhaps?

He unloaded the satchel and sat down with clear relief. I called for Lubbe to bring him some ale and he accepted it with gratitude and began to explain.

'King Henry, our late king of blessed memory, founded both Eton and King's College, but since his...his death, Mistress Shore, our circumstances have been less secure. It was his wish that we educate five and twenty scholars and care for a similar number of aged and infirm men. Not counting the servants, we have sixty-six persons to maintain and that includes ten teachers and six choristers. But in this year alone our income has dwindled from £1500 to £370. I should not complain for King's College is in an even sorrier state with so much building not yet complete.'

Had we reached the crux of this?

'You see, Mistress Shore, our trouble lies in the fact that the King's grace has diverted much of our income to provide for St George's College at Windsor for the rebuilding of the chapel, a matter very close to his heart, I understand.'

'Indeed, it is.'

His fingers plucked nervously at the folds of his habit. 'I believe his highness may have taken an unfortunate exception to the fact that we retained King Henry's image on our seal. We have now rectified the matter. What we were wondering, Mistress Shore, was whether our college might prevail on your kindness to speak with King Edward on our behalf and ask him to return some of our goods and lands so we may earn sufficient income to sustain the wishes of our founder.'

I liked this churchman's decency, not to mention his tolerance of someone like me.

'I can certainly speak up for such a worthwhile enterprise, Provost, but I think you overestimate my influence.'

A sweetness wreathed his features. 'Mistress Shore, from near and far I have heard of your kindness. Help us and you will ever be in our prayers.'

I smiled. Here was a priceless bribe to tempt a fallen woman – the prayers of an entire college!

He hauled his satchel onto his knee. 'I have a summary of our ledgers if you would like to see them.' He made use of my small table and spread the figures of the last ten years. 'I thought we had royal protection when their graces visited us in '71,' he said sadly, 'but, see, here and here, how our income has been diverted.'

Hmm, just mentioning King Henry could make Ned irritable, but this matter seemed to be fairly urgent. Already, the college was crusted with debt.

'I'll do what I can, Provost, but the King has gone to Pontefract and is not likely to be back in London for several weeks.'

When my visitor had departed, I gave the matter much thought and decided to create another precedent and seek an audience with the Queen. Mind, I had as much hope of seeing her as a blind beggar but, to my astonishment, one of her ladies actually came to King Street next day to fetch me – and to perhaps scout a little for her mistress.

Elizabeth Woodville's bedchamber was more opulent than Ned's and upheld her acquisitive reputation. The carpets, tapestries and stained cloths were the most skilled works I had ever beheld and the open shelves of the aumery were crammed with cups encrusted with jewels. The Queen lolled upon a daybed covered with priceless sables. She was pregnant again. A small pile of books with gilded clasps lay on a small table near her elbow next to a golden platter of almond sweetmeats. She might be listening to one of her handmaidens plucking a psaltery, but she looked as happy as a cow in a threadbare field.

I knelt on the fur rug next to her embroidered slippers.

'Ah, the Trojan mare.' A hand dangled provocatively in front of me and I had no choice but to kiss the lavish diamond that could have easily scratched my cheek.

'It is very generous of you to let me speak with you, madame.'

'Generous! Pish! It is only because I am bored. You might offer me some amusement, Mistress Shore, if it is only to cringe at the sharpness of my tongue. There's a stool behind you or does this require grovelling?'

'I hope not,' I replied brightly. 'I should very much appreciate your counsel, your grace.' I watched the perfect arches above her eyes rise in cynical unison. 'It is just that I have had a visit from Provost Westbury of Eton.'

The cupid's bow lips tightened. 'How very tedious. Wanting charity, I suppose, and favours of a more respectable kind than your normal truck.'

I resolved not to let her prick me. 'Wanting, yes. Wanting enough to sustain the purpose of the college.'

'And you have come to me with his plea. How very presumptuous of you.'

It was like walking against a gale but I plodded on. 'Gracious madame, I understand you have visited Eton College. Is this man's plea worthwhile, would you say? Are they striving to fulfil their purpose? If so, perhaps you would consider writing to the King's grace on their behalf? Their plight seems desperate.'

She threw back her head with a husky laugh. 'Lord help us, the King's concubine conniving with his queen. Next instant you will be suggesting we enjoy each other's company and attend church together.'

'Actually, that's strange that you should mention it...' I began, showing her a sparkle of eye.

Her lips twitched. The smile that lit her face displayed her stunning beauty.

'*Actually*,' she mimicked, 'you have amused me.' Then she was silent, watching me like a stalking cat, and I wondered if she was even considering my request, but then she surprised me. 'Yes, I have visited the college several times. They always made us welcome.' Languidly she picked up the plate, offering me a sweetmeat.

I took one with a smile, grateful as an exhausted diplomat offered peace after weeks of wrangling. She ate one, too, delicately licking the crumbs from her lower lip.

'The trouble is, Mistress Shore, there is only so much cake to go around. If you give more to one religious house, it means you have to take from somewhere else. Like my husband's time – if he is with you, he isn't with someone else – someone like me.'

I nodded. No knee-shuffling apology from me even if she deserved one. I assumed she would dismiss me after that swipe of paw but she did nothing of the sort.

'Very well, we shall play matters thus. I shall consult with Canterbury and raise the matter with the King.' Snapping her fingers, she sent a page to fetch her secretary. 'He's putting on too much weight,' she observed. 'You must have noticed with all the rolling around.'

'You mean the King's grace?'

'Don't be thick, woman, I'm not talking about the Provost of Eton, am I? Try and discourage his royal hungriness from consuming a second supper, will you! His horse will be grateful and I imagine you will be, too.'

'That seems a reasonable *quid pro quo*, gracious madame.'

She dismissed me then with an indolent toss of chin, but before I reached the door, she asked, 'Where is your Achilles' heel, Mistress Shore?'

The King's kindness had given me vulnerability; to lose his friendship would be to shut out the sun.

'In my heart, madame.'


'By Heaven, I have hungered for you,' Ned exclaimed, on his return from the north. Wasting no time, he set his arm about my waist and turned me towards the stairs.

'Ha, really?' I challenged, as we hastened up to my bedchamber.

All my delight in life tumbled back in full measure as I unlaced his shirt. Our lovemaking was urgent; our fulfilment divine.

'I have been remiss, my darling. You deserve to be rewarded for your patience,' he murmured afterwards, stroking my neck as we later lay entwined. 'Hmmm, how about a golden collar with matching eardrops?'

'Just being with you again is joy enough.'

'What, such a saint, so selfless?' He skimmed his hand down my thigh. 'Maybe I should ask the Pope to have you canonised. We can sell locks of your hair to every abbey in Christendom and make our fortune. Ouch! Think of the pilgrims. Hey, stop whacking me, you witch! Now come on, ask me while I'm in a giving vein.'

'Well…'

'See! I knew I could tempt you. There isn't a woman in—'

I silenced him with a kiss. 'I do have one wish,' I conceded, stroking my fingers through the royal chest hairs. 'I'd like one of your grooms to teach me how to ride.'

'What, a horse? Can't you be satisfied with riding me?' He eased me up astride him.

I leaned forward, drowning him in my hair. 'I mean a creature with four legs and a mane.'

'Ah, an ass like your husband,' he murmured, fastening his palms to adjust me better. 'Now, to the gallop, my Jane!'

But he had listened. He ordered his marshal to designate a groom to teach me and when I went to the stable for the first lesson, there was a lovely little mare named Bathsheba reserved just for me.

When I did not travel by river, I loved riding Bathsheba. Sitting in her red leather saddle made me feel like a lady and people treated me with far more deference; they touched their caps or cleared out of my path. I felt safer, out of the reach of cutpurses and carousers.

I wanted to be above other dangers, too. The Trojan Mare yearned to canter along the sand between the plains of Troy and the Greek fleet without attack so I decided to ask the advice of my Florentine namesake, Elizabetta, the mistress of Ned's banker friend, Gerard de Caniziani.

Amiable and rotund, she reminded me of how Margery Paddesley had been before bitterness had taken a chisel to her cheerfulness. Elizabetta gave me escort round her house, chattering the whole time in a motley torrent of Florentine, Latin and London servants' cant. When we finally sat down in her parlour to wine and almond pastries, I told her how I wanted to increase my wealth so I might be more independent.

'You can talk to Caniziani, Signora Shore, but I can tell you what 'e will say – tell the bel Eduardo to buy you a casa. A house in Charing, *sì*? Why you look at me like that?'

I chuckled. 'You give me good counsel, but—'

'But you have already thought of theess, *sì*?' She shrugged. 'What eez going on here in your block?' She tapped her temple. 'You do not want Eduardo treat you like a bobtail? You out of Bedlam?'

I laughed at her English but she was right. The memory of my father's whore still haunted me. 'Yes, ma donna, I think you have hit the nail upon the head. I like being the King's mistress but I do not want to be seen as greedy.'

'Bah, *meglio essere invidiati che compatiti*. Let the world envy you.'

I set my beaker down and leaned forward. 'What I wondered was whether you think the Medici Bank might give me a loan. You see, I already own a silk enterprise and I'm a freewoman of the city.'

She shrugged. 'If you must 'ave it so, Caniziani will lend you enough to buy Windsor Castle. I'll ask him, *sì*?'

Never trust a banker who is friendly with the king who is your lover.

Ned was angry. He strode into King Street looking like an apostle who'd missed the Second Coming. 'In God's name, Jane!' he yelled, flinging his hat at my tapestry of Dido and Aeneas. 'I will buy you Windsor-ruddy-Castle if you need it. Why didn't you ask me first?'

'I was trying to do things my way,' I muttered, struggling up from my curtsy.

The royal nostrils quivered. He glared down at me. 'Are you trying to undermine my credit?'

'Your pardon?'

'How do you think it cursed well looks if my mistress goes grovelling to the damned Medici for a loan to buy a house. Just a house, for God's sake.'

'I didn't grovel.' I argued, swiftly rising to my feet.

'Everyone grovels unless they've discovered some dirty secret about their banker. Christ Almighty, what will the Frogs make of it? That the King of England hasn't even a gomph stick to wipe his arse?'

'Ned!'

'I'm sorry.' He flung himself down on my only chair so hard it pleaded for mercy. 'What's eating you, Jane?' Heels slammed down on my footstool. 'Is my money not good enough?'

'No, it's not that, my dearest lord,' I laughed, kneeling by the chair. 'I was trying to stand on my own feet.'

Beneath his lashes, he dashed a sulky glare at my knees. 'You can't. You're my mistress. You don't *stand*, you *recline*. You're meant to ask for perfumes, jewels and…houses. Christ, Jane!' Hurt misted his hazel eyes. 'Don't you want to do this anymore? Do you still want Hastings?' He stared beyond me at the tapestry, as if imagining himself the lonely side of the triangle. 'Is that it?'

He thought that Hastings and I might still… Oh, God, surely not.

'But horns would never fit inside your crown,' I murmured lovingly, turning his face to me. I had to forgive his taunt even though it burned. 'Don't ever doubt me. If I had a coat of arms, I would steal your brother Richard's motto: *Loyaulte me lie*. As for Hastings, you might as well bid the Moon to flee the Earth's embrace. You come first with him, ever and always.' I nestled my cheek against Ned's breast. I could hear his heart. Oh Sweet Christ, what if it ever stopped?

Gently, his fingers stroked down my throat. Eventually he asked, 'Why, then?'

I looked up at him with all the love I could muster. 'I was trying to make provision. One day you will tire of me and there is no Guild of Mistresses to bolster my fall.'

'Jane,' he chided, running a loving finger along my lower lip.

'Oh, Ned, it will happen. Do you really believe we shall hobble to bed together thirty years from now?'

With both hands, he drew my face to his. 'I'll never tire of you.' He kissed my lips as though they were the most delicate flower petals. 'Love isn't just the laying, it's friendship, it's trust, it's laughter, and thirty years from now, if we both live that long, you will still make me smile.' I suppose I looked ridiculously enraptured by his honeyed words because he dissolved into laughter, grabbed me across him and shouted, 'and *then* we'll hobble to bed together.'

Pillow talk when your lover is mellow after a bout of sinful coupling is a smoother-out of quarrels. Ned agreed to loan me funds from his private purse; I vowed I should pay him back.

Before the winter could come on us again, I bustled and found a pretty stone dwelling near Aldersgate. My buried treasure for a rainy day. Meantime, I was content to dwell in King Street and let out my new city purchase to a wealthy widow.

In December my former maidservant, Isabel, came to tell me that she was free to join me. My grumbling husband had sailed to Antwerp with a royal letter of protection from Ned, a valuable guarantee of credit that would have his rivals in Brabant drooling with envy. Oh, I could have swung on the bell ropes of St Paul's. I need no longer fear encountering him in the city. Shore was finally *offshore!*

# IX

At least I was not a concubine confined in a pagan's seragalio. Ned did take me to Eltham and his other river palaces, but I had never visited Windsor, and Provost Westbury had pricked my curiosity. I longed to see this special chapel where the Order of the Garter ceremonies took place, and that summer I begged Ned to take me aboard his barge since he was going to Windsor on his way to Nottingham.

'I hate Windsor,' yelled Dorset as we rode beneath the castle gatehouse with the trumpets blaring. 'I always get lodged on the north side, it's gloomy as hell and the poxy rooks in the upper ward wake me up too damn early.'

'I'm glad something wakes you up,' muttered Hastings.

I had never been in a castle, except to visit the menagerie at the Tower of London. Windsor similarly had acquired towers and lodgings of every age and style as each king made changes, but it was King Edward III's stern, drum tower with a little watch turret stuck jauntily to one side of its battlements, like gloves on a hat brim, that my gaze flew to first.

Despite the masons' drays, the piles of timber and stone and general building mess across the lower bailey, a huge crowd had mustered to welcome Ned: the dean and canons, an 'anthem' of choristers, officers, garrison knights and menials. A festoon of masons even saluted from the scaffolding helming the chapel's great west window.

A page conducted me to my chamber, which was off the royal apartments and had once been occupied by Alice Perrers, mistress to Edward III. Judging by the furnishings, little had changed. While Isabel unpacked my coffers, the boy offered escort to the top of the Round Tower. I do not care for spiral steps, especially when they twist through several storeys, but the God's eye view had me gasping and not just from the climb. I had never stood so high in my life.

A dizzy drop below, a miller and his apprentices were heaving sacks through the upper postern, and further off servants were laughing as they carried fresh linen across the courtyard. I observed Dorset lolling against a doorway, still in his riding clothes, laughing with a servant girl, and further off one of the young choristers was giving a furtive glance behind him before he lifted his skirt and pissed. There was smoke from the town chimneys curling lazily into the air beyond the southern gatehouse and a nobleman's barge gliding along the river. Bridle paths and streams ran through the green of the pastures like silver threads and the shadows of the clouds sailed over the copses and fields with the self-importance of huge caravels. I supposed God could see every detail – the antlers of the deer grazing in the park, blissful as cows; the household of does and fawns plodding behind their lord and master along the edge of the woods, woods that stretched for twenty miles or more, woods where ghosts hunted by night and the king's men by day – a group of birdcatchers were striding across the pasture towards the trees

I lingered, exulting at the glory of the day until... O God! As a small bird flew high across the bailey, a slash of wings hurtled from the sky. So fast, so deadly. In an eyeblink, the little bird was snared in the cruel talons of a sparrowhawk. My body shuddered as though I felt the bird-claws ripping into my body, too, and I crossed myself with a desperate prayer. That vast sky had become a threat. I felt exposed, alone, so tiny beneath the eye of Heaven. It was a reminder that Life could flick his fingernail again and nothing would be the same.

Next morning, with great pride, Ned thrust open the scarlet doors, embellished with the gilded iron scrolls, and led us into his beloved chapel.

'This will be the mausoleum of generations of Yorkist kings,' he boasted, leading us from the bright July sunshine of afternoon into a mason's paradise. 'My Fontevrault.'

Hastings tapped his staff loudly. All hammering and yelling in the chapel ceased. In every direction, workmen tumbled to their knees on the gritty flagstones or saluted from the ropes and planking.

I could smell fresh timber. A fine dust hung in the air. The masons were working on the interior stone vaulting over the choir stalls, and most of the chancel and nave was hazardous with scaffolding. Because of the danger and lack of space, Hastings wisely closed the door on Ned's retinue, so there were just the three of us picking our way through shavings and offcuts, and Ned delivering a sermon on the differences between Taynton, Reigate and Caen stone.

The craftsmen were delighted to banter with the King, especially the fellow who was chiselling a row of angels. Ned clapped him on the shoulder and they had a wicked conversation about the heavenly choir.

Everything was rich in glorious craftsmanship. I could see why Ned needed to divert so much money to this enterprise. I was not a little envious that he was to able to fund such beauty, but I confess to pride, too, that it was my lover who was creating this jewel of architecture to awe the sons and daughters of the future. A pity I did not have a little child I could bring to admire his father's achievement.

When Ned had finished settling a few matters with the master mason, he led me to the shrine where, with the Pope's permission, he planned to inter the bones of St John Schorne, the village priest and healer who had once conjured the Devil into a boot.

'Don't you have the actual boot?' I teased.

'I'm sure we could find one. The Order of the Holy Boot, Ned?' suggested Hastings, inspecting the ceiling with sudden interest.

'I'll bestow the order of the boot upon the pair of you,' Ned muttered, and hauled me away to see King Edward III's sword and the fragment of the True Cross that had been pilfered from the Welsh (who probably hadn't paid for it in the first place).

Oh, I was so happy being with Ned and Hastings that I knelt and prayed with great gratitude, but then Ned pricked my happiness. Instead of letting me inspect the scurrilous scenes the wood-carvers had made for the misericords, he insisted on showing me the drawings for his death monument.

'It's to be in black marble and separated from the aisle here by a grille of gilded wrought iron, finest you can imagine.' He spread his arms high. 'And I'm going to have my effigy done in steel and silver gilt. That will be at this height, and down beneath, level with the aisle, I'll have a stone skeleton. Heigh, don't make a face, Jane. Kings have to plan for these things. What about your tomb, eh?' he chuckled, tweaking my nose. 'Have your feet on a little dog?'

'Don't be daft, Ned,' quipped Hastings. 'More like a brass showing her latest headdress.'

I put my tongue out at them.

'Well, mine is going to be the glory of England,' boasted Ned, and he tossed my veil over my eyes.

'Stop it!' I exclaimed, longing to return to the misericords. 'I hate this talk of tombs.'

'What about you, Will?' Ned jested. 'You are more likely to need one before us.' That was so crass, but Hastings did not look offended.

'I would ask that I be buried where I stood in life.'

'At my side?' Ned buffeted his shoulder. 'Alas, plot taken. The Queen will have to slide in there and she won't like a grave *à trois*.'

'At your feet, then.'

Ned's merriment ceased. For an instant these two men I adored so much stood staring at each other. Tears gathered behind Ned's eyes and then he flung his arms about his friend. 'By God, Will, I owe you so much. You shall lie in a chantry next to mine. Yes, it shall be so and all shall know it.'

Then he looked round at me.

'Heigh, Will, we've made Jane snivel, too.'


I was certainly in tears next day when Ned was brought back from the hunt on a litter. His horse had thrown him and he was put to bed in foul temper, aching and shaken, but at least alive.

Hastings had no appetite at supper.

'We were tempting fortune, talking about death so blithely,' he muttered, catching up with me on the stair landing after I'd left the Great Hall. 'England could have been a heartbeat away from a boy king and Lord Protector Uncle George.'

'But they'd have you,' I said, and kissed his cheek. It was the first time I had done so since we had been lovers. 'Have an early night, my lord,' I suggested kindly, curtsied and left him.

'You two do not waste much time, Mistress Shore,' drawled Dorset, emerging from the lower spiral.

'Oh really,' I groaned. 'Don't you have "friends", my lord?'

'"Friends", is it? Oh, I have "friends". Poor old man not up to it anymore?' he jibed.

'All the hunt are exhausted, my lord marquis.'

'Ouch, nurse! And this naughty boy didn't go hunting.' He slapped his own wrist and put an arm across to block me. 'Want to risk a night with me, then?'

'Oh, be hanged, my lord marquis!' I scolded lightly. 'You always whistle the same tune.'

'Darling,' he cooed, pursing his lips. 'They're getting old, but you and me…think of the joust we could have.'

'I haven't your imagination, my lord.' I extricated my person. 'Goodnight to you! Oh, a murrain on it! I've left my mantle on the King's bed.'

A lie, but I was not going to my quarters with Dorset on the prowl. The ancient lock to my door didn't work. So I argued my way past Ned's servants, slipped into his bed and cuddled against his hale side. He had been given some poppyhead infusion and was snoring like a creaking windmill so it was hard for me to fall asleep.

I lay staring up at the bed canopy. It was possible, I thought charitably, that Dorset's expensive doublets might button over some very deep scars. In his shoes, how would I have felt seeing my father's battle-hacked body carted shamefully home for a traitor's burial? Or my inheritance snatched away because Papa had fought for King Henry? And imagine a few years later, another reversal in fortune: landless at noon and by three o'clock the King's stepson! Heady liquor for a boy on the cusp of manhood. What did the boy feel as his mama suddenly bestowed all her attention on a handsome young stranger? Left out? And then the sneers of the ancient nobility and the accusations that his mother and grandam were witches.

It would be pleasing to do a spell myself and conjure Dorset and Hastings into friendship. No, I thought, falling into slumber at last. It was just too hard.

Ned was restored sufficiently next day to hear Mass in the make-shift chapel off the Great Hall, and then he was closeted with his brother-in-law, Lord Rivers, who was come that morning to make report from the young prince's household and the Council of Wales at Ludlow.

I was left at leisure to browse through the books Ned kept here. His best collection was at Richmond Palace, but there was plenty to amuse me. It was raining and the servants lit a fire to outwit the damp in the air. Once the smoke was gone, I closed the window light intending to sit upon the seat below so I did not need candles.

I had found a book that Ned had owned as a boy, *Liber de secretis secretorum*. The Latin was too much work to discover what the secret was, so I looked through a beautiful illuminated manuscript from Burgundy, and then settled into *De cas des nobles hommes et femmes malhereux* by Boccaccio.

About eleven of the clock, Dorset sauntered in. He had been riding. He did not disturb me but stood before the fire to dry his hose, staring down at the hearth. The air began to stink of wet wool. I was about to make some excuse to leave the room when Hastings came in. He was holding a letter and, judging by his scowl, primed for a quarrel. I kicked out my skirts to hurry out but he waved me to remain.

'I've been seeking you all morning, Thomas. This comes from Cecily. She says she hasn't heard from you for a month.'

The shrug of the satin pads that gabled Dorset's shoulders implied indifference. 'Women always say such things.'

'Cecily isn't "women". She's your wife.'

Dorset finally turned round. 'What am I supposed to do, Father Hastings? Bury myself in Devon at boring old Shute?'

'That's not the point, Thomas. You own the Bonville inheritance now. Time you took up the reins and showed your face once more to Cecily's tenants but, no, you are content to wallow in the income like a hanger-on.'

'I beg your pardon, my lord,' snapped the Queen's son. 'I can manage my own affairs.'

Hastings still had a burr beneath his saddlecloth. '*Affaires*, yes, that's about all you can manage, Thomas Grey. That and pissing. You need to grow up, lad. Cecily is only seventeen and she's already had your child and is carrying another.' He smiled with victory as Dorset jerked his head back in surprise. 'Ho, so you did not know you had another babe on the way?' He thrust the letter in Dorset's face. 'Read for yourself! She says she told you in the last letter she wrote you.'

Ready to bluster, the marquis reached out. 'Listen, it was not definite when she last wrote.'

'Definite?' sneered his father-in-law. 'A woman either has courses or she doesn't.'

Spots of scarlet bloomed beneath Dorset's fine cheekbones. 'You know full well what I meant, Father Hastings – whether the seed has set or not.'

Hastings' fingers curled into fists. 'She's your wife, not a jelly mould!'

Dorset carried the letter towards the window where I sat. I was surprised the sound of grinding teeth did not fill the angry silence. He might be keeping his temper, but the paper shook in his hand as he read. Hastings glared at his son-in-law's back with dangerous contempt and then looked across at me with a lift of eyebrow that invited my agreement.

I sent him a plea. There was a sensible limit to rubbing a young man's nose in his own mess, but, no, humiliation was on Hastings' agendum.

'What a worthless dag of a husband you are, Thomas Grey.'

In reply, Dorset tossed the letter to the floor and, to my surprise, hauled me up. I squealed and struggled, trapped at the waist. Hastings' eyes narrowed to serpent slits of fury.

'Look in your own mirror, old lecher,' Dorset taunted, his breath whispering past my cheek. 'Why don't *you* go and hang about *your* wife's skirts, or are her breasts too saggy for you? These are better sport, make you feel younger, eh? What a shame Ned made you give these up. Poor old Father Hastings.'

'Let me go, Lord Dorset!' I snarled. 'I am not part of your quarrel.' I wrenched free, but in escaping across the chamber, I left them facing each other like spurred cocks thrust into the ring.

Dorset stepped mockingly forwards. 'You're just an envious, old hypocrite, Lord Chamberlain. Too long in the tooth. Can't take late evenings. Can't take the wine.' His disdainful gaze fixed on Hastings's hose flap and he flopped his wrist in the older man's face. 'Can't fly the pennon any more.'

It was so fast! Hastings smashed his fist into Dorset's jaw and sent him sprawling. A footstool skidded beneath the marquis's knees as he fell heavily on his back. He rolled over, swearing, and hurled himself headfirst into my lord's belly.

Hastings went staggering back into the chair with Dorset hammering him. Down crashed a great candle stand and a pretty small table into the snarling confusion of sleeves and flailing limbs. I grabbed up a laver of wine and tossed the contents over their heads, but it made no difference. A pity. It worked with dogs.

Thank God it was only fists. A tapestry tumbled. Another skewed sideways. I did not know whether to bar the door and let them punch the anger out of each other or yell for help, but it was the fresh blood pulsing from someone's nose and the shattering of Ned's blue glass flagon made me grab my skirts and run to fetch... Well, I'm not sure whom I intended, but as I raced through the second chamber, I almost hurtled into Ned and his entourage. I took refuge in my king's arms with a sob of relief. Ned was no fool. He instantly drew me aside.

'Hastings...and Dorset...fighting,' I gasped.

'Just a private matter,' Ned announced loudly over his shoulder. 'You have leave, gentlemen! Not you, Lord Rivers!' He jerked his head in summons at his brother-in-law.

I could not believe they were still fighting. Ned took one look at the dishevelled chamber, grabbed the pair of them by the backs of their collars, banged their heads together and flung them apart.

'You break my peace and my— Hell, you broke my Schweitzer flagon!'

'I'll break his worthless head!' panted Hastings, trying to shake free of the guards who had seized him.

Rivers grabbed Dorset by the arms. 'Whoa, nephew!'

Dorset's nose was bloodiest, plopping onto his shirt and stomacher. One of Hastings' cheeks was bruised and there was a ring scratch down its fellow.

'By Our Lady, you can leave court, Tom! As for you, Will, you can go back to London and cool off in the Tower.'

'What!' His friend went white with rage.

'Yes, go and supervise the cursed mint!'

Hastings' mouth was a pen slash of resentment and he tugged his clothing straight and marched out head high.

Dorset was smirking. 'Just because I stole a mistress from him like *another* here I could name.'

'You know that's not the reason, my lord,' I exclaimed and turned to Ned. 'The quarrel was over Lady Cecily. Lord Hastings considered my lord marquis should spend more time with her.'

'Well, hop off and do so!' growled Ned.

Dorset could not criticise the King openly but he could do it obliquely by attacking me. 'You telltale old cow.'

'*Old cow?*' I walloped him across the face. 'I may have five years on you but that is all.'

He staggered back. 'She hit me, Ned.'

'And I'll put a boot up your arse. Get out of here!'

That left us alone with Rivers. He whistled with cynical amusement. 'This will set the tongues wagging.'

Ned answered him with two short words and left the room.

With a sigh, I began to set the chamber to rights. Rivers picked up the scattered books. He made a show of examining them for damage but he was more intent on manipulating me.

'Since you are playing the alarm bell so beautifully, Mistress Shore, perhaps you should warn Hastings that the activities of his officers in Calais on his behalf have not gone unremarked.'

I did not look up from gathering the shards of cobalt glass. 'I daresay I'm being as dense as a November fog, Lord Rivers, but what exactly are you talking about?'

He crouched down before me and offered a cupped palm for the fragments. 'As a housewife, I'm sure you understand skimming off cream.' He rolled the word.

'I'm out of practice, I'm afraid,' I crooned back and rose to my feet, smoothing my skirts. 'But – *as a housewife* – I have learned not to listen to idle gossip. I believe the King's grace has, too.' If Rivers wanted to plant the seed of suspicion against Hastings in Ned's mind, he could use someone else.

He straightened gracefully and stared down at me from his fine height with the sleepy languor he always affected. 'You should not have smacked the Queen's son, Elizabeth Lambard.'

'No, I agree with you, my lord, and I shall apologise next time I see him, but maybe if *she* had smacked him more, I should not have had to.'

He looked at me with blatant pity. 'I see in you a poor deluded creature, still clinging to the mane of a weary old warhorse in case our sovereign lord kicks you out.'

'Yes, that's me,' I said. 'But *he's always fought* on Ned's side.' *Unlike some.*

Rivers' eyes glittered. 'As I said, deluded. There'll come a time when you go grovelling to my nephew.'

There spoke the man who was tutor to our future king and it didn't bode well, least of all, for me.


Once he had his temper lidded down, Ned returned. The chamber was back to its rich, serene character and he thanked me for it.

'Brawling like schoolboys, I had to punish them,' he said sadly, dropping down into the chair. 'But did you see the hurt in Will's eyes? I hope he understood.'

'He'll come about.' I wrapped my arms about Ned's neck and kissed the top of his head. 'And I hope Dorset will forgive me.'

But I didn't believe in fairies either.

# X

Just before Christmas, George's wife died. She had never recovered from bearing a stillborn babe two months earlier. Then in January came worse news: Ned's brother-in-law, the Duke of Burgundy, had been slain in battle, and Ned, fearful that France would now gobble up Burgundy, urgently summoned his two brothers to court. But George would not come straight away. In his grief, he kept his duchess's embalmed body lying in state in Tewkesbury Abbey for five-and-thirty days. Then, when he did arrive at the council chamber, he was no longer in mourning but ardent to marry again.

'If he stayed off the malmsey, he might see the world like a sane man,' Ned exclaimed, pacing in my parlour in King Street like a caged beast. 'Want to hear his latest nonsense, Jane? He will neither eat nor drink under my roof. Says his son is a changeling and I am to blame. Heigh, yes, I'm in league with the fairies as well as Italian poisoners. Pah, the brat is simple.' He whirled his finger at his temple. 'Moon-faced, know what I mean?'

The duke's son and heir a village idiot! Oh dear!

'Weren't he and his wife cousins, Ned?'

'Second cousins, love. They had a papal dispensation. But I know what you are hinting. Curse of inbreeding, eh?'

'And your brother Gloucester is married to the other sister.'

He gave a huff of breath and shrugged. 'So the Pope gave him a dispensation as well. Necessity of state. The last thing we needed was George getting his hands on *all* of Warwick's lands.'

'Are my lord of Gloucester's children hale?' I asked, replenishing the cider in his cup.

'His bastards are. He managed three before he wed, so nothing wrong with him, but Cousin Anne's not a good breeder. They've only managed a son so far – bright enough, thank God! I'm going to make him Earl of Salisbury.' He took a swig. 'Hell and Ballocks! You know what, Jane? George reckons he's going to marry Mary of Burgundy. Imagine! He'd be Lucifer incarnate, allying with his greasy friend, Louis, to grab my throne. And now that Scots clod James has offered him his sister's hand as well. Whoresons, all of 'em! I might as well sit on the mouth of a cannon and light the fuse.'

When the royal council fisted the board in disapproval of his marital ambitions, Duke George left Westminster in a mighty fury. For a few weeks he simmered in Warwick Castle and then in April he sent his henchmen to abduct his wife's favourite tiring woman, alleging that she had poisoned the duchess. He had the poor woman hauled to Warwick town where he forced the local judge and jury to find her guilty. Then he hanged her.

Ned, furious at his brother's rape of the law, summoned him to answer charges. George ignored him and made much mischief. Slanders about the King's legitimacy flickered across England like sheet lightning in the summer clouds and Ned, give him due, weathered them until Harewell and Tapton, his spies in the duke's household, delivered a disturbing report. Some of George's retinue were employing the black arts against Ned and his son, Prince Edward, predicting that they would soon die.

That had Ned snarling. Several men, including George's close friend, Thomas Burdett, were arrested and tried by a commission, and a week later, on Monday, nineteenth of May, they were found guilty of high treason.

I tried to stay out of it, but on the morning of the verdict, two women, one veiled, the other with a hood covering half her face, came to my door at Westminster. Isabel brought them up into my solar.

The taller woman wore a starched coif. Her gown was of fine wool and the most perfect black dye I'd ever seen, save for Ned's doublets. Her eyes were beautiful, blue and sandy-lashed, and although her cheeks had the stretching that comes with age, she was remarkably attractive. A large, unadorned gold cross hung upon her bosom, but she wore no other adornment save on her ring finger and I assumed she was an abbess. Petitioners like her were the hardest to deal with. They did not like to be thwarted. When I made a courtesy, she merely inclined her head.

Her plain, younger lay attendant was round-shouldered and likely to acquire a hump if she lived long enough. Her cone head-dress was of modest proportion, she was wearing a silver collar with a pendant 'M' and a wedding band, and her gown was of amber damask over a brown petticote. Thumb-sized shadows underlined her eyes and her face told me Life had taken a whip to her.

They declined refreshment. The older lady sat straight, her stare roving over my furnishings. Clearly, the buttering up that tediously preceded a plea for help would not come from her. It was the younger woman who leaned forward.

'Mistress Shore, it is said that you have the stomach to speak out where there is injustice. Lord Hastings said you might be willing to help me.' She had a Midlands accent, Warwickshire perhaps.

'Come to the point, Margaret.' The older woman's tone was brisk but not without charity.

'My husband is Sir Thomas Burdett, Mistress Shore, one of the men condemned to death tomorrow morning, and I assure you I can think of no one else to turn to.'

I was speechless.

'I've tried to talk sense into Ned,' said the older lady. 'He won't listen to Will either and Elizabeth is about to give birth.'

*Ned*? *Elizabeth*? I stared at her, totally bewildered. She was too young to be one of Ned's sisters but old enough to be…*his mother*? Jesu! The well bucket hit the water and I tumbled forward onto my knees.

Her grace of York rarely set foot outside Baynard's Castle but here she was in my house.

'Your grace, I didn't—'

'Well, why would you?' she said matter-of-factly, flicking her fingers at me to seat myself again. 'And this is a matter of extreme urgency.'

'Mistress Shore, please,' pleaded Margaret Burdett. 'My husband is going to be executed for high treason and—' She clapped a hand to her lips as if the words already made her retch.

I blinked hard, feeling myself much moved to pity. Burdett would be hanged. They would hook his entrails out while he was still alive and then hack the body into four and stake his head on London Bridge.

'Dame Margaret,' I said helplessly, 'your husband was tried by—'

'Five earls, twelve barons and six justices in the Star Chamber,' cut in her grace of York. 'Yes, due process of law, Mistress Shore, and he was found guilty. However, it is still possible for my son to grant him mercy.'

Trying to talk to Ned about Burdett would be like sleeping with a candle on a haystack.

I lifted my hands in frustration. 'Your grace, I believe that no man should die so cruelly, but I have only been able to help people with petitions about small matters.'

Dame Margaret gave an anguished gasp. 'Please, the King's officers will take my children's inheritance. Our land, everything.'

I reached out a hand to clasp hers and waited until she had regained control before I asked gently, 'Do you believe your husband is innocent?'

She looked me in the face. 'He did spread sedition, but he believed what my lord duke said about—' She bit her lip, darting a wary glance at the duchess.

I guessed which slander she meant. 'But there were other charges?'

She nodded. 'Alas, it's true what he said about wishing the antlers of the white buck were in King Edward's belly because he had been pursuing that buck for years and, yes, it was the King who killed it during a hunt, but Thomas didn't really mean he wanted the King dead. He was just jealous when he heard.'

'And the sorcery? Didn't your husband's body-servant testify against him?'

'You mean Alexander Rushton, God forgive him, but I'm sure he was forced and they must have tortured Master Stacey, too, for him to accuse Thomas.'

I hoped not. Ned had always claimed he disapproved of torture.

'Stacey is a fellow of Merton College, Oxford,' the duchess informed me. 'Thomas Blake, the other condemned man, is the college chaplain.'

Margaret Burdett nodded. 'My husband met them four years ago when the duke commissioned them to draw up his birth chart, but I swear Thomas had nothing to do with any of their predictions this time.'

'And the duke has sent no letter to exonerate any of them?' I asked her.

'No,' she replied angrily, 'and it's too late now. It's not just, not just!' Her fists hit her lap. 'Why should my husband be the whipping boy? He's been stupid, yes, but he did what he was told. For the love of Our Sweet Saviour, Mistress Shore, I don't want him to die. But the King will not see me.' She flung herself on her knees before me. 'You are the only person left.'

I put my hands on either side of her shoulders and said solemnly, 'I'll do whatever is within my power, but pray don't raise your hopes.'

'Oh, thank you, thank you.' To my dismay, she kissed my hand as though I was a princess.

I looked across at Ned's mother. 'His grace leaves tomorrow for the Queen's lying-in at Windsor and that gives me little time.'

The duchess rose to her feet. 'Come along, Margaret.'

Burdett's wife took her cloak from me. 'I cannot thank you enough, you kind soul. God be with you, Mistress Shore, and grant you eloquence.'

I shook out the duchess's cloak to arrange it about her shoulders but she held up an imperious hand and bade Dame Margaret wait for her downstairs.

'Close the door if you please, Mistress Shore.' I latched it and came back to face her. We were both tall so she was able to look directly at me. 'You will be risking a great deal of displeasure if you intervene in this business.'

'Yes,' I said with feeling. 'And, pardon me for my frankness, your grace, but you have raised that poor dame's hopes too much by bringing her here. May I ask why?'

She gave me her cloak to put about her shoulders. 'Because, as you rightly pointed out, Burdett and the others are small fry. If they are executed, George may…will…do something else foolish and God knows where this may end.

'I don't know if you have met George, Mistress Shore. Oh, you have. And have you ever seen a ball of quicksilver? It's bright, shiny, a perfect sphere, but poke it and it changes shape, moves fast and then becomes a ball again. That's George. Irritable as a bull with a horsefly on its rump in May, but in June, talking, talking, talking, brimming with schemes that could encompass the whole of Christendom, by July, wallowing in self-pity and saying that the family hates him.

'He thinks he'd be a better king but he can't keep order on his own manors. And he drinks too much. How do you manage such a man? So, you see, it has to be Ned who makes the compromise, and I need you to point this out to him.'

'You do not ask much,' I said wryly.

'No,' she agreed with a smile. 'But Ned always calls you his Jehane d'Arc.' She tugged her hood forward over her starched coif. 'Now, do give your father my good wishes when you see him, Elizabeth. I have not forgotten his loyalty to my late husband.'

I curtsied. 'He will be touched that you remember him, your grace.'

She nodded to me to open the door for her. 'If you decide not to speak with Ned on this matter, I won't blame you but I'll be disappointed.'


I waited for a quarter of an hour outside the Lord Chamberlain's accounting room before one of his secretaries ushered me in.

Hastings did not ask me to sit down. 'You had unexpected visitors?' He signed a letter, then reached for another in the waiting pile.

'I did. Very elevated, in fact, and thanks to you, I find myself at a crossroads.'

'Now where have I heard that before, Elizabeth?' He looked up, wearing his busy Monday face. 'Ned expects you for a late supper – not too late, mind. He leaves for Windsor at daybreak.'

'Too much excitement in London?' I asked dryly.

His lips twisted. 'Something like that.'

'Why have you set me up for martyrdom, my lord? The rain will get in by the time Ned's finished shooting holes in me.'

'And you'll look very holy, my dear.' He saw I had the urge to throw his household book at him because his expression creased into a tepid smile. 'Your pardon. The reason is you are the only one left and you do a good sniffle when it suits you.'

'Ohhh!' I fumed and sat down on a secretary's stool and jabbed my elbows on the board so hard that the inkpots shook. 'Do I care?'

'Yes.'

I glared and he paused his quill.

'Elizabeth, this Plantagenet quarrel is like that Roman mountain that blew its rocky top off. People will get hurt needlessly.'

'Yes, we all know that, my lord, but there's no harnessing Nature. And if peacemakers are so blessed, why aren't *you* trying to talk Ned into signing a pardon?'

'I've tried.' He dipped the quill and resumed his task. 'Go home and get some rest before tonight.'

'Grrr,' I said with feeling at his bowed head before I let the secretaries back in.


When dung comes, it comes in spadefuls. I returned to find a monkey's tail of petitioners looping round the corner from my doorstep. Young and Lubbe were on guard and they hastened across the palace yard to escort me in. Scrolls and letters were thrust at me from all sides and my arms were full by the time I reached the stairs. But that was usual. Lubbe helped me unload.

'Your brother's 'ere, mistress.'

'I don't think so, Lubbe.' Petitioners used all kind of ruses to invade my privacy. 'My brothers never visit.'

'That's what we thought, mistress, but this 'un does have a look of you. Isabel's up there with 'im to make sure he don't snaffle nuffink.'

Isabel opened the door for me, a duster in her hand, and her eyebrows at a questioning angle. Fidgeting by the window stood my youngest brother.

'Jesu!' I muttered to Isabel, as she took my cloak. 'I hope nobody has died.'

Will watched open-mouthed as Lubbe deposited today's missives on my board. 'This is normal,' I explained coolly.

Lubbe lingered. 'You want the others shooed away until tomorrow, mistress?'

I shook my head. If Will was here to do a sermon on the mount, I'd need an excuse to dislodge him.

My brother came across and gave me a chaste kiss. He still seemed a stranger with the smell of church in his robes.

'What brings you?' I asked, drawing off my gloves. 'No fevers or fires, I trust.'

'No.' He scowled at the door. 'Is your maidservant right in her wits? She was watching me as if I was about to steal your silver.'

'Perhaps you have a furtive look.'

He snorted like Father. 'I haven't time for jests, Elizabeth. I need your help and the matter is vital.'

'Today is not a good day, Will.'

'It's about the hangings at Tyburn tomorrow morning and...' He hesitated. 'You do know about the high treason trial, don't you? They were—'

I ignored his disbelief in my intelligence. 'How does it concern you, Will? You're not asking to walk with them to the gallows, are you?'

'No, it's because a parishioner came to see me this morning. Her name's Marion Stacy. Stacey is—'

'An Oxford fellow. And this Marion is his sister?'

'No, his wife. He's to be hanged tomorrow, Elizabeth. There's no time for her to petition the King for mercy unless...'

I sat down and dragged my hand wearily down my face. 'Will, you don't know what you ask of me.'

'Please, Elizabeth, please save Stacey's life. I promised her you would. I know the man. He wouldn't...'

'He *did*. We are talking about high treason. Are you saying five earls, twelve barons and six justices are wrong?'

'Yes, I am. His wife saw him when the guards fetched him from the Tower. She says he was walking like a cripple and he looked so old, she hardly knew him. They tortured him, Elizabeth.'

'And suddenly your whore of a sister is the only person who can save him?'

A shameful scarlet flushed Will's face. 'If you want to bargain, I don't blame you. I promise to say nothing more about—'

'My sins? Well, I doubt there'll be any more after tonight. If I speak of this matter to the King's grace, I am likely to lose everything.' I spread my hands to include the Flemish tapestry of Dido and Aeneas, the finely carved aumery with the gilded salt and chased goblets, my costly gown. 'Would *you* risk all this, Will?'

My brother sat back in innocent astonishment. 'Really? I thought you and he were like that.' He held up crossed fingers.

I stood up and rang my little hand bell for Lubbe. 'I think you had better go now, Will. I have plenty to occupy me, as you see. It was good of you to call at last.'

The sarcasm ran off him like a raindrop on a cered mantle. 'Those people out there, they believe in you. I...I talked to them. They said no one is kinder hearted in all of London.'

I was touched yet I knew the limits of folly. 'But, Will,' I pointed out wryly, 'this is *Westminster*.'

*

Teweksbury mustard is foul stuff on its own. I took a spoonful to make me sneeze and cleanse my head, but it did not rid me of the knotted cord sensation. Had they done that to Stacey, bound his temples tighter and tighter? And who were 'they'? Every bridle path of thought led to Ned.

I made my way through to his apartments that evening with a heavy heart.

'Ah, I forgot the time, love,' he exclaimed, rising to embrace me. He looked at ease with his shirt loosely laced and an ancient, sleeveless doublet that he should have given to the poor and couldn't button anymore, stretched across his back. He gestured to the pile of papers. 'Clearing up a few matters before Windsor.'

'So I see.' He hadn't even touched the platters of cheese and fruit set out on the small table. 'Do you need to leave tomorrow?' I asked sweetly, poking at his chest. 'Her grace has not gone full term yet, has she? And don't queens shut themselves away for a month beforehand?'

His laughter rumbled beneath my fingers. 'Got me pilloried, eh? I'm going hunting. Clears the brain. I feel mewed up here like some damned hawk, but now that you've arrived...' His hands curved around my buttocks and drew me against him.

We made love among the parchments. A swift untying of points and tossing up of petticotes, and afterwards I fed him while he dealt with the last of the dispatches. Eventually he wearied and came across to the window seat. Flinging cushions about my feet, he made himself comfortable against my skirts.

'I wanted to ask you something, Ned,' I murmured, licking the quince jelly from my fingers. 'You may get angry.'

'Send you to the Tower?'

'Maybe.' I removed the platter from my lap. 'This trial that's been going on in the Star Chamber all week, I thought you didn't believe in torture.'

His back tensed against my leg. 'I don't.'

'But hasn't Doctor Stacey accused your brother's retainer under torture?' I held my breath to see how he reacted. This was hazardous, like walking through a marsh at night. I didn't want to lose this intimacy, risk everything for three men I'd never set eyes on. All the other times I had intervened had been small matters; this was treason.

Ned lobbed a cherrystone at the hearth. It missed. 'Must we discuss this? I'm going to be away for two weeks and you want to talk about the mongrels who tried to get rid of me and my son.'

O Jesu, this was folly, except that I could not stop thinking about the hooks and knives being whetted for the morrow. I stroked my fingers through Ned's hair. He relaxed again, letting his head fall against my knee.

'All London is going to be at Tyburn, my darling. Forgive me for speaking plainly but if the people feel that there has been injustice, there could be rioting.'

'Christ, Jane!' He swivelled round to glare at me. 'The people will cursed well riot if there *isn't* a hanging and drawing. Anyway,' he muttered, settling back again, the royal arms folded, 'it's not as though it's the first time Burdett and Stacey have been accused of sorcery.'

'Oh.' My fingers tensed for an instant and then I fondled his hair again. 'How so?'

The petulance eased. He took a deep breath. 'Before the Battle of Tewkesbury, remember how Queen Margaret's army landed at Weymouth and marched north? Because they were denied entrance into Gloucester, they couldn't cross the River Severn there and they had to march on to Tewkesbury where we defeated them?'

'Hm-m.'

'The man who wouldn't let them in at Gloucester was Richard Beauchamp, and a few years ago his wife had an affair with

Burdett. She demanded Burdett find an astronomer to see if her husband had long to live. Burdett went to Stacey. Anyway, to be brief, there was talk of witchcraft but insufficient evidence for poor old Beauchamp to make a charge.'

'So Burdett is hot-blooded as well as hot-mouthed?'

'Look at it this way, love, a shady lane breeds mud. I can forgive the bastard for wishing the buck's horns were in my belly. Hell's teeth, if you've been chasing a particular stag for months, you don't want some other knave blundering in to shoot it.' Another cherrystone flew across the chamber and pinged against the metal hearth screen.

'Under the 1352 Act of Parliament on treason, we can't convict Burdett for what he said about the buck unless there's evidence of conspiracy as well. Now, there are plenty of witnesses to testify that Burdett was stirring up unrest. Again, that isn't quite enough. Dogs that bark at a distance never bite. He wasn't waging war or trying to start a rebellion on George's behalf, see.'

I saw. For me, Burdett's loyalty to the duke opened up the question of when a retainer had the right to refuse his lord's commands, but Ned had not finished. 'It was Stacey's evidence that tipped the balance.'

'The black arts?'

'Yes.'

I tugged my hand free. 'But that evidence was given *under torture.*'

It was dangerous to let my disapproval show. Ned could shift easily from lover to king, winching the portcullis down with a heavy slam if I stepped too close to his conscience. Tonight the drawbridge was still beneath my soles. So far...

'Hang about, Jane, not on my direct orders, I can assure you. My officers obviously got over-zealous.'

'Not the Duke of Exeter's daughter?'

'No, it's barbaric. Not on my watch!'

I let silence be my ally. Ned's fingers were playing distractedly with the braid edging my gown. He was staring pensively, not at the tapered toes of his shoes, but across at the fireplace. Was he observing the iron tongs, thinking about the torture his men had used? The branding irons, the pincers to pull out a man's finger-nails or crush his genitals? Had he *agreed* to that?

Mistrust was plucking at me, or else the Devil himself was whispering: Go on, ruin yourself, Elizabeth Lambard. Tell this king of yours that you don't believe his word. Goad him until he yells at you and flings you out of his life.

Where do you draw the line between justice and compassion? I doubted there had been injustice in the Star Chamber, and what right did I have to interfere, to question that court's author-ity? For the sake of Margaret Burdett and Marion Stacey? Yes, I sympathised, but many cutpurses and murderers have wives and children. Without punishment of transgressors, the realm would descend into lawlessness.

'I'm not pardoning *any* of them, let's be clear on that!' Ned lifted an admonishing, inky finger. I caught his hand and drew his palm to my lips.

'Could you promise me that from this day forth no torture will be used on any prisoners in the Tower? You are too great a Christian prince to permit such savagery, Ned.'

He turned his body to me and, thank God, there was love not anger in his eyes.

'Please, Ned,' I pleaded, with all my heart and soul. 'Let justice always prevail, but not based on testimonies that have been wrung out of men's limbs like blood.'

'My sweet soft-hearted Jane.' His hazel eyes searched my face, then he lifted loving fingers to stroke my cheek. 'Yes, I can make such a promise.'

'You have to make sure your officers obey you,' I urged him. 'Otherwise it's...'

'Farting in the wind?'

I smacked him. He laughed, heaved himself up and brought the flagon over. 'I always know when you're up to something,' he muttered, refilling our cups and settling down again. 'Jane, the people's ungowned lawyer.' One hand curled about my ankle and stroked upwards. 'My warrior in skirts, brandishing her rolling pin for the humble and down-trod.' His fingers suddenly tightened, cruelly. The teasing was gone from his voice. 'Who put you up to it this time? Will Hastings?'

'Let us be satisfied with compromise,' I purred, clinking cup rims with him. If he was sincere, I had done more good than saving three guilty men. I must be content with that.

He shook his head. 'Not good enough, my lovely. I want whys and wherefores. Royal command!' He was quaffing his ale and watching my face.

'Really?' I challenged with good humour.

'Yes, really.' I heard the unpleasant edge of metal in his tone.

'You'll regret this.'

'Not unless you will. Spill!'

'It concerns someone's mother.'

'Ha, the biggest cannon to bombard a man? Were all three mothers grizzling on your doorstep?'

'No, only one. Yours.'

Ned choked. 'Mine? Mine out of Baynard's? Hell! Next thing it will be the Holy Apostles rowing Christ across the Thames.'

'Your stately mother brought Burdett's wife to my house this morning.'

'God's truth, the conniving...' He stumbled to his feet, cursing and slamming his fist into his palm and then, just like the waves that bruise the riverbank from the wake of a boat, his temper subsided. 'I'm sorry you have become involved, Jane. Mother should be talking sobriety into George, damn him, instead of plaguing you. He's the one letting his friend die. If he had shown some remorse for hanging his wife's servants, I might show these misguided traitors some mercy.' His eyes bore grimly into mine. 'Well, did Burdett's woman grovel?'

I nodded.

An unpleasant smile dimpled. 'But you haven't asked me for his life? Don't tread on quicksand, eh?'

I swallowed. 'My brother, the rector of St Leonard's, Foster Lane, also came to see me this morning, Ned. One of his parishioners is Stacey's wife, Marion.'

'Married! Poor old bastard, that's him done for then. He can't claim benefit of clergy now.'

I was aghast. 'You mean he wouldn't have been hanged?'

'Well, he will be now. Drawn and quartered! A pity you told me.'

The food lurched in my stomach. I somehow got to my feet. 'This makes me sick to my soul, Ned.'

'You started it, Jehane d'Arc.' He went to the board and pretended to sort the papers.

I did not know what to do. I didn't want to become a moth in the cold of the night, seeing the light through the cracks in the shutter, unable to reach him, but I did believe in Christian forgiveness even if I sometimes fell short. I took a gulp of wine. The fierce rustle of parchment spoke behind me. The King did not want to be challenged. He presided; he never rode to the tilt.

My voice was husky as though the words could not be brought forth easily. 'The week you became king, my lord, back in '61 when I was still a young girl.' Behind me, the royal hands paused. 'There…there was a London citizen called Walter Walker, whose son was to have the running of *The Crown Inn* at Newgate, and that man, well, he made a jest and said his son would inherit "the crown". Master Walker was put to death, Ned, because of you.' I turned to face him. I wanted to ask: *Did you know that? Did you let it happen?*

His expression was royal, unreadable, but his words…his words were tipped with steel. 'And do you know who arrested him and had him hanged, Jane? Sheriff John Lambard!'

I didn't know. My skin must have gone pale as ashes. I clutched at the table and missed. Ned rushed round and sat me down.

The tears came in such a tempest that I couldn't stop them. I cried – for poor Master Walker and the traitors who might be guilty but must suffer such a horrible death.

'No more!' Ned commanded softly, flicking the last drops from my cheeks. 'My dearest love, I promise you there shall be no more torture while I reign as king, but tomorrow morning justice shall be done.'

That Monday morrow in the darkness before cockcrow, Myddelton shook my shoulder as I lay in the King's bed.

'Mistress, his grace's servants will be here shortly. Best you go.'

I kissed Ned's forehead. 'Enjoy the hunt,' I murmured, 'and may Christ and his angels protect the Queen in childbirth.' Beneath my caress, Ned muttered but did not fully wake. 'Please tell his grace what I said,' I whispered.

Myddelton nodded. 'I'll see you back to King Street presently, Mistress Shore.' I heard him tidying the outer chamber while I dressed.

Because it was early and the stairs that led from the Painted Chamber were better lit, he took me out through the double doors. The guards saluted me. It could have been otherwise. I sent a prayer of thanks to St Mary Magdalen for my own survival.

*I cannot save the traitors*, I told her, *but maybe your saintliness could,*
*soften Ned's hea*—

'Jesu!' I squealed as a dark question mark of a man straightened
on the second landing.

'What the…?' Myddelton lifted the candlestick and we beheld
the long, thin face of the royal councillor, James Goldwell, the
Bishop of Norwich. 'My lord, have you been here all night?'

'Ye…N-no. That is, I…' Episcopal fingers were tugging and
smoothing as though he had been found *flagrante delicto*.

Myddelton's candle was shaking but discretion was one of his
polished virtues. He carried on past, but when I followed, Bishop
Goldwell held up a delaying hand.

'Mistress Shore, is…is that you?'

'Yes, my lord,' I said, making courtesy.

'I… I hope…that is…' The palace was still silent about us and,
as though drawing courage from that, he drew breath again.
'D-Did his grace the King sleep well?'

If it had been daylight, this cleric would have seen me blush.

'He did, my lord.' Two stairs down, I saw Myddelton's candle
wobble.

'G-good,' said my lord bishop. 'That's…good.'

And suddenly the hammer hit the anvil. 'Master Myddelton,'
I called, 'would you be so good as to wait for me downstairs, please?'
Once the candlelight reached the lower floor, I was able to ask, 'Is
this a mercy errand, my lord?' A sharp gasp and then he confessed.

'I'm here for Stacey. We were students together. The man's a
good scholar, Mistress Shore.'

'Is he married?'

'No.' Surprise edged his voice. 'Unless he's broken his vows.'

'So he is claiming "benefit of clergy"?'

'Yes, but no one wants to listen. It's like the rights of sanctuary
these days, almost eroded. However, if the King's grace would …'

'I'm sure his grace will respect your compassion, my lord.' But we were both thinking about Tyburn.

Downstairs, Myddelton coughed. I could hear the packhorses being brought into the yard, and voices upstairs; the body-servants on their way to clothe the King.

'My lord, if you would be advised by me, you must tell the King that Stacey has a sister in London who lives in St Leonard's parish. Not his wife but *a sister*. Her name is Marion. *Marion*. And, for the love of God, don't tell him I said so, my lord, or your cause will fail.'

'But, Mistress Shore, I don't understand.'

'Trust me.'

I heard the carts leave. Soon Edward, King of England, would be on his barge, and at the gallows, those who had slept overnight for the best view would be stirring. People would be waiting outside Newgate Gaol to jeer. The condemned would be carted through High Holborn to St Giles Hospital, where the holy brothers would give them each a great bowl of ale, their last drink upon earth and then…the rope, the whetted knives.

Close to eleven o'clock, I knelt at my prie-dieu and prayed for their souls. It was mid-afternoon when Lubbe reported back. I was sitting in the sun in the little courtyard when I heard his voice through the open door.

'The press of people, I never saw the like,' he muttered, collapsing onto a stool and propping his heels on the kitchen table. 'Give us some ale, Belle, then I'll front the mistress.'

'You can front me now!' I snapped, closing the door.

'And get your plaguey boots off my clean table,' grumbled Isabel.

Lubbe sprang to attention, his cap twitching in his hands.

'I don't want details, sirrah,' I said firmly. 'And no jesting! Was there a hanging?'

He held up two fingers but not in disrespect. 'Burdett and Blake, mistress. The works.'

I tried not to imagine. 'And Doctor Stacey?'

'They was all up there wi' nooses round their necks an' all, an' then Sheriff Colet rides forward with some bishop wot is waivin' a sealed message from the king's grace.'

I held my breath as he paused, grinning.

'Reprieved – "Benefit of clergy". Old fellow swooned when 'e 'eard an' the others looked fit to piss, saving your pardon, mistress. The crowd didn't like it. They wanted Burdett to be saved cos 'e was only followin' 'is lord's orders. 'E kept protestin' it weren't 'is fault, right to the last. Crowd got wot they wanted, though; a good showin'. Wouldn't 'ave done for the King to pardon all three. Very unwelcome that would've been, eh, mistress?'

I couldn't answer nor did I have to for there was a knocking at the front door. Young went to deal with it and staggered back with a basket of grumpy chickens.

'These squawkers are from the Bishop of Norwich, mistress.' Resting on top was a nosegay of wild flowers and in a very unlettered hand, a strip of parchment with the words:

*God blesse you and thanke you wyth alle my hert, MS*

# XI

The bells rang out that week to celebrate the birth of a third prince. Ned, offering his brother forgiveness, named the babe George. But the old proverb, *'Ale in, wit out'*, was proved true. When the duke heard about Burdett's execution, he galloped down to Westminster and charged into the Star Chamber, bellowing for the King. Of course, Ned was at Windsor, and instead of taking the matter to him, the duke harangued the councillors and made them listen to the testimony of some Franciscan preacher, who claimed to have heard the condemned men's confessions of innocence. The palace immediately sent a courier to Windsor.

Ned could be lazy as an old dog, but when he was stirred up, he could strike fast. He returned to Westminster in full Plantagenet rage, summoned the Lord Mayor, sheriffs and aldermen, and in the common hearing accused his brother of usurping royal authority, breaking the laws of England and threatening its judges.

I know his mother tried once more to mend the quarrel but George was unrepentant. In June he was taken to the Tower together with some of his advisers including Stillington, the Bishop of Bath and Wells, a former Chancellor of England.

The day following their incarceration, I received a letter from Bishop Goldwell informing me that last night Dr John Stacey had died in the Tower. His will named Goldwell his executor and all his goods and debts were left to his widow, Marion.

Ned had ordered his death.

I don't know how long I sat alone with the bishop's letter on my lap. For I was remembering how old King Henry had fortuitously 'died' in the Tower on the night of Ned's triumphant return to London after his victory over Lancaster.

I still loved Ned. You dance while the music plays, don't you? But in truth the shadow of the Tower cast a darkness over the entire kingdom.

George spent the remainder of the year in the Tower and then in the following January of 1478, when an icing of snow glistened on the pinnacles and turrets, the great lords rode into Westminster to witness the marriage of Ned's five-year-old son, Dickon, to the little Mowbray heiress in St Stephen's Chapel. A few days later they assembled in the chill of Westminster Hall to try George for high treason and Ned was the chief accuser.

For almost three weeks, the matter endured. I remember the New Palace Yard was perilous with black ice the day that Buckingham, steward of the jury, announced the sentence of death. I saw George brought out of the hall, his hands bound in front of him and his back rigid and proud. As if to rile him further, it was Rivers who was given charge of his escort back to the Tower.

During the next two weeks, while the unsigned warrant lay waiting on the royal council board, messengers carried arguments up and down the spine of England. From Middleham, Richard of Gloucester's home in Yorkshire, to Westminster Palace, from Baynard's Castle to Middleham, and Middleham to Westminster.

And from Westminster, a terse growl from the King was carried north once more. Gloucester and the Countess of York were desperate to save George's life.

'I do not know why he bothers,' Ned snarled as Hastings set the latest letter from Gloucester before him in his private chamber. 'They are closer in age,' I suggested, but the King was not listening.

'By Jesu, the pair of 'em came to blows in this very room over Richard marrying the other Neville girl. Remember that, Will?' Hastings nodded and Ned continued for my benefit. 'Tried to force her to take holy orders because he was damned if he'd share one inch of Warwick's lands with Richard. You call that broth-erly love, Jane?' He strode angrily to the fireplace and hurled the letter unread into the fire. 'And now my stubborn old mother has whistled me to Baynard's yet again. I'm the King of England, damn 'em! I've had enough.'

He obeyed his mother's summons, but her latest pleas for George's life fell like autumn leaves upon unfeeling flagstone and he returned to Westminster, stern and pale.

'Rather than keep your brother forever in the Tower, Ned, couldn't you compel him to become a Cistercian monk?' I suggested daringly that evening, as I rubbed a soothing, rosemary unguent across his brow. 'Hide him deep in some abbey on the Yorkshire moors. Surely your brother Richard would help you?'

From beside the fire where he was playing chess with Lord Howard, Hastings sent me a warning glance, which I ignored. Ned was not the only one who had endured a conversation with her grace of York.

'I'll bury him right enow.' Ned's jaw was clenched. 'He wants a crown, Jane. Well, he shall have a heavenly one. Do you hear me all of you?' he snarled, raising his voice. '*I will have no more traitors in this kingdom!*'

Two days after, on nineteenth of February, it was announced
that George had died. A private execution. 'Drowned in a butt of
malmsey', the Londoners jested. He was twenty-nine years old.
His coffin was taken to Tewkesbury Abbey for burial. I believe
there were few mourners. No one in his family spoke about it and
a pall of silence fell on the rest of us, but the tidings sent ripples of
shock throughout Christendom.

For a man to execute his own brother! Many Englishmen
said the Queen's family was responsible. Perhaps they were. Lord
Rivers took himself off on a pilgrimage to Compostela out of
gossip's slingshot so perhaps it was he who carried out Ned's
orders. I am sure some people blamed me.

I do know this: the ghosts who haunt the battlefields of Barnet
and Tewkesbury – those hundreds of fathers and sons – they'd be
still alive if it had not been for George's bitter envy. God forgive
him and may his restless spirit find peace at last.


After George was coffined and trundled off to Tewkesbury,
I found myself in a fierce quarrel with Ned.

The Queen wanted Mary, the young heiress of Lord Hunger-
ford, as bride for one of her kinsmen, but Hastings determined
to snare her lands for his son and heir. Without squaring matters
first with Ned, he secretly sent for papal permission and had the
children exchange betrothal vows.

'Why should Hastings not have an heiress for his son, Ned?'
I asked sweetly as we walked in the garden at Westminster.

'You should keep your cursed nose out of this, Jane,' Ned
growled, pulling his arm out of mine and kicking at the crinkled
leaves. 'I've just had the Queen ranting at me and I feel like
entering a poxy monastery. Anyway, I thought you did not believe
in childhood marriages.' He smacked his skull. 'Ah, thick of me

to forget, if it's Will Hastings, it's a different story. Just because he fished you out of your dull little pond, you don't owe him anything.'

'But you do,' I countered. 'With your grace's leave,' I curtsied and received a glare, 'I shall be pleased to receive your grace's company – when your royal temper has cooled.'

Yes, I was pushing my boat out into dangerous water again but I hazarded that Ned would come about. What I did not expect was a summons from Elizabeth Woodville.

I was escorted to her audience chamber where she was seated on her chair of estate beneath a scarlet canopy. She was flaunting her wealth. The cap below her stiff butterfly veil winked with precious stones. Pearls, each the size of a wren's egg, hung from the intricate golden collar about her throat. The latter showed her age. I had not really seen her close to since the death of her babe, George of Windsor. Her jowls were beginning to sag, her breasts had lost their fullness and from my position on the tiles, I could see her ankles were puffy.

Elizabeth liked to keep people on their knees when giving audience. Especially me. Her ladies were tittering already. They must have heard I was out of favour with Ned and vulnerable. However, it wasn't going to be a public lashing of words; Elizabeth gestured her attendants to withdraw to the back of the chamber and beckoned me to shuffle up the steps.

'Why have you interfered, Mistress Shore?' I presumed she meant in speaking up for Lord Hastings.

I stared up candidly into those hard, aquamarine eyes. 'I interfere in a lot of matters, gracious madame, but only where I find injustice or venality. I am sure your grace will agree that the King's justice should prevail at all times.'

'Ding-a-poxy-ding!' Her toe kicked my knee. 'Do your servants shine your halo every morning or does it have a perpetual lacquer?'

I persisted. 'If your highness would enlighten me, please?'

'You persuaded his grace the King to release Stillington from the Tower.'

Stillington? Surely she meant Dr Stacey and then I recalled recently receiving a letter from the imprisoned Bishop of Bath and Wells! Robert Stillington, that was his name. He had once been Chancellor of England but during the troubles with George, Ned had had him arrested. He had not been brought to trial on any charges.

'No, madame, I did not persuade the King to order his release,' I replied, showing polite surprise rather than remorse. 'The bishop wrote to me a few weeks ago enclosing a letter for the King's grace. I merely passed it on. I pass on many letters.'

'Mistress Shore.' Her impatience was scarcely reined in. 'You have displeased me greatly. You meddle in matters in which you have utter, utter ignorance. I have been very tolerant of his grace's affection for you, but in abetting Stillington, you have rendered yourself open to charges of high treason and, believe me, I shall not hesitate to have you dealt with, unless—'

'Madame, I've no—'

She slapped my face. 'Do-not-interrupt-me!'

The whispering at the back ceased. I sensed the gleeful voyeurs holding their breath.

Elizabeth's power over Ned was greater than mine, but a pox on that! Sincerity could be my buckler.

'Madame,' I protested, 'I do not comprehend what I have done to offend you.'

My bewilderment was honest and fortunately she believed me.

She leaned forward. 'Stillington is a poisonous mischief-maker.

He has spread foul lies about the King's birthright, and I have no doubt that he and George were behind the accusations of witchcraft brought against my mother a few years ago.'

My cheek was stinging and I could see her hand was still itching. I'm told that when you are in single combat, you watch your enemy's eyes so I did not abase my gaze but I managed an apology.

'I only passed the bishop's letter on, my lady. I did not read it or presume to speak on the man's behalf. I supposed him to be old and infirm so it seemed an act of mercy.'

She recoiled. 'Be damned to your acts of mercy, woman! Play angel to your little petitioners if it makes you feel holy but do-not-interfere-in-matters-of-state! I want your oath on this, Mistress Shore, or, as God's my witness, I'll bring you down!'

I left her presence, stunned and puzzled. A few days later Ned told me that ancient Stillington had been placed in the custody of the Bishop of Worcester, one of the Queen's affinity. He refused to tell me more but, by Heaven, if I had known then how much mischief that cursed old man would cause a few years later, I would have torn his letter in pieces and begged Ned to keep him in the Tower until he rotted.

I was not out of favour for long, but 1479 was a year when the pestilence took many lives including three of London's lord mayors. Seeing so many coffins carted through the streets frightened us all and there were few feasts and gatherings, but the following year, Ned's youngest sister, my lady Margaret, Dowager Duchess of Burgundy, arrived at Gravesend and came up the Thames by barge in much splendour. Even Richard of Gloucester broke off his campaign in Scotland to come down and see her for she was greatly beloved.

'Meg' was in England to gain Ned's help against King Louis. When she left London, she seemed happy with the agreements they had reached. Ned and the Queen rode with her to spend a few days on Rivers' manor at Ightham in Kent before farewelling her at Dover.

I was waiting desperately for Ned's return.

'There's something I have to tell you, my most gracious lord,' I exclaimed jubilantly. 'At last, I'm carrying a babe!'

You might have thought I had been invited into the Kingdom of Heaven by the Lord Christ himself, I was so ecstatic. It must have been when Ned snatched a wicked few moments with me that afternoon behind the large oak tree near Waltham Abbey. Strange that swift daylight intercourse might seed a baby when nights of languorous lovemaking in bygone years had proved fallow.

As soon as I began to feel the subtle changes in my body, I bade Ned be gentler in his thrusting.

'Pah, you have more love for this unknown brat than you do for me,' he grumbled.

'But, Ned, you know how much I've longed for a child and since this babe is half yours, you do not need to ram it in the head as if you are loading a cannon.'

I suppose he had sired many children, ten lawful – and goodness knows how many packsaddle babes – so one more meant little to him. Nevertheless, his ambivalence was hurtful and when my babe was five months grown within me, I decided to take no risks lest our coupling harm its anchorage. In May, when the court left for Windsor, I pleaded I was poorly and stayed back at Westminster.

A few weeks later I miscarried. A boy child. Losing the babe threatened my sanity. I was babbling that God was punishing me for my sins. Isabel sent for Mama and they persuaded me to go to Hinxworth, where the peace of the summer meadows might be balm to my troubled soul. And so I hid myself away to grieve.

Ned commanded me to Westminster in leaf fall. I made my preparations with apprehension, but the moment I passed through Bishopsgate, I rejoiced at the cluttered shop counters and the apprentices tugging at my stirrups. Hope rode pillion behind me; maybe I might bear another child before too long.

'Well, look who is back!' Dorset exclaimed as I quietly entered the inner sanctum beyond the Painted Chamber. He detached himself from his Uncle Edward's company and sauntered across to put his arm about my waist. 'You shouldn't have stayed away so long, my mistress,' he whispered. 'I fear me others have stolen your place. Isn't it time you and I kissed and made up?'

'Jane!' Ned came striding across and kissed me on the lips. 'Welcome back, my sweet.' He bade me stay for supper with him, but there was no lovemaking the instant we were alone together.

'Look at you,' he said fondly. 'Still my loyal, lovely Jane.' Then I was enfolded in his arms, my head snug against his breast. His breath was warm upon my hair. 'I am so sorry you lost our child, my darling. God willing we can make another.'

I doubted that. I rarely shared his bed. With me, he preferred to play cards, discuss the price of lambskins or his shipping ventures. Like Hastings, I was still one of the intimates who shared his supper parties, but I heard now that other – *younger* – women fed his lust. Women of doubtful provenance whom Dorset brought in for him. Flowers, picked young and wild, that only lasted a day.

I despised Dorset and the Woodville men more than ever. Whoresons! Fools! They were continually challenging Ned to prove his stamina – yes, until his true friend Hastings could bear it no more.

'It's as if Ned's trying to regain his lost youth,' he complained to me over hyppocras and wafers in his chambers. 'If he doesn't take heed, he'll end up with the pox and a rotting shaft. We need to keep him hale, Elizabeth. Imagine England without him!'

'He's trying to fight his age,' I said sadly. 'His physicians have convinced him that if he breathes the same air as those that are fresh and vital, it will invigorate him.'

'What nonsense! Intelligent company will do more for him than giggling numbskulls. I'm out of temper with him, truly. I'm getting too old to play watchdog.'

'No, you're not,' I said fondly. Since he had dismissed his servants so he might speak freely, I played the page and took the flagon across to refill his goblet. 'In fact, compared to Ned, my lord, you have hardly aged one bit.'

'Stop honey-tonguing me, wench. I'm getting thin up here.' He tapped the crown of his head. His silvery fringe hid some of the care lines in his brow but, yes, he was right.

'If you keep a hat on....' I teased.

'Fifty-two,' he groaned. 'Poxy Dorset would like to see me put out to grass.'

'I daresay 'Poxy Dorset' would like to see Ned put out to grass.' There, I had voiced my blasphemous thoughts and Hastings did not argue. Encouraged, I added, 'Don't you think it is time Prince Edward spent time with Ned and saw more of the world than Ludlow Castle? Forgive my frankness, my lord, but when the boy was here last summer, I could see how he had modelled himself too much upon Lord Rivers.'

Hastings pulled a face. 'All very well, Elizabeth, but the court is not a healthy place. What if the boy apes Dorset instead? At least at Ludlow, it's all books and learning.' He drew a deep breath. 'By Christ, I'd like to put my boot up Dorset's backside. If he calls me "Old Father Hastings" one more time...'

The Queen's kinsmen were trying afresh to disgrace Hastings with allegations that he was lining his own pockets in Calais and having secret truck with King Louis. They even buzzed it round the palace that we were once more lovers.

Every time I witnessed their foulness affecting Ned's thinking, I sought to deliver a draught of common sense. The King was no fool; he knew their mischief, but it sapped his energy when he should have had his mind on breaking Scotland and crashing through the sticky web that King Louis was spinning around him.

Indeed, it was the beginning of a cruel winter; the harvest had been the worst in years. As the trees became skeletons and the dank November weather seeped in at the cracks of the casements, I became concerned by the gradual changes I espied in Ned. He should have been preparing to join his army against King James in the coming spring, but there was an unhealthy lethargy slowly eating into his soul. He was no longer the energetic, carefree man with whom I had fallen in love.

He still could cut a splendid figure in his blue cloth of gold, with the order of the garter adorning his hose and the white rose diamond brooch upon his breast. Yet, when he wore his white damask furred with sable or his scarlet mantle with the purple lining, the colours aged him. Besides, there were other betrayals; his waist belt had only one hole left in the tongue, many of his rings were newly enlarged, dewlaps cowled his chin and there was a morose slump to his shoulders as though his great skeleton was weighed down by all that extra flesh.

I resolved that when the weather warmed, I would devise plentiful sports to tempt him into exercise. Perhaps he could invite the London aldermen to a hunt and feast at Waltham (the blessing of the oak tree might bring me a harvest) or ride again to Sandwich with Prince Edward to see his fleet of trading ships.

My other decision was to end the lease on the Aldersgate house and set up a household there with my servant, Young, in charge so I might increase my presence in the city. I also acquired more silkwomen and, like the wise bridesmaids in the parable, I increased my purchase of fine ornaments that might be sold easily if adversity struck.

At least Ned's health improved as the last snows melted, but then in May, when the petals of blackthorn were falling from the hedgerows, fifteen-year-old Princess Mary died and he grieved much for her.

Unwilling to give up his French pension, he stood guiltily aside while France made war on Burgundy. More and more he drank late o'night with Dorset, and in the mornings he would be like an ill-tempered bear snapping at the hounds that tried to rouse him. Rich foods no longer sat well in his belly, and sometimes during a banquet he would hasten to the latrines to be sick.

My temper finally boiled over. It happened one night after supper when Ned was clearly not feeling well. Myddelton was escorting me out through the servants' passageway when we encountered Dorset and Edward Woodville herding three young women towards the bath chamber door. The girls looked respectable. Clean enough, I suppose, but hardly more than fifteen or sixteen years old.

'You disgust me!' I snarled at Dorset and Woodville, blocking their way. 'You are ruining his highness's health and threatening the good of the kingdom.'

'Whoa,' sneered Dorset, swaggering in close and forcing me to one side the passage. 'If it isn't jealous Mistress Shore, *ageing* Mistress Shore!'

'If I am such a crone, why do you keep trying to bed me, Dorset? Go home, demoiselles!'

Of course, the wenches only tittered as Edward Woodville hurried them past. Myddelton – and I don't blame him – disappeared. Only over-confident addlepates like me dared run foul of the Queen's kinsmen.

'I despise you!' I snarled loudly at Dorset. 'You treat those girls like dumb beasts.'

'But they are strumpets, Mistress Shore, just strumpets.' Like you, his eyes told me.

'Then what does that make you, my lord?'

He struck me across the face for my insolence.

'Such a *gentleman*,' I sneered, raging that I had not the strength to ruin his grinning teeth. I must have raised my arm for suddenly a familiar voice said, 'If you must, Jane, don't draw your thumb in.'

'Ned! *Ned?*' I gasped in amazement. He had come round from the Painted Chamber with Myddelton.

'She's a damned fishwife,' complained Dorset, showing ruffled dignity.

'Never in my life have I hit a woman, Thomas,' said Ned in a dangerous voice. 'Apologise to her!'

'Apologise to an upstart mercer's spawn?' Despite his bluster, fear glittered in Dorset's eyes. Brandished before him was the calm, deadly will of a king who had never lost a battle.

'On one knee, sirrah. *Do it!*'

Slowly the Queen's son sulkily lowered himself to the floor. 'Your pardon, Mistress Shore.'

'Louder! As if you mean it.' Ned grabbed his hair and forced his head fiercely forwards. The marquis obeyed, grimacing in pain, and still the King did not let go. 'This *lady* has done more good than you will achieve in your entire, useless life and if I ever hear further report of you scorning her, I'll have you in the Tower faster than you can spit.'

'B-but you said you wanted girls.'

'No, lad, *you* said I wanted girls. I'm not in the humour tonight so take your arse hence. Jane, I still require your company! No argument, Dorset! Go and whine to your mother! Myddelton, find Lord Hastings and my lord of Ely. I am in the mood for *intelligent* discourse.'

When we reached his bedchamber, Ned almost collapsed in my arms and I bade his gentlemen help him to bed and bring hot bricks to ease his discomfort. By the time Hastings and Bishop Morton arrived, our king had fallen asleep.

# XII

Something dark was definitely cankering within Ned's belly. By day he put on a stoical face but by night he was almost crying with the pain.

'What is the matter with these physicians?' I exclaimed testily to Hastings later that week as I paced in frustration that I could do nothing to help the poor man.

Hastings shook his head wearily. 'Dr Fryse examined Ned's belly again this morning and he still thinks it might be an ulcer. He's given him more horehound and moneywort, and he's hoping whatever is at the root of this may heal itself. But if there is a clogging before the waste enters Ned's bowels, he may have to try a stronger purge – wormwood, bitter almonds and so forth. Hobbys is coming in to leech Ned this afternoon.'

Pah, this evil ailment was beyond a jar of leeches.

'God willing, it'll bring him ease.' I murmured. 'I've been trying to see a pattern. Eating briefly alleviates his discomfort but then the pain returns and only vomiting relieves it.'

Hastings sighed. 'It makes no sense to me either. Last night he left the board several times and came back and ate again.'

'If only he might eat in his chamber.'

'Appearances, Elizabeth. A king must show no weakness.'

'Why not?' I challenged. 'Oh, I suppose, the French might attack?'

He ignored my tantrum. 'Richard is coming down for Christmas. I'll ask him if he can take over some of the public duties so that Ned can have some rest.'

'Alleluia,' I muttered.

As if bodily pain were not sufficient, God had torment for Ned's mind as well. A week before Yuletide, Duchess Meg wrote to say France was forcing surrender upon Burgundy and the diplomats were already on the road to Arras to draw up a treaty. Worse, King Louis was demanding that the Burgundian heiress should wed his son the Dauphin and cede half her duchy to France as a dowry. The news shattered Ned. It meant that Princess Bess's betrothal to the Dauphin was finished and there was no need for King Louis to continue the fat pension to the English crown.

Ned was so angry with himself for doing nothing to save Burgundy that he barred his door and no one dared go near him. Next evening, however, Dorset and the Queen's brothers persuaded him that a good carousing might help him gain oblivion. If Hastings had known, he would have stopped them.

Before daylight next morning, Myddelton was banging on my door in King Street with a message from Hastings bidding me attend Ned straight away. I hastily pulled on some clothes, not bothering with a cap and veil.

'What's happened?' I asked Myddelton, hurrying to keep up with him as we crossed the frosty cobbles.

'I don't know, Mistress Shore, but the matter is urgent. Pray you, say nothing to the guards. My lord is trying to keep a lid on this.'

My imagination was crazed with possibilities as we ran up the stairs. The men guarding the royal apartments had orders to let us through. The Painted Chamber was deserted and ominously silent as we crossed to the other door.

Ned's room was strewn with bodies. For an instant I almost screamed and then I realised that three of them were snoring. Sir Edward Woodville lay belly up across the windowseat, Sir Richard Woodville decorated the daybed with a pisspot full of puke within hand's reach. Through the inner doorway I could see Dorset outrageously sprawled across Ned's bed, while my beloved lord lay like a beggar before the cold hearth. Beside him was an empty flagon rolled upon its side. Hastings was kneeling over him.

'O sweet Christ,' I exclaimed. 'Has he choked on his tongue?'

Hastings shook his head and snapped an order to Myddelton. 'Get back out and make sure no one comes in!' He looked up at me. 'I don't like this. He always holds his drink.'

'Ned, my love,' I whispered, falling to my knees. His face was cold beneath my fingertips so I grabbed his dressing robe and tucked it round him. 'Have you sent for his physicians?'

'Of course, and the Queen.' Ned's friend shook his head despairingly. 'Damn it, the Breton ambassadors are due this morning.'

'A murrain on them!' I muttered. 'Can you not say the King is indisposed?'

'He can't be.'

'For the love of Christ!' My temper was fraying. 'Give him some slack, my lord.'

'You don't understand, Elizabeth. He's England. If word he's failing—'

'Please!' I flung a hand up to silence him. 'Ned,' I whispered. 'Come, my love, wake up. *Ned!*'

My plea evoked a mumbled curse and my heart stopped lurching. Hastings whistled with relief and I realised just how much he had panicked. We all depended on Ned. He was the cornerstone.

'You are worried about Calais, aren't you?' I whispered to Hastings.

'I'm worried about every poxy thing. All that we've tried to do in Scotland. As for Brittany's peril, that's why they are here for his help. We need to— Oh, lad, we need you.' Like a desperate father, he pushed the hair back from Ned's forehead.

I glared at the soles of Dorset's feet. 'Tosspots!' I muttered. 'Have they no brains or do they pass one around between them?'

'Their brains are in their cocks. You know that.'

'Listen, voices!' I exclaimed, sitting back. 'The physicians are here, thank God!'

'Good, let's get him into his bed, if we can scrape that bastard off the coverlet.'

So it was that while Hastings had his hands full trying to haul an ill-tempered sot from the bed and I was kneeling on the floor with Ned cradled on my lap like a poor dead Christ, Richard of Gloucester forced his way in.

The last person we expected! Dusty-cheeked from the road, ebullient from his campaign against the Scots and clearly keen to spoon every detail into Ned, Gloucester halted in horror at the sight of his incoherent brother

'What in God's name goes on here?' The words hissed like water on red-hot irons.

'The King is ill, your grace.'

'Ill, woman?' His eagle eye took in the upturned goblets and his overturned in-laws. He dropped on one knee beside Ned and bent his head to smell his brother's breath. 'The King of England's stinking drunk.' He raised his head and looked daggers at Hastings and back at me. 'You bawd! You gormless, stupid bawd.'

I gasped, outraged by the calumny, but he was already on his feet yelling, 'How in Hell can you let him get like this, Will? Is this your loyalty, letting him run with swine and strumpets.'

For an instant, Hastings' mouth hung open in shock. 'No, Richard, it's not like that,' he began to splutter but the duke swung back on me.

'Get out of here, you cursed whore! I don't want to ever see your face again. Go!'

I scrambled to my feet, my trembling fingers clasped to my lips. Behind Gloucester's back, Hastings gestured me to quickly leave and I fled in anguish at the unfairness.

Have you ever tried to rid the ink from your fingers? How hard it is. If only I could have pumiced that foul impression from Duke Richard's mind.

For an hour I sat shivering before my fire. The sunne-in-splendour, warmth of my life and glorious light of my days, was dimming and I was already being cast into the darkness. Yet indignation can heat the body like a thousand torches. Summoning Isabel, I went to Mass at my brother's church where we lit candles for my beloved.

*England needs Ned*, I whispered to God as I knelt on those heedless flagstones, but was he listening? Had he already signed the next consignment for Hell?

*Item i: one king, adulterous and avaricious.*
*Item ii: a strumpet to follow.*

No, please God, no, no, no.

On my return from church, I found Myddelton in the kitchen warming his hands at the fire. His news cheered me; Richard had dealt with the Breton embassy and Ned was back in his wits and getting dressed. But then he gave me a sealed letter from Hastings. My lord advised me to lie low at my Aldersgate house until Richard returned to Yorkshire. I was displeased but what could I do? It would be a miserable, lonely Yuletide.

★

January was almost spent when Richard of Gloucester took his leave. The instant the duke's horse's tail disappeared through the clockgate, the King sent a servant hotfoot to fetch me back to Westminster.

I was so happy to feel the comfort of his arms and he held me so tenderly.

'I've missed you so much, dearest Ned. How are you, my love?'

He cocked his head and managed a rascally smile. His breath smelled clean but then I realised he had been chewing a clove to sweeten his breath.

'I am sorry, sweetheart. My brother was like a young dog yapping at me to rest. Easier to say yea and shut him up.'

I stood up on tiptoe and forgave him with kisses, but how I wished he had summoned me to the palace so I could show Gloucester my true livery of devotion.

'Your brother called me the foulest names, Ned. He blamed me for your drinking.'

His large hands curled delicately on either side of my face like soft, protective leaves. 'Hush, sweetheart, I told him it was not so.'

But yet my king had left me in brief widowhood at Aldersgate. Ah, I would not chide him. What was done was done. He needed cheerful company, not a watering pot, splashing over with self-pity.

'Your pallor is better, Ned. I warrant his grace's visit has done you good.'

He loosened his hold. 'Like a damned nursemaid. All possets, purges and hie to bed at owl's fart. Hell, even had Mother fussing and that's a bigger miracle than waking Lazarus.' He stood me away from him and thrust back his fur mantle. 'What do you think of my new doublet, mercer's daughter?'

Cornflower blue velvet furred with ermine. A kindly hue for him. Was I deluding myself he was getting better? The black he usually favoured would have made his poorly skin look stark and slack.

'I like it, Ned.'

Two rows of jaunty golden knopfs marched down his chest. Splashes of scarlet satin gleamed within hanging sleeves – sleeves bunched thickly at his shoulders to give him breadth. *To give him breadth?* My gaze crept to his belt. I had seen it before but never buckled in so much. 'Will persuaded me to order a new set of apparel,' he was saying. 'I can afford it, after all.'

'Yes, of course, you can,' I whispered and laying my cheek against his chest, I burrowed my arms around him beneath his mantle and for the first time, my fingertips met.


Throughout the following weeks, the court remained tight as a wary snail at Westminster. Ned gave few audiences and soon it became impossible to sheath the whispers that he was not in good health. Even the Queen bestirred herself. She did all within her power to heal him, ordering distilled waters, purges, infusions – borage, rose, thyme, valerian – to ease Ned's digestion. Slivers and morsels, mild and unspiced, adorned the royal platter. Alicorn horn and bezel stones, reliquaries containing saints' bones, all these she brought to his chamber. She conferred hourly with his apothecaries, physicians and chaplains, and I'm told the works of Galen lay open in her bedchamber.

But the pain increased. Little escaped Ned's bowels and there was scarcely room within his body for nourishment. He could only lie on his right side because of the pain and he would wake in the middle of the night, cradling his belly, and yell for his servants to bring him syrup of white poppy. Many a time during February and March, I would cross that freezing yard at the hour of ghosts.

His jester and I devised entertainments to distract him, dancers, players, tumblers, and oftentimes his children would come in with puppets and interludes. Little Prince Dickon was a merry prattler, but such children expect close listening and his father was too easily exhausted. By night, to shutter out the darkness and the agony, I told Ned stories of dragons and princes, tailors and millers' sons, or memories of happier times we had shared. As dawn brushed colour across the turrets of the city, he would fall asleep, but mostly he dozed shallowly and stirred unrefreshed, his eyes red-rimmed, with no peace for his bruised mind.

Across the Channel, King Louis was dying but no other news was good. In March we heard that my lord of Albany had made peace with King James so Gloucester's Scotland campaign had been for naught. England was bereft of friends and all the princely bridegrooms promised to the princesses had been just airy promises. Hindsight made me wonder if Ned's decisions that previous year had been made with the sickness already in him, rusting his judgment, and none of us aware.

'Those cursed foreigners all used me, Jane,' he complained, his tears almost unharnessed. 'I am become the laughing stock of Christendom, a toothless, clawless lion roaring at the wind.'

I dared not tell him the Londoners now spoke of him as 'Old Ned'.

'Nearly forty-one, Jane. Nearly forty-one, with a pain that WON'T GO AWAY.' In misery, he turned on his side and drove his fist into his pillow.

'Yes, it will, my dearest,' I lied for both of us, 'providing you take the medicines and behave yourself.'

'Where's the cursed sport in that?' Then suddenly he turned and his fingers fastened round my wrist with sudden urgency. 'Jane, Jane! Next fine day after Easter, we shall go fishing just like we did when we first met. I promised my girls I'd take them. Bess shall have a longer rod and Dickon may come if he promises to stopper his chatter.'

'Whoa, steady,' I exclaimed, glad to see him enlivened. 'Yes, we shall – if her grace agrees.'

'A pox on that, wench! Next fine day!'

Easter fell at the tail of March and Ned attended Mass in St Stephen's Chapel on Good Friday and Easter Sunday for his soul's good but at his body's peril. Past Fool's Day, the weather softened and a warmer breath stole over the land. Ned still pleaded to go fishing; he was obsessed with the notion. I prayed the Queen would put a dampener on such an outing. Amazingly, we held a little domestic council, she and I.

'Are the physicians wise in permitting this, your grace? April can be as moody as a pimpled youth.'

Elizabeth Woodville perused the sky. The scatters of clouds were idling. 'It would do him good, I think, Mistress Shore, for if we refuse, he'll be worse than a baited bear.' She snapped her fingers at one of her ladies. 'Fetch the children, and one of you, inform the Lord Chamberlain.'

'Shall you come with us, then, madame?'

The cherub bow lips almost smiled. 'Me, fish? My dear Mistress Shore, is the pope a woman?'

Never in the brief exchanges we had shared over the years was I permitted to feel at ease. This time she lowered her feline stare to my collar of pearls and sapphires. 'That is such a lovely piece. Did my husband give you that – or was it from Hastings?'

At a gilded hour that afternoon, when there was still good humour in the sun, the royal barge took us upriver. The princesses and little Prince Dickon were delighted to have their father's attention, and Ned laughed and teased them, hiding the pain. Watching, those who loved him could have wept.

As the shadows deepened and the breeze frisked up with a bite in its jaws, I pleaded with Ned to order the boats home. Stubborn man, he would not go back until one of us had hauled in a decent fish. Yes, he wrapped his thick mantle about him, but that was his only concession.

We delayed too long. The twilight turned chilly as a murderer's smile, and though Ned was furred thickly as a bear, he started to feel cold. By the time we arrived back in Westminster, he was shivery and the tips of his fingers were numb. The royal apothecary provided him with a yarrow infusion. We put his feet in hot water but it took a long time to have him warm again.

In the days that followed, he grew weaker, despite the fussing of his seven physicians. The death of his old treasurer, the Earl of Essex, rocked him further. My poor Ned, he had so much unfinished business. He realised he was the clay that held us together and tried to make things right. Although I was not there to witness it, for I could only flit in like a little bat when most of the world slept, I heard about the handshakes and fulsome promises of forgiveness made across his coverlet. And in my growing grief, I recognised my own fear. Once the masks were off, would the blades hiss out? I would have to find my way alone.

On Tuesday afternoon, Ned was given absolution, and Hastings sent across the yard for me. It irked me that I must be grateful for these precious moments but I was not the only one who had to lurk in the shadows. As I stood waiting for permission to enter the royal apartments, Myddelton shepherded a sombre youth and a maiden from the Painted Chamber. They looked in need of a kindly voice.

'Goodness me, I have not set eyes on you two before,' I said brightly, curious to their parentage for their resemblance to Princess Bess was at odds with their modest apparel.

The lad bowed. 'We are his grace's bastards, my lady. My name is Arthur and this is Grace.'

'Elizabeth Lucy's children,' explained Myddelton.

'Oh.' Words fled me, not because Mistress Lucy had been Ned's mistress before he wed – the embers of that affair were long cold – but that I should have no babe of his begetting. 'God keep you both,' I said huskily, and tried to put away self-pity. I hoped that Prince Edward was hastening from Ludlow and would arrive in time.

The guards let me in and I stood in the doorway, my optimism challenged like a tiny candle flame in winter's gust. Poor Ned was tucked into the great bed of state with a white cloth wound about his head and it was as though he already lay upon his bier in the abbey, for the window lights were shuttered against the outside day and two great stands of flickering candles stood either side the bed. Incense tapers sanctified the air and only the knavish smoke from a tumbled log on the hearth played heretic. The ceaseless whisper of prayers from two cowled friars was marred by the snores of my lord of Canterbury, slumped like a question mark on the only chair.

This inevitability of defeat was not my creed. I paused, arming myself once more with defiance. If Death stood in the corner, I would shake my fist at him.

Hastings rose from a stool by the bed and beckoned me across.

'Good morrow, lazybones,' I murmured cheerfully, leaning down to kiss Ned's moist brow. His eyes opened and a smile drifted like light brushwork across his pallid skin. I clasped his hand, trying not to cry at how weak his fingers were now. He tried to scuff my palm with his thumb as he always had but the effort was too costly.

'Jane, my…Jehane d'Arc.' I still winced when he called me that. 'I want your forgiveness, sweetheart.'

'For what, my dearest lord?'

His voice was the merest whisper, like the soft shiver of wind through pine boughs. 'The times I've played around.' A crinkly, sheepish smile.

'Of course, I absolve you a thousandfold, Ned.'

'But I hurt you, my Jane.' His hand reached out weakly towards my cheek and I stooped and carried his fingers to my cheek. 'What's to become of you, my little love?'

Oh, dear, foolish man to worry about me. 'Why, my liege,' I teased, 'I'll set up a stall in the seld for cakes and people will become so fat that they'll have to buy new girdles, too.'

Ned ignored my nonsense. He turned his face slowly to Hastings. 'Can she rely on you, Will? You'll see she wants for nothing?'

'I swear it, Ned.' Hastings crossed himself. 'To my dying day.'

'Good, that's good.'

'Ned, I—' I wanted to plead with him to fight on but I could see every painful breath was a battle he could lose at any moment. 'I...I love you, sluggabed.'

'Now...tell me a story, my Jane. As profane as you like.' His eyes slid wickedly across to the source of the gentle snores.

Fearful I would be shooed out, I looked up at Hastings but he nodded and withdrew into the shadows. The archbishop slumbered on.

'Harken, then, great King of England and Lord of Ireland, once there was a miller's daughter, slender as a willow sapling. Her eyes were the blue of a summer sky and her hair red as fox fur, and she could weave...' I watched Ned's eyelids grow heavy and his lips relax into a weary smile as he fell into slumber.

Once, I told myself silently, there had been a duke's son who became King of England and he was the handsomest youth in all of England...

And once there had been a mercer's daughter who loved him.

# Witch

# I

Ned died early next morning. Wednesday, the Feast day of St Mary of Cleopas. The tolling of St Stephen's bell woke me and my heart almost broke as I heard St Peter's Abbey join in the doleful clanging. Dong-dong-dong-dong-dong. Like drops of lifeblood splashing relentlessly into an ewer, one by one by one. Ned's pain was over. I should rejoice for him but to let go was so hard; to believe seemed so impossible.

The courtyard was raucous with shouts and the rattle of harness. I opened the window. Horses with rider leg shields attached to their saddles were being led in – post horses. Across by the mounting blocks, an impatient crowd of knights and esquires were yelling at the grooms to hurry. One after the other, the messengers spurred out through the archway, the stones thrown up by their horse's hooves already like earth on Ned's coffin. I envied Richard of Gloucester in Yorkshire. For a few more days, his brother would still be alive for him.

'Mistress.' I had not heard Isabel's knock. Kindly girl, she stood behind me with a cup of honeyed milk, teardrops on her cheeks. 'My Lord Chamberlain sent a page across. He says he will let you know when they have laid out his highness's body. I'm so sorry, Mistress.' The latch fell softly.

I leaned back against the wall with the beaker warming my palms, knowing that strangers' hands were eviscerating my lover's body as though he was a traitor, smoothing perfumed ointment over the skin that my fingertips knew so well, closing the eyes that had looked at me with so much love.

'Are you here watching us for a little space, Ned?' I whispered, blinking up through my tears at the pall of grey sky. 'Look, Heaven honours your passing, my darling. There is no "rising sunne" this morning.'

My brother William arrived. He said someone from the family should be with me. Cynic that I am, I believe he itched to ladle my soul back into the pail of righteousness. Nevertheless, I was glad of his consideration and compelled him to escort me across the yard. How amused Ned would be to see me linking arms with a priest. Except...

'Elizabeth?' Will sensed the sudden ebb of strength and shot out an arm to support my back. 'You do not have to do this now.'

'But I want you to meet him, Will,' I whispered. 'Maybe then you can tell Jack and Rob why I love...loved him so.'

Recognising me, the knights on vigil in St Stephen's Chapel permitted us the unique access to the King that had always been my privilege. Will accompanied me into the chancel, stunned that his sister should have precedence, but it only took the twitch of a hoary eyebrow from the kneeling Bishop of Ely to snuff out Will's confidence. I could feel his nervousness as we approached close to the bier.

Ned lay beneath a purple and gold cloth of estate before the altar with a crown on his head and scarlet shoes upon his feet. I stood in reverie touching the tapered leather of his shoes. Had it been permitted, I would have washed his feet with expensive perfume and dried them with my hair.

How hard to believe that his eyelids would never lift again, or the mouth I had so often kissed ease into a wicked smile. I bent to touch my lips to his forehead and froze, repelled by the waxy unguent. My brother, conscious of duty, was drawing me back to kneel, and yet I was trying to recall the fresh, clean scent that always thrilled my senses. Already the remembrance was elusive and I felt a surge of panic. I knelt. Frantically, I grasped for a lifeline of ancient prayer to speed Ned's soul and haul myself back to sanity.

Before long, my brother tugged at my sleeve. Discomforted by so many mitres, embarrassed that his sister was the harlot in this Gethsemane, he was impatient to be done. I let him steer me away. I no longer belonged here either; I would spend my night vigil alone and light my candles for Ned in my own darkness.

'Mistress Shore!'

I turned, in surprise. John Morton, the corpulent Bishop of Ely, had followed us out. He beckoned us aside. My brother would have kissed the episcopal ring but Ely kept his gloved hands clasped and unavailable.

'My dear child,' he said to me. 'I wanted to tell you that a few days ago King Edward, God keep his soul, remarked to me, "You know, John, many women I have had, but her I loved." He was talking about you, my daughter. Press those words in the book of your heart, and take them out in the winter of your years, eh? No, don't thank me.' He drew a blessing. 'Go with God, "Jane" Shore.' He waddled back into the chapel leaving Will open-mouthed and me so utterly grateful.

'That was so kindly of him to tell me that.'

My brother's indignation surfaced in an instant. 'Kindly, sister? Condoning your sin when he should be encouraging repentance. Oh, I know his sort, using Holy Church as the stairs to temporal power.'

'I think you are angry because he ignored you, Will. He deliberately tries to disconcert people but he has a delicious ironic humor and once you know him, he's good to banter with.'

'*Banter with?*' Fraternal disapproval; a shove of hands deeper into the sleeves of his robe.

'It would be heartening, Will, if at least one of my brothers acknowledged that I was more than a courtesan.'

'I am here, am I not?' But he clearly resented my credibility – I was just a family mess, ripe for a spring clean.

We might have continued in sulky silence except a familiar figure met us on the stairs – Edmund Shaa in his lord mayor's robes, leading a group of solemn aldermen.

'William, Elizabeth.' He left his companions, heedless that speaking to me might cause him scandal. 'This is a sad business, my dear,' he said, after offering me his condolences. 'And the new king only twelve years old. Who is to rule us?' He looked round at the trickle of bareheaded nobles and churchmen going up to pay their respects and lowered his voice. 'If you hear anything of note, Elizabeth, pass it on, my dear. These are difficult times and to be forewarned is to be forearmed. Remember, eh?' Then he nodded to my magpie brother. 'Take her home, Will lad, and get a pot of mulled ale into her. She's looking as white as a miller's apron.'

Endure a closeting with Will and a sawdust sermon on mending my ways? The last thing I needed, but since he seemed burrlike in his attention, I led him down towards St Peter's Monastery. I needed activity for my restless, grieving spirit. Besides, this was the beginning of farewell to Westminster; I should never stroll these paths again.

As we picked our way west along the muddy path that skirted the wall of the abbey garden, Will delivered his usual dose of comfort for the freshly bereaved. I did not listen.

We reached the little river that separated Westminster from the marshes of Millbank, and followed it southwards. A hopeful navy of mallard ducks kept us company, furrowing the water, desirous of their daily bread, but today my hands and heart were empty. A spatter of rain drove us to shelter beneath the willows where the tributary mingled its life with the Thames.

'Wasn't it generous of Mayor Shaa to stay and speak with us?' I muttered, trying to stopper Will's sermon.

'I confess myself astounded that the Lord Mayor of London should ask for *your* help, Lizbeth.'

'Don't be.' I walked back out into the rain and said over my shoulder. 'You know very well that plenty of people have come to my door these last few years and some of them are merchants like our father.'

He gave me a sharp look. 'Next you'll tell me you were responsible for sending archers to Brittany.'

'Oh, was it that obvious?' But seeing him so gullible, I protested, 'No, Will, I am jesting But I do admit that at times Ned did consider my couns...' My breath faltered as reality slapped me around the face like a tormentor. I felt fragile again.

Will's tilt of nose told me my reign was over and I should seek redemption. He scrambled back onto the path and hastened after me. 'I tell you this. I'd not wish myself in Edmund Shaa's shoes, wagering on to whom to bend the knee. Stay away, that's my advice.'

Stay away?

We walked in silence past the Exchequer. Candles glowed behind the diamond panes. 'Gentleman Usher No 5,' I murmured sadly. Will was right that I must put the past behind me. I tried to swallow, to keep hold, but then I came utterly unravelled, for there was tethered Ned's barge, empty of laughter, its lanterns staunched.

'We w-went fishing just last week, Will,' I whispered, struggling not to weep. 'Th-there was no g-gainsaying him.'

I expected censure but Will surprised me. 'Aye, the dying often
have these sudden whims. Last week I was confessing a sick man
and all he kept asking for was a beef pie from the *Dagger*. He
scarce had one bite but was dead two hours later.'

My brother came back with me to my house in Westminster
and stayed until almost curfew, talking about family matters. As
he was about to take his leave, there was a knocking below and
Isabel brought a cloaked man up to the solar.

'Elizabeth! I—' Hastings stopped short at seeing a priest with me.
As for me, I stared at him in astonishment that he had come there at
such a time. How desperate he looked, how sorrowful and stricken.
Grey stubble covered loose flesh. He had lost substance these last
weeks, forgetting meals in his losing battle to save his friend.

'B-Brother,' I said nervously, setting my hand on Will's sleeve,
'this is Lord Hastings. My lord, may I present my youngest brother,
William Lambard, Parson of St Leonards, Aldersgate.'

My brother stared from our visitor's distraught face to mine
and his body went rigid. 'I'll take my leave then,' he said coldly.
'My lord, sister.'

'I'll see you out.' I grabbed his arm on the stairs. 'It isn't what
you think, brother.'

But the look on his face was like a stern archbishop condemning a self-confessed heretic.

'Isn't it?'


'Christ's mercy, I had to get away, Elizabeth.' Hastings collapsed
on the settle before my fire and buried his head in his hands. 'I
can't believe it yet. It should have been me for the coffin not him,
not him. O Jesu, a man could not want for a greater friend.'

'Easy, my lord. Here!' I fastened his hands around a jack of mulled ale and knelt at his knee. He reached out a hand to my face.

'Damn fool I am disturbing you. I wanted to be with someone who loved him as much as I did.'

Poor Hastings. I scrambled up and wrapped comforting arms about him as Isabel had done with me that morning.

'Do not hold back your tears,' I whispered. 'There is no unmanliness in grief.'

I guessed all day he had gone about his duties, stern as a stone saint above a cathedral door, while the man inside him was howling to unleash his anger and sorrow. Now the façade crumbled and the trickle of tears became a torrent, tumbling down over his cheekbones and splashing into the blackness of his mourning.

When at last he straightened, knuckling the moisture from his upper lip, I summoned Isabel to bring us some refreshment. 'Have you eaten anything today, my lord?' I chided and he shook his head.

'No, Mama,' he mocked and blew his nose heartily.

'That's better.' I refilled the jacks. He was not looking so ashen now although his hand trembled as he drank. When he seemed calmer, I said: 'Tell me, my lord, how is the Queen bearing up?' My lover's wife deserved some charity on my part.

'Her?' He almost spat. 'The bitch! She was in last night with Bishop Rotherham haranguing poor Ned to sign a new will giving the kingdom to her charge.'

'And did he sign?' I asked in alarm.

'Thank the Saints, no. I sent Canterbury and Ely in to stop her mischief.' I watched his fingers rub anxiously across his forehead and I marvelled anew at how great a burden he carried on his shoulders. Loyal to Ned, even after death.

'I think it great pity that she did not summon the Prince of Wales to be at his father's bedside,' I said.

To my surprise, Hastings reared like a poked snake. 'God's mercy, Elizabeth, don't be so womanish. Do you not understand? That was my doing. I stopped her.'

'Your doing? But why, my lord? Surely both of them deserved that moment?'

He set his cup down. 'You think it reprehensible, but if the Prince were already here, we should have a coronation by tomorrow and the Woodvilles would be all over the kingdom like a plague of locusts.' I must have looked at him in utter confusion for he added, 'It's simple, my dear, if he is crowned before Richard arrives to take charge, the boy will have the authority to make his mother Regent of England.' I had not understood that the crowning was so crucial.

'And you know what that arse Dorset said to me an hour since, Elizabeth? "Things are going to change round here, Father Hastings. I'd make haste back to Ashby if I were you." Christ forgive me! I had to come away before I stuck a dagger in the sot. They want my head, Elizabeth.'

He was overwrought. I doubted even the Queen would go that far. Kick him out of office, perhaps, and appoint Rivers as King's Chamberlain and Lieutenant of Calais; yes, that could happen. Ned had foreseen there would be fur flying and claws out.

'I thought you all swore peace and brotherhood across Ned's coverlet, my lord.'

'Pah, with our fingers crossed behind our backs. We only did it to please him.' He flung himself from the settle and paced, clutching his temples as though he wanted to wrench out his mind. 'O Jesu, what a mess! What a damned cursed mess! Why did he have to die, Elizabeth? Why now? After all those battles and ne'r a scar! Why now, before his sons are grown?' He kicked the footstool over in his rage and stood before the hearth, his back heaving. 'You were right. Ned should have spent more time with the boy instead of packing him off to Ludlow. What does Rivers know about training a king?'

'You will have the chance, I'm sure.'

'I damned well trust so.' His breath grew more even. 'Well, I've written privily to Richard and Harry Buckingham, warning them they'll need to hurry to intercept the Prince on his way to London. It's the only way to rein in the Queen.'

'You've *already* declared sides?' I would have kept the playing cards close to my chest.

'What is the plaguey alternative, Elizabeth? Dorset lording it as High Constable of England? I'm not swallowing that. Over my dead body!'

Isabel's knock forced him into the semblance of calm. I opened the door for her and when she had set out the platters, I bade her fetch the valerian posset that she had infused to help me sleep.

'Let me stay here tonight,' Hastings pleaded.

Heavens, no, I thought. Gossip could have the Lord Chamberlain and Mistress Shore fornicating on King Edward's shroud soon as blink an eye. How Gloucester would love that.

'I thought you would be keeping vigil at Ned's bier tonight?' I prompted gently, rising to my feet.

Anguished blue eyes stared up at me. 'All night, too? I can't, Elizabeth. I'll not get through my duties tomorrow unless I get a few hours respite. My head feels like it's been scoured out. Anyway, I'm not needed. Stanley's in charge until daylight. I beg you let me stay just a few hours. I tried to snatch a few winks at the palace but every instant some jack comes knocking: "What about the mourning liveries, my lord?", "What about this?", "What about that?" Ask the damned queen!'

He was so wretched. How could I refuse? I shared the valerian with him, built up the fire and fetched down bed linen to make the daybed comfortable. I bade Isabel neither to clear away the platters nor disturb him in any way and then I went to bed.

The night was cold. I kept thinking of Ned's body lying in the chapel and his soldiers keeping watch at each corner, their heads bowed, their fists upon their down-turned swords. So much I thought upon the past, the happy times, and I wept, my fist in my mouth, for a king taken too soon, too soon.

And then I heard the sound of a man sobbing. The parlour was below my bedchamber and I defy anyone to say they could cover their ears to another's misery. Compassion, an unfulfilled motherly response, call it what you will, compelled me to pull on my wrap and go downstairs.

Gently I lifted the latch. The dying fire showed me the white of his sleeve, the glint of silver hair as he lay face down between the cushions, his body shuddering.

'My lord,' I whispered, kneeling to lightly touch his shoulder. 'Is there aught I may bring you? More valerian?'

He shook his head, gulping too much to find a voice. Oh, he needed so desperately to sleep and Sleep, elusive creature that she is, was being cruelly fickle.

I drew the blankets up and tucked them about him. I would have left him but he caught my arm. 'S-Stay a little.'

'Only if you promise to go to sleep now,' I whispered. I stroked his back like I might sooth a child frightened by evil dreams. In a soft, languorous voice I began to tell a story and slowly, slowly, the judder of his shoulders gave way to a peaceful rise and fall. Weariness had at last closed the shutters of his mind but I was left remembering the other unfinished tale told to a dying king and I could not hold back my grief. I tried not to make a sound but Hastings stirred.

'My poor Elizabeth!' His fingertips traced my tears and then he clasped my hand. 'God's mercy, woman, you're frozen.' He lifted the blanket, gathered me up against him and I wept, grateful for care. I became drowsy, reluctant to seek out my cold bed. The wool hose he wore was warm against the back of my knees and his breathing had become soft and regular. There was no sin, no desire. He snuggled against me like he would his wife so I did not leave but fell into a deep, warm slumber.

Later, it was a different matter. His right hand began to stroke across my belly. Drowsy, I thought it was Ned who lay beside me and then I remembered. God pardon my sin, but Hastings' hand awoke my body's desire. It was half a year since I had shared the royal bed and in the last seven years I had been faithful. No man but Ned had lain with me.

Truly, there was no disrespect to Ned's spirit intended. In our desperate, rapid lovemaking, there was healing for us both. Afterwards, I returned to my bedchamber guilty but consoled. I did not regret what happened but it would not occur again.

I dressed before daylight and went down to wake Hastings because he would need to steal back to the palace lest the scandal harm us both. Since my servants were still abed in the attic, I played my lord's attendant, carried up an ewer of hot water and offered to barber him.

Clean-shaven and smelling of Castilian soap, Hastings almost looked his old self. Sleep, and perhaps our coupling, had relit the lantern of his soul, for there was a vigour in his step.

'You should be canonised, Elizabeth dear,' he whispered, grabbing up his cloak from the settle. 'Hapless petitioners and sad chamberlains.' However, during the lathering, he had apparently acquired a conscience, for he added, 'I ask your pardon for what happened between us.' His blue eyes beseeched me for absolution.

'Call it mutual consolation.' In wifely fashion, I tidied his cloak across his breast making sure his collar of office was concealed. 'Now take care no one recognises you.'

He stilled my hands. 'Do you want me to send for your brother and assure him that—'

'I'm not a cut loaf?' I sighed. 'Ha! Whitewashing my brothers' opinions of me will take until Doomsday not to mention all the mops and pails in England.' I would not admit how much the disgust in Will's face had scalded me.

'But if I had not come here. What about your servants? Can they be trusted?'

'Enough, Lord Chamberlain! Go and arrange a coronation!' I chided amicably, passing him his hat and gloves.

He tucked them beneath his arm and kissed my cheek. 'Thank you for your charity.' But still he lingered, drawing on his gloves, his lips tightening as though he had some unpleasant confidence. 'Listen, I wish with all my heart you could come with us when we take Ned's body to Windsor, Elizabeth, but it's not...You understand?'

'I understand.' I expected no concessions. It still hurt to be the friend who would not be there. 'When is it to be? You haven't told me.' I suppose neither of us wanted to think about the finality.

'I cry you pardon. Ten days, I believe.' He put his fingers to the bridge of his nose, needing to calculate. 'Yes, just short of St George's Day.' It was hard for him to go on but he managed. 'A... week in St Stephen's, across to the Abbey and then from Charing to Syon, thence to Eton and finally, St Geor—' He swallowed, trying to regain his voice. 'I-I have to break my wand of office and throw it in his grave.'

'O Sweet Christ!' I remembered the three of us standing in the chancel and how I had hated the talk of monuments. 'Well, do not run yourself ragged,' I whispered, and shook him in wifely fashion. 'A pity Gloucester cannot be shouldering some of this.'

'He'll come south as soon as he can.' He kissed me on the cheek before he pulled his hood up over his hat to hide his face. 'I'll be

like a horse on a treadmill until the funeral's over, Elizabeth, but
if you need my help before I leave, send your man across. After all,
I promised Ned I'd care for you.'

Care is an ambiguous word and the slight flare in his gaze as he
said it mightily perturbed me. Would this 'good lordship' come
with obligations? Had he and Ned privily arranged my future like
some chattel to be handed down?

*Item i: I bequeath to my beloved friend my second best bed and also
one mistress with hangings attached.*

But maybe I was wrong.

'Thank you, my lord.' I curtsied, grateful to hide my face.
'Pray you, wait an instant.' I hastened up to my bedchamber and
from my coffer I took out the white rose from Ned that I had
pressed so long ago. For a moment, I hesitated, longing to keep
it as a remembrance, yet how else to show the world that a king's
mistress had a wand of office too. The right to grieve, the choice
to love, even if I was a woman. 'Please, will you cast this in Ned's
grave for me?'

And I laid the flower across his outstretched palm.

Call it common sense; by the time I had breakfasted, I'd reached
the decision to be quit of Westminster. I went outside, found
myself a splash of sunlight and sat down with my writing board.
My reasoning went like this:

i.   *I may be a whore but not by nature despite what my brothers think.*
ii.  *I should not have behaved like an alley cat even with grief as my
excuse.*
iii. *I shall not let the Queen or Gloucester rearrange my life.*

iv.   *I shall move out of here before one of them uses a broom on me.*
v.    *If H starts thinking like a reckless dotard and wants to bed me,*
*the scandal can be used against him by his enemies.*
vi.   *I am not going to let that happen. (I underlined 'not' thrice)*
vii.  *I am free to make my own decisions.*
viii. *I have resources and do not need a man to protect me.*
ix.   *I cannot be sure of that unless I try to stand on my own feet.*
x.    *God willing!*

So there it was, I was going to remove temptation from the palace doorstep and hasten to my house in Aldersgate.

And speaking of doorsteps: by ten o'clock, mine was a-buzz with blowflies – victuallers, who had smelled my demise, and wanted their bills paid lest I disappear into a purgatory reserved for royal mistresses. One had the gall to say I might pay by spreading my legs. Lubbe was hot to let the fellow's teeth become acquainted with his spine, but I wanted no bloody fracas. I was about to summon help from the palace guardroom when a larger pest dispersed them.

Dorset. No shutting the door in his face so Isabel showed him in. He sprawled, all sable and gilt, on the settle where Hastings had sat so bowed with misery.

'So, Mistress Shore, what's to become of you?'

I was careful to stand on the other side of the hearth. 'I trot into pasture like an old ambler?'

'Not thinking of a new saddlecloth, then?' A leery look, unsuppressed by sorrow, crawled over my body.

'No, my lord. And, to be honest, I find this conversation hurtful considering the man I love lies scarce cold across the yard.' I hope Dorset did not know about last night's visitor. Thank Heaven I had cleared the daybed.

He stood up and swaggered across. 'Oh come on, chickie, use your head.'

Count to ten before I knee him? 'My head, Marquis? I thought that was the last thing you were interested in.'

He had a crooked smile. 'Still playing me like a ruddy perch, eh? Just like you did the King, but a man can grow tired of waiting.' He ran a finger down my bosom. 'When I come back from the funeral, I want you in my bed begging for it. Understand?' He bent his head to kiss me. I let him but I did not kiss him back. He made a meal of trying to make me.

'Begging, Elizabeth,' he murmured, with a lift of lip. 'Naked and begging.'

Bastard! I was shaking. Shaking with fury, hurt, fear. I don't know how long I sat with my head in my hands before I made shift and went downstairs to tell Isabel and Lubbe to start packing. Then, trying to disregard the trembling of my fingers and another rush of grieving, I went to my bedchamber, unlocked the lodging inventory from my strongbox and carried it down to the solar. Unlike my Father's strumpet, I would take nothing that was not mine; I might be an adulteress but I was not a thief.

'Mistress.' Isabel stood in the doorway, fiddling with the hem of her waistcloth; usually a sign of courteous disagreement. 'I think you are doing a wise thing in leaving here.' She was bursting to say more so I set aside the papers.

'When I was over at the palace conduit this morning, there were two lads from Lord Hastings' employ, fellows I often have a mite o' gossip with, and they were a-saying that if the Queen becomes Keeper of the Realm, my lord has a ship standing by to take him and his men to Calais quick as a sneeze, and he'll hole up there. I thought as how I'd better tell you in case his lordship has been forgetful in saying aught.' She watched me squish my mouth sideways. 'So keep a-packing, shall I?'

'Yes, Isabel,' I answered grimly. 'Time to duck and make for the undergrowth.'

Oh, why did her news catch me on the raw? I was not some unjarred leech that needed to crawl from one man to the next, yet now I felt panic grab my innards, as though I was in open country, defenceless against attack. Would Hastings leave me with the kestrels circling?

All morning my little household laboured. Once the panniers were queuing in the hallway and the crammed wooden chest in my bedchamber stood ready for hauling on the morrow, I cajoled Master Beaupie from his perch at the Exchequer, and together we went through the inventorium so he might bear witness to my honesty. He paid me my allowance to the end of April and our business was done. Just one more night beneath the eaves of Westminster.

Heavy hearted, I walked round to farewell my little white mare, Bathsheba. She wickered as though she understood, gazing at me beneath her long lashes, but our discourse was interrupted by Princess Bess. She had just come back from riding.

'Jane? Is that you?' One of her plaits was out of its pins – a golden rope against her blue-black skirt. The cold wind had rosied her cheeks but her eyelids betrayed the scarlet of weeping. I hoped hard riding had given her comfort.

Shining up a smile so like her father's, she strode across to embrace me.

'I am making my farewells,' I explained sadly. Bathsheba blew a warm huff into the hollow between my neck and shoulder and nudged me for a precious withered apple.

'Really? I can ask my mother if you may still ride her.'

I shook my head. 'That's generous of you, your highness, but I need to set the past behind me.'

'Oh lordy, you're not going to do something rash and take the veil, are you? You are still prodigiously lovely, you know. Just seeing you makes me feel like a carthorse.'

'Nonsense.' I took her hands. We looked at each other in mutual sadness. 'Your father was so proud of you, dear Bess. It's a pity you cannot wear the crown. What is wrong with this ill-fangled world?'

Merriment crept into her eyes. 'Delicious treason, Jane. I'd make you my Lady Chamberlain. Oh, pest, I'd better go. I'm supposed to be fitted for my gowns. Blue velvet for the ride from the Tower and crimson for the coronation. Curse it, I'm crying again.' Knuckling her eyes, she turned away. 'Must go, Jane. Pray do not forget me.'


Have you woken to the sinister rustlings of human vermin? Fear of evil freezes you; your breath halts, every sense strains to discover truth amongst the overspill of dreams. I heard Isabel's stifled shriek, her limbs thrashing on the truckle bed and the cruel thwack of knuckles on flesh. My own scream jammed in my throat. I reached for my candlestick as a weapon but the cursed thing crashed down. A calloused palm sealed my mouth. I struggled to poke my fingers up my assailant's nostrils but he was more ox than human, and the press of sharp steel above my Adam's apple settled the quarrel.

A flagon fell near the other man's foot. 'Fuck it!'

Moonlight through the shutters betrayed my housewife's chatelaine lying on the oak chest. The whoreson espied my jewel coffer too and I cursed that I had already taken it from its hiding place. He bagged the gems that Ned had given me: the sapphire and pearl collar; the emerald clasp, all my ear droplets, Hastings' golden leaf necklace and every brooch save the amethyst still pinned to my yesterday gown. But not all; I managed to slide off the rings I was wearing and edge them beneath the coverlet.

Before the rogues left, they gagged and bound me to the bedpost.

'There, cunny,' the ox whispered and his fingers goosed me in farewell.

Not knowing if poor Isabel's neck was snapped, I worked at my bonds like a starving rat but God was merciful and my servant and friend recovered her wits, albeit with a goose-size egg bump. She freed me and downstairs we discovered poor Lubbe trussed on the cellar floor with rags bound into his mouth. A swift lantern survey around the house argued naught but my jewels had been stolen. Had Fortune seized a whip to force me to my knees? Foul, foul April!

With the slow dawn came enlightenment and Isabel's squeal of discovery from upstairs. 'See what I've found, Mistress! I must have knocked it from the fellow's hat before he hit me.'

I took the pewter badge from her. A pitcher and a magpie? The crow of Aesop's fables?

Before I reported the robbery to the sergeants-at-arms, I sought out the old groom who had taught me to ride and asked whether he recognised the badge. He did.

'Aye, some of her grace's retainers still use these. God's wounds, mistress! Do you need to sit down?' He steadied me.

The Queen's vengeance? I could go storming to her apartments. Is that what she wanted? There was a scaffold's width betwixt common sense and that folly. Better to load up the cart and gee up.

I returned across the Palace yard and, avoiding the creditors, went in through the back lane. Young must have arrived to help because my cart from Aldersgate was drawn up in the yard. All my servants were gathered in the kitchen. Isabel was sobbing in

Roger Young's arms, but they pulled apart as I stepped in. He was looking vexed.

'Don't tell me there's trouble at Aldersgate, too,' I exclaimed.

Lubbe swallowed his mouthful of food and jabbed a finger towards Young whose face had gone brick red.

'How about we start loading up?' I suggested, and when the others had gone about their business, I turned to Young and Isabel. 'What's the matter?'

'I'll fist the curs who did this to Belle,' he said savagely. 'An' I'm glad you're movin' to Aldersgate, mistress. I'll guard you both, never fear. But this business has brought things to a head.'

'Things?'

'I've asked Belle to wed me, mistress, an' I know I should've asked you first but seein' her hurt an' all, I've blurted it out. An' I'm resolved on it, mistress, truly. But she ain't said yes yet.'

Isabel was still dabbing her eyes on her waistcloth. 'Cos it's yes, you dafty, so long as it pleases you, Mistress Elizabeth?'

I hugged her. 'At least some good has come of this, Belle. Roger, I couldn't be more pleased. I'll ask my brother to call the banns.'

So the thieves provoked happiness as well as sorrow, and I tried not to feel bitterness against the Queen. Bitterness eats you like a maggot, beginning at your heart. That night as I knelt on my prie-dieu, I prayed for Ned's soul and I called to Heaven for justice and, as it happened, God had a case to bring as well.

# II

Despite the stink of the city, it was reassuring to step out my door into the city streets. It gave me a sense of anonymity – albeit false. Any dimwit could discover where 'Old Ned's Whore' was dwelling and I am sure my neighbours gaped behind their shutters when foreigners like Caniziani and the Spanish ambassador, Sasiola, called to present their condolences.

God be my witness, I offered these gentlemen no more than meat and drink but I was glad of their company during the week of Ned's funeral. The aliens and the unacceptable; we lepers had to close ranks. My friends were nervous. Whenever London grew uneasy, it took its temper out on the foreign traders' houses and the city was edgy, no mistake.

Strangers were pouring in for the coronation: barons and bishops, hoping for high office; merchants with strings of pack-ponies staggering after them; country jezebels who could be taken against any wall cheaper than pudding-ale; and, of course, the human rats, those who liked slitting throats and cutting purses.

Isabel cursed at the time it took her to stumble back the short distance with her water pails. I found Cheapside impossible – cobbles clogged with dung; wheels, hooves; strangers' boots that stamped and stomped, missing my toes by a hair's breath; horsemen's spurs that almost ripped my skirts; St Anthony's pigs squealing, let alone the touting and shouting, the spit, the curses and the piss. I found myself longing for the decorum bestowed by a king's close presence – the clean-swept cobbles of King Street and the orderly calm of Old Palace Yard.

But there was more than a greed for profit rattling the newcomers. Every hostelry clanged with knights and men-at-arms ready to clap their hands to their sword handles. From their surcotes and badges I knew some to be Hastings' retainers from the Midlands; others were the Queen's men from Northamptonshire and the southern shires. I felt truly sorry for Ned's son.

I had my own little struggles. The creditors found me again, one fellow claiming that King Edward had never paid him for my emerald clasp. Knowing Ned, that might be true, but the gem was among the stolen jewels.

'Go to the Exchequer then for payment, sirrah,' I told him, but he made a great to-do, yelling abuse at me until Young heard the furore and sent him on his way.

None of the petitioners I had helped came near me. People have convenient memories.

The Sunday after I had moved back, I encountered the Paddesleys on their way from Mass and they both looked pointedly the other way, noses uptilted, as though they had found something of uncommon interest alighting on the chimneypots.

The court returned the day after St George's Day and I dreaded a rapping on the door from Dorset's scoundrels, but mercifully the marquis was preoccupied with survival. However, a terse letter arrived from Hastings asking me why I had quit King Street without his leave?

When a man is put out, believe me, there are no grades of offence. Did I not realise it was inconvenient (to him, of course)? I replied that I should be pleased to call at Beaumont's Inn when he was less occupied and so forth. The 'so forth' part was phrased gracefully so as not to give offence. You cannot tell a lord that he needs to think with his brains not his lower organ. Dorset, I understood from Sir Edward Brampton, had finally discovered the difference.

It was Geoffrey Sasiola who kept me informed. He spent his time about the palace like a beekeeper waiting for the hive to swarm. From him, I learned that Hastings had stout allies on the royal council – Ned's former steward, Lord Stanley, and the Bishop of Ely. But the Queen had plenty of dogs to bark for her and Dorset was showing a lot of verbal muscle, especially as to whether the coronation should go ahead if Gloucester failed to arrive in time.

Sir Edward Brampton admitted to me he was impressed by Dorset's politicking.

'Bastardo! You know what 'e said to Lord 'astings theez morning, Elizabetta?' Brampton mimicked the marquis, one hand on his thighbone. '"By Heaven, are we royal councillors or mere ciphers for my lord of Gloucester? Well, I tell you this, my lords, we are important enough to make and enforce decisions without the king's uncle."'

Without Gloucester? It did not bode well.

Two days after the Feast of St Mark, I wakened to the sound of marching feet and watched from my window as the long caterpillar of the Queen's retainers passed, heading for the northern gate, proudly carrying Ned's pennons to his son. I hoped it was Dorset going forth, but it was his younger brother, Sir Richard Grey, who rode beneath the St George's cross. Later that morning, the criers were ringing their bells; the coronation day had been proclaimed. A week hence.

So soon? I just prayed that Hastings could keep his balance and protect me from Dorset's lascivious fingers. High time I called at Beaumont's Inn, and, by Jesu, I almost ran there! For just as I had been taking down my cloak from the peg, a letter arrived from Dorset summoning me to his presence that night. Oh, I would have scratched my face raw rather than play the naked games that he enjoyed.

What is wrong with the world that a woman cannot keep her independence but must be badgered? In such a mind I hastened off to Thames Street.

I had not bargained to find Beaumont's Inn a garrison. Men-at-arms were practising single combat in the courtyard and an assemblage of knights, esquires and dogs – most of Ned's former household – were noisily encouraging them.

'By Heaven, sirrah, this looks more like Westminster Palace,' I muttered to the porter, wondering if I could slink into the house unnoticed. Fine chance! I had a whole pack of gentlemen whooping after me into the hall.

'Come to buckle on a brigandine, Mistress Shore?' exclaimed one wit.

'Yes, sirrah, if you have any that will fit,' I replied.

'I'd say we all have something that'll fit you, sweeting,' chortled someone.

I put on my sternest stance. 'I came to hear about the internment of our late sovereign lord, whom God keep in his mercy,' I exclaimed, crossing myself. Instantly, every man's eyes snapped down in prayer. 'Now, gentlemen,' I said, after the moment of silent reverence. 'Am I to understand Lord Hastings is expected presently?'

'The old man's at the Star Chamber,' Ned's youngest esquire blurted loudly.

'No, he's not!'

The company fell into a shamed silence as their master tersely ripped off his riding cloak and flung it into the arms of his body-servant. My informant's skin turned the colour of dried blood. 'My lord, I did not mean—'

Hastings strode forward with a jingle of spurs, and the throng respectfully made way. Ned's death had hardened him. The benign lines, which had given his face nobility, had transubstantiated into an iron determination that I had never glimpsed before. His silver hair was slashed short and there was a wary narrowing about his eyes as though he expected trouble. I read a military captain's manner in the way he halted by the loose-tongued esquire.

'You spoke truth, lad. I am old by your standards but still a man. *Mistress Shore*?' He held out his wrist for me to go with him. It was blatant. With his pride at stake, I could scarcely refuse, and the hall was too hushed for my peace of mind as he led me past the high table. I hoped we might linger before the hearth and make some show of normal discourse, but Hyrst was bowing us into the withdrawing chamber.

I was not pleased. This behaviour would give instant vent to scandal so I pointedly kept my cloak on and did not sit down. Hastings saw nothing untoward in that since the fire had not long been lit. He was more intent on scolding me, and as soon as the door was closed, he confronted me like an angry lover.

'What has been going on with you? You don't tell me you are leaving King Street. You don't bother to visit here and explain.'

I did not like being out of favour with him. I owed him my good fortune, and if I lost his friendship, I would be facing the pointed end of Woodville malice on my own. But was he planning to flee to Calais if matters got too hot? Where would that leave me?

'My lord, I stayed away because I don't want to be accused of bed-hopping like a wanton flea, and I have a regard to your reputation as well as mine.'

'But *today* you are come.' He flung one glove down on the chair and drew off the other. 'It wouldn't be because Dorset has scared you?'

Blood drawn. Hastings' informants had been efficient.

'Yes,' I admitted, cradling my shoulders. 'He's being a vindictive whoreson. He wants me "naked and begging" but I assume you know that, too, my lord.'

'What man wouldn't?' he muttered with feeling, ignoring the jab at his omniscience. His blue eyes were no longer icy, but I stayed where I was making no move to kindle his impious thoughts, if such they were. He was watching my face as he flicked open the loops of his doublet, one by one. I looked away. The chamber was silent save for the hiss of sap from the fire. Then one of the logs tumbled from the irons. Its misdemeanour broke the impasse. He took up the tongs and crouched to set the log back among its burning brethren.

I let out my breath. This was a delicate game to play. I was so fond of him but the heat of carnality, the infatuation that had drawn me to Gerrard's Hall was long past. Explaining there were reasons of state that must limit our intimacy could take some skill.

He rearranged the wood above the kindling, playing with the fire. I cannot guess what was going through his thoughts. Maybe he, too, was reconsidering.

Hastings could survive the challenges that lay ahead. Age had not rusted him. I was relieved to observe the flexibility of his back as he crouched there, the precision and determination in the union of hand and eye. I defied Fortune to name me a more powerful ally, but she could be a bitch. After all, Ned had been struck down against the odds. Yes, England needed Hastings. I needed Hastings.

'Did...Did all go well in Windsor?' I asked him huskily, and I walked over to stand an arm's grasp away.

He nodded grimly, staring into the struggling flame as though he was seeing again the ropes hauled out, Ned's sword upon the coffin below, awaiting darkness. I imagined his pain at hearing the snap of the heralds' staves, knowing his fingers, too, must break his wand of office.

'Nothing was finished, of course. Nothing to mark his grave.' He gave a deep sigh and I did not know if it was the inevitability of death or bitterness against the maliciousness of life that moved him. 'I'll have to speak with our new king about the monument and get the workmen moving.' He grimaced. 'Persuading anyone to do anything is a cursed battle at the moment.'

'The royal council is being difficult?'

He clambered to his feet. 'Piss-weak, yes, girls the lot of 'em, and you'd think Dorset was the new king by the way he speaks to us.' He gave me a sideways glance. 'But I suppose I should be grateful to him. You are here at last.'

I was about to take issue when a Damascus moment over-whelmed me.

He stilled. 'What is it?'

'Maybe *this* is exactly what Dorset intended.' I glanced round at the door. Given enough ale, the men in the hall would all be blab-bermouths. 'What if I'm his Trojan horse, my lord? Maybe forcing me to turn to you is aimed at destroying your public honour and Gloucester's esteem of you.' Not to mention rending what little respectability I had left.

Indulgence softened Hastings' expression. 'Then you go out through the gate and come in the postern, Elizabeth.' A male solution offered with a speculative grin.

'Oh.' I sank down on the nearby settle, not sure whether to laugh or cry. The Gordian knot sliced with a thwack of words.

'It's all right, my dear,' he murmured, sitting down beside me. 'You are not on your own anymore.'

Call me too much a woman, but we all have moments of frailty and his kindness tripped me. Ned's slow death, my family's condemnation, Dorset's threats and the robbery. I dissolved into tears.

'They've thieved the jewels, too. The ones Ned gave me,' I sobbed, finally jettisoning all my resolutions not to tell him.

I felt the hand stroking my shoulder tense and heard his breath catch between astonishment and outrage. 'They? You mean the Queen and Dorset?'

'I...Yes,' I swallowed, my kerchief now a sodden ball between my palms. 'It...it was the next night after you stayed with me. I was packed ready to leave Westminster and get out of their sight, but two knaves broke in. My plate was downstairs in chests ready to be hauled, but they left that. They took my sapphire collar, everything in my jewel coffer. One of them punched Isabel, almost broke her neck.'

'In Heaven's name! They didn't rape you, did they?'

I shook my head. 'It was frightening enough, though.'

He sat back with a deep intake of breath and then he sprang to his feet and glared down at me. 'Hell take it, Elizabeth, if this was before I left for Windsor, why on earth did you not come to me straight away?'

I gazed down at my lap feeling deservedly chastened.

'Because I did not want to burden you.' I looked up at his snort of anger. 'And I can't be sure the Woodvilles were behind it but it's just that she, the Queen, I mean, remarked upon my sapphire collar. And there's this.' I fetched out the badge from my purse. 'Isabel found it in my bedchamber.'

He carried it to one of the candles. 'Yes, some of the Queen's Kentish affinity still wear these. By God, I'll have the Woodvilles' balls for this.'

'My word against hers, my lord?' I rose to my feet. 'No, pray you, let the matter rest. There's sufficient bad blood between you already and, besides, the case is too flimsy. I could not recognise the men.'

'Flimsy? Here is evidence, for Lord's sake.' He glared at the door. 'A cursed pity Catesby isn't here.'

'No, please, think upon it no more, my lord. I should not have told you.'

He stared down at me perplexed and then he relented. 'Give me time, Elizabeth, and I'll make sure you get everything back.'

I shook my head. 'The important thing is that you don't let the Woodvilles bring you down. Do you not see? Even the robbery may have been aimed at provoking you by harming me.'

He rubbed his fingers across his chin but he seemed to give the suggestion lodging, for he nodded and sat down upon his chair, slamming the wooden arms. 'Bitch! I'll be revenged on her, I swear it.'

I felt humbled, grateful, but I needed to distance myself to keep him safe, and yet being here felt secure as a citadel.

'My dear friend,' I murmured, lightly touching his shoulder. 'I'll not keep you further from your business, but dare I presume on your kindness further, please? Can you spare me some of your men-at-arms to guard my house?'

'Oh, Elizabeth,' he exclaimed guiltily. 'By Heaven, of course.' Then he was on his feet, taking my hands in his. 'You can have an entire army.'

'Hmm, that would shock the neighbours.' I tried to slide my fingers from his.

'Don't go yet. Please stay.' His gaze slid to my lips and he tightened his hold.

'My gracious lord, no. This is not wise.'

'Is honest friendship not permitted?' He saw me glance nervously away. 'Stay to dine. Out there.'

'But the smoke of gossip, my lord,' I reminded him. 'Even now we've been alone too long. Can you not see I'm the rift that could separate you and Gloucester? He already has me branded as a false friend to Ned.'

'My dear, I am not some inconsequential nobody. Gloucester needs me.'

'Please, send to Ashby for your wife to join you,' I whispered, giving his fingers a gentle shake.

'Why?' His face hardened.

'Because…because Gloucester flourishes his marital fidelity like a crusader cross and your wife is his cousin and a Neville.'

'Rein in on this, for Heaven's sake. You seem to see Richard as some sort of avenging angel, descending from the north all fire and brimstone? No, I'm not laughing at you, but we need to keep things in perspective.'

Well, I was! *He* was the one with a twofold agendum. He had the look of a man with kissing in mind, but when I did not lean towards him, he let go my hands.

'I'll dispatch some men round to your house, but first…' He rang the bell for his page. 'Bring us some malmsey and bid Sir Thomas Ferrers join us.' If that's how this must be played, his eyes told me reproachfully.

'A chaperone?' I sat down again, delighted to be outwitted.

'And you may clothe him in a coif and apron if it will make you feel more comfortable.'

I gave him a sheepish smile. 'I offer up my distaff in surrender.'

There was a swift arch of eyebrow, but he said nothing scurrilous.

Left alone for a few moments, I sighed and leaned back. The rumours that Hastings was preparing for withdrawal to Calais must be false. The Flemish tapestries had not been taken down nor the ornate cups fetched from the shelves.

For the first time in days, I could let down my guard, and by the time Hastings' brother-in-law, Tom Ferrers, sauntered in to keep me company, I was in a mood of great affability.

Pouring me some mead, he remarked, 'You know, Mistress Shore, it is a damned pity that William Hastings cannot be Keeper of the Realm for he understands far more of our late king's business than any other.'

'You do not think Gloucester sufficient for the task ahead, then?' I asked.

He pulled a face. 'Capable fellow, of course, but likely to stick in some of his northerners and that means tipping our late king's lads out of their saddles. They won't like that. Better if he went back to control the Council of the North again.'

Hmm, Gloucester was more likely to become a tinker than go along with that, and, presumably, in this ideal kingdom the Woodvilles were going to take a vow of silence.

'Buckingham's never held any high office, has he?'

Ferrers shook his head. 'Bit of a dark horse, that young man, but he is a duke.'

'Rearranging the kingdom, Tom Ferrers?' Hastings came back in with a brisk step. 'All's well, Mistress Shore. I've sent a half-dozen reliable men to safeguard your portals. Has she told you her jewels have been thieved, Tom?'

That was my business so I diverted the conversation. 'When is Prince Edward expected to reach London, my lord?'

A soldierly tension infused the room. Ah, this was why there was such a gathering of retainers here; they were waiting like hunting dogs for the horn.

Hastings shrugged. 'A day or so, I reckon. I've had word his retinue reached Northampton yesterday afternoon and both dukes have the intent of meeting him there by nightfall this evening.'

'Aye, town'll be packed like herrings nose to tail,' chuckled Ferrers. 'Reckon Grey and the London retinue will be there by now as well, eh, William?'

'No, they're still on the road.' Hastings' tone was smug. Clearly he had planned it that way, but I had misgivings. Northamptonshire was the Queen's home shire. If I was in her shoes, I'd have a few sidesteps ready. However, before I could set a burr beneath Hastings' girth, his page summoned us to join the company for supper.

I stayed until twilight. Hastings bade me farewell in the common view and Hyrst saw me to the porter's gate where three stout fellows were waiting with torches. Before we even reached Baynard's Castle, one of them took my arm.

'This way, mistress.' He pointed down the laneway towards the river. I thought he meant we should take a boat to Queenhithe and went with them cheerfully, but we walked no further than the postern.

'You're supposed to be seeing me back to Aldersgate,' I hissed.

'No, mistress, those were not our orders.'

I heard the bolts drawn on the other side and knew I had been outwitted. 'Then I'll make my own way,' I snapped, but their lord stood waiting for me. His fellows herded me in without a by-your-leave and disappeared into the darkness. Hastings drew me into his arms and stifled my protests.

'You tricked me,' I said after being thoroughly kissed.

'You asked for an escort. I gave you one. I thought we were agreed: "Out at the gate and…".'

'"In at the postern". Do I not have a say?'

'Not if I can help it.' But he sensed my reluctance and, perhaps to give me time, he led me under the trellised arches and out the southern gate to the riverbank. The breeze had stilled and the moon was a newly minted coin flicked up in a game of chance. We were seen; a waterman rowed close, the lantern bobbing on his prow, its cheerful light prancing upon the lapping waves. For some minutes, the oars trod water hopefully and then the fellow gave up.

Hastings didn't. 'Why are you so moral all of a sudden, sweetheart? We still have a few days until your Duke of Brimstone

arrives and I could do with some diversion.' I must have tensed for
he changed his ply. 'Forgive me, I spoke lightly.'

'I'm not an heirloom from Ned, my lord.' I drew away, frowning
into the darkness. Was Ned's spirit watching from beyond the stars
or standing beside us like a guardian angel? I shivered. Perhaps the
Devil was forcing him to witness our shabby behaviour.

'I keep thinking upon him,' I murmured, hoping that revelation might skew Hastings' plans for tonight.

'Yes, I realise how much you loved him.'

'And you love your Kate.' Another invisible presence.

He turned me to face him. 'I do and yet…Elizabeth, my dear
Elizabeth, I've watched you spread your wings like a butterfly
awakening from her slumber. From the moment I saw you on
the ladder in your shop and every moment since, your company
has given me the most utter joy.' His hair was a helm of silver; his
face was ageless beneath my fingers. 'Stay with me tonight,' he
pleaded, holding me against his breast. 'Tomorrow what you will,
but tonight I'll keep you safe against the darkness.'

To surrender would be to distract him from the dangerous
path he trod and jeopardise his reputation; to deny him might
also madden him, divert his thoughts when these perilous times
demanded a cool judgment.

Out on the inky water, a fish jumped into the alien air to avoid
death and fell back into its destiny.

'This night then, my lord, but tomorrow—'

'Tomorrow is…tomorrow.' Oh, I tasted the triumph in his kiss.
'I knew you'd see sense.'

He led me back with a cat's night sureness. We reached his
bedchamber. How ironic that my old ambition to lie here should
be finally achieved. Yet the room resembled a monk's cell. The
tapestries were furled in the corner like battle standards in the time
of peace. No costly brocade canopied the bed; no fine coverlet
draped the blankets.

The dissembling, poxy cur! So he was packed for a swift departure!

'Is this a spring-clean?' I asked dryly. 'Or have you turned Benedictine?'

'Undress me and find out, my darling.' he teased, pulling me to him. 'See if I'm wearing a hairshirt.'

I captured his hands. 'You wouldn't be packed for Calais, would you, my Lord Lieutenant? And what happens to "the woken-up butterfly"? Does she flutter along at the rudder keeping away from the seagulls or wait here to be gobbled?'

'I would have sent for you.' The rueful look had been quickly found.

'Oh, I've heard that one before.' I exclaimed angrily.

'*You* left Westminster without telling *me*,' he countered.

'Yes, but I only moved to Aldersgate, for Heaven's sake. It's hardly Jerusalem.'

We stared at each other like a couple of angry swordsmen and then I started laughing and his face softened. 'It doesn't matter,' I lied, but dear God, I hurt inside. I hurt so much. Was there no man in the world who could be true to me? Now I didn't have much choice but to pretend forgiveness.

In a couple of strides, he was holding me again. 'Oh, by Christ, I love you.'

What? The 'L' word? Useful to dredge up for mollification. I stared up at him in disbelief. First betrayal and now deceit, and I had stayed a loyal friend to him all these years.

'I have loved you from the beginning, Elizabeth.'

If I had not needed him, I would have slapped the earnestness from his face. 'If that is true,' I retorted, 'you wouldn't have sacrificed me to the King. He need never have known.'

'It was your decision.' He kissed me. 'And let's talk about now, shall we?'

Now? He wanted to lie with me again because I was available and he desired me. In return, I would receive protection – *on his terms.*

'My dear, I know you loved Ned, that you still grieve for him,' he was saying. 'But whatever is left for me, I'll accept with all my heart.'

He'd accept if I would give? Yes, I could give, but I did not want to take, to become tethered again like the Pole Star. I desired my freedom but I wanted to live to enjoy it.

'My lord,' I replied. 'A great deal is left for you, but by speaking so freely of love, you debase its currency. You always say you love your wife but you still betray her.'

'Well, I do love her,' he countered gravely although his hardening body told a different story. 'But, Almighty God be my witness, I need your love, too.'

You learn with men that nothing you say will make a scrap of difference. I pulled free from his embrace. I knew the sensible course. I had not been a concubine all these years to worry about coupling and I was very fond of Hastings, but I was under no compulsion to make it easy for him.

'Haven't I watched over you all these years, Elizabeth?' he exclaimed, still trying to please. 'For pity's sake, matching you with Ned was more than self-interest. Sometimes it crucified me seeing you together. *I love you.* I love you and I don't care a fucking kingdom whether it debases the currency or not.'

By our Saviour, how complex we humans are. I'm sure he believed what he was saying. For my part, I was sad I could not return his love in equal measure and that in my ignorance I had not guessed how deeply he'd cared for me.

Below the window, I heard the rattle of thin chains and cheerful barking. His servants were letting loose the guardian dogs. Without Ned, the human dogs were being unleashed, too. I must decide wisely.

'Elizabeth?' he prompted.

I remembered how he had stood in Shore's shop and transformed my homespun life into shining brocade with just a smile. Now his lips brushed my fingers.

'Sweetheart, I'm no monk and I've been too long from home. I'm lonely, Elizabeth, and I want you so much.'

Ah, so men speak of love and lure us to their beds. He pushed my hand down to free his prick.

'Perhaps you should have been born a Saracen.' I began loosening his clothing. 'A lawful wife in every shire and concubines along the Great North Road.'

'Too-com-pli-cated,' he said between slow kisses. 'That is so good.'

Our tumbling was satisfactory, not sustained and tantalising like those early lessons. Hastings was asleep in an instant leaving me to pad round to his side and pinch out the candles save one little nightlight.

This time I cuddled up to him. I thought about his Kate. Why had she not taken the reins and come to London? She was Warwick's sister, surely not craven-hearted. Or didn't she care? I would have covered those miles someh—

My reverie was broken by barking, shouts and running feet. Beaumont's Inn exploded into turmoil. Hastings sprang from the bed, hastily pulling on his underdrawers. Before he could investigate, fists pounded the bedchamber door. The light of torches showed beneath it. The Queen had sent her soldiers.

# III

'Will, open up!'

Hastings held a lethal baselard in his right hand as he set his other hand to the wooden door bar. 'It's Ferrers!' he whispered over his shoulder with a grin of relief.

'He's *lonely*?' I scrambled from the bed, grabbed my gown from the floor and joined him at the door. 'They may have a knife at his throat,' I warned, glancing about me. Perhaps I could jab a tapestry pole into someone's belly?

'My lord, I must speak with you.' The second voice was familiar but I could put no name to it; Hastings could. Once I had my gown over my head, he passed me the dagger and thrust the bar aside. I did not share his confidence. I tensed behind the door, blade at the ready. The torchlight lit Hastings' naked breast for sacrifice but his face showed no fear. In fact, he smiled.

Leather creaked as someone bowed. 'My lord. I have news. Good news.'

The lawyer Catesby. He stepped in, gritty-eyed, smelling of horse sweat and road dust, his red hair whipped and tangled. Hastings' men retreated back to the hall, laughing and backslapping, but my breath settled slowly.

'Well, have they secured the Prince?' barked Hastings.

'My lord, I have never seen the like. *Oh*, I beg your pardon, good day to you, Mistress Shore.'

'Day, is it?' I snapped. I felt like some Medea, standing behind the door with a naked blade, my hair wild about my shoulders and no modesty kerchief to scarf my cleavage. Despite his obvious fatigue, Catesby was still man enough to stare.

'For God's Sake!' snapped Hastings. 'Let's have your news, man. You may speak before Elizabeth.'

I did not want to know. Tension clung to the lawyer. It would be like tasting the metal as well as the brew.

I found it hard to follow the tale at first but the crux was this.

Two days earlier Hastings had sent Catesby up to Northampton where Gloucester, Buckingham and the Prince of Wales's retinue had agreed to meet. Lord Rivers and the boy were the first to arrive, but instead of waiting for the two dukes, Rivers hastened the Prince closer to London; fourteen miles closer, to the town of Stony Stratford, a long line of shops and taverns which straddled the highway north. Then he rode back to Northampton that evening to meet the dukes.

They all had supper together and then either late or in the early hours, Gloucester arrested Rivers. Both dukes then set off at sparrowfart for Stony Stratford to find the Prince.

'So now are we talking about what happened only yesterday?' I asked.

'Exactly, Mistress Shore. I rode hotspur to Stony Stratford with their graces and my heart was in my mouth for they had only three hundred men a piece, contrary to what you advised, my lord. When we entered the town, it was clear that Grey and the London retinue had arrived. Nigh on two thousand Welsh and Londoners, I'd estimate. The street was crammed with kettle-heads as far I could see. The dukes' retinues would have been outnumbered soon as blink.'

He waited for one of us to say, 'So what happened then?' Hastings obliged.

Catesby grinned. 'The bravest thing I ever saw, my lord of Gloucester calmly rode forward behind his heralds and the throng parted like the sea did for Moses. He just kept riding. Closer and closer he came to Prince Edward, and the Woodville retainers just stared in awe.'

I tried to picture it. 'I am confused, Master Catesby? Where was Prince Edward? In his lodging?'

'No, Mistress Shore, he was mounted up along with Grey and his household officers. They were tarrying for Lord Rivers. When the duke came within twenty paces of the Prince, he dismounted and walked through the crowd, right up to his highness' stirrup and there paid him homage. My God, such courage! Any man could have pulled a dagger on him but he showed not a shred of fear.'

'What about Buckingham?'

'Right behind Gloucester like a faithful dog. Grey could have had them arrested but he did not have the steel in him, just gaped like a man smitten by God. If it had been his brother, Dorset, matters might have gone differently.' The lawyer beamed smugly at the glee lighting Hastings' face. 'Then his highness demanded to know where his Uncle Rivers was. I tell you my heart was in my mouth once more. Before Gloucester could answer, Buckingham asked if the boy had breakfasted. The lad said no, so the two dukes swept him back into his inn to dine, with Grey and his highness's other officers trailing woe-faced after them.

'Since I was your embassy, my lord, I followed also. Next instant, Gloucester ordered Grey's arrest declaring that "the Queen's kinsmen had conspired to prevent him becoming Lord Protector and wilfully corrupted our late sovereign king, destroying his health and virtue".'

My hand crept to my lips in dread.

'A soldier to his backbone,' continued Catesby. 'Not a blow was struck. Not a drop of blood was shed. I never saw the like.' Esteem glowed in his face, but I felt misapprehension, an emotion Hastings clearly did not share.

'Excellent! I knew things would turn out all right. Richard has always been a cool man under fire.' He rubbed his palms together with a smirk the Devil would have envied. 'So, two Woodvilles under arrest already. Are they to be brought to the Tower?'

Catesby smiled like a conjurer about to lift the final walnut shell. 'This is the clever part. They're to be separated and sent to Gloucester's northern strongholds as hostages.'

Ha! The Queen would be spitting. All cunningly played (and I'll wager Gloucester had been one of those tiresome brats who beats everyone at chess). However, the thought that both the Prince and England might be stuck with 'Uncle Gloucester's opinions' for the next thirty years or more was a sobering thought.

'So where are his highness and their graces now? St Albans?'

'No, Mistress Shore, they went back to Northampton. To await word from you, my lord. They want your assurance that London is safe for them to proceed.'

'They've gone back up the road?' Hastings looked winded. 'With the Queen's retinue as well?'

'No, Gloucester paid them off from his own coffers. Every Jack of 'em will be high as kites by now, packing every tavern betwixt here and Stony Stratford. So that is my news, my lord. His grace has sent you this letter in his own hand and begs your apology for its brevity. He desires you dispatch a messenger to Prince Edward straight away.'

Hastings broke the seal. The message was short, the writing clear and Italianate. 'Yes, indeed. Assurance they shall have.'

He glanced towards the upper window light. 'Good, almost dawn. I can have a man with them by nightfall. Well done, Catesby. Go and get your head down. I shall see you are well rewarded for this day's work.'

His duty done, the lawyer had started to sag. To have galloped back all that way and much of it in darkness would have wearied any man. He bowed and rallied sufficiently to bestow on me an appreciative grin before he left us.

'That fellow will go far,' Hastings muttered as I helped him dress.

'Do you mean Gloucester or Catesby?' I muttered, but he made no answer, no doubt preoccupied with the message he would send the dukes.

Left on my own when he had gone to wake his secretary, I slid back into bed wincing at the cold touch of the sheets against my skin. I nestled down, shivering with cold and unease. What would the Queen do when she heard the news from Stony Stratford?

Hastings sent in some potage for me and returned with his servants to finish dressing. He was cock-a-hoop at Gloucester's strategy of taking hostages.

'We've already had a message from the Woodvilles,' he declared, rubbing his hands again. 'Lionel Woodville desires an audience with me. I'll wager you anything the Queen wants me to broker a peace between her and Richard.'

'I should go,' I announced. 'And I think we should not meet again until things settle down. I wish you joy with the bishop, but take care, he has a silver tongue.'

It might be wise to flee to Hinxworth until all the noble fur and hackles settled, whisk temptation out of Hastings' way. But then it struck me that riding north would not be safe with Grey's dismembered retinue tottering back.

At least I must keep a discreet distance. As Ned always said,

'Fortune's a fickle wench. She can knee you in the groin at any time'.

Catesby was returning to his lodging as I was leaving. He escorted me partway up Paul's Wharf Hill. The whites of his eyes were still flecked from hard riding, but he was like a man who had found the crock of gold at the foot of the rainbow. I wondered if Hastings had promised him the office at court that he so desired.

'May I say black becomes you, Mistress Shore. It bestows a barrier that beckons crossing.'

I laughed. 'I commend you on your stamina, Master Catesby. All the way from Stony Stratford and still game to flirt.'

'It must be your presence that so revives me. I see you've changed back to your old mount.' He nodded back down the hill to the roof of Beaumont's Inn. 'But, then, I guess there is little alternative for an ambitious woman.' I made no reply to that thrust. He said nothing more until we parted at the corner of Knightrider Street. 'We all cut our cloth to match the times, Mistress Shore. If ever I may be of comfort to you...'

'How kind.' I might consider him again as a lawyer; I'd never consider him a friend.

How quickly this fickle world can turn.

Later that morning, Hastings sent a messenger with a saddled horse for me and an urgent request that I ride to Beaumont's Inn. Something must have gone awry at Northampton.

The house exuded a tomblike quiet as Hyrst silently escorted me through the great hall. I assumed all the gentlemen had gone to prepare the palace for the young king, but something was definitely wrong. In the withdrawing chamber, my ebullient Hastings had been replaced by a morose figure, slumped in his chair with his chin on his chest and a mazer of wine between his fingers. He looked old and defeated. I could smell sweat, as though he had been riding hither and thither, and something else. Bruised male pride perhaps? Someone had badly riled him.

'So, didn't you make Lionel lick your soles?' I asked when he did not stir. Narrowed eyes and a sour curl of lip preceded his answer.

'Oh yes, he licked 'em until his tongue was raw.' He took a swig of wine and swirled the rest, staring into the depths. 'For two poxy hours. And you know what, Elizabeth? All the fucking time the mongrel was keeping me talking, that arsehole Dorset was at the Tower stealing Ned's coin from the Treasury.'

*Stealing*? I pulled up the stool and sat down beside him. 'How on earth—'

'Because he is still Deputy Constable of the Tower, curse it! By Christ, I never even thought he had the spine.'

My mind was reeling with the implications. It wasn't that I did not believe the story, but you could not move fast with a fortune in gold and no army to protect it. 'I don't understand. Where could he take it?'

'Onto a carrack, just before the tide turned. Edward Wood-ville's taken it to sea. Hired the ship from the Genoese apparently. Idiots didn't ask any questions. I've sent a letter in strong language round to their headquarters demanding they send another ship after it and order its captain to turn about.'

'And Dorset fled with his uncle?'

He shook his head, and took another swig. 'You haven't heard all of it yet. Oh God, Elizabeth, Richard was relying on me and I've let this happen. Pour me another drink, will you?' I refilled the wine cup and poured one for myself. Goodness, the French and Hanse pirates would be on their knees giving thanks when they heard of such pickings sailing their way. And Ned would rock his coffin over.

'There's worse,' Hastings growled. 'The instant I was informed, I rode to the Tower and while I was there, our bitch of a queen ransacked Westminster. The best plate, the tapestries, ornaments, anything that was not nailed down, all taken. It looks like a pantry after a plague of rats have been through.'

I sat back a-gasp. 'She's taken it on another ship?'

'No, crammed the goods into Westminster Sanctuary. Broke down a wall to do it. I have the place surrounded. She's holed up there with Dorset and the children.' Elizabeth knee-deep in coffers with bored fledglings? Oh please, yes, greed can be so uncomfortable.

'And the Great Seal?' I asked. No royal commands could be given without it. 'Is it with Chancellor Rotherham or you, William?'

'*Me*? I wish it were so.' Hastings thrust himself from his chair. 'No, the silly, old want-wit handed it to the Queen without a second thought. He's gone to get it back but, Jesu, what a mess, and there's me like a prize fool sending to the dukes to say everything is smelling of roses when there isn't any money to rule the realm.' His face tightened harshly as though his wounded esteem was a jagged rip in his very flesh. 'I tell you this, Elizabeth. I'll not tolerate young Richard reading me a lecture like some schoolmaster with a poker up his arse the moment he arrives.'

'Of course not,' I said soothingly, 'and I'll wager the Queen will come to terms. She may have the treasure but Gloucester has her brother and two of her sons, and I am sure you can negotiate a truce. Maybe Princess Bess can help. She adores her uncle.'

He snorted, unwilling to be mollified, so I gave him a motherly shake. 'Heigh now, are you not the great lord who survived the bloody fields at Towton and Tewkesbury, and yet you fear a young

friend's reprimand? Look at it this way, William, if it wasn't for
your warning, Gloucester might be under arrest by now, but you
and he are both at liberty and it seems to me the danger is over.
So long as Prince Edward is well, that is what matters.'

But what did the future hold? The Queen would not stay in
sanctuary forever, not with a henhouse of young daughters and
a chance to rule through her son. The moment the Prince was
crowned, all those who had opposed her would be sweating.

I returned to Aldersgate that night but I slept ill. I could see
that Hastings, Gloucester and Buckingham would have to protect
their backs from the Queen's inevitable vengeance. How in
Heaven could they outwit her? Killing the hostages would only
deepen the rift.

Next morning Hastings issued a proclamation that the young king
would ride into London on the fourth of May. The city calmed at
the news and everything seemed to go off the boil and cool down.
I sent Lubbe to Beaumont's Inn and he returned with a reassuring message from Hyrst informing me that his master and Mayor
Shaa had been collaborating on preparations for Prince Edward's
welcome.

Hastings called in on me at suppertime, wanting me back
at Beaumont's Inn, but I made it clear I intended to remain at
Aldersgate.

'You are not saying this because you think I'm too old for
you?' he asked, with the crestfallen look that usually aroused my
sympathy.

'What, suing for compliments when you've more vigour than
most men half your age?' Yes, men like to be told superlative lies
but this lay close to the truth. 'No, my great concern is Gloucester
and please don't argue me down. If he still has it fixed in his head

that I am one of Dorset's familiars, I had rather stay invisible until he returns to the north – for your sake and for mine.'

'He probably has agents in my household,' Hastings muttered. 'I've had people in his. Just a precaution to protect Ned, mind. I couldn't have *both* his brothers running round like lit firecrackers.'

'And you have a man in Buckingham's?'

'Yes.'

'And mine?' I had asked that once before.

'Ned, of course.'


On the appointed day, our young king rode into London with his uncles. I did not watch because the pain would have clawed great lesions in my heart. Instead, when I heard the peals of bells ringing out across London, I knelt on my prie-dieu in prayer for Ned's soul. For me there was only one sunne-in-splendour.

I learned later that all went merrily. Lord Hastings welcomed Prince Edward and the dukes at the hall of Thomas Kemp, the Bishop of London. Apparently there were no recriminations, no sense of young dogs criticising an old warhorse's stumblings, but kissing of hands all round and enough promises of loyalty to fill a great man's library.

The coronation was now set back until the twenty-second of June, but Hastings assured me it would be even more splendid for the delay. No one seemed to mind except, I guess, the Queen. Certainly, my silkwomen sighed with relief to know they had more time, and the guild workshops hummed with activity. London was like a millpond surface on a windless day. Like the rest of the city, I tried not to imagine what turbulence might lie beneath.

As for the great lords: Gloucester, now Lord Protector, unpacked at Crosby Place, where he always lodged, Buckingham took up residence at his Manor of the Rose down near St Laurence Poultney, and young Edward moved into the royal apartments at the Tower, as was customary for a king before his coronation.

It was as if there were two courts: my Lord Protector's, where the everyday running of the kingdom was enacted, and the King's council, where Hastings spent most of his time. Now, when he visited me, instead of worries, he brought cloth samples, and his conversation cantered upon the King. He wished to make himself as indispensable to the son as he had to the father, telling me he felt it was the best way he could serve England. Not unexpected. What great officer can let go of power?

# IV

By the end of May it was not just the summer air but also the Lord Protector's temper that began to heat. Neither Hastings nor my lord of Canterbury had managed to broker a peace with the Queen, and Gloucester refused to free her brother and son unless she consented to bring the children out of sanctuary for the crowning.

To my surprise, Hastings sent me a message that young Edward wished to see me. I was uneasy at obeying lest it annoy the Lord Protector, but how could I disobey a royal command? I clothed myself in a high-necked, modest gown and hid my hair beneath a cone cap with a folded back frontpiece fastened with a simple pearl brooch.

Crossing Tower Hill brought back the foul memory of being caught in the crowd with my brothers when I was a girl and forced to see a Lollard burned and it was a relief to enter the Tower bailey.

A score of carpenters were erecting pavilions between the royal lodging and the White Tower for there would be many young esquires made Knights of the Bath on the eve of the coronation, and the air was bruised with a great deal of shouting, sawing and hammering. The King was not at the royal apartments and I was directed back to the Lord Lieutenant's house where I found his highness in the garden with several young esquires and some of his father's former officers: Sir William Parr, Controller of the Household, Lord Stanley, the royal steward, and Morton, Bishop of Ely.

Our twelve-year old King was very gracious to me and I was permitted to watch as he shot at the butts. Seeing him concentrate as he positioned the shaft and pulled the bowstring tugged at my heart right tenderly for it hurt to glimpse expressions that were so much his father's. The lad was as tall as me and likely to equal Ned's height when he was fully grown. His hair, tied back in a tail, was still gilt, a beauteous colour halfway between his mother's flaxen and his father's brown. His looks would make a magnificent king and break many hearts and yet... Surely, his demeanour was far too grave for a boy of his age? No wonder, either, for his courtiers were so serious. Whenever his arrow hit the centre of the target, there was no whooping, only a dutiful clapping as though the activity was tedious and they all wished to be elsewhere.

To my astonishment, Edward announced he desired to see me pull the bow.

'Stand away, please,' he advised his attendants.

'Aye,' said someone. 'Who knows where a woman may aim her arrows.'

Edward stood close behind me, correcting my balance. 'I beg you to help me,' he whispered. Surprise made my shot go wide. 'Please keep making mistakes. *Put your thumb thus,*' he instructed loudly. 'I need to know Mama's plans and what she intends to do to free my Uncle Rivers. Can you go to the sanctuary and bring me her answer?' I deliberately shot badly so he might help me again.

'But, sire,' I whispered, 'you may easily send one of your gentlemen with a letter.'

My lesson was causing disapproval. I sensed Parr about to intervene. I aimed properly this time and my arrow caught the outer rim of the target and bounced off. Together, Edward and I walked across to retrieve it.

'I know you and Mama were rivals,' he whispered, 'but, please, good mistress, I know not who to trust.'

'You may surely trust Lord Hastings,' I answered.

'But Mama will not. Please, for the love you bore my father.' He stooped and picked up the arrow and as he passed it back, pressed a small ring into my palm. 'Show this to her as a token.' It was given in the nick of time; Parr insinuated himself between us.

'Your highness, Master Oliver will be expecting you. Time for study, I'm afraid.'

Edward nodded solemnly. 'Indeed. Farewell, Mistress Shore, God be with you.'

'And with you, my sovereign lord.' I curtsied, my mind rebelling at the task he had begged of me, but how could I refuse Ned's son, who was now the King?

As I passed Bishop Morton, he looked me straight in the face as if he guessed that more than archery had taken place and flicked his gaze meaningfully to the open window above us. 'May God *watch over* you, Mistress Shore.'

His warning was apt. As I entered the passageway, I met Catesby in company with Buckingham, which surprised me, but then I remembered that he had long been a legal adviser to the duke.

'Why, Mistress Shore!' said Buckingham, as I sank down, my demure gaze fixing humbly upon his expensive shoes. The shabbiness was gone now. Not a surprise; Gloucester had given him control of Wales.

'Your grace.'

'Isn't he a little young for your wiles?'

'Your pardon?'

'Our little king.'

I resisted the temptation to smash my fist down on his toes for such an insult. 'I trust your grace is jesting,' I replied sweetly.

A tepid smile climbed to his eyes and he moved on.

By Heaven, I flew outside like some poor sparrow frightened by a lurking mouser. What's more, a sinister Tower raven eyed me as I leaned against the stone rail edging the steps and I shuddered, despite the heat of the afternoon.

'Elizabeth?' Hastings' shadow fell across me. 'Oh, my dear, are you ill?'

I fanned my hand in front of my throat. 'It's a very warm day.'

'Bodes well for the coronation. Come, have a walk with me if you can bear the heat.'

Colour was back in his face and he had discarded his long black mourning robe for a honey jerkin and a loose blue mantle with slashed sleeves.

He suggested we mount the ramparts that linked the Garden and Lantern Towers, but even up there the air was sizzling and sluggish. I dislike days when the heat presses all colour from the land and the miasmas of pestilence began to stir. It had been hot like this in 1479. Besides, I had Edward's request scorching my mind. Should I tell Hastings what had been asked of me?

'My dear, I've decided that after the crowning, I'm going up to Ashby for the rest of the summer.'

I was pleased. He had been fretting about his half-built brick keep at Kirby Muxloe. It seemed patient Kate was weary of riding down to chivvy the master-builder.

'I thought you were indispensable,' I teased. 'Will his highness give you leave?'

'Already agreed. Richard intends to take him on a northern progress to York and I shall go with them as far as Leicester.'

That boded well. Maybe Gloucester might eventually free his hostages.

'You know, Elizabeth, it would please me if you were to go to your father's house at Hinxworth during the plague months. I shall know then that you're safe.'

I had not thought beyond June but I told him yes. Would Dorset be out of sanctuary by then? Yes, maybe I should go.

'Do you think the Queen will attend her son's crowning, my lord?'

Hastings smiled like a man who has everything in hand. 'The King won't forgive her if she stays away. He said as much to me.'

Below us a freshly painted barge slid from its mooring at the Tower Watergate. Buckingham, seated beneath a scarlet and black canopy, returned Hastings' salute.

I felt the duke's stare as keenly as though his breath was in my face. Would he tell Gloucester how he had seen Hastings and Mistress Shore standing so close?

'I cannot warm to that man,' I murmured, watching the unison of the oars dipping and rising; the stillness of the duke. 'Why didn't Ned have him on the royal council or give him high office?'

Hastings lent against the crenellations, folding his arms. 'A whole basket of reasons, my dear. He's the last of the House of Lancaster unless you count Tudor, over in Brittany, so it was politic to keep him dampened down, but, basically, Ned never liked him. The poor brat made a dog's breakfast of settling into court life, resented being the Queen's ward and having to marry her sister. No surprise, there – the Staffords are a haughty lot. Dorset and the other Woodvilles used to make sport of him. I always felt sorry for the boy, tried to give him a dollop of advice now and then.' I wondered how Buckingham felt about that.

'And now he has the administration of Wales, and Dorset and Grey are fugitives behind four walls and an army of kettleheads,' I muttered.

'Aye, that should content him. To my reckoning, he's always craved the respect people had for his grandfather, the first duke.'

Surely respect was something you earned? It did not necessarily come with a parcel of land or a wand of office. 'Do you *trust* him?' I asked.

'Put it this way, only Richard and I have ever shown faith in him. He owes us loyalty.'

If you grind Faith down to its essence, it is not based on knowledge but the trust of one's instincts. As for trust… I felt a terrible sense of unease. How had Buckingham once phrased it?

*Trust is an old-fangled word.*

# V

I took a boat to Westminster on the King's errand and was surprised to find how many onlookers were gathered about the ring of pikemen surrounding the sanctuary. When I stated my business to the sergeant in charge, he took me to his captain, John Nesfield, a strapping fellow with a thick Yorkshire brogue and a keen eye.

'Eh, not another launderer of the royal linen?' he challenged as I was compelled to stand before his board like a prisoner and then, glancing up, he realised the quality of my apparel and his curiosity quickened. 'State your purpose, Mistress...?'

'Jane Sands,' I lied. 'I am a former tiring woman of her grace Princess Elizabeth.'

To my relief, Nesfield agreed that I might enter. Under his supervision, two soldiers searched me with such uncommon diligence – one would have thought they were looking for veins and arteries. Then the pair accompanied me into the ground floor of the sanctuary where a monk received us and carried my request to the Queen.

The room where I was bidden to wait was spacious in construction but you could hardly see the flagstones. A staircase occupied one wall and the others were obscured by wooden chests carelessly piled high with bed hangings, footstools, games boards, cushions, pillows, crucifixes and rolls of stained wall cloths. I recognised the curtains from Ned's state bed stashed beneath a tangle of silver candlesticks. We waited; the soldiers with folded arms, and I with trepidation.

There were hasty feet on the stair. 'A visitor!' exclaimed Princess Bess, prancing down. 'Mistress...Sands.' Clever maid, she instantly played along and more besides. 'One moment,' she exclaimed excitedly. 'I must fetch the others. They will be so pleased.'

'My lady,' protested the youngest soldier, but she flashed him a look from behind her lashes and disappeared up the stairs. A few moments later, three princesses and Prince Dickon galloped down, followed by little three-year-old Bridget. Bess must have primed the older ones. After they had politely exchanged the time of day with me, those wicked darlings grabbed the pillows to wallop each other and gave chase, screaming and dodging around the soldiers.

'Your brother sent me,' I whispered, clasping my hands before my chin so Bess might see his ring.

She kept her smile merry but her tone was anxious. 'How is he?'

'Fretful. He asks to know your mother's plans.'

'Lord! I'm afraid there aren't any. None that she's told me. DICKON, stop making so much noise! I doubt she will come out until my brother's in the abbey with the crown on his head. CECILY, tell Kate to stop that squealing. I can't hear myself think.'

'And my lord of Dorset?'

'Tom's going berserk stuck in here with us. ANNE, you cat!'

'What shall I tell your brother, then?'

'I don't know. Can you come again? I can ask Mother. Sorry! SOMEONE stop Bridget putting sticky on Papa's chair.'

I shook my head. 'We can't risk this a second time.'

'Why ever not? We are not criminals and it's my uncle who's Lord Protector, not some enemy. Cecily, entertain our visitor. I have to fetch something.'

I heard her feet on the floorboards above and a man's voice, and then she was back, holding something up her sleeve. Cecily deftly moved in front of us and I found myself seconds later clutching a necklace.

'Tom says tell him to be patient.'

'*But—*'

Sunlight fell across us and Nesfield stood in the doorway. 'Such a caterwauling!' he chided, scooping up Bridget who was about to totter out between his legs.

Bess took her sister from him. 'Thank you for letting us see Mistress Sands, captain. You will observe and witness that I have given her a necklace. It belongs to her. I borrowed it some time ago and I shall swear so on a stack of Gospels if you require it of me, so you are not to take it off her, you understand. It is rightfully hers.'

'Eh up, let's have a look, then.'

I reluctantly opened my hand and probably looked astonished as he to see the confusion of sapphires. It was my precious collar.

He took it and whistled. 'This isn't some bauble.'

'I do not wear baubles, Nesfield,' retorted Bess haughtily. 'If my Uncle Gloucester wishes to make an issue of this, let him come and raise the matter himself. I think you'll find he will not dispute me.'

Her confidence awed him. 'I shall have to make report of this,' he warned.

'Of course, I should not expect otherwise but if I hear your men have taken this from Mistress Sands, you will find yourself with a very uncertain future. *I* have no quarrel with the Lord Protector.'

Nesfield let me keep the necklace but his men searched me, even more thoroughly, if that was possible. Thankful to be allowed to depart, I took a circumambulatory journey home in case 'Mistress Sands' was followed. I was angry that the errand had achieved nothing except that I had my necklace back and now knew for certain that Dorset had been behind the theft.

'Tell him to be patient.' What was that supposed to mean? Quite honestly, I believe Bess spoke the truth and they were all like insects sitting on leaves waiting for the wind to blow or leaf fall to arrive.

Next day I returned to the Tower only to find my way into the royal lodging barred by the sergeant in charge of the King's bodyguard. He demanded to know my business.

'Sirrah, when last I spoke with the King's grace, he commanded me to attend him again.'

'Well, I am afraid you are not regarded as worthy to come into the royal presence, Mistress Shore. The new High Constable's orders.'

Buckingham! After much argument, I had to retreat. Oh, I was shaking and my face was hot with fury, but Hastings was not at the Tower that morning and could not take my part. I'd have to confide in him, I decided.

Hastings was right wrathful when I came clean about my mission next day.

'I'll return the poxy ring and give the King your message. Young fool! He should have consulted me first, and you should not have meddled, damn it! If Richard and Buckingham want to make trouble for you, you've given them every reason to suspect you're thick with the Woodvilles.'

'I was obeying the King,' I snapped back, my breath short. 'We do have one, in case no one has noticed.'

We glared at each other and then the fierce ridges of his face softened.

'My kind Elizabeth,' he exclaimed, gathering me into his arms. 'But I want your promise. No more meddling.'

Three is a difficult number unless you are fortunate enough to be God, Christ and the Holy Ghost. History is spattered with messy triangles. Marcus Antonius, Octavius and Lepidus; Arthur, Guinivere and Lancelot; Ned and his two brothers; and now the triumvirate of Gloucester, Buckingham and Hastings.

The first week in June, as we walked in my garden, surrounded by the bees in busy hum as they milked the lavender and mari-golds, Hastings admitted that he was beginning to feel super-fluous. Now that the fine stitches of the coronation were in hand, he had lifted his head up for air and grasped that he was no longer part of the inner sanctum at Crosby Place.

'Look,' he said, breaking off a dead rose head. 'I'm the last one to want to hang about like John of Gaunt when I should be in my coffin and, yes, these younger men want to do things their way, but Buckingham has nothing on his ledger. He doesn't know a shovel from a sword. He's never dealt with the French or the Scots, what's he going to do – dance with 'em? Richard should be working with me, not him. And I've been given nothing for my support. He could have given me some reward for taking his side against the Queen.' He sniffed, like a neglected child. '*I* should have been made High Constable.'

'Yes, you should have been,' I agreed sweetly, 'but I think Gloucester showed good sense in making Buckingham Justiciar of Wales. Coming from Brecknock, he knows it well. You've never set foot there, have you?' I received a growl for my pains.

'I suppose you've heard the rumours that are flying around?' he muttered, as I led him into the shade of the loggia, where Isabel had set out ale and freshly baked gingerbread for us.

I had heard. Useless chaff! The old scandal that Ned had been sired by a common archer called Blaybourne and the gossip that Ned's secret marriage to the Queen had been unlawful. But the rumour that really dinged with the ring of truth was that Gloucester wanted to depose his nephews. Well, yes, he probably did after years of watching Ned, but it didn't mean he was going to tip Ned's son off the throne. How could he?

As if Hastings was reading my thoughts, he at last came to the core of his worries. 'Listen, I hesitate in worrying you with this, but Catesby came to see me yesterday evening. He truly believes that Richard will make himself king.'

My blood ran cold. Here was the Lord Chamberlain giving this nonsense credence. For a moment I made no answer. I knew the arguments. Child kings weakened a kingdom and my merchant friends were saying England needed a strong man to counter the grasping schemes of King Louis, especially now Ned's free trade agreement with France was in tatters. Surely young Edward, with his intelligence, would soon be old enough to lead the kingdom?

'Well,' I said aloud, trying to reassure myself. 'My Lord Protector will need a lawful reason.'

'That's the thorn, Elizabeth,' Hastings said, turning his face to me. 'I think he has one.'

'Oh, not that ridiculous archer nonsense. Why doesn't her grace of York make a public declaration denying the smears and...' I faltered in my babble. Something in his face frightened me. 'Oh God,' I whispered.

He rose to his feet, strode across the grass and slapped an angry hand against the pear tree before he turned. 'Remember how determined Ned was to have you? He was like that about Elizabeth Woodville, willing to make her queen so he could get his leg over. Well, I remember that before he became king when he was about eighteen, he was hot as mustard for another young widow,

Eleanor Talbot, the daughter of the Earl of Shrewsbury. A very pretty girl. He was always galloping off to see her just like he did later when he was trying to lay Elizabeth, but on one occasion when he visited Eleanor, there was a priest among his escort.

'Ned had a wild, rebellious look that day. I asked him if he wanted me to ride with him as well. He laughed and said he was going to the gates of Paradise and St Peter only allowed one man in at a time.' He raised his eyebrows at me. 'What does that sound like to you?'

'A betrothal,' I whispered dully. Just as binding as my betrothal to Shore had been.

'Exactly. If it's true, Elizabeth, it makes Ned's sons bastards unable to inherit.'

His mouth a grim pleat, he stared upwards, where a flock of jackdaws made a black whorl against the wild sky.

I pressed my fingers to my lips and stood up, my mind running amok with the implications, past and future. 'George knew, didn't he?'

'Yes, he knew, Elizabeth. He was threatening to beat the matter into the open. That's the main reason Ned had him sentenced to death. To protect the succession.'

'But if this first betrothal took place, what, in 1459 or '60, why did Lady Eleanor never speak out?'

Hastings shrugged. 'She took the veil. Maybe she loved the Lord Christ better. Anyway, she's long dead, but the priest who rode with Ned is still kicking, oh yes. Did well for himself with Ned's patronage. First, bishop and then Chancellor of England.'

'Not Bishop Rotherham!'

His laughter was wry. 'No, my sweet goose, Bath and Wells! Robert Stillington. You've probably never set eyes on him. Ned had him imprisoned after George's trial and for the last few years Bishop Alcock's had charge of him.'

No, I had never set eyes on Stillington nor did I want to. A loss of temper was imminent; I felt like I had as a child when my brothers left me out of their secrets. 'You've always known this?'

'*Guessed,*' he corrected. 'If Stillington testifies, it places Richard in a hellish quandary. The duke's a stickler for upholding the law. If the law says the princes are bastards – and, of course, no one wants George's boy – then Richard is legally obliged to take the crown. Catesby thinks he will.'

'Does that mean that Stillington has spoken out?'

'What do you reckon, my dear? I know he's been to Crosby Place.'

It is an understatement to say I felt sympathy for Gloucester's dilemma and plentiful compassion for Ned's sons. I was remembering the Queen's fury with me for my part in freeing Stillington. It all made sense now.

I had one question left: 'What are you going to do?'

Rebellion relies on arithmetic. Numbers on the board. Numbers in the field. Hastings had already done his sums.

'Even if I can muster two thousand, I haven't sufficient support among the nobility to protect the princes. Stanley may stand by me, and a few of Ned's household knights, but that's it.'

'What about Lord Howard?'

He made a face. 'No chance there. He'll claim the Duchy of Norfolk if Prince Dickon is disinherited.'

'And Buckingham will support Gloucester?'

'Does the Earth move round the sun? Harry wants the Bohun inheritance returned to him. Only a king can grant that.'

'There is still the Queen and her affinity,' I muttered, but imagining Hastings giving the kiss of peace to Dorset was like expecting a couple of snarling dogs to share a bone. Besides, one sinister move from the Queen and Gloucester might behead his hostages.

'I have affection for Richard. I've known him since he was

scarce out of swaddling, but to stand by and see Ned's children pushed aside, that's a great matter.'

'Oh dear,' I sighed. 'Look, Catesby could be wrong. Stillington may have said nothing at all and if he does, Gloucester may still honour Ned's will.'

Hastings wrapped his arms about me and drew me close. 'Let us be realistic, my dear. Would you?'

History is full of times when people sit on their hands. Gloucester did nothing untoward or in haste, so on the second Thursday in June, Hastings and I risked a late supper together at my house. He did not tell me whether he had been in secret communication with the Queen. Nor did I ask. If the Lord Protector was going to continue purring like a contented uncle, there was no reason to unsheathe the daggers.

Buckingham, however, was a different animal. Maybe if Hastings had understood how much hate had fermented in that young man, he might not have been so blithe as we lay between the sheets that night.

He was still in cheerful mood next morning and ate a hearty breakfast. At nine, his retinue arrived at the garden postern. He had a meeting at ten in the White Tower with Gloucester, Buckingham and the King's council.

'It is Friday the thirteenth so ride carefully,' I admonished, as we strolled arm-in arm along the path. 'Especially maids emptying chamber pots.'

'I promise to doff my hat to every upstairs wench 'twixt here and Billingsgate.' His eyes smiled down into mine before he kissed me.

'May your meeting go well.' I straightened his chain of office, glad he was also wearing his precious crucifix.

After he had ridden off, I shook myself to business. Because the times were so hurly-burly and I was not on the Lord Protector's good lordship list, I decided to bury my sapphire collar and the rings I had left, so I put on my broad-brimmed hat, smuggled my small coffer outside and stowed it in my trug beneath my gardening gloves. There was a tubful of lavender from King Street which begged planting and could serve as marker for my treasure. Hercules, a gelded black mouser, who had been left behind by my tenant, kept me company and batted my soles as I knelt at my task. I hummed as I dibbed, replanting some pinks and hyssop next to the lavender.

It was not a summer's day of silvery haziness but rich and intense. The early breeze had cleansed the air of the city's cooking smoke and the sky shone as blue as Our Lady's mantle. Hoverflies dallied above the camomile, a humblebee was harvesting the nectar from the marigolds, and several ladybirds were trundling up and down the stems of the rose briar hunting out the juicy aphids clustering the buds. Their scarlet and sable liveries reminded me of Buckingham's retainers but, beguiled by this little kingdom of insects and flowers, I was in too serene a mood for distress as I eased out the wisps of grass that were vying with the beans.


Thirteen men at Christ's table and one of them a traitor. At half past nine I was still in the garden pulling up milkweed and thinking about the Friday of Our Lord's last supper when my house echoed with a fierce assault on the doorknocker. I started to my feet. I was not expecting visitors and there was no one to answer the door because Isabel and Young had gone to a cousin's funeral. I raced to the garden gate, crept up the lane and peered around the corner. Half a dozen pikemen in black brigandines were hammering the front door.

'Open in the name of the sheriff!'

With a gasp I ducked back, grabbed up my skirts and ran away. Perhaps a neighbour saw me or the soldiers were ordered to break in at the back for they came charging round. Three hurtled after me. I dashed round the next corner and up the steps to the nearest alley. I needed to double back south to St Martin-Le-Grand and plead for sanctuary. I tore through Goldsmith's Hall, dodging clerks and liverymen, then round the back of Foster Lane, and helter-skelter round the drays and barrows until some pesty apprentice grabbed and tethered me by my hair. I struggled and smashed my sole into his shin, but I did not have a fraction of his strength. The soldiers took over.

'Where's your mistress, you filth?' bawled one, twisting my arm up behind my back so cruelly that I yelped. 'Answer, damn you!'

'Gone to a burial,' I squealed. 'Now-let-me-go! I'm just a servant, see!' I brandished fingernails clogged with earth.

The other pikemen arrived. By then we were surrounded by passers-by, the men leering and the housewives hostile because of my hair loosened like a whore's.

'She says Shore's wife has gone to a funeral.'

The sergeant gave the man a cuff on the ear. 'This *is* Shore's wife, you dolt.' Wide-eyed, my captor let me go. I pulled my kirtle straight and tossed my hair back over my shoulders, but what came next shook me to the core.

'Shore's wife, we are arresting you for treason and witchcraft.'

# VI

*Witchcraft!* Indignation, bewilderment, terror, panic – all these emotions surged through me as the marching cage of soldiers forced me south to the nearest wharf. I moved like a mechanism, my mind in shock. They flung me into a boat, and with a soldier jammed against each of my shoulders and the sergeant glaring from the middle plank, I had no chance of drowning myself. I could only watch helplessly as the two oarsmen swung the boat eastwards. As we neared London Bridge, the truth hit me like a pail of icy water. They were taking me to the Tower!

No, wait! I momentarily calmed. Hastings would be there. He'd intervene. Then my blood froze. God ha' mercy, maybe arresting me was some attempt to destroy him. I stared in panic at the severed heads above the drawbridge, and then I remembered how once, crossing London Bridge, I'd seen a woman sitting dazed in shock. Passers-by had told me her son had thrown himself into the river and she had just heard the news of his death. Perhaps I could pretend shock, too?

The prow was turning towards the Tower.

'Jesu! Is *that* where you are taking me?'

'Well, we ain't taking you to Calais, darlin'.'

I keeled forward in a faux swoon and when they hauled me up, I sat like a frozen corpse, staring ahead. At the Tower Watergate, no amount of yelling and prodding made me shift a muscle. When they yanked me to my feet, I kept my eyes vacant.

'If this is a prisoner, her name must be recorded in the Tower register,' said someone in authority.

'Not this time,' argued the sergeant holding my arm. 'It's just a woman.'

The Bell Tower was pealing noon as they marched me into the lane between the wards. I was hauled up the stairs of the Garden Tower and thrust into a chamber, bare as I remember, though I durst not look about. I just stood there in the middle of the floor with my back towards the door. They left me alone but I sensed them watching through the grille. At least I could move my eyes now. I do not know how long I stood there. Someone unlocked the door eventually. I heard the clank of scabbard against greaves followed by the creak of leather and shuffling footfalls.

'So this is the famous Mistress Shore?' A common fellow stuck his face in mine. The gaoler? I nearly gagged; his breath was like a privy. 'So, wot do we require first, sir? Splinters 'ammered under them nails?' He waggled his knuckles beneath my nose. 'Wot's the matter with 'er?' he asked, peeved at my lack of response. 'Most of 'em are shakin' like St Vitus by now.'

The officer observed me for several heartbeats and then they both left. I heard his voice low and authoritative outside the door.

Did people in a daze move about? How much longer could I stand like this? O Christ, help me! Was I now Gloucester's hostage for Hastings' compliance? 'Stand by as I depose my nephew or we'll shove your whore head first into a barrel'? Or would I be tortured to give evidence against the Queen?

The Bell Tower gave tongue again. Not an hour chime but a frantic alarm. The guard outside the door clattered down the stairs. I could hear shouts. Armed feet. Had Hastings ordered the dukes' arrest in the King's name? This would be the day. Yes, in the White Tower, where he knew the garrison. Yes, yes! God make it so. Ned! Ned, can you hear me? Guard your son and stand by your friend!

The city churches took up the alarm. Ah, soon, this madness would be over. Hastings would come for me. I heard horses galloping. More shouts.

No one rescued me. All Hallows on Tower Hill struck one before the telltale noise of feet on the stair forced me to resume my dazed stance.

'Mistress Shore.' The hint of Northamptonshire was familiar. So was the musk he wore – Catesby. 'Mistress Shore, you can stop this mummery now. We don't need your testimony. The traitor William Hastings was beheaded half an hour ago for treason against the Lord Protector.'

Indeed? Oh yes, and Christ and his angels have been sighted off Gravesend. I did not flinch.

'The old man's dead, Elizabeth. See!' Catesby flourished Hastings' precious crucifix before my eyes.

Hastings dead?

Dead?

I broke my trance. I began to scream.

And scream. And scream. And scream.


Within the hour I was dragged to another wall tower and down a dank staircase to a chamber, lit by cressets. At one end stood a brazier of burning coals with branding irons sticking forth, and from the beams there dangled leather harnesses and chains. Hooks along the walls carried all manner of pincers and manacles. The foul stench of past horror clung to the smoky air.

A bare-chested, muscular oaf in a half-mask with a leather apron over his hose was waiting beside a bed-size wooden frame that had mysterious wheels and cords at either end. Seeing an exhausted woman with tear-stained face, he rubbed his hands.

'Here's a pretty chicken. These lads been making you cry, have they?'

My guards grinned and retreated to the door.

Christ protect me! I stared at the apron, noting the hideous spatters. Was this the fiend who had beheaded my good and kindly Hastings an hour since?

'Don't hang back, sweetheart.' He drew me across to a huge aumery, shaped like a coffin. Nail-heads studded the door, and he unlocked it to reveal their shafts sticking out, row upon row, like hefty bodkins. 'Feel inside, mistress. Go on! I won't do nuffin'. Feel inside!'

I reached in, feigning an indifferent expression. Merciful Heaven! The entire back of the cupboard was crisscrossed with nails. Were people shut into this monster? It was an effort not to retch.

'Or maybe you'd like to grow a head taller, mistress.' He tugged me over to the other apparatus. 'Meet the Duke of Exeter's daughter.'

*I promise you there shall be no more torture.* Ned, why didn't you destroy this device of the Devil? Or did you lie to me?

Feigning disdain, I stroked a fastidious finger along the inner frame. It came away dusty, and my heart lurched with relief.

'Dear me, sirrah, this looks like it hasn't been used since King Henry's time. In fact, I know it hasn't. King Edward thought it barbaric. He told me so himself.' I stooped and looked underneath. 'Hmm, I'd check it for woodworm if I were you.'

My host's jaw slackened at my audacity but then he resumed his obnoxious litany, ignoring the sniggering guards. 'Over here we 'ave branding irons, knotted cords to squeeze your skull and pincers to remove your nipples. And, of course, your nails. Well, we can pull 'em out, one by one. Saves you the problem of cleaning 'em.'

'Would you like me to spew on your floor now or later?' I asked sweetly. 'What, are there no mops and buckets here?'

The hangman looked nettled that his tour had not distressed me. 'Take her away,' he yelled, holding up crossed fingers. 'This one's a witch. She has the evil eye.'

Oh God, the word 'witch' shook me to the core. The guards scoffed, but when they had me outside the door, they would no longer look me in the face. I was marched to a tiny cell along the passageway. Not 'Little Ease' where a man can neither sit, lie or stand but, nevertheless, damp and cheerless as Hell. A drain served as privy and I could hear the rats scurrying along the sewer.

The soldiers took my belt, stockings and garters although there was no nail or beam from which I could hang myself. They did leave me a candle, and one guard was posted to watch me through the grille. Lest I commune with the Devil? Fine chance! Even God had his hands over his ears.

My back to the door, I threw up over the drain as quietly as I could.

Former prisoners had gouged their names. I started to add mine with a fragment of stone. I had reached the 't' of Elizabeth when my eye strayed to two names I recognised. Dick Steres, the skinner who was executed for treason at Smithfield, but the other scratch-marks made my blood run even colder: Margery Jourdemayne, the Witch of Eye, burned at the stake for sorcery against King Henry. There was the year: 1441. What a fool I'd been to play haughty with the gaoler.

In utter despair, I slumped down against the chill wall. I had no appetite, my throat was raw, my head ached as though the knotted cord was already biting into my flesh and I was chill to my very soul. Was this how Holy Job had felt, tormented by God?

Christ and his saints have pity! Ned's wife was out of reach but his mistress was the perfect whipping child. A woman, a whore, already a prisoner. Who better to drag to the stake for witchcraft?

I turned the stone within my fingers. Could it cut through to my veins?

I did not care to live but neither did I wish to burn.

Survival is a cruel instinct. Before I could play the Almighty with my own body, I was led out, not back to the torturer, but to a partitioned upper room where a notary sat with a writing board on his knee. On the other side of the travers, two hefty women stood waiting. Wives of the gaolers, I suppose, each wearing a sprig of St John's Wort for protection against my sorcery. They made me strip naked and each of my garments was taken for examination. Then they made me stand near the windowlight while they searched my skin for the Devil's marks. Thanks be, I had no warts, but what if they called a mole a teat? As they finished with each of my parts, they reported loudly to the notary. Oh, the humiliation!

When that was over, while one of them distracted me in conversation, the other jabbed a bodkin into the flesh of my behind. I squealed and nearly slapped the hag.

'That's a good honest pain,' she said. 'Be glad of it.'

She gave me a thin shift to wear and a stool to sit upon. My clothes were not brought back. I was shivering, expecting to be dragged down to the torture chamber, but they informed me the proctor from the Bishop of London had arrived to question me.

He looked to be afflicted with worms, more a cadaver than a man. Ascetic, taut, tonsured, with the usual pendulous earlobes that accompanied age. If I had guessed his agendum first away, it might have gone harder with me, but sometimes Our Lady protects dimwits. He summoned the notary to join us and after confirming my identity and making me swear on the Holy Book, he began his questions.

'Did you ever meet with the Widow Grey, lately styling herself Queen of England?'

What, did he think the Queen and I drew up a bedchamber schedule?

'I was the King's concubine,' I replied.

'Woman, you must provide an exact answer or we shall put you to the question downstairs.'

The threat loosened my tongue: 'Only once did I seek an audience with her grace and that was on behalf of the Provost of Eton College that she might ask the King's grace to restore his patronage.'

That raised the eyebrows but he rallied. 'You never met with her by night?'

I bit back a sarcastic answer. 'No, I avoided her like the plague.' I did not mention that I had discussed Ned's health with her. I could see where this might lead.

'And the Queen's mother, Jacquetta? Did you ever meet her?'

'No. She died before I came to Westminster.'

'We have evidence that you desired to bewitch the Lord Protector.'

'Evidence! What evidence?'

'It is not necessary for you to know.'

'Then you debase the law, proctor,' I exclaimed with heat. 'Everyone has a right to know who accuses them and what is alleged. How otherwise can I refute the lies being told against me?'

'It is for us to decide who is telling the truth not you.'

'I loved King Edward, God rest his soul, and he would stir in his grave if he knew of this evil accusation against me.'

O Sweet Jesu! I drew a sharp breath as my memory stirred. That day Ned had introduced me to Gloucester. *She has bewitched me.* Was it Ned's words that had brought me to this trial? Had one of the many servants who stole in and out like wraiths given testimony? Or the Lord Protector himself?

As if he read a garbled version from my thoughts, the interrogator asked: 'Did you ever hear King Edward say that the Queen or her mother had bewitched him?'

'No, Father.'

'Did he ever say to you that you had bewitched him?' *My Jehane.*

'Actually, he did, but it was as a lover speaking lightly.' I tried to decipher the priest's reaction. Had I just announced my death sentence?

'You are wise to give us the truth, my daughter. Go on.'

'There is no more to say, Father. I needed no sorcery. I loved King Edward with all my heart and he loved me. You may find a palaceful of witnesses to tell you that.'

'Can you deny you had power over him?'

'Yes, I can. He was my king and sovereign lord.'

'Yet you influenced him to change his mind when others asked you to intercede for them?'

'Only where a cause was just. For instance, if you had come to me seeking help and I had pleaded on your behalf with the King's grace, would that have been sorcery?' His silence made me speak further without forethought. 'It is my understanding that witches only seek to do evil. God be my witness, I only ever desired to help good men find justice.'

'How do you presume to know what witches seek? Have you consorted with other witches?'

'No!'

'Do you confess your sins as a fornicator?'

'Yes,' I sighed, 'I confess my sins.' What did they want me to do, wear a rayed hood from now on? Live outside the city walls? Make confession every day? 'Yes, King Edward and I were lovers, but I am *not* a witch!'

'Did you and Thomas Grey, lately styling himself Marquis of Dorset, make any wax dolls or participate in any rites of sorcery?'

'No.'

'Did you and the traitor Hastings or any of his household make any wax images, draw up horoscopes or participate in any rites of sorcery?'

'No.'

It was all written down but interrogation was repeated two hours later and again two hours after that. The same questions. The same answers.

That evening I was permitted a visitor of my own flesh and blood. My brother Will bravely came to see me after he had learned from Mayor Shaa of my arrest. He stood in the heart of the little cell and scolded me for not heeding his counsel. With no choice but to listen, I huddled miserably against the wall, conscious of the agonised prayers gouged into the stone behind my back.

'All you say is true but don't let them burn me, Will,' I pleaded. 'Surely the Bishop of Ely will speak on my behalf?'

'Didn't they tell you he's mewed up here as well. So are Lord Stanley and Oliver King, the Prince's tutor. You are in dire trouble, sister.'

For loving Ned and Hastings?

'There are many I've helped when I had the power, Will. Is there no one to bear witness on my behalf?'

'What? Risk the ill favour of the great lords who are now the authority in this land just to defend a sinful woman? Use your head, Elizabeth?' He crouched before me and chafed my cold hands. 'It is a different world out there.' I must have looked so devastated for he added cheeringly, 'Be brave. There's still Lord Mayor Shaa. I'll see what he advises. Do you want me to send for Father?' I shook my head.

We knelt in prayer, then he kissed my cheek. 'Better go, eh? I've a sermon to write.'

'On unbiddable women?' I muttered, swallowing my tears. 'Wait, Will, there's something I must tell you in case we never meet again. Something you must tell Jack if I am sentenced to die. I don't want him to remember me as evil.'

Will listened with growing indignation as I explained about Father's thieving mistress and how I had given my savings to save the family's reputation. 'The Shaas can confirm I'm speaking the truth, Will,' I assured him. 'Anyway, I made Father promise that once he had money in hand again he would buy a house in Hertfordshire for Mama and turn the shop over to Jack.

'Why on earth didn't you tell us, Elizabeth? We're your brothers. We had a right to know.'

'It was between Father and me. I didn't want Mama hurt. Anyway, both Rob and Jack were overseas at the time.'

'Yes, but—' The guard clanged in, growling at Will to leave. My brother ignored him. The wheels of his mind were turning fast. He looked so devastated. 'Then we owe you everything. I couldn't have finished my studies if you hadn't made that sacrifice, could I?' The soldier shoved him to the door. 'And Jack wouldn't have the shop and—'

'It doesn't matter, Will,' I cried as the lock clanged shut. 'And don't blab to Jack unless…' I broke off, trying not to cry.

'Be brave,' he shouted through the wood. 'I'll pray for you this night.'

I hoped he would. But was anyone except the Devil listening?

★

The proctor appointed to defend me came to my cell that evening. A whey-faced young man with a laugh like a he-ass. Myopic, too, forever craning forward, screwing up his eyes and drawing his lips into a tight 'o' of concentration.

When I asked him for the true gravity of my circumstances, he overwhelmed me with 'ifs' and 'buts'. The gist seemed to be that, depending on the testimony of witnesses and the suspect's responses, there were eleven levels of action that might be taken against witches.

In passing sentence, the bishop would be required to judge whether the suspicion of sorcery was light, strong or grave; whether the witnesses' intent was to defame; whether I had confessed; whether I was relapsed, penitent or impenitent. An appeal against an adverse sentence was possible but it depended on whether the judge deemed the action frivolous or lawful and just.

All clear as mud.

'Now I need to ask you some important questions, Mistress Shore. Have you ever cursed a herd of cows?'

'Not recently.' But seeing he took my wit at face value, I swiftly made denial. Then followed an interrogation that in lighter circumstances would have had me doubled with laughter.

Had I caused lightning and hailstorms? Had I changed anyone into the shape of beasts, sacrificed babies to the Devil, impeded procreation, bewitched anybody into inordinate love or extra-ordinary hatred?

'No, never.'

The final question terrified me: had I caused any man to lose his virile member?

Of course I had not, but what if Shore was brought from Antwerp to testify?

With the questions done, my young advisor warned me my head and body hair might be shaved, pins stuck in me to test if I felt pain and my body examined for extraneous teats where incubi might suck.

I was tempted to retort that every man I knew had two of them upon his chest. Instead, I pointed out that this examination had already been done.

'Nothing was found.' I said with confidence.

He looked at me with pity. 'I have argued that you should not be "put to the question" again, Mistress Shore, but it is still a possibility. It was also suggested that some of your household be brought to give evidence.'

*Brought?* The word reeked of Buckingham.

'I have nothing to fear,' I declared. Yet in my heart, I was terri-fied that if I saw Isabel tortured, I might babble the sky was green or that Buckingham was Christ come again.

Once more in the cell, I was left with the stub of a candle, the patter of rats and a sleepless night of fear stretching through the cold hours into morning. Cradling my knees, I sat against the wall, grieving and crying out silently to the shades of Ned and Hastings for justice. Yes, I had sinned with them, I admitted to God. Adultery many times over. Yet I was always faithful, I'd never betrayed either of them. But to burn for witchcraft...

When you face death, you begin to cast away old values. In looking back over my life, I realised that night how much vanity I still carried; how I feared the hurt to my pride if they degraded me by shaving off my long fair hair and yet, when we face God's throne on Judgment Day, of what significance are grey eyes, blonde hair and breasts that others envied?

The memory of seeing a poor Lollard burned when I was a child came back to me. Jesu, to be hurdled through the streets and bound to a stake with wood beneath you, to feel your flesh melting, to smell your own skin starting to smoulder. How long would the pain endure? How long before the smoke suffocated you?

I was in such cruel reverie when the bolts scraped back and Master Catesby stepped in, wrinkling his nose. 'Good morning, Elizabeth.'

A cloak lay over his arm and he was carrying my gardening shoes.

'Well, look who the Devil has blown in,' I snarled, observing the glint of embroidered shirt above his satin stomacher, the emerald and pearl brooch upon his hat and the extra rings adorning his hands. 'Have you come to gloat, you foul traitor?'

'You spread your legs to the wrong man, Elizabeth.' He handed me the shoes. 'Now let's see if you can charm a bishop.'

# VII

When we entered the boat, I expected to be taken to the Lollards' Tower at Lambeth Palace, but instead I was taken to St Stephen's Chapel, Westminster, to stand trial before Thomas Kemp, the Bishop of London.

Devoid of tapestries and sparse of furniture, the palace had a hollow, eerie feel. It was early, there were few servants about and even they looked furtive. Outside the chapel stood the sheriff's soldiers, waiting to swoop on me like kites once my conviction was secured. They eyed me contemptuously. I suppose I looked a gutter slut with no coif to cover my head like an honest woman.

Incense from early Mass hung in the chapel air. The board set before the bishop's chair stood where Ned's body had lain before the altar. I sadly knelt and crossed myself, beseeching Ned's spirit to protect me for I felt so defenceless.

Catesby was openly gloating at my discomfort nor did I like the inscrutable, covert looks that the interrogator and other magpie clerics were casting my way.

Do we have guardian angels? I hoped mine had woken because my young proctor arrived yawning. Hardly a silver-tongued Cicero.

They made me stand while we waited for the bishop. I prayed silently, fervently, imagining the beads sliding through my fingers, petitioning Our Lady and St Mary Magdalen to give me strength.

At nine o'clock Bishop Kemp hobbled in with sticks, his face strained with the effort. Pain makes a testy judge. His crepe-skinned hands shook as he shifted his papers before him but his gaze was sharp enough. Firstly, he called for a stool to be brought for me and then he studied my person: the hands without jewels clasped upon my lap; the tendrils of long hair uncombed since yesterday, the soil of my garden still blemishing the wizened leather of my shoes.

The charges were read: that I had conspired with Hastings and the Queen in sorcery against my Lord Protector; that I had carried messages under a false name; that I had accepted a jewelled collar from Dorset to pay agents to spread rebellion; that I was guilty of leading the late king into debauchery by which lewd living the days of his life were shortened; and that he was forced to oppress his people by taxes to pay for my services and feed my insatiable appetite for riches.

I pleaded innocent of treason and sorcery but guilty of carnality. I had thought out some arguments to defend myself but Bishop Kemp warned me to hold my peace. Nor was I requested to give evidence because he had already read my deposition.

He peered cantankerously at Catesby before he exclaimed: 'There is much here confirming this woman's adultery, but are there any present that will give testimony of this woman's *good* character?'

Who would?

'I shall speak for her.'

A murmur of astonishment rippled through the chapel. At first I did not recognise the short churchman who stepped forward and placed his hand upon the Gospels.

'I am the Provost of Eton College,' he announced, swinging his gaze round over the entire assembly. 'I can tell you Elizabeth Lambard is a sensible, intelligent woman of generous and charitable disposition. Without her intervention – which was given freely without thought or request of any reward – I doubt Eton College would still exist.

'And, my lord judge, I know this is hearsay, but Mistress Shore's reputation for compassion stretches beyond the walls of this palace. Many there are who would be beggars had she not begged on their behalf.'

Oh, I could have thrown my arms around the provost's neck as he stepped down.

'I will speak for her good character also.' James Goldwell, the Bishop of Norwich, stepped forward to take the oath. 'This woman was a goodly influence upon the King. There is no malice in her.'

Good men, brave men, to speak for me. And then there was one more, a man who had respected Hastings and sworn allegiance to Ned's son – Bishop Kemp. Too old to fear the dukes and too wise to make that obvious, my judge, bless him, had the common sense, authority and courage to dismiss the charge of witchcraft on lack of evidence. But my relief was short-lived.

'However, as to this grave matter of conspiracy,' Kemp continued, blinking at the court, 'it is not within the jurisdiction of Holy Church to judge whether this woman is guilty of treason.'

Dear God! Was he saying a civil court could still find me guilty?

'On the charge of adultery, however, since the plaintiff admits by her own mouth that she is a sinner...' He rambled on about virtue and those in authority setting a good example.

I closed my eyes in pain.

'My daughter, *I repeat my question*: have you anything to say in your defence? Stand up and address the court. *Mistress Shore?*'

I was being given a chance to speak? I shook off my daze and glanced to my proctor for advice.

'Say nothing,' he mouthed as I stood up. But I knew his counsel was wrong. I let silence have its way as Ned always had done before he spoke. I stared around the faces watching me. There was not one woman present among these male custodians of temporal and spiritual law.

'My lord bishop, I know full well that the Lord Protector blames me for the decline in the health of our late sovereign lord, King Edward. But I ask you: is a lowly woman like me more powerful than Almighty God?' An ugly gasp came from the throats around me. 'For surely it was God's will that King Edward died too soon for England's good?'

A precarious argument but they were listening. I could have sliced a knife through that silence.

'And if you say the fault *is* mine, are you not belittling our late king? This may be a trial of my reputation but it is also a trial of his. Do you remember him as a feeble-minded dotard? No, I think you do not. Surely then in condemning me, you condemn King Edward's judgment? Yes, I loved him, I was true to him and if love be a sin, then I am guilty.'

There was a silence until that bastard Catesby began a slow mocking handclap as he rose to his feet: 'This woman is a liar and a whore. Upon my soul, I swear she lay with the traitor Hastings the very day King Edward died. Let her deny it under oath.'

I shook with shock at his venom but Bishop Kemp slammed his hand down upon the board.

'Enough! Master Catesby, you are not requested to give testimony. Notary, strike that out!' Looking back, I'd swear he was protecting Hastings' memory and that meant clearing the court lest Catesby prove persistent.

'I shall make the judgment of this court known to his grace the

Lord Protector and he may proceed as he sees fit. In the meantime, the prisoner shall be given into the authority of the Sheriff and delivered to Newgate Gaol. Court dismissed.'

*Newgate!* The prison for criminals who were taken out to be disembowelled and ripped apart? *St Mary Magdalen help me!*

And she did. She sent a lightening bolt of courage through my sinews.

'Your pardon, my lord bishop, but as a freewoman of the City of London, I claim my right to be taken to Ludgate.'

Kemp might have been thinking about a late breakfast or maybe he relished thwarting the two dukes' plans. He waved a dismissive hand to the men-at-arms.

'So be it! Ludgate. Sheriff Whit, remove this woman hence!'


Ludgate Prison! Rebuilt about twenty years earlier, London's cage for debtors, trespassers and frauds. I had visited poor widows here but never thought to find myself behind these iron gates. The quadrangle, which lay at right angles to the city wall, was some thirty-five paces long by two score wide and this was where the prisoners spent the day. At night they were locked into a large chamber upstairs. There were a few private cells if you had the means to pay.

I was dragged into the head gaoler's room and forced to stand before him. He dismissed my guards. 'I see you've naught to buy you comfort, Mistress Shore, so it'll be bread and water unless...' A rub across his codpiece underscored his meaning. 'This great fellow is longin' to follow the path of royalty.' To my horror, he started letting down his flap.

'What?' I scoffed, grabbing up a stool. Within seconds I fled the room, leaving him staggering – and legless. So was the stool.

\*

Word of the notorious Mistress Shore's imprisonment spread swiftly. By noon a crowd had gathered outside. Will arrived, bringing cheese and ale. When he saw my state of dress, he went hotfoot to my house. Alas, he found it locked up with wooden bars across the doors. Then, bless him, he went to Jack's and cajoled a gown, coif and clean chemise from Eleanor, my sister-in-law.

When I was decent once more, he and I sat down in a corner of the yard.

'What's happened to my servants? Isabel and Young were at a funeral when the soldiers came for me. Have they been taken as well?'

'I don't believe so. Your neighbours told me they've seen neither hide nor hair of them since yesterday morning.'

Yesterday? Was it only yesterday that Hastings died?

For a while we sat in silence, then he said, 'By the way, Lord Hastings' body has been taken to Windsor. I watched his funeral barge go past this morning. People are angry about what happened.'

'Yes,' I agreed sadly. 'He was much loved. Even more than Ned at times.'

Seeing I was managing to hold myself together, Will glanced around to make sure no one could overhear. 'There's something else. When I went to see Mayor Shaa this morning to find out where you were, he told me a few things in confidence. It seems your "friend" became so incensed at the meeting in the White Tower that he drew his dagger on Gloucester and there was a right to-do. Yelling and so forth. Enough to have the guards draw their swords and rush in.' He paused. 'Can you bear the rest?'

'Go on.'

'Shaa rode to the Tower with his soldiers as soon as he heard. He said Gloucester was looking white and shocked when they spoke together but Buckingham was calm as anything. The benches and papers were all over the place although that could have been done later. But what Shaa reckons, judging by the bloodstains on the flo—' He grabbed my shoulder. 'Steady, Elizabeth, hear me out! Shaa reckons his lordship was killed up in the meeting room, before he was beheaded.'

'Before?'

'Yes, in the heat of the moment. The official proclamation is that Lord Hastings committed treason and was taken down and beheaded. Don't glare so. It *was* treason. Shaa reckons he was either dead or dying when they dragged him down.'

'He died unshriven, then?' I said dully.

'It was swift and clean, Elizabeth. A soldier's death. Only Shaa's opinion, mind.'

'But why would the dukes twist the truth, Will? I don't understand.'

'Look, if a man is cut down in an argument, whoever killed him can be held responsible and there must be an inquiry by the coroner. But if a man is beheaded for treason, it is done by the authority of the law and no individual can be blamed. That's why they could not hold a trial. His lordship was already dead. Shaa reckons Buckingham was very quick-witted to work that out.'

'Unless he intended it that way from the start,' I suggested with bitterness. 'And if Hastings could not be provoked to lose his temper, I'll wager they planned to force a false testimony out of me.'

My brother thought about it and said, 'It's not good, Elizabeth, none of this.'

No, it wasn't. I might have only hours to live.

'If I am to be…b-burned, Will, please, will you make me a promise? Could you…would you, stay near me to the end?'

★

Will, bless him, stayed that night at the prison. He paid for a cell for me and slept across my door so that the gaoler would not pester me, but early in the morning he left to celebrate Mass, and I was in fear again. My instinct told me that if the knave took me against a wall of the quadrangle in daylight and full common gaze, no one would give a tinker's cuss; they'd probably want their turn.

After those years with Shore, I was adamant that no man would take me against my will again, so when I espied a fist-size stone, I grabbed it and kept tight hold. Being hanged for murder was a loathsome thought but compared to burning...

The other prisoners were curious about me. Like timid beasts with an exotic creature in their midst, they edged nearer to where I sat. One pretty girl, fair-haired, grey-eyed, told me that she was Mistress Shore and that she loved King Edward more than any soul on earth. I listened fascinated until the head gaoler cruelly cuffed the poor wretch away. Then he came down on his haunches behind me and gifted a breath of onions and rotting teeth.

'Now you tell me somefink, darlin', did the Lord Protector wan' yer an' you said no? Is that what this is really abaht? Or wuz it *yer* wanted 'im?'

Before I could snarl an answer, a horn sounded outside the gates and everyone in the courtyard came alert like wild creatures sensing danger. It was the other sheriff, former linen draper and now wealthy mercer, John Mathew, who rode in. There was a warrant tucked into his belt, a rope looped round his saddle pommel and a dozen pikemen at his horse's heels. I started to shake as though I had the ague.

My gaoler laughed nastily. 'Well, they're not wastin' time. It looks like today yer kiss the Devil's arse. They'll have the faggots piled for you.' He grabbed my head and forced a kiss on my mouth before he swaggered out to meet the sheriff.

# VIII

With a sense of inevitability I watched the warrant handed over and Sheriff Mathew's gaze seek me out. I cursed that it was he who had come for me since he had never forgiven my father for opposing his acceptance into the Mercers Guild.

At a nod from him, his sergeant-at-law hauled me into the gaolers' room off the courtyard. The head gaoler and the soldiers crammed the doorway. For a moment, I thought they were going to rape me, one by one.

'Kirtle off,' the sergeant ordered. 'Shift only. Head uncovered. Hair loose.'

'Never!'

'Put it this way, you'll burn quicker.' The gaoler exchanged grins with the others. 'Yer hair will sizzle in no time.'

'To Hell with that!' I snapped, but with the pack of them threatening to manhandle me, I had little choice but to disrobe and unplait my hair.

'Barefoot! Take off them shoes!'

Anger was a crutch when my mind was crippled with the horror of burning at the stake. I turned my back and removed my garters and hose. 'Why hasn't a priest come to shrive me if I am to die?' I snarled over my shoulder.

'They do it next to the bonfire,' the gaoler chortled. 'Keeps the crowd nettled up, don't it?'

My immediate fear was that the soldiers were going to strap me to a hurdle and drag me through the streets, but they bound my hands with the long rope and tied the other end to the sheriff's stirrup. Thus I was pulled out into the street like a common whore in just a cotton shift with only my loosened hair to give me modesty.

I would not weep at this gross humiliation. It was taking all my effort just to keep upright. The knobbly cobblestones hurt. My feet would be bleeding if I had to walk all the way to Smithfield, but better bloody soles than my back hurdled skinless. My anxious thoughts were so cantered on the horror awaiting me that I did not notice at first that not only were we heading towards St Paul's but also the shops of Bowyer Row and Ave Mary Lane were bolted. Then enlightenment came like a reprieve. Today was the Sabbath! There were never executions on Sundays.

I stopped stock still. 'Sheriff Mathew!' I cried out, pulling against the rope.

'Ooooh, Sheriff Mathew, coo-ee, coo-ee,' mocked the crowd.

Irritated, he turned his head with a haughty look. 'What is it, woman? If you need to relieve yourself, do it now.' His words shocked me but I had a more pressing matter.

'I want to know if you are going to burn me?' The soldiers and people laughed.

Mathew held up his hand for silence, and drew his lips together with false pity. 'Foolish creature, whatever gave you that notion?'

'The gaoler said—'

'"The gaoler said",' he mimicked. 'One can tell your brain is only between your thighs. You're to do penance as a strumpet, Elizabeth Lambard.' He kneed his horse forward.

They were going to stone me? Like Father's whore? No, this could not be. No, no!

'I'm a freewoman of the city,' I protested, pulling back with all my strength, but Mathew ignored me.

'Wotcha doing later after they've sloshed the shit off you, darlin'?' yelled an apprentice in Poulterers' livery, swaggering alongside.

'Penny a screw now?' jeered another.

'Surely you're worth at least a groat,' I jibed, swallowing my tears. The jest worked; they became kinder. It was a mercy to enter the cathedral away from their taunts. Except I was wrong in that as well.

There was no holiness in St Paul's that day. Here was Mathew's haughty hate made hundredfold. If my hands shook as I carried the burning taper up the nave, it was because I had never known until now how much these self-righteous London worthies loathed me. Smug, disdaining to show overt glee, they stared ahead as I passed: I had become filth to be sidestepped by their clean-heeled virtue.

Bishop Kemp, flanked by a line of priests on either hand, was waiting for me on the chancel steps below the Rood screen. If he had not already acquitted me of witchcraft, I might have turned and hurled my defiance at the gloating hypocrites. Let them haul Gloucester in here, too, make him do penance for the bastards he'd fathered. Hypocrites! But as I knelt on the steps and saw the poor Lord Christ nailed in agony upon the Rood above, my indignation seeped away. What was my humiliation compared to His? Thus, I made my confession in a contrite voice, and Bishop Kemp set his hand upon my head in forgiveness and decreed that I must go forth and show to the people that I was a self-confessed sinner and truly penitent.

As the clergy escorted me out behind the processional cross, I kept my head high, yet without my headdress and robes, and

I tasted shame like ashes in my mouth. People who knew me stared stonily ahead. Hands that once reached for my help were tightly clasped in pious prayer. But as I passed level, I know they looked. The men's glances fingered me lasciviously through my shift, while the wives, assuaging envy, cast daggers of malice at my back.

My pride, false and treacherous, armoured me as far as the west door, but when I glimpsed St Paul's Yard and heard the roar that went up from the mob, I nearly retched in shock. It was my childhood horror of Tower Hill come alive. This was no ordinary Sabbath crowd such as pelted my father's mistress, but a rabble, already five or six deep, surrounding the great yard. The lords' and guilds' stands, set either side the cathedral's southern door, were filling fast. My horror grew. The open space that I must walk was vast, about four hundred paces in length; God knows how wide.

The circle of soldiers was struggling to hold back the crowd as more people poured in through the archways. Faces packed the windows of every house and turret. Some youths were clambering across the roofs of the shops and gatehouses. Others were straddling tree branches, hanging onto ladders or perched on barrels and crates. Making the round where I must walk were barrow-men, ladling out excrement into pails and selling bags of stones.

As if to torment me further, the sheriff's men hauled me aside, hiding me within a thicket of pikes while the worthies hastened from the cathedral. Then came the blare of trumpets and I heard curses and hooves. Had Lord Protector Gloucester come to see me shamed? I knew then the price of my years of glory was this: Gloucester's retaliation against the Woodvilles for thieving his brother. I was the whipping child, the abscess of Ned's adultery that must be aired and cleansed by public scorn. This wasn't about me, I tried to tell myself, but it was no comfort. The baying crowd would not care. They were here to mock and make sport.

However, it wasn't Gloucester causing the upheaval but his bootlicker, Buckingham, and in his fulsome retinue I glimpsed faces from Beaumont's Inn. Curse them! More than a score of Hastings' henchmen.

There were angry shouts. The soldiers about me craned to see the quarrel. Buckingham's pack must be forcing their way into the crowd about the nobles' stand.

I was trembling. Wretchedness overwhelmed me. Mourning the men I loved, what did pride matter? Let the people spit and hurl piss at me. If public repentance was what God wanted, shouldn't I welcome it? Call it expiation. And yet? And yet degradation before hundreds of people?

About me, my guard slammed their halberds in attention. That whoreson Mathew had ridden across to see if I was still standing. His smile was cruel. Mine was icy and resolute. The essence that makes us what we are, that won't let go against the odds, kept me on my feet.

Mathew deliberately withheld me as if I was the fiercest bitch at a dogfight, all to whet the people's appetite, and when the rabble's impatience was ratcheted to breaking, he spurred his horse forward into the centre of the yard and held up a gauntlet for silence. I heard my name and the monstrous epithets that followed. The crowd roared its hunger.

My guards, feeding on the jeers and huzzahs, made great show of stepping aside and lowering their pikes to prod me forwards. A cluster of churchmen was waiting. One gave me a fresh-lit taper. Another raised the brass processional cross. I was to walk behind him with two priests following me swinging censers and chanting prayers.

I crossed a heart that was trying to flee my ribs, and took the first step. The gritty cobbles made me totter and it was hard to retain any dignity. I fixed my gaze on the rope sandals of the cross bearer. The priests were keeping their distance, ensuring that I could be easily pelted without the filth spattering them.

God was in no mood to forgive. This might be June, but a sharp breeze stabbed west across the open yard. It smacked the blood into my cheeks and tossed my mantle of hair back from my breasts. No longer shielded, I felt my nipples chill and pucker against the thin cotton so I lifted the taper higher trying to hide my breasts with my elbows. I almost set fire to my hair, my hands were trembling so.

O Christ, is this where life had brought me? All effort, fore-thought, charity to others, loyalty and love to Ned and Hastings, all gone for this? I hadn't been capricious or vengeful or greedy or— O Jesu, forgive my sins! Redeemer, stretch out Your hand to me. I have sinned. I have sinned. I have sinned.

My body was tense, ready to flinch at the first stone, but the people close by fell eerily silent as though bewitched. Eyes glassy and wide, lips gargoyle slits of indecision, they stared as I passed, the pails of shit and piss hanging in their hands, their children tugging at them in puzzlement.

Maybe I could survive this? Maybe there was respect for Ned left in their hearts, but men in black and scarlet were moving through the crowd, ahead of me – Buckingham's dogs, inciting the people to stone me.

'Your taxes went to clothe this slut!' bawled one of them, lobbing a stone over the people's heads. It fell short and a child started screaming. The crowd turned, snarling.

'The bread from your children's mouths. Stone the old goat's wh—' The man was sucked down into the heaving mass. Fists rose and descended.

The cross bearer, knowing his duty, swung round on me.

'Witch! Fornicator!' he snarled loudly, brandishing his cross to stir the people, but they still stood stunned as though I was some exotic beast parading past. I could only thank God as I reached the south-east corner unscathed. Facing me now was the nobles' stand.

A pailful of piss and turds splashed my path. I faltered.

O Ned! Help me!

*'Heigh, what's a bit of muck?'* I remembered his laughter in Eltham meadows as I fell from horseback into a ripe cow turd. *'Gold comes from muck, Jane. Adam came from muck.'*

But my heart knew he lay lifeless, walled in beneath his chantry. And my beloved Hastings, neck severed, eyes open in shock, lying at his feet.

I'm alone. There's no one to care anymore.

Mathew's horse danced beside me. 'Keep moving, strumpet! You want this to take all day?'

I shook my hair forwards and with my eyes downcast, I walked towards hateful Buckingham.

'God save young King Edward!' yelled a brave woman's voice. 'When's the crowning?'

'Where's good Lord Hastings?' shouted another voice. Boos and hissing came from the crowd. Through my strands of hair, I glimpsed the duke rise. His companions sprang to their feet, jeering and fisting the air at me.

Dared I? Yes, I lifted my head, stared at Buckingham as I passed and holding my right hand at my side, lifted my third finger.

The common people who saw cheered. The rest watched in silence.

I reached the cathedral's south door and lowered my eyes again in penitence, relief flooding my soul – until a giggling child threw a spatter of pebbles. No, it wasn't over. I still had to pass the guilds' stand.

Was Jack here to witness my humiliation? Had he told Father and Mama?

I'd broken God's commandments, defiled my family, shamed my husband and the guild, striven for luxury and riches. For what? To die a street slut? How Margery Paddesley must be smirking.

I looked up and saw her ahead, watching me. Margery, the Lord Mayor's daughter, hefty, scarlet clad, white jowled, staring, drawing breath. Paddesley and Shelley either side her, making haste to stand, saliva ready in their mouths.

*Now it comes.* I stumbled, missing my foothold on the uneven ground. *Keep walking, count. Try not to think.*

Margery shifting to— My breath snagged.

Dear God, she was jabbing the men back with her elbows, standing up to – *Clap*?

Margery? Applauding me? Paddesley trying to pull her down, her slapping him away, her face anxious, earnest, defiant. Around her, guildsmen's backs stiff with shock.

Dame Juliana Shaa heaving herself up and, O Lord, regardless of her husband's reputation, clapping as well. Alys and the Shelleys' daughter. The men outraged. Merciful God, other guild wives, each pair of hands beginning to move. Applauding.

*Applauding*? They're applauding me!

Tears choked my throat. Gratitude almost burst my heart asunder. Then the stand was behind me. Paddesley yelling, Juliana serene as an ancient keep.

Passing the common people again. A few more steps. One, two, keep counting, three, four.

I collapsed on the cathedral steps. Mathew was shouting orders. The soldiers grabbed my arms and hauled me towards a cart. Hell erupted around us as they flung me face first into the back. Yells and shouting, Mathew trying to control his horse, its hooves rearing and crashing. I shrank back as a pack of youths fought towards the cart. They were knocking the soldiers aside, unyoking the horses. Then they seized the pole and swung the cart around.

Numb with horror, I was on my knees, gripping the wooden sides as the cart hurtled at the archway to Carter Lane. Women and children scattered like terrified chickens. The soldiers were giving chase, their voices hoarse.

But this wasn't a mob wanting to burn me, I realised, my heart lifting. The youths running beside the cart were the street lads for whom I had found apprenticeships, and they were laughing, urging each other on, high as kites on ale and exuberance.

I struggled to keep my balance as we rattled into Creed Lane. This was wild, insane. Maybe tomorrow Gloucester would have me burnt, but I was laughing with triumph and a prayer of gratitude for God's mercy as we reached Ludgate.

The gaoler's jaw almost hit his bootcaps. 'Was there a postponement?' he demanded, marvelling at my unscathed bosom as he unlocked the gate.

'Like the coronation?' I retorted tartly, and my escort cheered.


That evening my foreign friends arrived with firkins, capons and minstrels. Greased with bribes, the gaolers let them in.

'Today was quite remarkable,' Caniziani remarked as he and Sasiola stood with me upon the city rampart that was part of the prison. They had watched my penance together from a friend's house in New Change.

'All beyond my understanding,' I murmured, savouring my wine. Tonight I rejoiced; tomorrow fear would return in cruel measure.

Caniziani liked to put matters in perspective.

'In my opinion, two things saved you, Elizabetta. Firstly, the people's love for Eduardo and his sons, who I think will never wear the crown.' He set a finger upon my lips. 'Let us say no more on that for you are not yet out of danger, hmm? And, secondly, your beauty and humility.' He read my astonishment.

Beside him, Sasiola nodded. 'People see beauty as the sign of a pure soul.'

'But—' I protested.

'No more, Elizabetta. You wish your head to swell?'

'No, but...' I could only shake my head in disbelief for words were beyond me.

Defiance comes in many guises: like the laughter and music in the yard below. I hoped some doughty soul would brave the dukes tomorrow and tell them how last night we danced the *saltarello* in the yard of Ludgate Gaol.

# Herself

# I

Ned's upright brother left me in prison. I daresay he had other matters on his mind, like thieving his nephew's crown. The morrow after my penance, the Queen foolishly surrendered little Prince Dickon to him. Perhaps she thought he might release Rivers and Sir Richard Grey, but the child joined young Edward in the Tower, and the following Sunday Sir Edmund Shaa's brother, Friar Ralph, gave a sermon at Paul's Cross implying the boys were bastards.

I still had the charge of treason hovering over my head like a monstrous bird of prey, and Ludgate, with the gaoler eyeing me like a cat with a titmouse, was no Paradise, so I decided to send a petition to Lady Anne, Gloucester's wife, begging her to intercede.

'Waste of time,' groaned Will, as he watched me sign the letter to her grace. 'She's Lady Hastings' niece, and seeing that you were fornicating with—'

'Oh, hush,' I chided, heating the sealing wax he had brought to seal it. 'If you don't ride at a quintain, you'll never hit it.'

★

Gloucester hit his quintain. The third week in June, Buckingham addressed anything that could be addressed: the Lords, the Common, the Guilds – and the rats from the sewers, I daresay – and on the Thursday he led a long crocodilus of lords and citizens to Baynard's Castle where he petitioned his cousin of Gloucester to accept the crown. With an army of northerners freshly arrived from York camped out at Smithfield, and the news that Rivers and Grey had been executed, no one was going to speak up for Ned's young boys in the Tower. This time the coronation would go ahead – with a different king. I wept when I heard, but there was nothing I could do.

I do not know if the queen-to-be was moved by my petition, or whether Gloucester was so euphoric at his new fortune that he could be merciful, but he agreed to my release providing it was into my father's care.

'I am past thirty,' I exclaimed to the sheriff's sergeant when he came to oversee my release. 'I do not need to be handed back to my family like a disgraced child.'

'Mistress Shore, if you are over thirty, I'll eat my hat. You don't look a day past five-and-twenty.' That buffeted the wind out of my indignation.

In Father's absence, it was Jack who arrived to take custody. We had not spoken for seven years. He was so like our father at the same age save he wore his hair longer and he'd acquired a stomach to match the stout pouch on his belt.

'This is a disgrace,' he muttered to Will as the three of us walked to the gate under the stares of the other prisoners. 'I run a respectable household.'

'It's a disgrace that a grown woman cannot be treated with dignity,' I retorted, my spirits bolstered by my return to freedom.

'What are you going to do – lock me in your cellar if I try to return to my house?'

'You haven't got a house, Elizabeth, neither have your silk-women. The crown has seized all your possessions.'

'WHAT!' I squealed. I could have scratched Gloucester and Buckingham's eyeballs out and hurled them to the nearest pig.

'What did you expect, sister? Traitors' possessions became the property of the crown. Even the clothes you are wearing are borrowed from my wife.'

'Jack, no! Surely my release means I've been acquitted?'

'Acquitted! Don't make me laugh, Elizabeth. Why do you think I have charge of you? One false step and you'll be back in Ludgate. I'm standing warranty for you, didn't you know that?'

Will put a hand on my shoulder. 'Let's get you home.'

'Home!' I echoed bleakly. Back to Silver Street as though I was a wicked child. 'And who has *my* home?'


Jack's wife, Eleanor, was stern to me at first, but when she saw with what joy I greeted my nephews and nieces, her manners grew easier, and within a few days I was no longer tainted in her eyes but a welcome sister-in-law.

Margery came to see me the moment she heard I was out of Ludgate. I found myself greatly in her debt for she explained that she had helped my silkwomen move to temporary lodgings in Basinghall ward not far from the Guildhall, and she had also reap-pointed my book-keeper.

'Only until you are back on your feet, of course, Lizbeth, and I am just the whitewash. It's really Father who is helping them, but we cannot let that be known, not with him being newly knighted by the King, so do not breath a word of this to anyone. Now I must go. There is so much to do with the coronation in just a few days.'

The coronation! London could think of nothing else. The Saturday after I was freed, King Richard III was crowned in great magnificence in St Peter's Abbey, Westminster. I truly pitied Ned's poor sons in the Tower hearing their uncle ride out to his coronation, but the law had upheld Richard's title. The only man who might have rescued them was Dorset. He had broken sanctuary on the day of Hastings' death. However, even if he managed to outrun the dogs King Richard's men were using to hunt him down, I doubt he had the fire in his belly to succeed. In any case, who would help him? The kingdom was already settling down to its new master.

Jack had no complaints. He had done well with orders from the court so he participated most willingly in the coronation procession. When he came back from the abbey, puffed up with pride like a courting pigeon, wanting to tell us what King Richard had worn, I lost my temper.

'I hope that cursed crown gives him the biggest megrim in history! Pah! I really wish I was a proper witch so I might curse him to Hell!'

'Elizabeth!' Eleanor looked utterly shocked. 'If the King's friends heard you...'

'Yes, I'd be ashes by breakfast.'

Jack was inured to my tantrums. 'Save your scowls, sister. Quite frankly, I could not care a mouse's turd who wears the crown except it be a man of good sense, who protects our trade. I' faith, I'd rather have a hawk like Gloucester than the Woodville jays, all glitter and warble. Say nothing and think what you please, that's my motto. Like Will says, you should not have got embroiled in Lord Hastings' treason.'

'There was no treason, Jack.'

'Elizabeth,' he admonished, holding me by the shoulders. 'What did I just say? Hold your tongue and cover your heart!'

*

I was not the only one to be dispossessed. The Woodville family lost all their manors. To his credit, our new king did not seize any of Hastings' lands and he must have been right fond of Lady Kate, for later that July he issued a proclamation that no one was to harm her and she was allowed to keep wardship of her children. Buckingham must have gagged at that for I'm sure he coveted Hastings' estates.

Looking back, I wonder how many of Hastings' men changed their cotes before their master was murdered? Were they all ladder-climbers like Catesby? If I ever met that cursed Judas again, I'd jab my fingers in his eyes. As for that serpent Buckingham, if I were King Richard, I'd watch my back.

Nightmares had plagued me since my penance. I would awake sweating, believing myself in the Tower cell or walking Paul's Yard. I had also acquired a terror of going forth in public. Eleanor was very understanding and patient. The first day she took me out into the street was the worst. Heavily veiled and with Jack's children holding my hands, I managed to walk halfway to Foster Lane but I was shaking and ill by the time we returned to Silver Street. Next day we ventured further and gradually I began to acquire some sovereignty over my panic. Will helped me, too, coaxing me to speak my fears aloud as though by airing them in the sane air of day would cleanse the fear away. The other healing to my soul was my old friend Margery.

The second time she visited, she offered the kiss of peace, even though Paddesley had forbade her to visit again. I was so grateful for her courage. She also brought gowns that no longer fitted her and made me try them on straight away so she might pin where we should take them in.

'I was so jealous as a girl,' she admitted as we sat sewing next day in Eleanor's solar. 'There you were, always so lovely, the apprentices worshipping you like a goddess, while I waddled at your side unnoticed. And then, of course, you won the King.'

'You make it sound like a game of cards, Meg. I hardly had a choice.'

'Pah to that! Anyway, I'd have done the same in your shoes.' She bit off a thread. 'Does Jack know about…you know…your Father's affair?'

I shook my head. 'And he never will, I hope.'


In late July, when the new king and his retinue set forth on a meandering progress northwards, and Buckingham sloped back to Wales hauling Bishop Morton with him for safe keeping, I felt a greater sense of freedom. At last I was able to see what could be done to regain my possessions. My goods alone were worth three thousand marks.

'Forget it!' Jack advised. 'There isn't a lawyer this side of Paradise that will take your case.'

However, who should come inquiring for me at Silver Street but my servants, Isabel and Roger Young. We exchanged news of our adventures. They had been hiding at his uncle's house in Kingston, too frightened to return to London. Lubbe had avoided arrest as well and was gone back to his mother in Croydon.

I was glad to see them. Of course, with my house and goods thieved by King Richard, I had no means to employ them now unless…unless, as Isabel pointed out, I could get my sapphire collar back. Well, I had been a king's mistress; now, I might prove a thief.

'Sneak into your own house?' Jack snorted, when I aired my plan. 'Maybe I should have you housed in Bedlam. Listen, we know that your place was thoroughly searched. They probably found your necklace, seeing it was mentioned at your trial.'

'But you could be wrong, Jack. My valuables might still be there.'

'Still be where exactly?' asked Will.

'Under a lavender bush,' I admitted sheepishly. I did not mention that what concerned me more was a packet of early letters from Ned that were peppered with endearments like '*Beloved mistress, who hath bewitched my soul*'. Innocent loving words that might still bind me to the stake.

I had an ally in my resourceful Isabel. She found herself employment with my former neighbour, and while renewing acquaintance with some of the servants in the street over a flagon of pudding ale, she discovered who had usurped my property. Another poxy lawyer – God curse him! Some 'Yorkshire Catesby' who had arrived in Gloucester's retinue and was working for the new Lord Chancellor.

According to the tidbits Isabel had garnered, every day, except the Sabbath, the lawyer walked down to Puddle Wharf and took a boat to Westminster. He did not keep a dog, his servants shopped in Cheapside on Tuesdays and bought fish in Billingsgate each Friday morning. On the last two Sabbaths, he and his servants had worshipped at the Goldsmiths' church of St John Zachary in Maiden Lane. Well, come next Sunday, I hoped there would be a long, enthralling sermon.

Acquiring hose and doublet when you haven't two pennies to rub together required a loose interpretation of the verb 'to borrow'. I lie, it was done honestly; I cajoled Jack's youngest apprentice into lending me a worsted cap with earflaps, his dark blue tunic and a pair of woollen hose, which proved right ticklish.

I confided in no one but Isabel and she insisted on helping. On Sunday morning, I pleaded the custom of women and stayed home while the rest of the household went to Will's sermon at St Leonard's.

I was still unused to going out alone so I was grateful for Isabel's company. Arm-in-arm, we set forth. At least in my boy's garb no one would mistake me for Mistress Shore, but I felt strange being able to stride out manfully with no petticotes rustling at my ankles. But we had only gone a few paces when my wretched hose began to slide and I had to go back to the house and tie the aiglets tighter.

My strategy was for Isabel to stand watch at the corner of the lane while I tackled the lavender bush. I hoped then to break into my house by wriggling through the pantry window. Its formidable grille was actually loose. A blade could prod up the inside catch, and I had a key to the inside door. If any of the household returned early from Mass, Isabel would immediately knock at the front door and distract them by inquiring where she might find Mistress Shore.

First we knocked to make sure no one was home and then I let myself into my garden. The sowthistles and hyssop were high but someone had plucked the gooseberries and picked off the dead marigold heads. My little lavender bush looked none too healthy. I set to work swiftly with the trowel I had purloined from Jack's yard and heaved a sigh of relief that the coffer was still there. But it proved empty.

For an instant, I sat back on my heels in shock, but then I pulled myself together and patted the earth back. The sheriff's men must have noted the fresh dug earth. Ah well, no time to indulge in a tantrum; I needed to get into my house.

Will's spare key to the back door no longer worked and a new iron grille was nailed across the pantry window. I frowned and eyed the upper casements, wondering how I might try the blade trick on my bedchamber windowlight. Then I remembered that when I had first inspected the house there had been an old ladder slumbering, forgotten, in the briars along the back fence.

It was still there but required much untangling. An outpost of snails no doubt were cursing me in their slow way as I wrenched it forth. The wood was splintery. Some of the lower rungs were rotten and loose, but I tested the others and they felt sound enough.

I was glad of my boy's garb as I climbed, and it proved a precarious business to slide my little sheath knife in beneath the catch and then to abandon the ladder and clamber across the sill. My heart was making more noise than my house as I landed upon someone else's travelling chest and stood listening warily for an alien footfall or familiar creak upon the stairs that betrayed another's presence. Then, reassured, I looked about me.

God damn him! The thieving slobberer of Gloucester's bootcaps was using everything of mine: the blue bed curtains and coverlet with the oak leaf embroidery, my silken, diapered pillows, the best ewer and jug, the towels. His mantle and hat hung upon my wall peg; a pair of riding boots was neatly placed beside my bedsteps; his leather strop hung beside the mirror where I used to braid my hair, and a razor and lathering cup stood where I had lain my combs and stored my perfumes. Mongrel!

At least the room was perfectly kept; evidently he loved neatness or else employed a diligent servant because no crumpled shirt or discarded hose cluttered the floorboards. No sign of a wife either – no stray stocking ball beneath the bed or a scatter of hair pins on the shelf. Well, I was glad. Somehow the thought of a woman using my possessions was worse.

For an instant, I sadly stroked my fingers down my bed hangings and then a mew outside the door tore at my soul. Hercules!

I *had* to let him in. Gathering the purring bundle into my arms I let time roll back for a luxurious, indulgent instant, imagining that I heard Ned's foot upon the stairs. But, alas, the sand was running too fast through this morning's hourglass.

My bedchamber held two hiding places. One was in the panelling behind my bed canopy, but I had left nothing there. What
I sought was cleverly concealed in the curved lid of my clothing
chest, which still stood at the foot of the bed.

Kneeling before it, I eased back the heavy lid. An aroma of
rosemary and meadowsweet, probably sprigs I had gathered last
year, was invaded by a teasing musky scent, which rose from the
several shirts folded on top. So the knave liked to smell good.
Well tally ho for him! I was tempted to delve down and see if my
kirtles lay beneath his garments, but the lid held the more important treasure.

Hercules sprang onto the narrow edge of the chest. I shifted
him, leant forward and saw the telltale force marks on the wood.
Someone had found the hiding place.

'Oh!' I snorted, cursing my enemies to Hell, and then— '*OH!*'
Something sharp was prodding my ribs and someone's foot was
anchoring the skirt of my tunic.

'Lift your hands, stand up and turn very slowly,' commanded a
male voice with a Yorkshire twang. Was this the whoreson, who
had been given my house, or one of his serving men? Either way
they deserved a knee in the groin, but the way things were going
I'd be back in prison by dinnertime. I hoped his balls shrivelled!

My garment was permitted liberty but the blade tip kept pace with
me. I turned and swallowed. An unsheathed sword was pointing at
my throat. The man was about my age. No milk and ginger north-
erner here, but dark brown hair and blue eyes – intelligent eyes –
and…yes, a good quality doublet. It had to be the lawyer. I stared
back miserably with Hercules arching against my calves.

'Please sir, forgive me, sir,' I wailed, dropping back to my knees
and wringing my hands. 'I dunno wot got inner me. Please, don't
turn me in, sir.'

Hercules sprang out the way as the sword tip slid past my left ear. With a deft movement, the blade flicked my cap away. My foe's lips twisted with smug triumph at my tight-coiled braids.

'You forget, Mistress Shore, that your face is famous. Not to mention the rest of you.'

'Damnation,' I muttered.

'In fact, you've been in my thoughts a great deal, madame, and not just because of St Paul's Yard.'

'Oh?' I muttered loftily, my face heating. Was he going to demand a tumble in return for letting me go? Scowling at the naked blade, I muttered, 'Is that really necessary now or does it make you feel safer in such threatening company?'

He tucked the sword under his left arm and offered me his hand. With a sigh of resignation, I accepted. His fingers were neither flabby nor moist, but pleasantly strong.

'Your house is quite delightful, Mistress Shore.'

I bit back a tirade on arse-licking lawyers who accept other people's houses without a qualm of conscience, but something needed saying. 'Oh, I am so pleased,' I retorted witheringly. 'Perhaps you'd like to purchase it honestly?'

'I do admit to feeling guilty. Lying between your sheets, learning the perfume of your clothes, reading the pages where your books fall open, I feel as though I already know you.'

Lord, this was becoming far too intimate.

'You are a fascinating woman, Mistress Shore. Thank you so much for your treason. I cannot think of anywhere else in London where I would rather live.'

The stinking son of a pox-ridden pimp! Why didn't he grind his boot heel in my face as well!

'My pleasure, sir,' I replied loftily. 'If you will now allow me to go on my way…' I indicated the ladder.

'Without what you came for? That would be churlish of me.' He tossed the sword on to the bed and folded his arms. Free of the weapon, the fingers of his right hand tapped consideringly against his sleeve. I recognised a bargaining look and braced myself. 'I'm prepared to compromise, Mistress Shore,' he said at last. 'You can have either the letters or the sapphire collar.'

*Either!* I hope the Devil fried his nether parts.

'They *both* belong to me, sir, and I consider you a knave and a thief to withhold them.'

'On the contrary, madame, everything you own now belongs to me with the exception of your own person, of course. As I said, I offer you a compromise.'

It was some sort of test. Selling the necklace would make my life easier. I would no longer have to wear a borrowed gown, I could buy gifts for Eleanor and the children, and go about. But the letters – all I had left of the happiest times of my life.

'The letters, if you please, then,' I said gravely.

Taking the keys from his belt, he opened his travelling chest and lifted out a strongbox that seemed to lack a lock until he slid back a piece of the carving and inserted a smaller key. Inside were several bundles of papers. He held out mine. I had never tied the bow of the green ribbon that way. He must have read them or someone else had.

'Thank you,' I said coldly and cradled the packet to my breast like a precious infant. Then I curtsied with a glare. 'Good day to you, sir.'

'You may use the stairs,' he exclaimed, concerned to see me make for the window.

The perverse demon in me needed to prove something. 'But they are *your* stairs.'

'And it's *my* plaguey ladder.' He grabbed my wrist and thrust me towards the door. 'Don't be so stubborn.'

'Stubbornness is all that your king has left me.'

'Really? It sounds like wounded pride to me.'

I felt like giving him two fingers but that would show how much he'd riled me.

'Good day to you, sir,' I snarled and flounced out.

'Mistress Shore!' I halted on the stair but I did not look round. 'My name is Thomas Lynom, Mistress Shore.'

'And mine is Elizabeth Lambard, Master Lynom,' I said haughtily to the ceiling above me. 'It is only my enemies who call me Mistress Shore.'

Do not suppose I did not curse Master Lynom thoroughly on the way home but, as Isabel pointed out, I was fortunate that he had not marched me to the sheriff. Why had he not? What kind of cat-and-mouse game was he playing?

As we reached Silver Street, my world was rocked again; a filthy beggar grabbed my arm.

'Alms,' he pleaded, his eyes wild.

I shook him off as though his touch was scalding. Although I did not mind being charitable, I disliked being touched by strangers, especially when it was almost the pestilence season. Isabel took him to task but he pursued us right to Jack's door and we had to shut it in his face, a face that haunted me. I could not think why, but I had other matters on my mind.

While Jack and his wife were gone to Clerkenwell Fields that evening, I read through each of Ned's letters. There were twenty-four in all, mostly written in the first year that we had been lovers. Ardent letters from Calais, St Christ-sur-Somme, Amiens, Picquigny that still brought a blush to my cheeks. No wonder Thomas Lynom had eyed me with speculation.

It was the endearments that concerned me, garlands of words like: '*Beloved witch of my heart who hath me in your thrall*' and '*utterly under yr spell, my sweet sorceress, Yrs, N*', *Edwardus Quartus* written

beneath with a magnificent flourish. These letters I placed in one
pile.

The later ones that began, '*Most Dear Elizabeth*' and ended
with '*Please can you ask Myddelton to have especial care to my hound,
Smoky, that was ailing Tuesday last and see whether he still be off his
food*', I stacked separately, then I carried the first pile down to
the kitchen and burned them one by one, with tears pouring
down my cheeks. Far better I burned Ned's letters than his words
burned me.

# II

The beggar! In the middle of the night it dawned on me who he was.

Next morning, when I went out with Eleanor and the children, he was huddling from the drizzle beneath the jut of our upper storey, waiting to ambush me. He had cast dust into the birds' nest of mussed hair to hide his ash blond colouring, and I suppose that was why his unkempt beard was filthy too. His grimy, tattered tunic was as ancient as any beggar's and his fingernails were clogged and torn.

'Largesse,' Dorset pleaded, as he tottered after us. 'Charity for the love of God.'

'Pray go on,' I said to Eleanor. Jack had allowed me some pin money so I made great play of fumbling in my purse.

'I thought you in Brittany with Tudor,' I whispered, pretending to count out my coins.

'With Gloucester's men watching every wharf, hunting me like a wild beast? That's why I've come back in.' His bony fingers snared my wrist. 'I've been eating the crumbs of horse bread from the gutter. Horse bread! Help me for the love of God!'

I narrowed my eyes in warning, for Eleanor was waiting at the corner. 'Here.' I tipped the little money I had into his dirt-rimmed palm. 'Meet me outside St Leonard's Church in Foster Lane at noon. I'll bring you food.'

It was dangerous to help him, but he was like a life rope to the past, and even if I despised him, to see any man brought so low was pitiful.

At noon, I set out for Will's church. It had a small yard about it and Dorset was already there, warming in a patch of sunlight. By the way he tore into the bread and cheese, I knew he had not lied, and now I had time to observe him, I could see how his bones threatened to pierce his skin.

'Eat slowly,' I pleaded, 'else you'll throw the whole lot up again. Here!' I passed across a leather bottle of ale.

He took a swig, closing his eyes and savouring it as though it was some heavenly elixir. Only when he had eaten every crumb did he speak again. 'Pity about the old man. Just when he was ripe to come to terms.' I must have looked slow, for he swiped his knuckle across the hairs on his upper lip and added, 'Father Hastings, Elizabeth!'

My wounds were too raw to tolerate a dissection.

'Buckingham wanted him out the way,' I declared firmly. 'There was no treason.' It had become my creed, but reading the scorn in Dorset's face, I knew I faced a heretic.

'Sweet Christ!' I snapped. 'Does it matter?' I wanted to scream: *if you had gone to Stony Stratford instead of thieving Ned's treasure, your stepbrother would be wearing the crown and Hastings might still be alive.* But I was guilty as well: if I had stayed away from the sanctuary… If, if, if! The detritus of 'ifs' would clog the Thames.

He took another swig and shook the bottle to see how much was left. 'We are going to get my brothers out.' Disbelief must have flared in my face, for he added, 'In Christ's name, Jane, at least give me a bed for the night! You don't have to share but…' The leer vanished. His gaze flicked like a hunted animal's to something over my shoulder. 'God's sake! There's some turd watching us.'

I swallowed fearfully and slowly turned my head. Of all people, it was the lawyer, Thomas Lynom, leaning upon the churchyard wall.

Quick-wittedly I smiled, waved, and said through my teeth, 'He's Gloucester's man. Get-out-of-here!'

Dorset had the sense not to panic. He slithered back, saluting me so his face was half-hidden, snatched up the leather flask and loped off, round-shouldered, in the other direction, out to Pope Lane. I stood up, shaking the crumbs from my skirt, and walked towards my enemy as though I had promised him a dance. How much had those keen eyes observed?

'You seem to have a soft heart for beggars, Mistress Lambard.'

'But no alms to give them, alas.' I beamed up at him with a confidence that was only skin deep. He looked very fine in his red mantle and matching hat with its turned back brim, but in the hedgerows scarlet is a warning of poison within. 'My brother is the priest here. I sometimes help him with his charity. Were you passing by?'

His grin was disarming if you did not note how his eyes were still observing the far side of the churchyard. 'No, I came to seek out your brother and ask where I might find you.'

'And now you have.'

'Perhaps if you are finished with…your *charity*, I may escort you to your house?'

'You are living *in my house*.'

He held up his hands. 'A poor choice of words. I apologise. Then may I escort you…somewhere?'

'I purpose to visit a friend in Silver Street,' I lied. He opened the gate for me to join him. 'So you haven't gone north, sir?' I remarked dryly as we walked together. *North with your bloody-handed master.*

'No, too much work here, Mistress Lambard. I'm employed by the new chancellor.'

'Ah, Bishop Russell,' I said knowledgeably. 'Yes, I've met him. He is…a most learned and diligent man.' *Godly, too, until Gloucester bribed him with the chancellorship!*

'I think so, too. England is in good hands.'

*Pah!*

The conversation hobbled, with me trying to avoid its hidden holes and puddled furrows. I would have sworn on saint's bones that either Lynom planned to solicit me – tup me for each sapphire – or else he was hoping I'd lead him to Dorset. This morning had been a close shave. Not one I wanted to repeat.

We reached Silver Street. 'Here is my destination.' I murmured politely. 'Thank you for your company.' I curtsied shallowly and turned away, only to have an afterthought. 'By the way, Master Lynom, you will need to eat the colewort before it goes to seed and the walnuts need picking for pickling and compote.'

'How very wifely of you. I'll tell my servants.' He put a swift, possessive hand upon my arm and grabbed me aside from the oncoming cart of horse dung. Oh, very husbandly! But his next words chilled me to my heart:

'Now, tell me, before we part! Did you burn your letters?'

I flinched in shock, my cosmetic cheerfulness gone in an instant.

'Well, did you?' he asked sternly, with a glance around to ensure no one was close. 'Did you?'

*It was not his business!*

'Yes,' I mouthed reluctantly, blinking hard. The pain of destroying them still hurt.

'Good, I am relieved to hear it. You are a sensible woman, Mistress Lambard. Here's your reward.' I watched in a daze as he tugged something from the breast of his doublet. He dropped a leather drawstring bag, still warm, into my astonished hand, closed my fingers over it and walked away.

'Elizabeth?' A woman's voice made me turn. 'Ah, it is you!' I was clasped to the maternal bosom of Margery's mother, Juliana Shaa. Then she stepped back, observing me with amusement. 'Well, well, it gladdens me to see you with roses in your cheeks but I should have thought you'd had enough of lawyers. Especially that one!' Thomas Lynom was still in sight, striding along with an easy gait and the confidence of a man who has the best in life.

'Because he has my house?' I asked distractedly, my mind beginning to whirl faster than a cutler's grindstone. God help me! Had the dissembling cur made copies of my letters? When would he wind me in?

'Yes, he has your house.' Old Juliana observed the man's fine calves with an appreciative eye. 'But didn't you know about his new appointment, Elizabeth?'

'What appointment?' I asked with a horrid, sinking feeling.

'Oh, my dear, have a care!' Her eyes were no longer smiling. 'Master Lynom is now King Richard's Crown Solicitor.'


Alone in my tiny bedchamber I opened the drawstring bag. The new Crown Solicitor had given me back my sapphire necklace. I could not believe it! Later that day two menservants arrived bearing three of my gowns, two pairs of shoes, several bosom kerchiefs and two sets of silken chemises. Blushing, I sent a concise but gracious letter back. Thanks were all I offered. He wanted me in the palm of his hand. He knew too much. His testimony could destroy me. What other game was there?

When Jack announced at supper that since the plague month was almost upon us, he desired Eleanor, the children and I to leave within the week for Hinxworth, I almost threw my arms about him with relief. Dorset and Lynom would be left behind.

At Hinxworth we celebrated Lammasday and I made little star and dragon loaves for my nieces and nephews. Whitewashing out the ugly bits of the past weeks, I confessed to Father and Mama that Bishop Kemp had made me do a penance. I did not say it had been in front of the entire city nor, thank God, did they question me further.

The remainder of summer sped by. Jack fetched Eleanor the week before Michaelmas. He had missed her, even though he complained about a wife whose cheeks were brown as a milkmaid's, purple-fingered children and a half-dozen panniers of blackberries.

I tarried another month. Mama, bless her, wanted me to stay forever. Heaven forbid! I considered myself too young to be put out to rural pasture like some old mare, and by October I was fretting for the city. So was Father. Although the roads were muddy with the rain, he announced he would escort me back to Silver Street. He missed the excitement of rushing to the quay to bargain when a cargo vessel was sighted, or chewing on market matters with his friends.

On the surface, we found the city quiet. The great lords were still absent from Westminster, but there was a sinister rustling in the kingdom's undergrowth. Lord Howard, now the Duke of Norfolk, was acting as the King's Justiciar. Of late, his affinity included large numbers of armed men, and people were asking why. The very day after we arrived back, messengers in his grace's insignia were riding hither and thither, and Lord Mayor Bilisdon was summoned urgently to attend the duke.

'It won't be about the price of gold, neither!' declared my father and he high-tailed it round to the Shaas to find out which wind was up my lord of Norfolk's tail, for although Sir Edmund Shaa had finished his mayoral year, he was still at the heart of civic matters.

'You'll never believe it!' Father exclaimed on his return, herding the family into the solar and closing the door. 'There's word of rebellion throughout the southern shires. The King's in a pother and heading back as fast as he may. Would you believe, he sent for my lord of Buckingham and the duke refused to come! There's tales coming in from all over that Buckingham's allied himself with the Woodvilles and intends to restore Prince Edward to the throne.'

Oh yes, and the Sultan of Turkey's become a Christian!

'I don't believe it, Father,' I exclaimed. 'Why on earth would he? King Richard's made him wealthier than Croesus. It doesn't make sense unless… Of course, he wants the crown. He is the last lawful heir of the House of Lancaster! Ned was right never to trust him.'

My menfolk ignored my logic; any mention of 'Ned' was an embarrassment.

'Buckingham is married to a Woodville, Elizabeth,' Eleanor pointed out.

Jack chewed his lower lip. 'Can he do it, though? Has he sufficient men?'

Father sniffed. 'He has to march from Brecknock – damned end of the earth, and he's never fought a battle. As for the Woodvilles, unless Dorset has slunk back ashore, they haven't any leaders. It'll be naught but gentry and farmers unless there's some great traitor who hasn't shown his hand. I reckon, King Richard will swat 'em like fl—'

The knocking below halted him.

A knocking with a sinister urgency that made my blood run cold.

# III

That night I was back in Ludgate Gaol on suspicion of treason. Who had I lain with this time? Buckingham?

Thanks be to God, the head gaoler was not on duty when Sheriff Mayhew delivered me there that night. Next day on the Crown Solicitor's orders, I was taken from the yard and informed I was to be locked into an upstairs cell, where I was to await his interrogation. *Thomas Lynom's* interrogation? The damned man was stalking me. Or *storing* me. A potted mistress to be knifed out onto his bread? Well, I was not playing that game! And this upstart whoreson's foolish order to keep me solitary would render me vulnerable once the head-gaoler came back on duty.

The cell proved a dark little room, furnished with only a crudely joined stool and a necessity pail. An arrow-slit in the ancient wall let in a cross of meagre light. For some there might have been naught to do but listen to the mad girl, who thought she was me, singing tunelessly in the yard below, but I was so afraid that the head gaoler would come to rape me that I took up position in a corner with the stool in my grip. For the rest of the day and through the night, I tried to stay awake, tensing every time I heard footsteps approaching. By the time that Gloucester's familiar deigned to confront me the following afternoon, my nerves were a-jangle through lack of sleep and I was more than ready to scratch his eyes out. A brave man or else a fool, he bade his notary wait outside and entered my small cell alone. Water dripped from his heavy cloak, the leather of his boots was dark with wet and, despite a hood, his fringe of dark hair clung to his forehead like sculptured curls.

'Good day to you, Mistress Shore. It's raining hard out there,' he remarked amiably as though I had invited him into my parlour for some mulled wine and tartlets. 'Exercising with the stool, are you?'

Teeth clenched, I set it aside. I was determined not to let him provoke me, but he was looking me over with a grin. 'I hope you are proud of yourself!' I hissed, backing from him as far as I could. 'You have my house, my goods. What more will please you? A pot of my ashes?'

'I see you are in your usual fine fettle, Mistress Shore,' he answered, shrugging off his cloak. There was nowhere to hang it and, with a grimace, he folded it carefully and dumped it by the wall before he turned his attention back to me. 'You are being held at the King's pleasure. I suggest you adopt a more conciliatory manner, throw yourself on his mercy and tell us all we need to know.'

Had the Crown Solicitor been a stranger to me, some eminent, solemn greybeard who had bothered to come clad in a lawyer's gown, I might have conducted our discourse with greater care, but this was Lynom. His vitality, his cocky scarlet doublet, symbolic of his sudden rise to riches – not to mention the fact that he was sleeping in my bed, had read Ned's letters and was eyeing me with much amusement – made me forget all courtesy.

'His mercy!' I sneered. 'And the princes in the Tower? Do they live at his mercy, too, or are they to be murdered like poor King Harry so none can rescue them?'

Ha, that made Lynom as angry as a poked serpent. 'Keep your cursed voice down or you will be for the bonfire!' he warned. 'And you have my word that the Lords Bastard are in good health.'

'Your word?' I enjoyed seeing him battle to bridle his temper.

'Yes, Mistress Shore, I was at the Tower with the Lord Chancellor yesterday and saw them for myself. As for King Harry, since it was your royal lover had him murdered, do not talk to me of my king's faults!'

'Ha! And your precious Gloucester did the deed on my Ned's orders.'

'No, that is an evil nonsense, and such accusations do you no good at all. Now I suggest you take a few moments to calm yourself before you make your deposition.' Confident I would comply, he leaned his shoulders back against the door and folded his arms; his entire stance a reminder to me that I was in his power. I glared at him and turned away, cradling my shoulders. Behind me the room was silent and growing colder. I bit my lip and shivered, close to tears. Why was I being so unwise? But what did it matter what I said? I knew how Ned would have acted now – ruthlessly! His brother would be no different. If Gloucester managed to keep the crown, there would be no more pardons. As though he read my thoughts, my inquisitor stirred. 'By the way, Mistress Shore, you are not the only person to be arrested. Everyone known to openly sympathise with the Woodvilles has been detained.'

'And there was I about to lead my army to meet up with Buckingham's, Master Lynom,' I answered dryly, turning to face him. 'You must be so pleased to have captured me in the nick of time.'

The upstart sucked in his cheeks and with a lift of eyebrows that said on-your-head-be-it, he flung back his knuckles against the door, summoning his notary to enter.

The young man fussed about, setting candles upon the window

embrasure, arranging the stool so he might sit where the light was greatest, taking off the ink phial that he wore about his neck, and readying his writing board. All the while Lynom watched me with narrow eyes as though I was an unjarred spider, and I stared back haughtily, my chin raised.

'Let's get this over with, shall we, Mistress Shore?'

In reply I swished him a mock curtsy but he merely nodded. The lawyer rather than the retainer was back in charge. Behind the tightening of lip and the hardening of his gaze, I could see the Inn of Court discipline snapping into place.

'Mistress Shore, have any of the Woodvilles or their henchmen been in communication with you?'

Hmm, so this could be more about catching Dorset than punishing me. It made sense. Snaring such a prize might earn Lynom a knighthood. Well, I took my time in considering my answer. It was a pleasure to ratchet up his impatience but, in truth, I was wondering *what* to answer. I could have negotiated; my freedom in return for a description of the new beggar on the streets of Farringdon, but I had some honour left. And trust Lynom? Pah to that!

'Go jump in the Thames, Crown Solicitor!'

The notary started to write and I gave a gurgle of laughter at the lawyer's furious expression.

'Godssakes, man! Use your wits!' he exclaimed, and then to my great amazement, his mouth twitched into better humour, and with a sigh and shake of head, he clasped his hands behind his back and we waited while the ink dried and the words were scuffed from the parchment. But it was not amusing. Lynom was at the top of the new king's dungheap. I don't suppose he had crawled there through treachery like Catesby but by winning cases to enrich his master. Two things I needed to keep in mind: never to underestimate this lawyer's cunning and always to remember

that Gloucester wanted Dorset's head on a pole on London Bridge
for the crows to peck at! Next to my beloved Hastings'. Three
things! O God, let me remember that most of all.

'Let us continue, Mistress Shore.'

Perversity seemed the best ploy, but my eyes were gritty with
weariness and my head ached.

'Have you had any recent communication with Lady Cecily,
Dorset's wife?'

'Ah.' I smiled as I watched the quill-tip dip and hover. 'I cuck-
olded Kate, her mother, and since then, of course, Cecily and
I have been bosom friends. I'm standing godmother to her next
babe.' I sidled across to the notary and purred, 'Aren't you writing
that down?' Then I grabbed the inkpot and hurled its contents at
Lynom's middle. 'Do you think me such a fool! Go to the Devil
with your poxy questions, you son of an evil whore! I don't care a
damn in Hell who wears the accursed crown! Why do you bother
with such foolish questions? Your king wants me burned as a
traitor and he'll see it done when he returns, so go and—O God!'

Lynom was staring down in dismay at the black stain wounding
his scarlet stomacher. He looked so little-boy hurt, so astonished.

'I'm so sorry,' I exclaimed, my fingers shaking at my lips. 'I
didn't mean—'

'You are your own worst enemy, Mistress Shore.' He grabbed
the latch and flung the door open. 'Get out!' he snarled at the
notary and the young man fled.

'Please, please...' I pleaded as Lynom reached for his cloak.
My common sense was telling me I had misplayed this so badly.
Catching his sleeve, I cried, 'Please understand, I haven't slept all
night.' He shook me off. 'Please,' I pleaded. Tears had begun to
trickle down my cheeks. I fell to my knees and clutched at the skirt
of his doublet. No doubt he thought me despicable, but I felt so
empty, so vulnerable, and my pleas poured out unbidden. 'Please,

I beg you, don't leave me here. The head gaoler has vowed to rape me.' He pulled away from me and I dropped my forehead to my knees in anguish. 'Please, Master Lynom,' I sobbed into my skirt. I do not know if he heard my muffled words, but I sensed him stare down at me for a long hard moment before he left the cell.

'Lock her in!' I heard him snarl at the under-gaoler. 'No one – no one! – is to have truck with her without my permission.'

I should not have behaved like a fishwife or a waterpot, but everything had overwhelmed me.

Lynom made sure the head gaoler never troubled me again. I was taken to a larger cell but more closely kept. A guard was appointed to keep vigil outside the door and to accompany me when I was marched down to the yard for exercise. Exercise? A brief walk around once a day. Cruel, when all I longed for was to be in my own garden and feel the sunlight on my face.

Oh, I spent much of those lonely days in prayer. *I shall cease meddling*, I promised St Jude and Our Lady. *Small things shall suffice me from now on*, I assured God. And my despair grew like the mould upon the walls.

Will was given permission to make short visits providing he consented to be searched. The cheese and viands he brought me were delivered gouged with knife slits, and the laundered undergarments that Eleanor's servant delivered at the gate arrived well fumbled.

Jack made no effort to see me. He was angry, fearful that any day he might be asked to pay a fine for my alleged misbehaviour. Nor would he make any pleas on my behalf, unlike Father and Alderman Shaa, now a knight, who each wrote a petition to the King.

It was too early for an answer or to know if King Richard would survive. He was in the Midlands – no doubt snarling this way and that like a wounded boar waiting to see from whence the dogs would spring. It was a week later, judging by the nicks I had made on the wall, when Lynom came to visit me again. I was resolved to be bad-tempered but he looked tired. I guessed Buckingham's treachery was conjuring up sleepless nights for all of Gloucester's bootlickers. There were dashes of silver glinting in the brown hair that showed beneath his low-crowned hat, his stubbled cheeks needed a shave and the grey fustian doublet did him no service. I smiled, wondering if he dared not wear good clothes to visit me.

'I'm glad to see you in better humour, Mistress Shore. I thought you might be waiting with an artillery of inkpots.' I shook my head, realising how much I had missed the challenge of his presence. 'Here!' He was shrugging off some sort of leather quiver from his shoulder. Curious, I watched him carefully upend it and shake out a slender sheath of rosemary and lavender. 'From your garden. Best I could find. All the other flowers are spent now.'

Tears blurred my sight. 'More precious than any imperial crown,' I murmured, breathing in their fragrance. 'Thank you.'

Perhaps this was to lull me into gentleness for his visit, and yet, beneath the shadow of stubble, his skin was flushed as he turned to hang the quiver on the doorlatch 'It stopped raining at last. Today's the first fine day we've had for three weeks.'

'The weather doesn't concern me, Master Lynom.'

'It should,' he answered. Jubilance was gleaming in his eyes. 'Buckingham and Bishop Morton are holed up at one of Lord Ferrers' manors beyond the Severn.'

I had no idea where the Severn was. 'I don't understand, sir.'

'The river has flooded, you see, the worst for years. Buckingham can't get his army across.'

'To join the Woodvilles, you mean?'

'To join anyone. I expect your brother has told you there have been isolated risings. Tudor's off the south coast with a fleet from Brittany, so we know his mother, Lady Margaret, has been involved. As for Dorset...' He paused, his blue gaze rising to fix mine. 'He is still at large in the West Country.'

The West Country? Well, God be thanked! But I dared not show my relief in case this was Lynom's trickery. He was certainly watching me like a mouser poised to pounce. Was I supposed to fling my wrist to my forehead and swoon in disappointment that Dorset was no longer in kissing distance?

'Well, I daresay he's hoping to get funds from his wife,' I muttered.

'You think he's gone to Shute?'

'Pray don't get excited, Master Lynom. He may have gone to the moon for all I care.'

'Is that the jilted mistress talking?'

'No, it's the prisoner passing the time of day.' I smothered a yawn and received a scowl for my pains.

'Tell me the truth and I'll pester you no more.'

I folded my arms. 'You wouldn't believe it, anyway.'

'Try me.'

'I'm sorry, sirrah,' I announced. 'You're too much like Doubting Thomas and I don't do miracles.' I turned my back and to my dismay heard the door slam behind him and the key turn.


Lynom gave orders that I was to receive no more visitors and he left me to stew in my own company for the whole of next day. A long time when you have nothing but walls to stare at and one pannikin of gruel. I was not used to hunger.

He came next morning just before noon.

'There is a hot beef pie outside the door.' Yes, I could smell it.

'Yours if you will answer my questions, Mistress Shore.'

I smiled sweetly. 'Oh, I'll answer questions exquisitely, but you'll need three pies. I do nothing by halves.'

My answer was calculated to throw him; he would not know whether I was playing games or going crazed. What threw me was that he was actually assessing me like a diligent physician with that damned, feigned caring mask that could disarm me if I did not keep my guard up.

'You're looking too pale.'

'Yes, it's all the fashion in Westminster sanctuary.'

He was scratching his forehead. 'Three pies?'

'Yes, conjure me three pies this instant and I swear I'll sing like a thrush.' I laughed, knowing full well that there was only one.

He took a deep breath and slapped his gloves against the door. There was a rattling outside and a guard came in with a tray. Upon it was a large platter bearing – a napkin, two mazers and a flagon of wine. And three pies. I looked at the pies, my lips open in astonishment.

'You gave your word,' he pointed out. 'Eat your fill and then we'll take a walk upon the ramparts.'


I shaded my eyes against the dazzling daylight as we climbed the dog-leg of stairs. This was a calculated cruelty on Lynom's part. Feed the bitch, take her out on a leash then chain her up again. Except that he longed to pet this contrary creature. I could sense he was paying attention to my ankles as he followed me up the steps. That male perusal had been evident from the first time we met – a weakness I could deliciously exploit.

As if they agreed with my fresh purpose, my fellow prisoners down in the yard were watching our progress. When lewd suggestions began to accompany their whistles, Lynom imperiously flicked his fingers and in an instant his escort had their halberds horizontal and were shoving our whooping audience into the shadow of the building. And just to be certain of privacy, his hand beneath my elbow urged me further along the rampart that led onto the gatehouse.

That gesture of power, that flick of command, left finger-prints on my spine. I missed my powerful protectors. Not just the security their authority gave me, but their air of possession, too. Oh how fickle we women are, delighting in the command a man may have over us, but only if we will it so.

When his hand left me, in mutual agreement we stood side by side, like two foreigners gazing out upon the city. I tried not to be conscious of the man beside me, to wonder what it would be like to lie with him. Was that his purpose? To seduce me? But he made no such move. I should have known he was subtler than that and so we lingered, quiet with one another.

Above my beloved London, the sky was April in October, huge cushions of cloud flung across a pale blue coverlet shot with smoky threads. The air was chill or was it my unused limbs that had cooled too much?

I could not bear to look east; towards the Tower where Ned's poor boys were just embarrassing remnants locked away, unloved. Did poor Hastings' blood still stain the cobbles? I shuddered, trying to keep my wits. Yes, safer to look out across at the Holborn rooftops. Count the chimneys and… God in Heaven! How could it have all ended like this?

Did I want to live? Is that why this mind-gaming lawyer had brought me up here, to whisper that he could release me into the pack-horse queue, the bustling river of life flowing through Ludgate? At what price? It did not need a sideways glance beneath my lashes to know he was observing me with speculation just as Hastings had that first time.

*Tomorrow shall be my dancing day*

To dance to Lynom's playing or dance on the gallows, was that my choice?

'I do not know London like you,' he remarked, leaning lazily back against the wall. 'Even more churches than York but I wager you cannot name every spire.'

'You know I can,' I said softly. I cradled my body, closing my eyes in pretence of delight at feeling the sun's warmth kissing my brow.

'You are still a beautiful woman, Mistress Shore.'

I opened my eyes and beamed at him. 'And you are still a lawyer.'

He laughed. 'We could pretend.'

'What, that I am ugly and you are a man without an agendum?'

'I cry you mercy. Suppose for a few moments that we are two pilgrims met by chance upon the road to Walsingham. We might walk and talk.' He held out his ungloved hand to me.

After playful hesitation, I placed my hand upon his wrist. He spread his hand, curled his fingers to entrap mine. I did not comment but I let my free hand scuff the wall as we walked, letting the rough stones remind me this was a prison. Otherwise, it was too luxurious: that womanly feeling beside a tall, fit man.

Ned, Ned! If I close my eyes, can I imagine your hand beneath mine?

I tried, but my breath encountered the scent of cedar, leather and spice. Through my fingertips pulsed the energy of an attractive man and my body was already lighting candles to welcome him. Was this his conscious purpose? Or an alchemy beyond phials and measurements?

'Well, sir pilgrim,' I said huskily. 'We must discuss the weather, the state of the road, the expense of hiring horses. I should ask you where you are from.'

'Sutton-upon-Derwent, south-east of York. And you, madame?'

'Oh, a London hatchling. And your wife, sir? She is not with you.'

'I have no wife, madame.'

'A widower then? How sad. But children, I presume?'

'Nor children.'

'I cannot believe that. At your age?'

'What?' he replied indignantly, losing his part. 'Why am I supposed to have children at my age?'

'You're good looking. Ah, you must be a priest. I did not notice your habit beneath your mantle, sir, forgive me.' I snatched back my hand in despair. 'What's the point of all this? Make me feel safe before you interrogate me again? Oh, stop your wretched games, sir. Take me back to my cage and shut the door! No, I'll save you the bother.'

I ran back to the stairs and hurtled down. Back inside my cell, I slammed the lock shut and burst into tears. When Lynom tried to open the door, I shoved it against him.

'Stop behaving like a damned shrew,' he snarled, heaving the door and me back sufficiently to ensure his access.

I let go the door timbers, grabbed up the last pie and hurled it. This time Lynom ducked. 'Leave-me-alone!'

Then, because he refused to obey, I slumped down the wall and dragged my knees against me. 'Go and get the stake organised. I've always known I'd be burned one day.'

'You're being ridiculous.' But the way he said it had a hollow ring and he couldn't look at me.

'Oh God,' I whispered. He was going to take his copies of Ned's letters to the King.

'You're a difficult woman to help, but why am I surprised.' He let me stew in the corner and took a turn about the cell, his steepled hands tapping against his lips as he arranged his process.

'Let's begin yet again, shall we. You've had your three pies so keep your promise. And make it honest. Are you listening? Do you understand?'

I nodded reluctantly .

'Very well.' Taking my arms, he assisted me up and sat me on the stool.

'The beggar in the churchyard? Did he give you a message?'
I shook my head.

'Who was he, then?'

'Dorset.' I saw Lynom's body jerk as though I'd punched him.

'What!' he yelled. 'That was Dorset?'

A lawyer flagellating himself? Now there was a wonder! 'I gave him food, sir. That's what you do with beggars, isn't it?'

'Is it or do you fuck them?' Now he was looking at me as if I was a dog's retching. I didn't like it. 'You're not just a whore, you're a human flea. High odds, Mistress Shore, but such rewards, and I daresay the danger quickens you, too – the aphrodisiac that gives the extra edge. King Edward, then Hastings, and if the Lord Bastard had remained king, you'd have been Dorset's mistress, ever at the hub of power.'

That hurt like a lash. Had I been standing I'd have slapped the cur. Instead, I smoothed my skirts. 'Unfortunately your arrows fall short, Crown Solicitor. I thought you wanted honesty but it seems you prefer the fable.'

'Really?' The cynicism was forced through clenched teeth. Why was he being so vehement? Ah yes, the royal tap on the shoulder was no longer likely. Or had he expected kisses on the battlements?

'I'm a one-man-at-a-time woman.'

'Are we talking by the day or the hour?'

Why so hot? 'By the reign, sirrah,' I answered. 'King Edward, then Hastings, but never both. And never Dorset in a million years.' But Lynom turned away, tossing back his head in disbelief.

'Upon Ned's soul, I swear it.' I protested, springing to my feet. 'Dorset and I were always enemies, although God forbid he will suffer a traitor's death.'

The Crown Solicitor was scowling, pinching the bridge of his nose, trying to bend the truth to his liking. My answer had not met his ripe hypothesis.

I sat down again. My head ached. Lynom's venom was preferable to Catesby's cruelty, but I was still a creature in a cage to be poked and teased.

'I'm sorry if I insulted you, madame,' he apologised, but the swift bow of head was arrogant. He paced towards the door, his left thumb tapping his clasped hands behind his back. 'You say you and Dorset were enemies?'

'Yes,' I confirmed wearily. 'He and his uncles were forever slandering Hastings and I. He tried very hard to lure Ned's love away from me.'

Lynom swung round to face me. 'You mean he loved the King?'

'Not that kind of love. Dorset never loved anyone but himself. Mayhap adversity has whittled him into a better man. I can tell you it is not doing much for me.'

He ignored that tantrum. The gloves of the interrogator were comfortable once more, fitting without a wrinkle. 'Let us return to you and Dorset, shall we? Why has your name been coupled with his?'

'Has it? I hope not. Ah, maybe in Yorkshire. Your master was always under the misapprehension that I was one of Dorset's intimates, beguiling Ned into debauchery, but, believe me, it isn't true. Ned and Hastings kept me safe from him. I was never in the Woodvilles' camp.'

'But Dorset asked you to sell the sapphire necklace to raise money?'

'No, it was mine, the Queen ordered it to be stolen from my house in King Street after the King died. Princess Bess gave it back to me when I visited her. And there was a witness to that, Captain Nesfield. She told him it was rightly mine.'

'I know Nesfield. He can make a deposition.' Again, I sensed something unspoken. Could I have convinced him at last of my innocence?

'You are looking as though you've walked into a post, Master Lynom. I can swear to all this on the nearest saint's bones.'

'Then I had better find some, hadn't I? For I shall be most disappointed if you can't, Mistress Shore.' He took up his gloves to leave. 'And if it's the truth, it will not hurt you.'

God willing!


'Be careful of Lynom,' Jack warned me when he came to visit next day.

It was a Sunday and because of Will's commitments and Lynom's order that only my brothers might have access to me, Jack had to bring me my food and he was not pleased at the inconvenience. 'I don't like being searched as though I am some common felon,' he sulked as I tucked into the cold beef. 'Crown Solicitor's orders, indeed! Northern upstart!'

'That was delicious. Please, thank Eleanor,' I answered, dabbing my lips with the napkin.

'It won't do, Elizabeth. The man's had agents asking about you all over the city these last few days. What's more, every poxy alehouse from here to Greenwich is taking wagers whether you'll let the old greybeard tup you. I can't show my face in the street I'm so ashamed.'

I was used to scandal but I was truly angry to hear that people were ridiculing Lynom.

'You're only worried about your bond,' I retorted. 'Perhaps you'd better sell my necklace.' I didn't remind him it was evidence.

He folded his arms. 'More lip from you, sister, and I shall.'

'And Lynom's not a dotard, Jack. He's my age and—'

'Bah, old, young, why would a high-flying lawyer like him be messing so much with the likes of you if he wasn't keen to get his leg over? Or is that already done?' He whirled his forefinger round his left little finger. 'Got you round here, hasn't he?'

'Has he? You underestimate me as always, Jack. If I can beguile a king, I can certainly deal with a crown solicitor.' I hoped.

He shook his head at me. 'You've really dragged us in the dirt this time. At least they're calling you Shore on the proclamation, not Lambard.'

I felt an invisible icy fingernail drag down my spine.

'Proclamation, Jack? What proclamation?'


I expected Lynom to distance himself, but he came to see me next day. There was a heaviness in his face that I had never glimpsed before. He did not remove his cloak so I guessed he would not remain long within my contaminated presence. Maybe this was the last time we would meet.

'I have heard there's a proclamation, Master Lynom. It would be useful to know the exact wording.'

His mouth tightened and from out of his hanging sleeve he drew a small roll of parchment. 'I had this copied for you.'

I hoped my hand would not tremble as I took it from him.

The proclamation had been issued in Leicester. King Richard was offering a £1000 for the capture of Buckingham and 1000 marks for each of the bishops, John Morton and Lionel Woodville, and the great rebel, Dorset, 'who holds the unshameful and mischievous woman called Shore's wife in adultery'. I read on in increasing horror; the words 'Traitor, Adulterer and Bawd' scorched my sight. Jack had spared me that.

'Oh, Christ Almighty!'

'Here!' Lynom pushed the stool beneath me and lifted the parchment from my lifeless fingers.

'It's as good as my death warrant, isn't it?' I said.

'Yes,' he said, making no excuses for his master. 'Yes, it possibly is.'

# IV

Lynom muttered something before he left me but I was too stunned to listen. I sat staring at the wall as though my wits had gone, too weary to conjure up useless hope. Why had God bound me so cruelly to Buckingham and Dorset's wheels of Fate?

I do not know how long I sat there in a daze — hours, for sure — before the bolts rattled back and Lynom stepped in again. His clothing smelled of the outside air, his hair was ruffled, and his face showed exertion.

'Elizabeth, are you ill?' He unstrapped a flask from his belt and pressed into my hands. When I made no move, he fastened my fingers round the leather sides and lifted it to my lips. Aqua vitae. It burned my throat and brought me back to living.

'I'm here to help you.'

Ha! He had sufficient evidence to burn me as a sorceress. Table the copies of Ned's letters, dump black Hercules on the judges' bench. Easy! As for treason, my own admission that the beggar was Dorset was sufficient.

'Indeed, Master Lynom? Help me? I think you should wish yourself a thousand leagues away.'

But he stood there, looking down at me with goodly concern. 'Can't you bring yourself to trust me?'

How I wished I might. In a different world.

'Isn't your king's trust sufficient, sir?'

He ignored that comment. 'Well, I have news to cheer you. I've just come from Westminster Sanctuary and I've spoken to Nesfield and Princess Elizabeth. They confirm everything you have told me. That is why I am willing to help you.'

I did not answer. My instincts were telling me he was sincere yet it was in his interest to please King Richard and escort me to the scaffold.

'Madame?'

O God, give me reason. Could I trust him? Had the return of my clothes, my letters, my necklace been part of a clever stratagem at first or… Or just decent human kindness? And maybe in that moment, I knew that slowly, unwittingly, I was growing to care very much for this man and if…if Lynom's promise to help me was golden and true, then I would be heartless to embroil him further. Shakily I rose to face him. 'Don't sport with me any further, Crown Solicitor. The King thinks me evil, the King wants me silenced and he will have it so.'

'As I've said before, you misjudge him as you misjudge me, I think.' He reached out his gloved hand and lifted my face. 'Trust your instinct, Elizabeth, please.'

Could I? My head ached with too much thinking. Down in the yard, the head gaoler was bawling foul abuse at my fellow prisoners. I wanted to cry. Their world, my world, all was so wrong, so wrong. No future for any of us.

'Elizabeth.' Lynom's hand was on my sleeve. 'Listen, I have brought the notary back. You must make a deposition. What you told me earlier. Begin at the beginning.'

I let him sit me down again and I missed his touch when his hands left me.

It was the same notary. He came in warily and kept his distance this time, guarding his inkpot.

Lynom began to interrogate me in a gentle manner and listen to what I told him with his full attention. Not with judgment this time, either. It was a slow business with the notary scratching away in the corner. And as we waited for the man to finish each of my answers, Lynom's blue eyes met mine with understanding and gazing back, I found myself wishing for all the world he were neither a lawyer nor King Richard's creature.

Only the curfew bell brought respite from his questions.

'You've done well,' he exclaimed, signalling the notary to leave. 'We'll finish this tomorrow. Try to get a good night's sleep, Mistress Shore.'

'Wait, sir. I have a question.' He halted at the door and turned round to face me. 'If …if we had met as pilgrims on the road to Walsingham, would you have asked me to dine with you?'

Despite a weariness that equalled mine, his blue eyes kindled a sinful smile. 'Yes, I probably would and mayhap much else, besides.' For an instant, I swear he desired to vanquish the pace of floor between us and take me in his arms. 'And would you have agreed?'

I smiled. 'Yes, I believe I might have, Master Lynom.'


Will was sceptical of Lynom's sudden conversion to the Order of St Elizabeth Lambard. My basket of daily bread arrived with my brother next day together with a warning on leading men into temptation. By 'men' he meant Lynom.

'You should not be encouraging a crown solicitor to take such a personal interest in your circumstances, Lizbeth,' he lectured me as I ate.

'The Crown Solicitor, Will, is not in swaddling bands,' I retorted, brushing the crumbs from my lips, but my brother had his holier-than-thou earflaps turned down.

'Indeed, no, sister, but God has given him better tasks to do than hang around your skirts. He has been telling me that speaking with the prisoners here has convinced him that changes need to be made. He is going to propose to the King that a suspected felon's property should not be seized when he's arrested. No, let me finish,' Will insisted, as I drew breath. 'He also considers that if a man's friends and family are willing to put up a bond, then a man should be at liberty until he is tried. Once the present troubles are dealt with, he is hoping that King Richard will consider placing these proposals before Parliament.'

I was speechless. St Thomas Lynom might be donning a halo in the mornings but it was still in front of *my* looking-glass.

'Lizbeth?'

'Oh, I hope the King will listen,' I murmured. 'And I am listening, too, Will.'

'Amen to that, then,' applauded my brother, 'for you are still a daughter of Eve and your wiles are awakening Master Lynom's lust. Do not lead him into sin. Remember, his duty is to God and his king and not to you.'

With that, he thumbed a cross on my indignant brow and took his leave.

I think his warning had come too late to purge any thoughts of lust or love from my mind or body. I had begun to listen for Tom Lynom's boots upon the stair like a little dog cocking her head for her master.

Lynom visited that evening just before curfew. He brought wine to share and looked pleased with himself. I sat down upon my palliasse and hoped he had good news.

'I've found several of the Lord Bastard's former attendants willing to verify that he sent for you,' he informed me as he filled my cup. 'Things are beginning to look up.'

I was grateful but I was not saddling my hopes. A vengeful king could override justice.

'All thanks to you,' I replied, lifting my wine in libation to this legal demi-god. It was good to relax my fears for a little space. 'Did you know you are slowly restoring my faith in lawyers. It's like the road to Damascus.'

He had become used to my humour. 'Then you should be blind by now.'

'That's not what makes you blind, Crown Solicitor,' I purred.

'Shrew,' he replied kindly, propping himself against the wall and taking a swig.

'You've had a busy day?'

'Does the sun stop moving?' He wiped his knuckles across his lips. 'And there seems to be a sudden dearth of wherrymen tonight. I waited half an hour at Westminster.'

'It's St Crispin's Day.'

'So?'

'Maybe they are all getting their shoes mended or celebrating Agincourt.'

He shook his head at my folly. 'Buckingham's been caught near Shrewsbury, by the way – on the farm of a servant. The fellow turned him in for the reward. He's to be taken to the King at Salisbury.'

I did not answer. Could Gloucester forgive? I doubted that. The betrayer betrayed.

'By the Lord, what a damnably odd world this is.' Lynom languidly traced the uneven surface of the wall. 'The King gave him trust, love, authority, made him his right-arm man. I wouldn't have risked all that. What's your reckoning?'

I sighed remembering Hastings' assessment. 'Maybe all Buckingham wanted was respect and all he ever expected was dislike.'

'That's a strange answer. Richard gave him respect a thousandfold.'

'In here.' I pointed to my heart. 'Buckingham didn't have it in here. You do.'

He pulled a face. 'Even though I'm a lawyer.'

I bowed my head to him in sport and he came to stand looking down on me.

'I've been wondering something else. When you are acquitted, what will you do?'

Acquitted? Ha! 'Offer my services to the Archduke Maximillian or King James of Scotland,' I teased.

'Hell, I believe you could,' he laughed. 'But, indulge me, could you live an ordinary life?'

'Of course,' I said, savouring my wine. 'It wasn't easy, being one of the King's mistresses. Lonely, most of the time. But two of the greatest men in the kingdom gave me love and valued my opinions. That was a gift beyond riches.'

'And you loved them both.' Had Lynom ever loved? I wondered. It was not the first time that thought had tiptoed through my mind.

'Yes, sir, I did.' I rose to face him. 'In truth, I didn't want to become Ned's mistress, not really. It just happened, but it was the only way I could free myself from Shore.'

Lynom's eyes widened. 'Hell, you did it for that?'

'Mainly, but I was seeking affection, too.'

If I took a step closer, this lawyer would kiss me, no question. Instead, I took a turn about my tiny kingdom, out of arm's reach.

'Don't tell you didn't want the power and riches?' he asked.

'I confess I enjoyed both, but being trapped in here has given me perspective. I thought riches would hedge me against adversity but with one stroke of a pen, pfft. All gone to a stranger.' I watched guilt redden his face. 'And don't apologise. Look, if I walk out of here, Master Lynom, it will be with nothing but my brothers' charity, and yet, you know, it doesn't bother me anymore.'

'It bothers me.'

'Because you have all my goods?' I stepped towards him.

'There, I absolve you.' He snared my hand as I traced a cross upon his forehead.

'Elizabeth?' My name was a caress upon his lips.

I knew Lynom wanted to lie with me. He knew my body ripened towards him, understood the play of power between us. Except…in the world outside he might cavort with whomsoever he pleased, whereas I…I slept in prison with King Richard's hatred watching me like an invisible presence. Waiting.

'Elizabeth?' It would only take a kiss to ignite an affair between us. An affair? A very short affair? And then?

The curfew bell began to ring from St Mary's.

I tugged my hand free and stepped away. 'Goodnight, sir.'

# V

Buckingham was executed in the market place at Salisbury on the Feast of All Souls. I could not forgive him for destroying those whom Ned had loved; he would surely roast in Hell. The news of his beheading terrified me. It meant the King would soon be back in London and I'd be put on trial. Lynom had said nothing to affright me, but I knew that if Dorset had slipped through the net, I would be the scapegoat. There was a precedent: Lord Rivers and Sir Richard Grey had been hostages for the Queen's good behaviour, but after the alleged plot between Hastings, the Woodvilles and I, they had been executed.

That night, fear of death was my bedfellow once again and the following day no better. I could not get warm, despite the extra blankets Will had brought me. Calling in on his way back from the Chancellery, Lynom found me shivering and unable to hide my utter despair.

'We have to get you out of here,' he muttered. 'Some of the other prisoners are coming down with gaol fever.'

'Why do you bother with me?' I cried, turning my face to the wall as he crouched to chafe my hands.

'Firstly,' he declared, 'it's the turnips. Secondly, the lavender bush. Thirdly, uncommon sense.'

'Wh-what?' I turned my face, confused and a little angry that he was mocking me.

'I feel guilty at eating your turnips.' He slid a finger beneath my chin. 'And the rest. Cheer up!' He hauled me to my feet. 'I've brought you a present.'

A trivet! The apparatus to warm a small pan of spiced ale. I watched with tears trickling down my cheeks as he struck a flint and set the pan in place. 'Have you warm in no time.' Then he gathered me into his arms, chafing my back vigorously until I squealed for mercy.

'So, the lavender bush?' I asked him as I struggled to keep my sanity. My sanity, yes. Oh, I realised that I had slowly been falling in love with him. His many kindnesses had battered down the keep of my mistrust and the way he looked at me whenever we were together now was undermining the towers and walls that I had set between us. It had always been there, that...that alchemy, except I had refused to acknowledge it.

'Ah, the lavender bush.' The answer waited while he transferred the warmed ale to my cup. 'Well, you looked so damned adorable kneeling there, but what I liked was that after you'd unearthed your coffer, you patted back the earth apologetically around the roots so the bush wouldn't die.'

'It was so no one would notice.'

'You do argue. Tell me it was not done with consideration even though your business was urgent.'

'You watched?' I sniffed back my tears. This was absurd. Lynom's caring about my silly lavender was making me cry more. And he was wearing his stupid grin.

'Aye, and in case you are wondering why I never answered the door when you knocked that day, it was because there's been this widow in the street forever pestering me because she knows I lack a wife.'

Why had he paused? What was he going to say? What mischievous Divinity gives a man's smiling eyes the capacity to stir a woman's blood, set her pulse racing and excite her heart?

'And...and the uncommon sense?' I gasped, my voice scarcely my own.

'Why, because you had the courage to destroy King Edward's letters even though they were your most precious possessions. And, Elizabeth...'

I blinked up at him through my wet lashes.

'I hoped perhaps that in burning those letters you were setting the past behind you.'

'For what purpose?' I asked huskily.

He lifted his hand to my cheek, touching the moisture of sorrow as though it was precious to him. 'So that maybe you could fall in love again. With me. And though I am neither a king nor lord—'

'Whoa,' I exclaimed, setting my fingers upon his lips, my heart both joyful and frightened by this madness. 'Trust a lawyer to think of precedents.'

His laughter warmed my fingers and he snatched my hand aside and kissed the palm. 'Wretch, let me finish. I was going to say you wouldn't have to share me, Elizabeth. Is that a convincing argument for you? I'll make a deposition now if you like, swear on the Gospels if it pleases you. I have adored you from the moment you entered my life. I love you, Elizabeth Lambard.'

I stared at him, my breath caught. 'You love me?'

'Unquestionably.'

King Richard's Crown Solicitor in love with scandalous Mistress Shore? With me?

I must have looked moonstruck. I felt all manner of emotions. Amazement mingled with joy, but fear and uncertainty too. Love gives us such power over others. This would make him vulnerable.

'Is the jury still deciding in that contrary head of yours, Elizabeth? Is your heart free to love again.'

I was wary of telling him my feelings. Not yet. I wanted to protect him.

'My beautiful Elizabeth?' I recognised the urgency in his voice, read the hunger in his eyes, and I felt an answering desire. 'I want you so much.'

I was no virgin, no wife, no mistress to any other. Why, I could please myself and him. And suddenly withholding did not matter anymore. What was it Ned had said: *'Take my hand and dance, Mistress Shore, dance before the music is over.'* If this intimacy between captor and prisoner was a temporary foolishness, I no longer cared.

'Thomas Lynom.' I wrapped my arms about his neck.

We kissed. He with as much skill as Hastings and more sweetness than Ned. And then in a trice he had the blankets on the floor, for the palliasse ropes would not have carried us both, and he was thrusting up my petticoats and kissing me between my thighs. I do not know who was more hungry, he or I. I was burning for him when he took me. It was a relief, such wondrous pleasure, to feel him slide inside me, and there was no closing of eyes, no looking away. We were gazing in triumph at one another as we came to that little death.

And when we were sated, he collapsed on his back with a gasp of satisfaction and a smile that would have reached to Canterbury.

'You are good,' I said. 'Very good.'

'Better than the King?' he asked.

"Better than your one, that's for sure.'

He rolled on top of me. 'Had you ever kissed a lawyer before?' he murmured against my lips.

'No,' I gasped. 'I swore I'd never let one...' He stifled my answer and then he slid his palms about my cheeks and made me look at him. 'I am in earnest, Elizabeth Lambard, and you don't believe me, do you? I-love-you.'

Men can lie, but Lynom… There was truth in his face and he wanted the same from me.

Prison, too much time to think, to fret, to ache, to regret, to dream, to… O God, how complex we humans are. I gazed at my captor, unsure, uncertain, humbled, dazed, stumbling.

'Tom,' I pleaded.

'You want me to say it thrice. Come, love me, Elizabeth, as I love you.'

One word, a nod? Was it so much to give? Instead I retreated again. How could I burden him with loving me?

'No, sir,' I pushed him away and sat up. 'This is a mistake. I have only a past, no future. Loving me will destroy you. And I'm not being cruel. I…I respect you too much to encourage you in your folly.'

He shook his head and the love shining in his eyes made my heart ache more. 'Too late, I'm afraid. And it's not infatuation. I'm too old for that.'

'Oh, Tom' I whispered. No man was too old to be infatuated, but if his love was pure, I did not deserve his trust. Tears overcame my search for uncommon sense, grief for a future that would never be.

'Come here!' He drew me back into his arms, offering a loving harbour for a little space. 'I knew you'd argue. Could have put money on it.'

I mopped my eyes with my sleeve. 'Isn't there some wench pining up in—'

'Sutton-upon-Derwent,' he said in a thick Yorkshire brogue that made me smile. 'There now, you are feeling better. As I said, there's no sharing for you this time. No other women in my life. Hell, imagine two like you.'

I fisted his shoulder in play, unable to…well, how can you put into words how wonderful, miraculous, humbling it is to have another human being care for you against all odds?

'Tom, for the little time I have left, I give my heart into your keeping.'

'Good enough. But all this talk of dying.' Now it was his turn to take a step back. I thought he was regretting his recklessness, but it was duty that was tugging him away. He had lied about sharing. He had a loyalty to the King. 'The Chancellor, sweetheart…I have to go now.' I think he read the sudden bleakness in my face.

'Of course.' We stood observing each other like some gauche, young couple. 'You are a good man, Tom Lynom,' I said.

'I'm persevering,' he said. 'I'll call in tomorrow evening. Don't go away!'

But next day he came rushing in at noon as though he was bursting with child.

'Buckingham confessed his alliance with Elizabeth Woodville and Margaret Beaufort before he died. He denied your involvement.'

I swayed, thankful, so thankful.

Elizabeth was out of reach, but Lady Margaret…? I remembered her smallness, the mouse eyes always watchful. I heard Ned's chuckle: '*If I had fallen in love with plain Meg, we might have united Lancaster and York. But, heigh, I didn't.*'

'Will Lady Margaret be executed?' I asked.

'Headed? Lord love you, no. Her husband, Lord Stanley, is in favour again so she's to be given into his hands and strictly…kept. Elizabeth!' Of a sudden, the Crown Solicitor was gripping me by the shoulders. Some revelation had exploded like Greek fire in his mind. 'That's the answer, my love.'

And he left before I could question him further.

★

With the Feasts of All Saints and All Souls over, Will had more time to stay with me.

'They say that Buckingham pleaded to see the King, hoping to sue for mercy, but Richard refused to see him.'

'I doubt there will be any reprieve for me, then,' I said sadly after we had prayed together. 'If the King believes Dorset and I were lovers, maybe I'm some sort of hostage. I reckon if Dorset and Tudor cause more trouble, I'll be sentenced.'

'If it is God's will, then—'

'Tomorrow shall be my Dancing Day?' I finished wryly. 'But what if God and I do not share the same agendum, Will?'

Hurling a don't-mock-the divine scowl at me, he rose from his knees. 'Trust and faith, Elizabeth. Maybe this imprisonment is a candle to bring enlightenment to your soul. Anyway, I've things to do. Jack will visit you later.'

'I don't want to see him, Will.'

'I think you should, Elizabeth, he has something to say to you.'


Jack looked as uncomfortable as a chicken in a fox's jaws. Was it the stairs that had made him pale?

'You're not ill, are you?' I anxiously gestured him to my three-legged stool. Had the physician found a lump beneath his skin or... 'It's not one of the children, is it?'

'Woman, will you let me get my breath!' And get some words strung together, by the look of him. 'Lizbeth, I said something to disparage you last night.'

I managed to laugh. 'You're not the first or last, Jack.'

His hands fumbled with his hat brim. 'Sir Edmund Shaa grabbed me aside afterwards and chewed my ear for it, calling me ingrate, and when I asked him what in God's name he meant by it, he raged some more. The crux is that he told me what you did for Father and how our family would have been paupered but for you. No shop for me, no living for Rob, no priesthood for Will and no house at Hinxworth. So I'm truly sorry, Lizbeth. All these years since Shore turned you out, I have thought ill of you.' He rose awkwardly. 'Can you forgive me?'

Tears gathered behind my eyelids. 'You had a sister who would not play by the rules, Jack. It can't have been easy. Besides, I have to thank you for standing bond for me. Pax?' I held out my arms.

For a moment he hesitated, turning his hat in his fingers and then he tossed it aside and hugged me to his heart.

'Pax, Lizbeth.'


Tom had a cunning edge to his expression when he visited me after supper. He had found a fur-lined mantle that Ned had given me and insisted I kiss him for it. I did so willingly and might have given him greater thanks but he set me gently back. Clearly there was more to this visit because he began to prowl about the room as men do when they are about to lecture women.

'Elizabeth,' he exclaimed, 'I've been thinking a great deal about the problem of getting your property back and how to convince the King you're no longer a threat.'

I waited politely for him to come to the point, expecting some legal argument, but he looked round at me with the mischievous expression that lawyers wear when they are about to surprise a jury.

'Since Lady Margaret's lord is now her gaoler, why not you and I?' All could be resolved if you agree to marry me.'

My gasp might have been heard in Southwark. Marry? King Richard's Crown Solicitor? I shook my head in wonder. No man spoke lightly of marrying. Thomas Lynom was offering me his life, casting away all he'd achieved. His commitment to me greater than to his king. It was old-fangled chivalry and a gift too precious to accept.

I shook my head and said gently, 'You and your sense of fair play, Tom. If it will ease your conscience, I'll write a will before they dispatch me bequeathing all to you, even Hercules and the mice in the cellar!'

His forehead creased but thankfully he was amused. I should have hated to bruise him.

'No, be serious, Elizabeth,' he said, folding his arms in business-like mien. 'If you were at liberty now and I asked you to be my wife, would you consent?'

Marry again? I had never thought to do so. Could I be all his? In accepting, I was giving away my freedom, dubious as it was. But Tom wasn't Shore. With Tom, there would be a meeting of minds, a house joyful with laughter, maybe a child. The loving family I'd always dreamed of.

'Yes,' I said slowly. 'In those circumstances, yes, I might.'

'See! he exclaimed. And, then, it was as though sunshine lit the shadows between us. Oh, God forgive me, I shouldn't have agreed. I was a contagion that would infect him, yet he seemed so determined, so resolute.

'My beautiful, darling Elizabeth. This may be the very way to free you. I'll write to the King. I swear I'll get you out of here.'

I shook my head sadly, but his loving kindness had already warmed the lonely places of my life. At last there were no words, only lips and touch. The feel of his arms protecting me against the cold, against the world. I forgot the cell about us. There was only him.

I have never known a man to give so generously. Such love was in his eyes, such love I gave from mine, that in our coupling was a sweetness that I had never known before, and the resonance, a feeling of great wellbeing stayed with me, as though his touch on the strings of my soul still lingered.

*Sing, oh! my love, oh! my love, my love, my love,*
*This have I done for my true love.*

We exchanged vows and then we prayed that God would bless us.

A week later, Tom's footsteps raced faster than ever upon the stone stairs.

'Read this!' he exclaimed joyfully. 'It's the copy of a letter from the King to Chancellor Russell.'

Had Tom been given some higher post?

*...our servant and solicitor, Thomas Lynom, marvellously blinded and abused with the late wife of William Shore, now being in Ludgate Gaol by our commandment, hath made contract of matrimony with her, as it is said; and intendeth to our full great marvel, to proceed to effect the same. We, for many causes, would be very sorry that he be so disposed; and pray you, therefore, to send for him, that ye may goodly exhort and stir him to the contrary.*

The letter drooped in my fingers. I needed to tell Tom to quit my life.

'No, don't be in the dumps, read the rest!'

*And, if ye find him utterly set for to marry her...'*

My heart began to race.

*...then if it may stand with the law of the church, we be content (the time of marriage being deferred to our coming next to London) that,*

*upon sufficient surety being found of her good a-bearing, ye do send
for her keeper, and discharge him of our commandment by warrant
of these; committing her to the rule and guiding of her father or any
other, by your discretion...*

Laughing, he swung me into the air, round and round and
round.

'You're to be freed, Elizabeth.'

One month later Tom and I were married at the door of St Leonard's Church with Will to bless us, and my family to hear our
vows. Chancellor Russell gave the sermon and Sir Edmund Shaa,
Dame Juliana and Margery were among the guests. Juliana swore
she would be godmother if I should soon conceive a daughter.

Her remark set the wheels in Tom's mind a-turning. 'Lizbeth,'
he murmured that night as he slid naked into our marriage bed
and pulled the bedhangings to against the cold. 'Should you like
to have a babe?'

I had been thinking about that, too. 'I know there's a risk at
my age, my love, but I cannot imagine anything I'd like better
– except, of course, being with you!' Wrapping my arms about
his neck, I drew his face to mine. 'What say you we go about the
enterprise without delay?' I suggested, running my finger teasingly across his lips.

'You might need a lawyer for this,' he murmured, turning his
head to kiss my palm.

'I've always needed a lawyer, Tom, but it has never been the
right one until now.'

'Let me be the judge of that,' he laughed. 'Shall we get started,
Mistress Lynom? You know I like to take my time to perfect each
clause.'

After our lovemaking, as I lay cuddled in my Crown Solicitor's embrace with Hercules a warm snail shape next to my feet, I thought about this fresh beginning. Perhaps I should consign 'Mistress Shore' to the keeping of the moonstruck young woman at Ludgate. The irony pleased me; I could brush off my unholy reputation, pick up my skirts and whirl into the dusty corners of England's history where no diligent chronicler could seek me out.

Tom was fast asleep when I stole to the casement and opened the shutters. Above the frosty gables of London, the giant Orion brandished his cudgel of stars at the western sky.

'Thank you,' I whispered gratefully to Heaven, and turning my face towards Westminster, I smiled and blew a kiss of farewell to the spirits of the men I'd loved.

## History Note and Acknowledgments

In 1972 the real Mistress Shore was finally unmasked, thanks to the excellent research of Nicholas Barker. In an article in *Etonia*, he informed the world that she was neither a goldsmith's wife nor baptised 'Jane'.

Two documents had come to light: the papal letter of Sixtus IV permitting Mistress Shore's case for divorce to be heard; and the will of John Lambard, drawn up in 1485, in which he left 'Elizabeth Lyneham, my daughter' a set of green velvet bed hangings and a stained cloth [painting] of St Mary and St Martha. He also left bequests to 'Thomas Lyneham gent.' and 'Julyan Lyneham'. We do not know if Julyan was Elizabeth's baby or Thomas's child by a former marriage, but he/she was obviously a recipient of John Lambard's affection.

So how did Elizabeth become 'Jane'? The documents of her time referred to her patronisingly as 'Shore's wife' and her first name was never mentioned. The man who christened her 'Jane' was the unknown author of the play *The First and Second Partes of King Edward the Fourth, Containing ...his love to fayre Mistress Shoare*, performed in 1599, long after Elizabeth Lambard's death.

The information about Elizabeth's father getting into hot water over the house in Wood Street is true, but I have invented the reason why. His showing Elizabeth to her suitor Shore is fiction, but it was inspired by Sir Thomas More's admission that he exposed his two sleeping daughters to a prospective husband.

After the divorce, William Shore returned to England in 1485. He died in 1495 in Derbyshire. There is a brass memorial on his tomb in Scropton Church, and a copy of his will (c1494) is held in the Public Record Office at Kew. John Agard was one of his executors.

Elizabeth's resting place is harder to determine. The brass memorial to her parents in Hinxworth Church shows her kneeling behind her mother, so maybe she died at Hinxworth. It is hard to believe that she ended her days old and penniless as Sir Thomas More alleges in his *History of King Richard III*.

And Thomas Lynom/Lyneham? King Richard's letter to him is authentic and, yes, Thomas did marry Elizabeth and survived the change of dynasty. During King Richard's reign, the bail system was inaugurated and legislation was passed to prevent felons' goods becoming forfeit before conviction, so Lynom as Crown Solicitor could well have influenced the King to make these changes. *The Calendar of Patent Rolls* mentions his pardon after King Richard III's death, and records that in 1486 he was the receiver for Richmond and Middleham castles (the latter was Richard's home in Yorkshire). Richard had granted Lynom a property at Sutton-on-Derwent, Yorkshire, but in 1518 this land reverted to its former owner because Lynom was 'now deceased'. However, there is another 'Thomas Lyneham gent.' who became a commissioner for several shires and served as clerk controller of Prince Arthur's household at Ludlow. This 'Lyneham' was a commissioner for Worcestershire in March 1531. I am still trying to discover whether his will has survived and where this successful public servant was buried.

A list of Lord Hastings' possessions dated October 1489, found among the papers of his son, mentions a flat diamond ring and a cross purportedly containing a fragment of the True Cross, and I have mentioned these in the story.

As far as Mistress Shore's character and appearance, the only source is Sir Thomas More's *History of King Richard III*, which was written between 1513 and 1521 in King Henry VIII's reign. More served as a page in Cardinal Morton's household so perhaps most of the information about Mistress Shore comes from Morton. More talks of 'those that knew her in her youth' and there may have been many older Londoners who remembered seeing Mistress Shore do penance. The comment that there was 'nothing in her body that you would have changed, unless you would have wished her somewhat higher' could have been said in irony about a tall woman. What puzzles me is that if More claimed she was still alive when he wrote his book, why did he not interview her? Did she refuse to speak to him? Was she not coherent? She would have been in her early seventies.

I have searched for mention of her in official documents but there is only Edward IV's 'protection' of William Shore and Richard III's 1483 proclamation against her.

However, what royal mistress could ask for a better reputation in posterity than Thomas More provides:

> But the merriest was this Shoris wife in whom the king therfore toke speciall pleasure. For many he had, but her he loved…she never abused to any mans hurt, but to many a mans comfort & relief: where the king toke displeasure, she would mitigate & appease his mind: where men were out of favour, she wuld bring them in his grace.

If you are searching for Mistress Shore's London in today's city, many streets follow their old medieval lines and you can enjoy a coffee in the crypt of St Mary-le-Bow, the church where her divorce case was heard. Gerrard's Hall no longer exists; its stones were ground up to make the prehistoric beasts at Crystal Palace. The façade of the London Mercers' former hall now embellishes Swanage Town Hall in Dorset.

My thanks to: Jenny Savage for sleuthing through legal archives; David Beasley, Librarian of the Goldsmiths' Company;

Joanna Loxton, Assistant Archivist of the Mercers' Company; and Paul Darby, Matlock Local Studies, Derbyshire, for providing a family tree of the Agards.

As for other useful sources: Tudor historian John Stow's *The Survey of London*; 'The Map of Modern Early London' at http://mapoflondon.uvic.ca/; the biographies of Edward IV and Richard III by Charles Ross; *Richard III* by Paul Kendall Murray; John Schofield's *Medieval London Houses*; and articles on the Woodvilles and Hastings families published in the *The Ricardian, Journal of the Richard III Society*. All these have lit my path.

I owe a lot to fellow Ricardian, Julie Redlich; to my writers' critique group for their valuable comments; and my wonderful 'guinea pig' readers – Margaret Phillips and Angela Iliff (UK), Jane Dowler (Canada) and Jean McClenahan (Australia). Thanks to all of you!

If you would like to read any of my other novels that are set in the Wars of the Roses, you are most welcome to drop in at www.isoldemartyn.com.

— Isolde Martyn, October 2012

# Glossary of Medieval words

ambler – horse very good for fast walking gait
arras – wall hanging
aught – anything
aumery – open cupboard/dresser
Brecknock – Brecon, Wales
brigandine – soldier's protective jacket
broadcloth – everyday cloth
caravel – ship
chapmen – travelling salesmen
cod-piece, cod-flap – inset in men's legwear
cog – small ship
cordals - laces
cote – coat
destrier – warhorse
diapered – over-stitched
doolally – northern slang for mad★
enow – enough
ewer – basin (style: an ewer)
fent – modesty insert in 'V' collar
frontlet – wire piece in headdress
fustian – mock velvet
greaves – thigh armour
jack (1) – fellow
jack (2) – leather tankard
jade – woman
jezebel – wicked woman
henin – steeple headdress fashionable in Burgundy
houpelande – man's long robe

inn – alehouse, but also a lord's hall

lairy – Derbyshire slang for wild, disorderly

Lammas Day - 1st August

laver – large bowl for hand washing

liveryman – member of a guild

lirapipe – hanging sideflap of a man's hat

madder – red dye

mark – 13s 4d or 8 oz silver

mawther – woman*

Michealmas – 29th September

milksop – cowardly person

musterdevillers – probably grey cloth

naught – nothing

parlour – sitting room

points – laces that held a man's hose to his upper clothing (gypon)

pricket –candle spike

proctor – church lawyer

rose noble – coin

sallet – helmet

settle – long seat with high back

shawm – musical pipe

solar – upstairs south-facing parlour

slibjib – Derbyshire slang for weak-faced man*

stained cloth – a painting

stomacher – worn between shirt and doublet like a waistcoat

the Staple – wool merchants' company

tabor – small drum

tansy (as in colour) – yellow

tartarin – rich cloth

thwang – northern slang for toss*

timbrel – tambourine

tippet – narrow, outer hanging sleeve

tisshew – gauzy fabric
trencher – bread that can be used as a bowl
turkisse – turquoise
warden and subwarden – officers in a guild
Winchester geese – Southwark prostitutes
werrat – northern slang for noisy brat, possibly used in the fifteenth
    century

# THE PRINCE DEMANDS AN HEIR...
# AND WHAT HE WANTS, HE GETS!

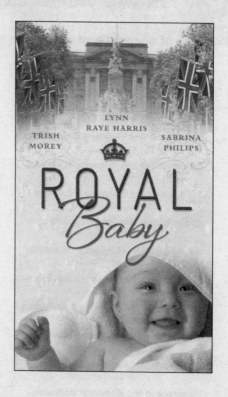

Let us treat you like a queen—relax and enjoy three glamorous, passionate stories about privileged royal life, love affairs...and scandalous pregnancies!

**www.millsandboon.co.uk**